The Experts Praise

DERANGED

by Jacob Stone

"*Deranged* is a dark and different serial-killer novel that will haunt the reader long after the book is closed and back on the shelf. Author Jacob Stone transfixes us with dread— and something more. He has the rare capacity to startle. Read if you dare."
—**John Lutz**

"*Deranged* is a fascinating and exciting blend of misdirection, topsy-turvy, and violence."
—**Reed Farrel Coleman**

"Gutsy and written with such casual grace, as if the author were sitting across the bar from me, telling me the story. *Deranged* just might be one of the most compelling, thrilling, and truth be told, at times look-away-from-page-frightening serial-killer novels I've read in a long, long time."
—**Vincent Zandri**

"Los Angeles has seldom seen such grisly fun. It's James Ellroy meets Alfred Hitchcock in a bloody yet bizarrely humorous romp on the psychotic side of the street."
—**Paul Levine**

Deranged

A MORRIS BRICK THRILLER

JACOB STONE

KENSINGTON PUBLISHING CORP.

www.kensingtonbooks.com

LYRICAL UNDERGROUND BOOKS are published by

Kensington Publishing Corp.
119 West 40th Street
New York, NY 10018

All Kensington titles, imprints, and distributed lines are available at special quantity discounts for bulk purchases for sales promotions, premiums, fundraising, educational, or institutional use. Special book excerpts or customized printings can also be created to fit specific needs. For details, write or phone the office of the Kensington sales manager: Kensington Publishing Corp., 119 West 40th Street, New York, NY 10018, attn: Sales Department; phone 1-800-221-2647.

PUBLISHER'S NOTE
This book is a work of fiction. Names, characters, businesses, organizations, places, events, and incidents either are the product of the author's imagination or are used fictitiously. Any resemblance to actual persons, living or dead, events, or locales is entirely coincidental.

LYRICAL PRESS, LYRICAL UNDERGROUND, and the Lyrical Underground logo are Reg. U.S. Pat, & TM Office.

First electronic edition: March 2017

ISBN-13: 978-1-5161-0180-1
ISBN-10: 1-5161-0180-4

First trade paperback edition: March 2017

ISBN-13: 978-1-5161-0183-2
ISBN-10: 1-5161-0183-9

Dedicated to Michaela Hamilton

Chapter One

As usual, Henry Pollard made sure that he was so gentle that he could've been cleaning dust off a dragonfly's wing as he sponged the soap suds from his wife's ruined body. He tried not to think about how much Sheila had physically deteriorated, but at times he'd let his guard down and his thoughts would absently drift to the subject, and it would stun him. The accident happened five years ago, back when his wife was only thirty-three. A robust woman brimming with strength and good health, and at five feet six inches and one hundred and forty-five pounds, she certainly wasn't overweight, more buxom and full-figured. To Henry, she had been breathtakingly beautiful.

The accident had left Sheila paralyzed on her right side, with her body twisted in an unnatural way. It had also left her with a weakened heart and a damaged liver. Four months ago, she had shriveled down to just seventy-four pounds, but it was better now that she was voluntarily eating again and he no longer had to force-feed her. When he last weighed her three days ago, she was back up to eighty-three pounds. It was still an unhealthy weight for her, but at least it was better.

Once Henry finished rinsing the soap off of her, he wrapped a freshly laundered plush Egyptian cotton towel around her body and patted her dry. He grimaced as he studied her hair. It looked grimy to him. Felt so too. Before the accident her hair was a source of pride to both of them. Thick, long, and curly, and with a golden luster that so perfectly accentuated her round, apple-cheeked face. He had grown to hate washing her hair. Not because it forced him to accept how brittle and gray her once luxurious hair had become, but because every time he did so long strands of it fell out. Of course, she no longer had a round, apple-cheeked face either. Now her cheeks were sunken, the flesh badly desiccated.

He decided washing her hair could be put off for another day or two, and instead wetted a comb and ran it through her hair, untangling several stubborn knots. Sheila's left eye winced as he did this, but otherwise she sat stoically without uttering a sound. When Henry was done, he grimaced as he saw that the comb had pulled out many more long strands of his wife's hair. He turned his back to her so he could block her view and keep her from seeing all the hair she'd lost. After he had the comb cleaned out, he lifted her from her seat in the bathtub and carried her to the bedroom so he could dress her. Henry might've looked squat and doughy, almost like a badly formed lump of clay, but he had immensely powerful hands and arms, and he could've easily lifted Sheila even if she had weighed three times what she did. After he had clothed her in a yellow summer dress that was the same color her hair had once been, he put her in her wheelchair and rolled her to the kitchen.

"I've got a lot to do today, so I'm not cooking you up a breakfast," he said. "A smoothie will have to suffice."

Even with the paralysis on her right side, Sheila could talk, although with great difficulty, but she didn't bother saying anything. Only stared at him with a woodenness that made her look like some sort of gnarled gnomelike carving. Henry could tell, given her mood, that she wasn't going to be saying a word to him regardless, and so ignored whatever emotion lurked behind her glasslike eyes.

He poured a glass of orange juice into the blender, then added a banana, half a container of yogurt, strawberries, a spoonful of honey, and a mix of vitamin and protein powder, and blended it all together. He took a swipe of it with his finger to make sure it tasted okay, then poured it into a plastic glass, stuck a straw in it, and placed it in a cup holder so Sheila could drink it. He then left his wife so he could gather what he was going to need for the day.

The chisel and hammer were new. He'd bought those two months ago at a hardware store in San Marcos, outside of San Diego, and, given the dark sunglasses he wore and the fake beard and mustache he had disguised himself with, it was doubtful the clerk would be able to provide an accurate description of him, assuming she even remembered him. That in itself was doubtful since she'd been in her early twenties, and Henry was mostly invisible to women of that age. He put the tools in a backpack that he'd had forever, wrapping them in rags and placing them on a change of clothing that he packed earlier, then threw in a roll of duct tape that had been lying around the house and a nine-inch long piece of iron pipe that he'd found near a construction site. The only other things he needed were his iPhone and a pocket knife, both of which were in his pants pocket, and a stand that he needed for his iPhone. He couldn't believe that he almost forgot the stand. That would've been disastrous. He found it in the guest bedroom closet and added it to the backpack, then left the backpack by the door leading to the garage. With all that done, he went back to the kitchen to check on his wife.

Sheila had barely made a dent in her smoothie. It would be a while before she'd finish it. Henry checked his watch. He had about twenty minutes before he had to leave, and grabbed an apple and settled down at the kitchen table. He took out his iPhone so he could look over his notes and the photos he had taken. In his mind, he played out what was going to be happening, and got so absorbed in his thoughts that he forgot about Sheila until she made a slurping noise indicating that she had finished her smoothie. Henry put his iPhone back in his pocket and wetted a paper towel so he could clean the remnants of the drink off her lips and chin.

"It's going to be a long time before I'm back," he said. "Probably not until nighttime. Should I put you back to bed or sit you in front of the TV?"

As he expected, she didn't answer him. Henry rolled her into the living room and placed her in front of the TV. He didn't bother asking her what she'd like to watch, and instead put on the History channel. Let her learn something.

Henry felt a tinge of guilt over how long he was going to be leaving her alone, but what else could he do? He certainly didn't want to arrange for an attendant. Better for the world to think that he had spent the day with her. Still, he was going to be worrying about her until he returned.

A stony resolve hardened Henry's face. Without giving Sheila as much as another glance, he grabbed his backpack and hurried into the garage. It was going to be a long day all right. After five long years, the Skull Cracker Killer was going to be making a reappearance. With a vengeance.

Chapter Two

The killer chastised the two bodyguards for letting him inside the house.

"Just 'cause I'm dressed like a cop, you shouldn't let me walk in here without first checking my identification," the killer said. "Come on, fellas. We've got the Carver saying Lawrence Tungsten's going to be his next victim, and that maniac's already killed all eight other people he's promised to kill. You guys have got to be more on the ball here."

One of the bodyguards—a chunky man in his fifties with a shaved head—stood frowning with his arms crossed over his chest. The bodyguard closest to the killer—a kid in his twenties with a mullet—rolled his eyes and muttered, "Okay, okay."

"Well?"

The mulleted bodyguard took a deep breath, not bothering to hide his annoyance. "Let's see your identification," he said.

The killer smiled. He removed his fake police ID from his wallet and handed it over. Mullet gave it a cursory look before offering it back.

"That's it?" the killer asked incredulously. "You're not even going to call my precinct to make sure I've got a legitimate reason for being here? Or even to verify that I'm actually a cop? Damn it, fellas, this Carver is a depraved and relentless killer. You think it's beyond him to get a fake police ID? Or a fake patrolman's uniform? If you two jokers are planning to keep Tungsten alive, you better do better."

Shaved Head gritted his teeth. Mullet's cheeks turned bright red. He asked, "Okay, what's your precinct's phone number? I'll call them."

The killer made a face. "Forget it," he said. "If I was the Carver, you two would already be dead now, or at least as good as dead. Just hand me back my ID."

The bodyguard cursed softly under his breath and proceeded to hand the killer back the ID when the killer surprised him by grabbing his wrist and jerking his body forward. Mullet yelped out in surprise, and his partner tensed, but didn't reach for his gun.

The killer said, "If I was the Carver I could've planted a knife in your heart before you realized what was happening." He nodded to the other one, "And you, great reflexes standing there like a dummy." Then to both of them, "Come on fellas, are you two begging to get yourselves and Tungsten killed?"

"Try that again!"

The killer made a face. "Forget it. You two are hopeless. Where's Tungsten now?"

Mullet muttered sullenly, "Upstairs in his study."

"And you two just left him alone up there? Really? Did you at least check that all the windows were locked and the curtains drawn?"

"Will you get off my back already!"

The killer shook his head, not bothering to hide his disgust, which appeared genuine and not manufactured. "Unbelievable. I'll tell you what. I'll go upstairs and check on him myself."

The killer took a step toward the staircase before stopping to stare with amazement at both bodyguards. "Really? You're going to let me go up there by myself? Are you two that incompetent? If you had any training, one of you would stand guard down here, the other would accompany me and make sure I'm not planning any funny business."

Mullet was seething while Shaved Head had tuned the killer out. Too chastened and angry to speak, Mullet started to lead the way upstairs, and the killer snorted out derisively, "They didn't teach you at your clown school not to turn your back on a possible suspect? Even if I were really a cop, I could still be the Carver."

Mullet froze for a second as he made sense of what the killer had just said, but before he could otherwise react, the killer had taken out a very sharp-looking hunting knife and ran the blade across the bodyguard's exposed throat. Blood spurted out as if the jugular had been sliced open. Before anything else could happen,

Morris Brick, who'd been sitting off to the side with the director, let out a groan. He couldn't help himself. The director yelled, "Cut!"

The actors who played the killer and the second bodyguard stopped then to look at the director. The actor who played the bodyguard with the mullet and sliced throat had moments earlier crumpled to the floor. He got to his feet and gave the director a questioning look.

"Jerry," the actor with the mullet said, "I thought it went well?"

"You guys nailed it. Seriously, great stuff from all of you. And Aiden, wow, the way you made your cheeks blush red like that on cue, amazing. But I need to consult with Morris, so everyone, let's take a half hour."

The actors and crew dispersed, leaving Morris and the director named Jerry alone. Jerry said, "So talk to me, Morris. You groaned. What was that about?"

Morris showed a placid smile, and spread his hands out in front of him in an apologetic gesture. He said diplomatically, "This scene wasn't in the script you sent. Some of the exchanges between the Carver and those bodyguards caught me by surprise."

The truth was Morris found the scene, as well as much of the movie, utterly ridiculous. Before starting his fledging Morris Brick Investigations (MBI) ten months earlier, Morris had been a Los Angeles homicide detective for fourteen years, and was the lead investigator for three high-profile serial-killer cases, all of which he solved, and which earned him a celebrity status both in town and nationally. This was his second Hollywood consulting job, and both were good money, and his hope was that they'd provide exposure for the firm. The first movie wasn't that bad, at least if you squinted enough, but this one so far was showing almost no resemblance to reality, even though the producers who hired Morris claimed they wanted authenticity. What they really wanted was Morris Brick's name attached to the property.

This movie, *The Carver*, was based on the Heath Dodd killings that took place in Miami. Even though the consulting contract only required Morris to provide feedback on the script, spend two days on the set, and allow his name to be used in promoting the film, the first thing he'd done when he took the assignment was to spend a week researching the killings. After that, Morris flew to Miami so he could meet with the lead investigator and prosecutor, and later was able to arrange an interview with Dodd in prison—the only interview that Dodd had so far been willing to give. While Dodd was clever and superficially charismatic, he certainly wasn't glib. And while it was true that Dodd would announce to a *Miami Herald* reporter the names of his next victims, he would pick common names shared by dozens of people in the greater Miami area. Sometimes Dodd would only use a first initial. None of his victims were wealthy enough to hire private bodyguards, and the police were spread too thin to provide protection to all of the potential victims.

Jerry said, "I know, I know, that scene's new, and none of that actually happened, but I felt the film needed some jazzing up there, and given Dodd's hubris, the scene feels truthful to me, at least to the spirit of things."

"Now that I've had a chance to think it over, you've got my blessing," Morris said.

Jerry seemed satisfied by that, but still, he raised an eyebrow. "You're not just trying to humor me, are you? After all, I distinctly heard you groan."

"It was more me thinking out loud. But maybe if you cut that last piece of dialogue, the one where the Carver all but tells them he's the Carver, and instead leave it simply with him cutting the bodyguard's throat the moment the bodyguard turns his back to him—"

"Morris, babe, I don't know. I really like those lines. I don't want to lose them."

Morris kept his placid smile intact. "Keep them. You've got my blessing, Jerry."

Chapter Three

Henry rang the doorbell three minutes early. A valuable lesson he had learned as a young boy was that people appreciated punctuality. When the realtor, Corey Freeman, answered the door he looked surprised.

"Leslie Gorman?" Corey asked.

"You seem surprised," Henry said, smiling in his pleasant manner. He really did have a naturally pleasant smile and gentle eyes that would usually put people at ease, and they did the trick here, at least enough so that Corey stepped aside allowing Henry to step past him into the house. The front entrance was mostly obscured by a fence and flowering bushes, but the less time he could be seen by someone passing by, the better. With only a slight hesitation, Corey closed the door.

"It's my name that confused you, isn't it?" Henry said with a wink. "Leslie? And also my voice. At least my phone voice. I've been told at times I sound like a woman over the phone." He chuckled good-naturedly. "I can't hear it myself, but that's what I've been told. I'm sorry if you're disappointed."

Corey laughed at that. "No siree, very glad to meet you, Mr. Gorman." He held out his hand, which Henry warmly took.

"Leslie," he corrected.

"Leslie," Corey agreed. His smile faltered as he gave Henry a quick, surreptitious look up and down, most likely attempting to appraise Henry's net worth based on his inexpensive and worn clothing. Of course, he couldn't have known that Henry wore what he did because he planned to dispose of the clothing later. "You said over the phone that you currently live a fair distance west of Los Angeles?"

"Simi Valley," Henry said, which was true.

"I see." Corey cleared his throat and in as diplomatic a voice as he could muster said, "Venice is a far more expensive community. I'm afraid you might be in for a shock when you see what you get for your money here. I, um, just want to prepare you."

"Not to worry. I did my research before calling you."

Corey acknowledged that with a nod, but he still wasn't convinced. "You're really paying for location and the Venice experience. But it's hard to beat this area." He hesitated before adding, "The banks are getting stricter these days. You're going to need ten percent for the down payment."

Henry showed a smile that would've made the Cheshire Cat envious, and his eyes twinkled with a gentle charm. "My wife and I came into a good deal of money a few years back. We have more than enough to pay cash for this house and a half dozen more like it," he said, which was also true.

That brought a quiver to Corey's lips and a gleam to his eyes. "Let me show you around then," he said, the excitement of a possible sale ringing in his voice. "This house might be small, but it's a gem. Solid, well-designed, and the great room, which I'll be showing you soon, gets a wonderful amount of natural light. As you can see, the owner has already cleared out, so you'll need a little imagination to picture what these rooms will look like furnished, but it will be quite a cozy home. Do you and your wife have children?"

Henry shook his head, which made the gleam in Corey's eyes all that much brighter since that answer increased the chances he might be interested in purchasing the place. While the den could've been converted into a bedroom, no matter how much you talked around it, it was really only a one-bedroom house, and would be cramped enough for two adults, let alone adding any kids to the mix, and one could only imagine the size of the mini rhinoceros-like kids this chunk of a man would spawn. Of course, Corey couldn't have known that Henry had no intention of buying this or any house no matter how the rooms were laid out, or whether or not the kitchen had been recently remodeled with top-of-the-line appliances. Nor could he have known that Henry had completely tuned him out, at least until they entered the great room, which was the nicest room of the house. Corey was pointing out the skylight, explaining how it could be opened and closed with a remote control, when Henry interrupted him by pointing to the floor and asking what that *thing* was. The way he said *thing* made Corey shudder. The room was empty yesterday when he showed the place. Could an animal have gotten inside and died? *Please*, Corey thought, don't let it be a dead rat, like what he found two weeks ago when he showed that house on Thornton Place. He steeled himself and reluctantly looked down at what Henry was pointing at, but there was nothing there. Before he could say anything, he simultaneously heard and felt a loud *thunk* vibrating violently inside his skull, and then there was only blackness.

Chapter Four

One of the few advantages of having a wide, pudgy body like Henry's was that you could hide a nine-inch iron pipe under your shirt without anyone noticing it. The realtor had been right. The great room did provide a good amount of natural sunlight, and Henry waited until they had entered that room before tapping Corey on the top of the skull with the pipe. It worried him the way the realtor had collapsed to the floor. He needed Corey alive and conscious, and if he had killed the man or knocked him into a coma, this would all be a waste.

Henry breathed out a sigh of relief when Corey began moaning. When he had first arrived at the house, he hid his backpack in bushes outside the front door, and he left the realtor so he could retrieve his backpack. He was gone for no more than thirty seconds, but when he returned Corey was on all fours, struggling to get back to his feet. Henry sat on Corey's back, collapsing him back to the floor. The realtor put up little resistance as Henry pulled his arms back and wrapped duct tape around his wrists. He considered doing the same to Corey's ankles but saw no reason to bother with that.

The realtor yelled for help. It would've been easy enough to shut him up—duct tape or one of the rags Henry brought would've done the trick—but he didn't bother with that either. Given how Corey lay on his belly, his voice had no real strength to it, but even if he could've let loose like Pavarotti in *La Bohème*, nobody passing by outside would've heard anything. While Corey yelled himself hoarse, Henry hummed to himself Musetta's Waltz from *La Bohème* as he placed his iPhone stand on a built-in bookshelf and fiddled with it, adjusting the angle so that his iPhone would be able to record what was going to happen. Once that was done, he took the chisel and hammer from his backpack.

After all of his yelling, Corey's voice had become little more than a croak, the type of noise a rusty hinge might make. He was sobbing as he implored Henry not to hurt him. "Why me?" he pleaded.

That was a hard question to answer. While Henry could've told him that it was just bad luck, that wasn't true. Corey was chosen because of his age, sex, and several intangibles that couldn't quite be put into words. There might've been thousands of others who could've been chosen instead, but still, it wasn't random. There was nothing Henry could've said to make the situation any more palatable for the guy, so he didn't bother saying anything. Instead he used the chisel and hammer and went to work.

It didn't take long for Henry to break apart Corey's skull or for Corey to quit struggling. He still twitched now and then, but once Henry used the claw end of the hammer to dig out lumps of Corey's brain, the twitching came to an abrupt end.

Once Henry was done, he checked the video recording he had made with his iPhone. It would suffice for what he needed it for. He gave a quick, cursory look at the mess he had made. As with the old nursery rhyme, *Humpty Dumpty,* nobody was going to be putting Corey Freeman back together again.

Henry used his pocketknife to cut the duct tape from the dead man's wrists. He then brought the hammer and chisel to the bathroom sink with the idea of washing them off, but the water must've been turned off for the house. He should've been better prepared and brought a gallon jug of water with him. Oh well, it didn't matter. He'd wrap them up in one of the rags he brought, and later when he incinerated his clothes, he'd throw the rag into the furnace also. Not that his clothes got any blood or gore on them. Still, better to be safe than sorry in case anyone spotted him nearby wearing them. He inspected his hands, and they were spotless.

After a quick change of clothes, Henry stored everything away in his backpack, then used a rag to wipe off any surfaces that he might've touched, not that it mattered. There were probably fingerprints from dozens of different people that could be lifted from the scene, and besides, his weren't on record. Still, as he liked to tell himself, better to be safe than sorry.

Henry stepped quickly outside and hid behind the property's fence until he was sure nobody was in sight. Then he took off, moving in a half-jog until he was two blocks away before settling into a more normal pace. After walking several more blocks, he found himself on the boardwalk, and soon melted into the crowd.

Chapter Five

Henry texted Susan Twilitter that he was running twenty minutes late and for her to order him a cheeseburger with sautéed mushrooms and a Coke, and that he would meet her at her booth. Susan didn't know him as Henry Pollard, nor as Leslie Gorman, but as Howard Donner. He could've shown up on time since he had three hours to kill after killing Corey Freeman—time that he ended up spending at the Santa Monica Pier playing skee-ball and sitting on a bench looking out over the ocean—but he didn't want to be seen walking into the restaurant with her. When he did show up at Susan's booth, he was twenty minutes late on the dot, and the food had already been brought to the table. Susan seemed both relieved and surprised to see him, almost if she didn't really believe he'd be coming, even though he had replied to three text messages from her assuring her each time that he was going to be there. It was sad in a way that she would be so worried about being stood up by the likes of Henry.

"You look like you didn't believe I was really coming," he said pleasantly, his thick lips twisted into a warm smile.

"What? No, not at all. I trust you, Howard. I've been looking forward to seeing you, that's all. And I was worried that your food would get cold, but it was brought out only a minute ago."

That was another reason Henry planned to be twenty minutes late. So that his food would already be at the table and the waitress wouldn't see him with Susan. He scooted in next to her and peered at the small garden salad that sat untouched in front of her.

"Is that all you're eating?" he asked. He wrinkled his nose. "I don't think that's going to be enough. You'll be needing your energy, especially with all the activity we have planned."

She blushed at that and ran her hand down her flat belly as if she were smoothing out her shirt. "I'll be fine," she said. "After all, I have to watch what I eat so I stay attractive for you."

"Ah heck, Susan, you could eat a dozen hot fudge sundaes and you'd be thin and beautiful."

"You're so sweet."

"It's the God's honest truth."

And it mostly was, although Henry stretched things with the *beautiful* comment. At forty-three, Susan was somewhere between slender and bony, with broomstick-thin legs and arms, barely any ass, and not much of a chest. Plums, at best, if he were being generous. Henry liked a woman to be more full-figured with some meat on their bones, like Sheila had been before the accident, and not have a boyish figure. Still, Susan did have a nice smile, and with her blonde hair, catlike brown eyes, freckles, and slightly upturned nose she could be very cute. Even with his gripes, she certainly rated significantly higher on the attractiveness scale than he ever would, and while she might not have been his ideal of feminine beauty, he could see how there'd be men out there who'd find her pretty, at least if they could overlook her barely ripe plums.

"How a pudgy schlub like me found someone so ridiculously hot and sexy is a mystery," he said.

He was laying it on as thick as he was partly because of that miserable little salad she was going to be eating for lunch. A few leafs of wilted iceberg lettuce, three pieces of cucumber, a couple of shriveled and pathetic-looking slices of green pepper, and two cherry tomatoes. What a lousy thing to be having for your last meal. The thought of it saddened him, and made him want to be extra nice to her during her last few hours alive. He added, "And so youthful looking. Not a day over thirty. I swear to God."

That one was a straight-out lie. Susan had her share of wrinkles, and with years of desperation seeped deeply into her flesh, she looked every bit her age. Still, it got her beaming, and she reached under the table and rested her hand on Henry's thigh. Her smile turned wicked. "It's so dark in here we could almost do the dirty deed right here without anyone knowing."

The back room of the restaurant being kept so dark was one of the reasons Henry had chosen this place. Being able to slip in through the back door without being seen was another reason, and the parking garage half a block away that didn't use security cameras was yet another. He and Susan had started dating three weeks ago, seeing each other secretly in dark restaurants and out-of-the-way places because Henry claimed he was preparing to divorce his wife, and that if his wife found out he was involved with her it could severely affect a settlement.

"Millions of dollars are at stake," Henry had told her, which would be true if he was actually divorcing Sheila. "My lawyer is getting all the *i*'s dotted and *t*'s crossed, and as soon as he gives me the go-ahead, we'll go public, but until then I've got to be extra careful."

So far things had been mostly chaste between them. A stolen kiss, a quick embrace, held hands, that type of schoolyard thing. The last time they met, Susan had told Henry that she was ready for them to be intimate, and their plans for after they finished their late lunch were to go hiking in the Santa Monica Mountains to a hidden and isolated spot Henry knew about so that they could get intimate there. In a way, that was all going to be true. Henry was going to take her to a spot he'd found off a little-used trail, and he couldn't imagine anything more intimate than what he was going to be doing to her. In many ways he regretted what was going to happen. Over the last three weeks he'd grown to like Susan quite a bit. She might've been a bit neurotic at times, but aren't we all? Besides, she was a nice person, had a good heart, and if he was really looking to divorce Sheila, he could imagine himself becoming romantically involved even if she wasn't physically his dream girl. Who was he to complain? He'd found out early in life that he was physically most girls' cruel joke. There was even a minuscule chance he might've changed his plans for the afternoon if she had reprimanded him for calling himself a *pudgy schlub*, but as nice as she was she probably knew she couldn't do that with a straight face. No, there were forces greater than himself at work here. The words "the things we do" whispered in his head.

He forced those thoughts out of his mind, and addressed Susan's joke about consummating their relationship right there at the booth, saying, "Don't tempt me. You're going to give me a stroke with thoughts like that." Then turning serious, he asked, "What do you see in me? You're a beauty while I look like a big block of cheddar cheese that's been melted in the sun. What are you doing with me?"

Calling her a beauty was an exaggeration, sure, but even with her barely ripe plums and nonexistent ass, most guys would rate her at least a six, while he'd be lucky to rate a two from any woman. She took her hand from his thigh so she could hold one of his thick meaty hands with both of hers.

"Howard, please, don't ever say that about yourself. You're the most gentle soul I've ever encountered, and you've got the kindest, most beautiful eyes. And you know what they say about the brain being the most powerful aphrodisiac? I've never met a man whose brain turned me on as much as yours."

He had to fight hard to swallow back a giggle when she made that comment about his brain, and somehow he forced himself instead to simply nod. She let go of his hand, the two of them seemingly losing themselves in their private thoughts. While Henry chomped away on his cheeseburger smothered in sautéed mushrooms, he caught a glimpse of the intensity burning in Susan's face, and noted the pinkish hue that was now coloring her cheeks. She really believed what she said, and he knew that she was deep in thought over what she was expecting to happen later that day. If only she had refuted his crack about himself resembling a block of melting cheese. That was one last lifeline he had thrown out to her, but it was too late now. What was going to happen was inevitable. As he masticated and swallowed the last remnants of his cheeseburger, he absently whispered to himself, "The things we do."

"What was that?" Susan asked, a nervous eagerness burning in her eyes.

Henry smiled at her. "Just telling myself for the thousandth time what a lucky guy I am to have met you."

She took hold of his hand and gave it a squeeze. "What a sweetie you are. Ready to go on our adventure?"

Henry left thirty dollars on the table, which would more than cover their bill. "I'm going to hit the little boy's room," he said. "I'm parked in the garage next door. How about I meet you inside the pedestrian entrance?"

Susan smiled thinly at that. "So we're not seen walking out of here together."

"A necessary precaution, but just for a little bit longer. My lawyer's promising me he's going to have everything in order by next week."

"Okay, okay, I understand." Her look shifted subtly, becoming somewhat guarded, accusatory, "You're not still sleeping with your wife, are you?"

That certainly came out of left field, and made Henry raise an eyebrow.

"No, that hasn't happened in years, and I assure you will never happen again," Henry said, which was the absolute truth.

Susan couldn't deny the obvious truthfulness in Henry's tone, and she accepted what he said. Whatever momentary doubt and distrust had surfaced vanished just as quickly. Henry gave her a warm smile as he left the booth and headed straight to the men's room. For a long moment he stood in front of the mirror and grimly stared at the cruel joke genetics and the universe had played on him. Not that he looked grotesque or frightening. Instead he looked utterly harmless and also completely unappealing sexually. Like he could be any woman's best friend, just not someone they'd ever have romantic thoughts about. It still amazed him that he'd ever found Sheila, or that Susan responded to him the way she did three weeks ago when he was out hunting for a potential victim and approached her while she sat on a bench by one of Santa Monica's walking trails.

Once Henry felt that he had given Susan enough time to leave the restaurant, he washed his hands, splashed some water on his face, patted it dry, and then left to meet her at the garage. When he stepped outside, he took three steps and froze before he realized what he was doing. Things weren't the way they were supposed to be. Susan stood on the sidewalk gabbing with a woman around her age. Or to be fair, the woman was the one gabbing with Susan.

Somehow this woman sensed Henry standing frozen in place, and turned to face him. Just as quickly, she looked back at Susan and when she caught her helpless expression, she made sense of the surprise she'd seen in Henry's face and Susan's reaction. Loudly enough for Henry to hear, she told Susan, "Caught you." Then she turned and took several quick steps toward Henry and held out her hand.

"Gail Hawes," she said introducing herself, her lips twisted into an amused grin. "You must be Susan's new friend."

Before Henry quite realized what he was doing, he took her hand and muttered that his name was Howard Donner.

"Pleased to meet you, Howard," she said, obviously tickled pink with herself. "Well, I'll leave you two to go off and do whatever it is that you have planned."

She grinned from ear to ear as she nodded so long to Susan. Henry seemed incapable of movement, at least until this woman disappeared from sight, then he slowly lumbered forward. Susan waited for him, her expression brittle.

"I'm so sorry," she said in a hushed voice. "Gail and I have known each other forever, and while we were sharing a bottle of wine a couple of days ago, I told her that I've been seeing someone special, but that we had to keep it secret for now. I also let it slip that we were going to be taking things to the next level soon. But I didn't tell her your name or anything about you. I swear. She figured it out from our reactions."

Henry tried to sort through this new development. Gail had stared straight into his face. She didn't know his real name, but she'd be able to describe him to the police, and Henry had no doubt that it would be an accurate and detailed description. But still, it would be weeks, maybe much longer than that, before Susan's body would be found, and even much longer after that before they'd be able to identify her, especially if animals got to her remains, so he should have more than enough time to take care of this Gail Hawes.

"I know how important it is to you to keep us secret for now," Susan said. "I know how much it will cost you if your wife found out about us. But Gail's one of my best friends. She's not going to say anything to anyone. Your wife's not going to find out about us from her. This really shouldn't be a big deal, and it certainly shouldn't interfere with our plans for today."

Henry only half-listened to what Susan was saying. He realized he might not have nearly as much time to take care of Susan's friend as he first thought. This woman might try calling Susan soon, maybe even later tonight, to find out how things had gone with her secret lover, and if she was unable to reach her she might try calling the police next.

"You look so troubled. Are you okay? Are we still doing this? If it will make you feel better, I can call Gail and make her swear she won't breathe a word to anyone."

Henry was so absorbed in his thoughts that he had momentarily forgotten about Susan keeping pace alongside of him. They'd reached the pedestrian entrance for the parking garage, and he held the door for her. He still wasn't sure what he was going to do. Forget about all the time he'd spent searching for such a perfect victim as Susan, there was also the three weeks he'd invested in her and the perfect plan he came up with, and he hated the idea of throwing that all away. He still had time to sort it out in his mind. It was going to take them at least two hours to reach the isolated spot in the Santa Monica Mountains where he'd been planning to kill her. Once they were alone up there he'd make a decision. Maybe divine inspiration would strike him.

"No need to do that, Susie darling," he said. He took a deep silent breath through his nose and let it out slowly, his facial muscles relaxing and leaving him smiling in an unconcerned, pleasant way. "We'll go on our hike as planned, and I'm sure everything will work out just fine."

Chapter Six

It was late in the afternoon, and Morris stood in front of one of the food tables, ostensibly trying to decide between a custard-filled and chocolate-glazed donut, but really deep in thought over plans he had with Natalie that night. He'd had enough of *The Carver* and was looking forward to calling it quits for the day and meeting up with his wife at their favorite restaurant, The Banyan Tree Grill, where he planned on ordering the pan roasted Statler chicken with garlic and Cipollini onions.

A familiar-sounding voice interrupted his thoughts, saying, "Man, you've been studying those donuts like you're expecting to pick them out of a police lineup later." This person laughed, and added, "If memory serves, those are the same ones they had out first thing this morning, so I'm betting the custard ones have to be rancid by now, maybe even deadly. Much safer to go with chocolate-glazed."

The reason the voice had sounded familiar was because it came from the actor who was playing the killer. The actor grinned as he held out his hand to Morris. "Philip Stonehedge," he said.

Morris accepted his hand. "Well, of course, I already know who you are. Morris Brick, but please call me Morris," he said. "Thanks for potentially saving my life here. Or at least my stomach."

"Happy to have done so. And Morris, I likewise know all about you. I can't tell you how excited I was when I heard you were going to be consulting on this film. Like everyone else in Los Angeles, I was held captivated during the Hillside Cannibal murder trials last year. Really remarkable how you caught that sicko." Stonehedge turned apologetic as he added, "I know we're on break here, but I'd be eternally grateful if you gave me a chance to pick your brain. I need to better understand the Carver."

Morris checked his watch. They had twenty minutes before they were supposed to return to the set. He nodded, and somewhat reluctantly decided it wasn't worth grabbing a donut and risking ruining his appetite for his dinner out. Besides, as he'd been telling Natalie, he could stand to lose a few pounds, so he ignored the rumbling noises his stomach made and settled on a cup of coffee, bypassing the cream and using skim milk instead. Stonehedge, who was leaner than an anorexic marathon runner, did Morris one better by only grabbing a bottle of water before leading the way to his trailer just outside the set. A minute later they were settled inside it, with Stonehedge offering Morris the sofa while he took the leather armchair.

"So what do you think so far?" the actor asked.

Morris sipped his coffee before commenting, "It's interesting how they're jumping around with the scenes they're shooting. Six months ago I consulted on *American Killer*, and the days I was on set they shot the scenes sequentially."

Stonehedge smiled thinly at how skillfully Morris had sidestepped the question. "That's Jerry's doing," he said. "He wants us to shoot all my killings first to help me get in touch with my serial killer side, so to speak, but it's not helping." A hint of desperation gleamed in Stonehedge's eyes as he leaned forward, resting his arms on his knees. "I'm lost here, Morris. I feel like I'm flailing around in the dark, and I need to find my motivation so I don't come across as a cartoon character and completely embarrass myself. I'm desperately hoping you can give me some insight as to why Dodd killed. I mean, is it as simple as that he's a twisted maniac? Is that all there is to it? Am I complicating things trying to find a deeper reason for him doing what he did?"

"Dodd's certainly a twisted maniac."

"Yeah, that much is obvious."

"But he also has a compulsion driving him to kill. You can think of him as an addict who can only get the high that he craves by killing in a way where he thinks he's outsmarting everyone and getting away with it. And once the high wears off, all he can think about is getting his next high. I have no doubt that right now as he sits on death row, he's suffering from withdrawal."

"That's what he told you? I read that you met with him in prison."

"He wasn't about to admit something like that to me." Morris took another sip of coffee, his eyes glazing as he thought back to the unsettling hour he had spent with Heath Dodd. "I'm sure he told himself that he wanted to see me only so he could convince me that he was framed by the police, even though he was caught red-handed during his last murder. But that had nothing to do with what drove him to see me, and that was to convince me that the real killer had to be more clever and brilliant than any of the serial killers I had encountered. There's no question Dodd's a piece of work, and at times I could see in his eyes his craving to kill. Although he tried hard to hide it, he was as jittery as any other addict badly needing a fix."

Stonehedge's head slowly moved up and down as he mulled that over. "What caused him to start killing in the first place?" he asked after a long moment.

Morris shrugged. "A more interesting question to me as a for-mer homicide detective would be when did he start killing, because I'm sure he had victims long before the world ever heard of the Carver. Maybe he experimented first with stray dogs and cats, but I would think the odds are good he killed his first person while he was a teenager, probably picking as early victims prostitutes, drug addicts, and transients—people whose deaths would mostly go un-noticed. As to what drove him to kill in the first place, who knows? There's some thought that serial killers have a chromosome abnor-mality that causes their homicidal tendencies. Others think it's due to brain injuries. Whether it's either of those, or something else en-tirely that drove Dodd, I couldn't say."

Morris's cellphone buzzed. Caller ID showed *Los Angeles's Mayor's Office*. He frowned at the phone for a moment, then told Stonehedge that he had to step outside and take the call. The actor nodded, deep in thought over what Morris had told him.

Once Morris was outside, he answered the call.

"This is Doug Gilman from the mayor's office," the caller said. "We met at your retirement party."

Morris remembered him. When Gilman had approached him at his police retirement dinner, Morris thought he had to be an actor who for some reason crashed his party. Gilman was young, only in his late twenties, and had that hungry Hollywood look about him. Outgoing, assertive personality, a perfect head of hair, teeth that were far too white and straight, and the type of bronze tan that you only get from frequent sessions in a tanning booth. But he wasn't an actor, and after only a few minutes of talking with him, Morris recognized him as someone highly ambitious who would probably be mayor someday. And no doubt governor also.

"What can I do for you?" Morris asked.

"We've got something for you. How quickly can you get to Venice?"

"It depends on what you have."

"What we have is something you and MBI are going to want, but I can't tell you any more until you sign an NDA. Are you near a fax machine?"

Morris told him he was on a job, and that he'd call him back once he figured out how Gilman could get him the nondisclosure agreement. It didn't take Morris long to track down a fax machine in one of the studio offices, and after he had the agreement signed and faxed back to the mayor's office, he called Gilman back.

"It looks like the Skull Cracker Killer has resurfaced," Gilman said. "And our luck, the psycho decided to move to Los Angeles."

Chapter Seven

When Morris met Doug Gilman at the murder site, the first thing Gilman did was let it slip that he'd been promoted to the mayor's deputy assistant since they last met, the pay raise for which must've accounted for the expensively tailored suit Gilman wore, as well as the equally rich-looking gray leather dress shoes he had on.

"No doubt due to your forward thinking," Morris said.

"No doubt," Gilman agreed. "I warned you at your retirement dinner you'd be hearing from me in the future, and when I realized what we were dealing with here, I wasted no time convincing the mayor that for the safety of the community, we needed to get you and MBI leading this investigation."

The two of them were alone near the front foyer while the police, forensics, and crime scene investigators mulled about in the back of the house where the murder took place. Gilman gave a quick look to make sure there were no prying ears nearby. Lowering his voice, he continued.

"I'm sure it must come as no surprise that there was resistance from your former boss. The commissioner is still nursing hard feelings about you taking a few of his detectives with you when you formed MBI, and as you can guess he didn't like the idea of having his department sharing the spotlight with you on such a high-profile case. But after a persuasive argument and a few moments of reflection on the commissioner's part, he turned out to be quite reasonable on the matter."

Gilman didn't bother mentioning the obvious, which was the only reason Hadley had backed down and agreed to let Morris and MBI be given the investigation was that it was the politically astute thing to do, which was the same reason Gilman was able to convince the mayor as well.

A little over six years and two months ago the Skull Cracker Killer began terrorizing New York City, killing nine people over a fourteen-month period, and then seemingly disappearing five years ago. The New York police and FBI had tried to keep a tight lid on the details of the murders, and the Skull Cracker name came from a reporter, not the authorities. This happened when the traumatized janitor who had discovered the first victim commented within earshot of this reporter that the poor guy wouldn't be able to have an open casket after the way his skull had been cracked open like an egg.

If this was really the same killer at work, and these killings followed the same pattern as what happened in New York, then there were going to be two more murders very soon, if they hadn't already happened. Morris knew this because a well-defined pattern emerged with the New York killings. Always three in a very short time span: the first victim being a white-collar man in his forties; the second, a typical housewife-type, also in her forties; and the third, a young woman in her twenties, always a blonde. By hiring Morris, the mayor and police department were shielding themselves from the heat that was going to be coming when the next bodies were found. If Morris was successful in tracking down the killer, the mayor would get the praise for having had the foresight in hiring Morris, but if Morris failed, which was likely given that the NYPD got nowhere with their nine murders, then it would be Morris whose reputation would be tarnished, while the mayor would still look like a mensch who did everything he could for the people of Los Angeles.

"How sure are you that this is SCK?" Morris asked, using the familiar acronym for the Skull Cracker Killer.

Gilman smiled grimly. "Unfortunately, pretty sure. You know Detective Annie Walsh, right? She's the homicide detective who picked up the case, and when she saw what was done to the victim, she sent photos to the FBI to check whether they had any other murders matching the grisly characteristics of this one."

"And of course they did," Morris said with a sigh. "Nine others."

"Yep." Gilman's grim smile tightened, leaving his lips bloodless. "There's a chance it's a copycat. Someone who found out about the

SCK's complete modus operandi, and not just about what was done to the victims' skulls. The FBI is sending us Sam Goodman, who was the profiler who worked the murders in New York, and he should be flying into LAX at ten o'clock tomorrow morning. But it doesn't matter whether it's a copycat or the original SCK. If it's a copycat, he'll still probably be killing his next two victims very soon. We need to catch him pronto."

Morris and Gilman had talked during Morris's drive to Venice, but all Gilman had told him about what was done to the victim was that it was gruesome. When Gilman handed him a small stack of crime-scene photos, Morris had to agree with Gilman's assessment. After carefully studying them, he handed them back to Gilman.

"I'm guessing the killer used a chisel and hammer to break apart the skull," Morris mused as he considered what must've happened. "And the claw end of the hammer to dig out the brain?"

Gilman blanched at the question, his skin showing a tinge of green. Morris noticed Gilman's reaction and reminded himself that he was talking to a political underling and not a cop. Maybe a very ambitious political underling who had gotten knee-deep in the details of this case so that he could convince his boss, the mayor, to hire Morris, but he certainly wasn't someone used to dealing with a murder victim whose skull had been obliterated so grotesquely.

"Never mind," Morris said. "I'm sure forensics can give me those types of details, and the FBI profiler can enlighten me as to what was done to the New York victims. Assuming I accept the job."

Gilman took a few noticeable deep breaths and wiped some perspiration from his forehead. He had recovered from whatever queasiness had temporarily hit him, although a faint greenish hue still showed in the hollows of his cheeks. He asked Morris what objections he'd have about taking the assignment.

"MBI would need to bill at our full rate. No discounts."

"Done."

"I'd have to be able to bring the full team onboard."

"Also done."

"And have complete control over how the investigation is handled, as well as get whatever support I need from the police department. And I decide what is released to the media."

"Done, done, and mostly done," Gilman said. "There are certain public safety issues that have to be taken into account as to what's given to the media, so there will have to be some give and take on that regard. But Morris, we're certainly not going to undermine you, nor are we going to interfere. So do we have a deal?"

Morris needed only a moment to consider the question before putting out his hand. "Deal," he agreed.

Gilman took his hand with the enthusiasm of a business tycoon who'd just closed a multimillion-dollar deal. Somewhat smugly, he gave Morris an appraising look.

"We'll iron out the details as to what needs to be released, and we'll hold a press conference soon to announce that the city has hired you to lead up this murder investigation. How about you swing by your home and change clothes?"

"No need. This is the nicest suit I have."

Gilman raised an eyebrow at that. "You're kidding? That looks like a suit you must've bought when you first made detective."

"The very same one. Fits like a glove," Morris said, patting his stomach.

This was mostly true. Morris had actually bought three suits the day he made detective, and the suit he had on was one of those three. What he'd said about the suit fitting him like a glove was a hundred percent accurate. All three of them were a half size too large for him when he'd bought them off the rack twenty years ago, but since adding fifteen pounds around his middle, they now fit him almost as well as if they'd been custom made, if not a little snugly.

"Morris, we don't have much time, but I could send you to my guy at Maximillian's on Rodeo Drive and see if he can get you an Armani off the rack, and maybe a tie that's in fashion, all on the city's dime. No offense, but there's going to be a tremendous amount of media attention on this, and even given your stellar reputation, the better you look, the better we'll look for hiring you."

Morris smiled thinly at Gilman's insistence that he buy more fashionable attire. Gilman certainly wasn't the only one. For a long time, Natalie used to do the same before finally giving up a couple of years ago. Whenever she would suggest that it was time for him to retire his old suits and buy some new ones, he'd always comment back that it would be a pointless thing for him to do since you can't make a silk purse from a sow's ear, and she'd roll her eyes and tell him that he was being stubborn only to be a pain in the ass, then she'd get angry and reprimand him for calling himself ugly.

Well, he certainly wasn't handsome, not with his big ears, thick, long nose, spindly legs and short, compact body. Maybe more comical looking than unattractive. In many ways Morris proved the old adage about a dog owner resembling his pet, since he looked quite a bit like his bull terrier, Parker. Of course, that old adage fell apart completely when it came to Natalie since she was a slim, petite, dark-haired beauty with mesmerizing large brown eyes. In Natalie's case, no dog would fit the bill. A cat might, at least if it were sleek and feminine-looking enough.

Morris wasn't just being stubborn, though. While he was generous with family and friends, and many times with strangers, he was extremely frugal when it came to himself, and his old suits were comfortable, still in good shape, and fit just fine. That was part of it. But another part of it was his pop, who had also been a Los Angeles police detective. Like Morris, his pop had bought three new suits when he earned his detective's shield, and never bought another one. Those were the only suits he wore the rest of his life. It had been twelve years since his pop had passed away, and Morris missed him. Something about the pride his pop took in only needing to own those three suits made Morris want to do the same.

Morris felt a catch in his voice as he told Gilman that he wasn't about to go shopping for clothes now. He added, "If my needing a new suit and tie is a condition for being hired, you're going to have to find someone else."

Gilman seemed surprised by Morris's reaction. He took a half step back and held up his hands in a sign of surrender, "Wow, Morris, I apologize if I've offended you. Not my intent, just trying to be helpful. But if it means having you work this investigation, you can wear a *mawashi* if you want."

Morris must've shown his puzzlement, because Gilman smiled and explained that a mawashi is what you call the loincloth that sumo wrestlers wear. "I learned that when I visited Nagoya three months ago as part of a cultural exchange. That's our sister city in Japan. Are we good now?"

Morris nodded. "We're good."

Chapter Eight

Gilman needed to make arrangements for the press conference. Before he left, he told Morris that Commissioner Hadley was in the back of the house with the other police and crime scene specialists.

"I texted him that you've taken the job. You don't need me to go back there and introduce you, right?"

Gilman was trying to be nonchalant about asking this, but Morris could see his uneasiness. It was obvious Gilman didn't want to go near the corpse, that seeing the photos and hearing the details of the murder was about all he could handle. Morris told him he'd be fine, and not to worry about anything.

After Gilman left, Morris called Natalie to tell her what was happening, and that he wasn't going to be able to make their seven-thirty reservation at the Banyan Tree Grill.

"I'd hate for you to miss out also," Morris said. "I know how much you were looking forward to it. Why don't you see if Rachel's available? This reservation was damn hard to get, and it would be a shame to waste it."

Rachel was their twenty-three-year-old daughter who was currently a second-year law student at UCLA. While Rachel inherited Morris's stubbornness, fortunately she physically took after Natalie. A slim, petite, dark-haired beautiful girl, although with Morris's flinty slate-gray eyes.

"You just want me going there so I bring you home an order of their pan-roasted chicken."

"I certainly wouldn't complain if you did. Or if you also brought home a slice of their flourless chocolate espresso cake."

"Ha! I thought you've been talking about losing ten pounds."

"I can start tomorrow." Morris made a harrumphing noise and

added defensively, "You wouldn't believe the willpower I exhibited today at the studio. Food tables laid out with free donuts and other sweets, and I resisted them all. A lesser man would've cracked."

"A slight exaggeration."

"Only slight."

Natalie made a *hmm* noise at that. "My poor hubby. It must've been torture," she said. "I'll see what Rachel has to say. But if I pick you up a slice of that cake, it will only be so I can have a taste." Her tone turned more pensive as she asked, "I remember reading about those murders in New York. How sure are you that it's the same person?"

"At this point, no idea. I haven't dipped my toes into the case yet. But be careful out there. And tell Rachel to be careful, and if for some *fercockta* reason she's been thinking of dying her hair blonde, tell her not to."

Morris could just about hear his wife shudder over the phone, or perhaps he only imagined it.

"That's right," she said in a softer, more fragile voice. "He always killed in threes. His next victim is going to be a woman my age. And the one after that, a girl Rachel's age, although with blonde hair."

"If it's the same person. I'll have to ask you not to share this information with anyone. Not even Rachel."

"Aren't they going to be warning the public about this?"

"There'll be a press conference later tonight to announce that MBI has been hired to lead up the investigation, but it's undecided whether we'll be tying this murder to the Skull Cracker Killer, or what details we'll be giving. All that has to be figured out over the next few hours."

"So you'll be having a long night?"

"One of many I suppose."

"Try not to get home too late." She hesitated before adding, "I don't want that pan-roasted chicken giving you indigestion. Or the chocolate espresso cake. You know how you get when you eat after midnight."

Morris promised he'd get home as early as possible, and if he got home after midnight, he'd save the take-out food for breakfast the next morning. After he got off the call, he followed the hubbub to the back of the house where a good deal of activity seemed to be taking place. Morris recognized everyone there except one of the crime-scene guys. He nodded to Hadley who was talking to the medical examiner, Dr. Roger Smichen, a tall, cadaverous-looking man with a head as bald as an egg. For a long moment, Hadley glowered at him, red-faced and jowly, before consenting to nod back.

"Brick, glad to have you and your firm working this," he said in a gruff, unhappy tone that showed he wasn't at all glad. He cleared his throat and told Morris he'd let Smichen fill him in on what was done to the victim, then walked away to converse with Detective Walsh. Walsh gave Morris a signal to indicate they'd talk soon.

Morris had known Smichen for over twenty years, and Smichen always possessed a naturally dour disposition, although at times would show a sense of humor as dry as a martini that had only been given a whiff of vermouth. The ME wiggled his fingers at Morris so that Morris would join him by the body, and Morris followed him to where the corpse lay crumpled on the floor. The broken up parts of the skull were also on the floor and had been pieced together like a grotesque jigsaw puzzle. Less than a foot away from the dead man's left ear were clumps of brain matter.

"I thought you left the force and started your little investigation firm so you wouldn't have to deal with murders like this," Smichen said.

"And yet here I am."

"Yes, here you are," Smichen agreed, shaking his head dismally.

"Was he alive when this was done to him?"

"Unfortunately, yes. None of this was done postmortem. Obviously, there was a tremendous amount of damage to the skull, but I found a curiously shaped hematoma and several flakes of rust, which makes me think the victim was first hit on the back of the skull with a rusted pipe."

"He was hit from behind?"

Smichen nodded as he pulled on his lower lip. He did a deep-knee bend and pointed with his index finger into the open cavity where there was no longer any skull, indicating the spot where the victim would've been hit. He grimaced and gingerly held his hip as he straightened back up.

"Hmm," Morris murmured as he tried to picture the blow. "The victim must've been bent over at the time."

"Possibly. I'll see if I can determine that when I get back to the lab, but possibly."

"So the killer either held a gun to this poor guy and made him bend over, or he asked him to look at some spot on the floor, and then bam, smacked him with a rusty pipe. Any signs of a struggle?"

"None. No defensive wounds either. I did find adhesive residue on the victim's wrists. We'll be figuring out what left it, but a good guess would be after the victim was knocked to the floor, his wrists were taped together behind his back, leaving him helpless."

"And then what? The killer takes a chisel and hammer and breaks apart the skull? Then uses the claw end of the hammer to dig out pieces of the brain?"

Smichen gave Morris an appreciative look. "Very good. At least that would be my rudimentary guess. But again, I need to get this back to the lab before I can tell you for sure."

"Assuming that's what happened, how hard would it be to do something like that?"

"Not that hard, at least not if you're determined and have a strong stomach."

Morris briefly closed his eyes and visualized the murder taking place. "At what point would the victim die?" he asked.

"Not while the skull's being broken apart. He'd probably go into shock once the brain is disturbed, but death wouldn't occur until a good part of the brain was removed."

Smichen again pulled on his lower lip, revealing receding gums. At that moment he looked more cadaverous than at any time since Morris had known him.

"I hope we don't get any more like this one," the ME said.

Morris agreed, but the odds were likely there were going to be two more very soon. A woman in her forties, followed by a blonde girl in her twenties. Unless this wasn't the real Skull Cracker Killer. Or unless Morris and MBI got incredibly lucky.

Chapter Nine

After Morris finished up with Roger Smichen, he next talked with Detective Walsh to get the lay of the land. As with the ME, Morris had known Walsh for a number of years. A tough-as-nails police officer who was bulldogged when it came to investigating her cases. Morris had tried recruiting her for MBI, but she turned him down, telling him that someone needed to stay on the force to catch the bad guys.

"Corey Freeman," Walsh said, telling Morris the name of the victim. "He was a realtor working at Lacey Properties here in Venice. The house is for sale, and Freeman's body was discovered when another realtor was showing the home to a couple—"

"Are they being kept under wraps?"

Walsh nodded. "For now, yeah. They're at the Santa Monica station on Olympic Drive. Before we let them go, you'll get a chance to talk to them, and let them know what they can and can't say. We received the call about the body at four. Uniforms had the site secured shortly after that, and I got here not much later, probably quarter past. It wasn't hard to figure that I needed to get the FBI looking at this, and so I sent them the same digital shots that I think you've seen."

"Yeah, Doug Gilman had a set of prints made and showed me them when I got here."

"Okay, so those photos show how it looked before the ME and forensics team arrived. They didn't change it too much other than seeing how the skull pieces fit together. It didn't take long, maybe a few minutes after I sent those photos in, for me to get a call back from a field agent named Charlie Higgins telling me this looked like SCK. Higgins was one of the agents who had investigated the murders in New York. Other than that, we've got uniforms canvassing the neighborhood for witnesses, and Greg Malevich is trying to find out who Freeman was supposed to meet here."

Morris knew Malevich. A big, blustery guy, but also a solid detective.

"We need to find out what time Freeman stepped into this house," Morris said. "We'll see what Roger comes up with for time of death, but I'm sure it will be at least a four-hour window, and knowing when Freeman came here will help a lot."

"We're still in the dark about that. Just like we are about who he was showing the house to."

"If he was even showing the house," Morris said, frowning. "He could've brought the killer here under a completely different pretext. Or maybe Freeman came here to show the house to someone else, and the killer knocked on the door and asked for a quick look around." Morris sighed and rubbed his eyes as more possibilities came to mind. "We need to get all parking tickets from the area pulled over the last week."

Walsh agreed that made sense. The reason for looking for a week's worth of parking tickets was in case the killer had come to the neighborhood other times, either for casing the house or as part of his planning.

"How about a four block radius? Maybe we'll get lucky with this."

"Sure, I'll put a call in first thing tomorrow morning."

"We also need Freeman's complete schedule for the last month. If he was in fact here under the pretext of showing the killer the house, this might not have been the first house he showed him. The killer could've been planning to kill Freeman at an earlier date, but was interrupted."

"I'll talk to Greg and ask him to dig for that information." Walsh showed a half grimace, half smirk. "Just our luck, huh? This psycho finally decides to crawl out from whatever rock in New York he's been hiding under the last five years, and he has to come out here."

"If it's really SCK."

"Ten to one it is."

Morris almost took Walsh up on that, but he'd never been much of a betting man. Besides, assuming the killer was going to keep killing, their best chances of catching him was if it really was SCK back at work. At least that way they'd have an FBI profiler who'd been studying the murders, as well as a small mountain of other investigative groundwork, and they wouldn't have to be starting from scratch. And if it was SCK responsible for this killing, finding out why he'd been dormant for five years could be what breaks the case open.

Morris decided he'd better get on the phone and talk to Detective Greg Malevich directly. They had no time to waste with this.

Chapter Ten

Henry ended up not killing Susan.

He certainly considered doing it, though. For the full two hours it took to hike the trail, he tortured himself over whether he could get away with murdering her, and even after they'd arrived at the hidden and isolated spot he had discovered a month earlier, he continued to struggle over the matter. His distress must've shown plainly on his face, because Susan's heavily-lined brow scrunched up as she looked at him worriedly and asked if he was feeling ill.

They were overlooking a ravine as they sat together on a blanket that Susan had brought. Henry finally made his decision then.

"A little lightheaded," he lied. "And a tad peaked too. Ah, I'm sorry *honey lips* (a pet name he had given her during their second date), but this hike might've been too much for me. Or maybe it was the cheeseburger I ate for lunch. Whichever it is, I'm not feeling quite up to snuff."

"Oh no!"

He found it endearing that she seemed so genuinely concerned about his well-being. But that wasn't why he decided not to kill her. Once he was finally willing to face reality (because it was getting *awfully* tiring swimming aimlessly in the river de-Nile), he accepted that he couldn't kill Susan unless he also got rid of Gail that same day. How could he reasonably plan on doing that when he didn't even know where she lived? Yeah, he could've tied up Susan like he did Freeman and forced her to divulge her friend's address, but even if he did that how could he trust what she told him? There'd be nothing to stop her from intentionally lying to him, or simply babbling out a wrong address in her fear, and whatever she told him he'd have no way of verifying whether it was true. And even if it were true, this Gail Hawes might be married or living with someone or have roommates, which would complicate things. It very well might not be that easy to kill her—it might be something that he'd have to plan out over days to do it safely, possibly even weeks. All of which meant Susan was going to stay alive for now.

He found it a relief to finally arrive at a decision, but also incredibly disappointing, since this was such a missed opportunity. He had picked the trail because it was so little used these days, and as expected they came across no other hikers that afternoon. Up until the moment they left the restaurant everything had gone exactly to plan, and then they had to run into that busybody. That loud, grinning, meddling woman. Not only would he have to skip killing Susan, but he wouldn't be able to bring anyone else to this perfect spot for murdering, at least as long as Susan remained alive. A heavy sigh rumbled out of him as he accepted all this, and his sigh caused Susan to look at him with even more alarm.

"Nothing to worry about," Henry assured her. "I'll be fine with some rest, although I'm afraid I won't be up to being intimate this afternoon, at least not without risking my heart giving out. Sadly, we'll have to wait until another time."

Now not only did Susan look alarmed, but also frustrated, which further endeared her to him, although he still would've killed her if he didn't have to worry about Gail ruining his plans. But still, Susan might be the only person alive who would sincerely be disappointed over not having sex with him. It was doubtful the same could ever have been said about Sheila, and Henry had had no sexually intimate experiences before his wife.

"Should I call for help?" Susan asked.

Henry smiled and shook his head. "It wouldn't do any good. There's no cell phone coverage up here. Besides, I'll be as good as new with a little rest now and a good night's sleep later. I promise."

"But what about the hike back to the car?"

"It's all downhill. I'll manage."

She didn't seem to like his answer, her concern for him wrecking her face more than her wrinkles. But what could she do? Carry him down the trail?

"Why don't you lie down? We can snuggle at least."

Henry lowered himself so that he lay on his back, and Susan nestled against him with her head on his shoulder and her knees bent and resting on his thigh. Before too long, Henry draped his arm around her. Once he decided not to kill her, he almost weakened and went along with their plans to become intimate. He hadn't had sex since Sheila's accident, and it wasn't as if the two of them were all that sexually active before then. Once every two weeks if he was lucky. So the thought more than crossed his mind to just go ahead with it, but what kind of monster would that make him? To have sex with a woman that moments earlier he'd been planning to murder in a gruesomely horrific fashion? How sick would that be?

Susan pretended it was an accident when her hand brushed against the stiff bulge that had been growing in Henry's pants, even though her hand had lingered far longer than it should've for that to be the case. Her voice sultry, she asked, "Are you sure you're not up to us getting naked and doing the dirty deed? All you have to do is lay back, and I'll do all the work."

Gawd, it was tempting. Even with her barely ripe plums and skinny ass, it was tempting. But the idea of Susan seeing him naked made his hard bulge as soft as a blob of pudding. It was one thing for her to imagine what he might look like without clothing, but it would be another entirely for her to see him that way. It was difficult enough the first time he allowed Sheila to see him naked, and they were in love! He had no doubt that Susan would be utterly disgusted. That his flabby, pudgy body would look far worse than whatever she might've been imagining. Besides, he had made vows to Sheila. For better or for worse. He was going to remain faithful, even with what had happened to her.

"Better for us to just lie like this," he said. "But another day. I promise."

She didn't argue. Her hand had lingered long enough to have felt the bulge in his pants soften. So they lay together, occasionally smooching, until the shadows from a nearby sycamore had crept over them. Henry didn't consider the smooching betraying his wife since he had no choice about the matter, at least not if he wanted to keep alive the possibility of breaking apart Susan's skull on a future date. He also didn't want to raise any suspicions, so the smooching was necessary to maintain the role he was playing.

When they decided to head back down the trail, Susan at first insisted that she carry Henry's backpack, but he wouldn't hear of it.

"No way, *sugar lips*! I'll be dead and buried before I'd let a beautiful sweetheart like you haul my backpack down this rolling hill that they have the audacity to call a mountain."

She blushed at that. "But Howard, dear, you're not feeling well!"

"I'm feeling well enough," he claimed. "Besides, it's just a stroll back to the car. Nothing to worry your head about."

Susan wanted to argue further, reminding him that it would be a two-hour hike down occasionally steep inclines, but she saw the futility of doing so. Henry had no intention of letting her get anywhere near his backpack, let alone carry it. The hammer and chisel were wrapped in cloth so she wouldn't hear any metal clinking, but the weight of the backpack would make her curious, maybe even curious enough to peek inside, which would leave Henry no choice but to drag her off the trail and break open her skull, even if it meant having Gail calling the police later that night and sending them on a hunt for his alias, Howard Donner. Possibly the police wouldn't take Gail's call seriously, at least not at first, but they certainly would after they found Susan's remains. Then their hunt would be for the Skull Cracker Killer, and they could very well have a police sketch to help them with their hunt. Or maybe even a photo. It wouldn't surprise Henry if Gail turned out to be as sneaky as she was meddlesome, and for all he knew she might've clicked a shot of him with her phone when he wasn't looking. But Susan never touched his backpack, so none of that was necessary.

Even though they were going down instead of up, it took the same amount of time to make their way to his car as it did when they'd traveled up the mountain to the spot Henry had chosen. He figured that Susan was intentionally slowing down their pace for his benefit, and he played along, exaggerating the way he huffed and puffed at times. While any small amount of physical activity tended to make him perspire like he was melting away in a sauna, he was actually in remarkably good shape even given his squat, pudgy body, and as his dad liked to say, he was as strong as an ox.

Since it was expected (and again, he didn't want to raise any suspicions), he took Susan to a casual but nice restaurant in Santa Monica where they were seated in a private booth and the waiter barely paid them any attention, although Henry still made sure to bury his face in the menu, or to turn toward Susan whenever the waiter was nearby. Afterward he took her home. When she invited him in to have a snifter of cognac (her idea, Henry preferred beer) and to see the inside of the town house that she rented, he relented. It was dark, and no one was hanging around outside, so he felt confident he could do so without anyone seeing him there.

It was late, a couple of minutes after ten o 'clock, before he arrived back at his modest ranch-style home in Simi Valley. Sheila was of course where he had left her. One sniff was all he needed to know that she had soiled herself, which was what he had expected to find. He avoided her stare, and channel surfed through the stations until he found what he was looking for. When he was driving home, he'd heard a news report over the radio about a realtor being murdered in Venice. While the report didn't provide any significant details, it did say that the police would be holding a press conference at ten o'clock, and Henry wanted to hear what they had to say.

Henry caught the press conference from the beginning. They didn't say much about the murder, only that they suspected the realtor had been lured to the murder site by someone posing as a potential home buyer. They certainly didn't say anything about this being the work of the Skull Cracker Killer. Maybe they hadn't made that connection yet. It would make sense if that were so. For the past five years Henry had been impressed at how the New York police had kept what had been done to the victims mostly bottled up. Word might've leaked out early on about their skulls being cracked open, but it was what was done to the victims' brains that would give people their real shivers. Heck, if the press had ever gotten wind of that part of it, they would've had a field day with it. So yeah, these Los Angeles police had no clue yet what they were dealing with. They would eventually. Some smart guy in the FBI would make the connection. Henry's lips tightened into a hard grin as he imagined what would happen then.

The rest of the press conference pretty much followed along the lines of what Henry expected. They gave the address of the house where the murder took place and showed photos of the outside of the home, and asked the public to call a special number if anyone had seen a suspicious person near that address that day. They didn't narrow down the time that they were interested in, which meant they didn't know when Freeman had arranged to show Henry (really Leslie Gorman) the house. The police all but confirmed that when they also asked for anyone knowing Corey Freeman's plans that day to call the special number.

The only curveball the police threw was at the end when they introduced a private consultant who was going to be handling the investigation. That seemed odd to Henry, although from what they were saying about this man, he was supposed to be a hotshot ex-cop. Henry would've known this guy Brick was an ex-cop even if they hadn't mentioned it from his cheap suit and the way his hair was cut short making it look like a bristle brush. Not very physically imposing, although he had that hard-nosed cop look about him. It was his eyes that gave Henry pause to worry. Tough, slate-gray eyes shining with intelligence. Those eyes made Henry especially glad he'd decided what he had about Susan. As much as he needed to kill again, Henry accepted that he was going to have to be extra smart about it and not take any chances.

That ex-cop Brick didn't say much at the press conference, only that people needed to take precautions, and if they spotted any suspicious activity they should call the police. No kidding. *Nothing but a bunch of hooey*, Henry thought after the press conference had concluded and he had a few moments to digest what was said.

Sheila hadn't spoken a word to him since he'd returned home. Without looking at her, he could picture in his mind the way she sat twisted and crippled in her chair, her eyes harsh and accusatory. He squeezed his eyes shut to get rid of that image, and without saying a word he connected his iPhone to the TV and played back the recording he had made of what he had done to Corey Freeman. Only after his wife had watched the murder, did he pick her up and carry her to the bathroom so he could clean her up and dress her in fresh pajamas. While he had used a sponge on her body, he had been gentle enough so that he could've been cleaning dust off a dragonfly's wing.

Chapter Eleven

Long Island, 1979

Henry could not pay attention to a single word Mr. Shapiro was saying. He wasn't very good at math, and algebra with all of its x's and y's and z's only confused him, but that wasn't why Mr. Shapiro's voice had become only a soft drone that he barely noticed. No, the reason for his inability to focus on anything his math teacher was saying was that Sally Klosky took the desk directly in front of his!

Normally, it was hard enough in class to concentrate knowing Sally was in the same room as him, but before today she always sat on the other side of the room so he couldn't see her unless he craned his neck so that he was looking behind his shoulder. He would never dare do that and risk having Sally catch him sneaking a peek at her. While it would be torture knowing she was nearby, he was still able to function, at least sort of. But now she was so close to him that he could reach forward and touch her. And he could smell her! He breathed in deeply an aroma of apple blossoms from her shampoo mixed with a whiff of the spearmint gum she was chewing, as well as a hint of her musty body odor. On any other girl maybe that smell wouldn't be so wonderful, but coming from Sally it was the most intoxicating odor he could imagine.

Henry was convinced Sally Klosky was the most beautiful thirteen-year-old girl who ever lived, and anyone trying to argue otherwise just didn't know what they were talking about. That would be like saying that *Star Wars* wasn't the greatest movie ever made. Or Spider-man comic books weren't the best. It just wasn't something open for debate. Everything about her was perfect. Her golden, curvy hair that rolled past her shoulders like finely spun silk, her adorable button nose, her peaches-and-cream complexion, the tiny dimple in her chin, that slight overbite that would show when she'd chew on the end of her pen. And her dreamlike body. He would blush deep red whenever he thought of the way she looked in her tight T-shirt and shorts during gym class.

Sally Klosky had Henry's heart and soul and was the only girl he could ever truly love, no question about it, even if he could only do so from afar. Except now it wasn't from afar! She was at most two feet away from him. A mere twenty-four inches, maybe less! At first that knowledge had caused a feverish hotness to flush his face and for his heart to pound away so hard that it left him dizzy. Then he realized the opportunity that he'd been presented with, and he moved his desk and chair just enough so he could see her in profile, and then he went about sketching her. Henry might not have been very good at math, but he'd always been a wiz at drawing. People, animals, inanimate objects like cars and spaceships, it didn't matter. He could draw anything. His art teacher liked to say he was a natural.

Henry had already finished four sketches of Sally, and was starting his fifth, and he had to admit they were pretty good if he did say so himself. It would've been impossible for him to fully capture her immense beauty—not even Rembrandt or any of those other old-time dead painters would be skilled enough to do that, but he was pleased with his results so far. He had plans for what he was going to do with them. Later that night he'd start working on a new comic book, and he'd make Sally his superhero. Maybe when he was done with it he'd summon up the nerve to show her his work, and maybe if he did a good-enough job, it would help him win her heart.

Henry was adding the finishing touches to his fifth sketch of Sally when his notebook was lifted away from him. He stared in horror as Mr. Shapiro held his notebook and looked over the sketches he had drawn. As his horror grew, he silently pleaded for Mr. Shapiro not to tell Sally what he had done. It would be worse than death for him if that happened.

Mr. Shapiro shifted his eyes away from the notebook to give Henry a severe stone-faced look, and Henry felt his heart just about stop as he tried to will himself to die, not thinking he could survive what was coming.

Mr. Shapiro, in an exceedingly dry voice, said, "Mr. Pollard, I was curious what you were so assiduously scribbling in your notebook, and you can only imagine my surprise to see that you were in fact taking copious notes from my lecture. It is always rewarding for a teacher to find a student so attentive."

Henry blinked several times, not quite believing what he had heard. Mr. Shapiro handed him back his notebook.

Raising an eyebrow, Mr. Shapiro said, "I will assume that moving forward you will continue to pay rapt attention on the classwork. Isn't that true, Mr. Pollard?"

At first Henry couldn't make sense of what had happened, and then he understood the mercy Mr. Shapiro had shown him, and he nodded his head furiously.

Mr. Shapiro gave Henry one last severe look before continuing with his explanation of how x could be derived from y and z given the two equations. Henry felt like a condemned man who'd miraculously been given a last-minute reprieve, and he forced himself for the rest of the class to ignore Sally's presence, not even allowing himself a whiff of her fragrance. When the class ended, Mr. Shapiro asked Henry to stay behind so they could speak for a few minutes. Once the rest of the students had filed out of the classroom, Mr. Shapiro signaled for Henry to sit in a chair across from his desk.

"You do realize this is a math class and not art?"

Henry gulped as he fought to keep from crying.

Mr. Shapiro let out a sigh, his stern expression softening. "You are talented, I'll give you that," he said. "But I can't have you spending class time drawing your fellow students, no matter how pretty they are. If I were forced to flunk you, it would not only reflect poorly on you, but on myself also. Do we understand each other?"

Henry felt tears leaking from his eyes and worming their way down his cheeks. "I will try harder, Mr. Shapiro, I promise." He choked down a sob before blurting out, "Thank you so much for not telling Sally. I might've died if you had."

"Yes, Mr. Pollard, I understand. Death by humiliation. Not the most pleasant way to go." He paused, then added with a wistful smile, "I assure you almost every single math teacher alive can sympathize. And Mr. Pollard, I assure you also that you will certainly be trying harder. We will pick a day where we will meet after school each week so that we can bring your work to a passing level. Agreed?"

Henry nodded energetically. "Any day you want. Can I go now?"

Mr. Shapiro gave Henry an uneasy smile. "Just one more minute," he said. "This may be a difficult lesson to learn, but Mr. Pollard, in life one must temper one's expectations. One must be realistic, or we open ourselves up to crushing disappointments. For example, I don't foresee you ever being an A student in math, but with enough hard work you should be able to earn a C. There's nothing wrong with that. No shame whatsoever. Everybody has different aptitudes, different strengths, as you clearly have a strong aptitude in drawing."

"I understand."

Mr. Shapiro's wistful smile weakened. He left his chair and sat on the edge of his desk so he was closer to Henry, his smile growing sadder as he continued to stare down at his student.

"The same can be true with affairs of the heart, although there the disappointment may be even more painful. Youthful crushes are natural, but as painful as they may turn out to be, they're ultimately fleeting. Miss Klosky is very pretty, no doubt, but have you considered talking with Miss Bower? She's a very nice girl. Smart, a good heart to her."

Henry's cheeks burned red as he realized Mr. Shapiro was telling him that Sally was well out of his league and that he should instead focus his attentions on Nancy Bower, a pear-shaped girl with braces, greasy hair, and bad skin. At that moment he never hated anyone more than he did Mr. Shapiro. Tears of anger welled in his eyes, but he'd be damned if he'd let Mr. Shapiro see him cry. He did, however, want his math teacher to hear the biting hatred in his voice as he thanked him for his concern, and then he was out of his chair and rushing to the door. Mr. Shapiro tried saying something else to him, but Henry ignored whatever it was and slammed the door shut behind him as he stepped into the hallway.

He was so caught up in his hurt that he didn't notice that Mark Angler, Brad Black, and Tony Fausano were waiting for him. These three had tormented him since fifth grade when they nicknamed him the *hog ogre* after their teacher had read the class the book, *Zeralda's Ogre*.

He noticed them, however, after one of them tripped him and sent him sprawling to the floor. Before he could gather himself another of them ripped his notebook out of his hands. A coldness filled his head and his world came crashing down around him after he'd gotten to his knees and saw that Brad Black was looking through his notebook. Brad flashed him the nastiest smile Henry had ever seen.

"I knew a dummy like you wouldn't be taking any notes," Brad said. "What were you going to do with these drawings? Beat off to them later? Huh, is that what little hoggies like you do?"

In a blind rush, Henry was on his feet, charging Brad, but Mark and Tony grabbed him and held him back. Brad ripped the drawings from the notebook and walked up to Henry's face, his nasty smile turning into an exceptionally ugly leer.

"What do you think you were going to do just then?" Brad demanded as he held a fist up to Henry's face and his spittle flew into Henry's eyes. "You were going to fight me? If you tried that I'd punch you in the face so many times I'd pulverize it, maybe even make it uglier than it is now, if that's possible."

"Please, just give me back my drawings," Henry pleaded.

Brad snorted out a laugh, then turned and yelled out, "Hey Sally, want to see what the hog ogre was doing in class?"

To Henry's increasing dismay, Sally was standing only twenty feet away with several of her friends. At this point, he was begging Brad and the others to please let him go and to give him back his drawings, and then he was silently begging God for Sally not to come over, but none of his begging did any good. Sally and three of her friends wandered over, but all Henry could focus on was Sally, and how her beautiful face was marred by confusion. He'd been trying to break free of Mark and Tony's grasp, but he gave up then.

Brad handed Sally the loose-leaf notebook pages, and as Sally looked at them with an inscrutable expression, Henry prayed that she'd recognize how devoted he was to her and that his love for her was pure, and that she would recognize the goodness in him, even if he did look like a hog ogre. It seemed like an eternity before she stopped studying those sheets of paper, although it could've only been seconds. During it all Henry's insides had turned into a cold queasy mush, and he prayed that she'd say something kind, or at least look at him with kindness. He didn't care any longer whether his love for her remained unrequited as long as he could continue to love her. When she finally looked at him, she did so with an inscrutable expression, and then as she stared into his eyes, her face contorted into something that wasn't so beautiful any longer.

"Yuck," she said.

She ripped the drawings up and let the torn-up pieces of paper flutter to the floor. She must've walked away with her friends then, but Henry was blind to that. He pulled himself free of Mark and Tony's grasp, which wasn't so hard since they were laughing themselves to tears. Then he ran from them, and kept running even though he was badly huffing and puffing shortly after leaving the school grounds. He was a mess, tears and snot streaming down his face, but he didn't stop running until he'd covered the full three miles from the school to his house.

Chapter Twelve

"You need to talk to your son!"

Mr. Pollard had just stepped through the door after a long day of working for the New York City Transit Authority. He was amazed his wife even heard him seeing that she was in the kitchen preparing dinner and she had the TV set in there blasting away. The woman must have hearing like a bat. That was all he could think of. He breathed in deeply and smelled the sausage, peppers, and onions that were cooking. Well, that was one good thing at least. He joined her in the kitchen, and after lowering the volume of the TV, he nuzzled the back of her neck while she busied herself with the homemade sauce she was preparing. She acted as if he wasn't even there. He gave up and took a beer from the fridge.

"He's my son now, huh?" he said. "I thought he's always your little angel." Sighing, he asked, "What did the boy do?"

"He got into a fight with other boys in school." Her voice turned brittle as she added, "And he cut three of his classes."

Mr. Pollard took a long pull on his beer, then wiped his mouth with the back of his hand.

"Doesn't sound like that big a deal," he said.

Mrs. Pollard turned to give her husband a severe look. "It is a big deal," she insisted. "Henry won't tell me what happened, but I could tell that he'd been crying. You need to get to the bottom of it."

Mr. Pollard took another pull on his beer while his wife stood her ground, her arms crossed over her chest. Anyone looking at them would have a hard time reconciling them as Henry's biological parents, at least at first. Mr. Pollard stood six feet, four inches tall, and was a large, barrel-chested, broad-shouldered block of a man. While his skin was naturally pale and his features could be construed as doughy and a bit lumpy, he was good-looking in a rough and tumble sort of way. His wife in contrast was barely five feet tall; a diminutive and very pretty redhead. It would take some doing, but if you had enough of an imagination and you studied them carefully you'd be able to see where bits of Henry came from, and the only conclusion you'd be able to make was that Henry had been badly shortchanged genetically. Almost any combination of genes from his parents would've resulted in a good-looking kid, and Henry got the one in a million mixture that didn't.

Mr. Pollard blinked first in the mini-staring contest he had with his wife, realizing quickly enough that if he didn't give in she'd let the sausages burn.

"Okay, I'll talk to him," he grumbled, letting out a heavy sigh of defeat.

"Henry's in his room." A worried look weakened Mrs. Pollard's expression. "He insists he's not hungry and won't be eating dinner. Something's wrong."

Mr. Pollard nodded. Sausage, pepper, and onion smothered in his wife's homemade tomato sauce was not only his favorite, but Henry's. While he thought his wife babied Henry too much and that boys Henry's age needed to be able to work out their own differences with fists if necessary, he had to admit that if Henry voluntarily missed tonight's dinner, there had to be a problem. He polished off the rest of his beer and left the empty bottle on the countertop, then headed off to his son's room. He didn't bother knocking on the closed door, and just walked in without warning while Henry was doing one of his drawings.

In his no-nonsense tone, he demanded, "Tell me about this fight you had today."

Henry looked ashen as he tried to bury the drawing he'd been working on within a stack of other drawings.

"Nothing happened."

This was said so sullenly that Mr. Pollard eyed his son carefully until he could intuit the meaning. "Some boys picked on you, huh?"

Henry looked utterly miserable.

"And you didn't fight back?"

Henry gave him a crestfallen, helpless look that answered him as well as any words could have.

Mr. Pollard nodded to himself. "It's my fault, not yours. I should've taught you how to fight by now," he said, although as far as he was concerned it was really his wife's fault. She was always babying Henry, always insisting that their son was too sensitive to get into fights or do anything where he could hurt himself, which was ridiculous. Thirteen-year-old boys are supposed to get into fights! They're supposed to roughhouse and get scrapes and bumps and bruises! Mr. Pollard closed the bedroom door so his wife wouldn't be able to hear them.

"You let other boys pick on you and it never stops," he said secretively once he was sitting on Henry's bed. "Here's what you do. Tomorrow you pick out the meanest of them and you beat the bejesus out of that boy. You do that and the rest of them will leave you alone forever."

Henry gave his dad a look as if he were crazy. "I can't do that."

"Sure you can. You're as strong as an ox, Henry. You get that from me. All you need to do is get your hands on that boy, and the fight's over. Stand up, I'll show you what to do."

Reluctantly, Henry did as he was told.

"Okay, you got short arms, so you want to get close to that boy and then start pounding away. Clench your fists as tight as you can and use short punches. Don't pull your fists back any farther than your chest. Let's see what you got."

Mr. Pollard held both palms up to his son, and Henry half-heartedly punched one of them.

"Come on, you can do better than that. Let it rip. Fast and furious, and twist your body into each punch."

Henry started punching his hands, at first reluctantly, but then a crazed intensity took over.

"Ow, ow, ow, you're breaking my bones. Don't stop, though . . . Ow, ow, ow. Holy cow, you're one strong kid . . . A natural mauler. You're going to make mincemeat out of that bully. He won't stand a chance."

Henry had thrown around forty punches in rapid succession before he started slowing down and his punches became sluggish.

"That's enough for now, killer," Mr. Pollard said with a renewed sense of pride. "I almost feel sorry for that bully, but that boy deserves every bit of the lesson you're going to be teaching him."

Henry stopped punching his dad's palms. His stubby arms fell slack, and he started looking mopey again.

"I don't think I can do this," he said dejectedly.

Mr. Pollard good-naturedly tousled his son's hair. "Sure you can, and you will. Henry, I have complete faith in you. Believe your old man, it will be over before you know it. And then the rest of those kids will know what they're dealing with." He paused before adding, "You're going to need your strength for tomorrow. You're sure you don't want any of that sausage and pepper mom's cooking up? It sure smelled good."

Grudgingly Henry admitted that he could eat.

"Good. Let's go to the kitchen and help mom set the table. And don't mention any of this to her. No need for her to worry, especially since it's going to be that other boy who'll be getting knocked on his butt."

Mr. Pollard draped his arm around his son's shoulders and walked with him to the kitchen. He'd almost asked Henry about the drawing Henry had been working on when he came into the room. Before his son had shoved it into a stack of other drawings, Mr. Pollard had caught a glimpse of it, and it looked to him like a picture of a blonde girl having spikes driven into her eyes. He might've been mistaken, though, and besides Henry had quite an imagination and was always drawing weird stuff.

The next day after opening bell, Henry was walking to his locker when Brad Black sidled up to him and called him an ugly little hoggie. Brad was probably going to say more, but before he could Henry turned and punched him in the stomach with every ounce of strength he could muster, and Brad went as white as a sheet and his body sagged. The next moment, Henry was shoving Brad into an empty locker. Brad was a tall, skinny boy, and while the lockers were five feet long from the floor to the top shelf, they were also very narrow and weren't made to have teenage boys shoved into them. The sides of Brad's head got scraped pretty badly and a piece of his left earlobe was torn off. By the time the assistant principal, Mr. Aronson, had pulled Henry away, Brad Black had been completely forced inside the locker, and later had to be cut out by the fire department.

The school originally talked about suspending Henry for the rest of the school year, but after hearing from other students how Brad and his gang had picked on Henry for years, his suspension was shortened to two weeks. When Henry returned back to school, no one picked on him anymore. Further, if he had paid any attention to Sally Klosky, he would've noticed that she now looked at him with a renewed interest. But he no longer paid any attention to her. As far as he was concerned, she no longer existed. His second day back, he sought out Nancy Bower during lunch and asked if he could sit with her. She told him she'd like that.

Chapter Thirteen

Los Angeles, the present

The lights were off when Morris unlocked the front door to his house, which made sense since it was three minutes before midnight. He was tired and hungry, and his stomach had been rumbling for hours. Earlier he had to snack on something if he was going to make it through the press conference without passing out from hunger, and he knew Natalie would've wanted him to have something healthy, like an apple, while he was craving potato chips, so he compromised and had both. But that was five hours ago, which meant all he'd had that day other than the apple and chips was a tuna-salad sandwich. Now as he opened up the refrigerator, he prayed silently that he'd find a take-out bag from the Banyan Tree Grill waiting for him. When he saw the bag with the restaurant's logo, he silently whispered his thanks.

Inside the bag was an order of the pan-roasted chicken and a slice of chocolate espresso cake, and, as Natalie had threatened, a small spoonful of the cake had been dug out, really only a nibble. Of course, he wasn't about to eat any dessert with espresso in it after midnight, he'd save that for breakfast tomorrow morning, but it would be something to look forward to. Morris again whispered his thanks as he moved the chicken into a pan so he could reheat it. He had just closed the oven door when he heard a soft padding behind him, and then the excited piglike grunts his bull terrier, Parker, made.

Parker wagged his tail furiously while his rear end wiggled like a crazed whirling dervish, all the while the dog making more of his piglike grunts. Morris got down on one knee so Parker could push his cement-hard head into Morris's stomach while Morris scratched Parker behind his ears.

"You just woke up, huh?" Morris commented in a soft whisper as the dog stretched and nearly unhinged his jaw as he yawned. "Let me guess, you smelled the food and thought you could weasel a midnight snack out of me?"

Another of Parker's piglike grunts.

"Yeah, well, not the Banyan Tree Grill chicken. Sorry pal, you're out of luck there."

"Who are you kidding?"

Morris looked back to see that Natalie had joined him in the kitchen. She had a tan cloth robe wrapped around her slender body and fuzzy pink slippers covering her small feet. At ninety-five pounds she wasn't about to make a lot of noise moving about the house, but it was because of her slippers that Morris didn't hear her enter the kitchen.

"Ha! If Parker thinks he'll wear me down, he'll soon find out who's boss," Morris said. "He's not getting a morsel of that chicken."

The dog let out another grunt over hearing his name. Natalie laughed. "We both know who's boss, and we both know you'll give in like you always do," she said. "Although I can't blame you. We've got a champion moocher on our hands."

"We'll see." Morris gave Parker's muzzle several rubs with his palm, then straightened up. "I'm reheating the chicken at three fifty for fifteen minutes. Sound good?"

"I'd add two ounces of water so it doesn't dry out, and cover it with some foil."

Morris embraced his wife and gave her a kiss. Parker, jealous of the attention, attempted to bull his way between them.

"I tried to be quiet," he said. "I apologize if I woke you. And thanks for picking up the food."

"You didn't wake me. I couldn't sleep. Hon, you better take care of the chicken, otherwise it might be too dry for Parker. We both know he's getting at least half of it."

There were two grunts this time: the piglike one from the dog, and a harrumph of protest from Morris. He left his wife so he could add the water and the foil to the pan he was reheating, then sat down at the kitchen table. Parker plopped down by his feet while his wife got behind him and kneaded her thin, delicate fingers into his neck muscles.

"Did Rachel accompany you?" Morris asked.

"She was busy studying so I took Claudia."

Claudia Franzetti was an osteopath who had an office in the same building where Natalie had her therapist office. "A nice woman," Morris said. "I hope you had an enjoyable dinner."

"Delicious. The swordfish was excellent."

Morris raised an eyebrow at that. "You didn't order their famous pan-roasted chicken? Sacrilege!"

Natalie dug her fingers a bit deeper into Morris's neck muscles. "I hate to break this to you, hon, but not everybody has to order their favorite dish every single time they dine out. You do, of course. You're such a creature of habit. At Banyan Tree, it's the pan-roasted chicken, at Bernie's Deli, the corned beef on rye, at Seven Star, the kung pao chicken, at Masala Dhaba, the tandoori lamb, at Lucca's, the lasagna."

"It's not so much that I'm a creature of habit, it's more that I know what I like," Morris argued. He took a deep breath and let it out slowly through his nose. "That feels really good. You've got magic fingers, Nat."

"The reason you married me."

"One of the reasons. The fact you're a knockout didn't hurt."

Natalie moved her hands down to Morris's shoulders. "You're so tense," she said. "A little less so after working on your neck, but still it's almost like I'm trying to massage stone." Her voice grew softer as she said, "I'm surprised you took on this investigation. I thought you were done with serial killers. Especially after that Vincent Rubosto monster. That case took so much out of you."

Vincent Rubosto was the Hillside Cannibal, and was a particularly noxious and aberrant personality who'd murdered and ate the internal organs of all eleven of his victims. Morris shrugged. "The name of my company is Morris Brick Investigations. We handle investigation," he said.

"Don't be smart with me. What you've just signed up for is a far cry from the movie and TV consultations and the handful of background checks and burglary cases you've been working on."

"I know. I certainly didn't expect to be offered something like this, and if you'd asked me yesterday if I'd willingly take on another serial-killer case, I would've said no. But when this was presented to me, I couldn't turn it down."

"Why not?"

"The idea of stopping this psycho seemed too important."

"Hmm," Natalie murmured as she considered this. "I could see how you'd especially feel that way after spending a day watching them film that idiotic movie. Is the rest of your team onboard with taking on another serial killer?"

"I called them, and yeah, they all want to do this."

Natalie continued to rub Morris's shoulder for several more minutes before announcing that her hands were getting tired. She joined Morris at the table, and looked preoccupied as she sat across from him.

"Don't worry," Morris said. "I won't let the investigation wear me down."

"You did those other times."

"Yeah, I did." He winked at his wife. "But I'd like to think I've learned something over the years about taking these cases too personally. I'll make sure to keep more distance this time, I promise. Besides, I've got a feeling that we'll be catching this psycho soon."

Natalie looked at Morris as if she didn't fully believe him on either count, but whether she was too tired or thought it would be pointless, she kept her arguments to herself. After several minutes of silence, Morris asked whether she had warned Rachel not to dye her hair blonde.

"She's not going to dye her hair."

Morris knew his wife too well to know what she was really saying, and he felt a jumpiness in his stomach. "You didn't warn her," he complained.

"No, I didn't, and for good reason. All I told Rachel was that MBI was hired to investigate today's murder in Venice, and that you'd be taking part in the press conference the police department was giving." Natalie showed Morris a weary smile, and added, "If I had told Rachel anything else, she would've cross-examined me until she had ferreted out the truth. And if I had told her anything about this Skull Cracker Killer targeting blonde girls, and she knew the city wasn't warning other girls about that, she would've dyed her hair blonde in protest. As it was, our daughter demonstrated her future prosecutorial skills by giving me the fifth degree over why the city would hire a private firm to investigate a murder. You should be amazed that I didn't crack."

Morris knew his wife was right. If Rachel had gotten even the slightest hint that blonde girls in their early twenties were more at risk of being targeted by this killer, she would be dying her hair out of solidarity. There was no reason for him to feel the uneasiness he was feeling. They didn't even know yet that this was SCK, which was why they had decided only to warn the public about taking necessary safety precautions, instead of panicking every woman in her forties and every blonde girl in her twenties. Besides, there was no reason Rachel would dye her hair, even though she had done it twice when she was an undergraduate student at Stanford—once dying her hair green, another time a shocking pink. And even if she were a blonde and this was SCK, the chances of her being picked by him given the thousands of other blonde girls in Los Angeles were minuscule. Still, as tiny as the possibility was, the idea of either Natalie or Rachel being targeted by SCK freaked him out. Even if he accepted that he was only being paranoid and that his wife and daughter were going to be safe, knowing that women like them were potential victims of this psycho angered him, and that was also partly why he took the job.

As Morris sat momentarily lost in his thoughts, he looked up and saw that Natalie now understood why he wanted to hunt down SCK. He was going to explain himself, but he was saved by the bell when the oven timer went off. He got up from the table so he could get the reheated pan-roasted chicken that he'd been dreaming of all day. Parker rolled to his feet and let out one of his pig grunts, knowing he was going to be getting his midnight snack.

Chapter Fourteen

Sam Goodman's plane arrived on schedule at LAX, and he looked no worse for wear when he walked into the MBI office suite on Wilshire Boulevard after his six-hour-and-twenty-minute flight and thirty-eight-minute cab ride. Morris already had the rest of the MBI team assembled, along with Dr. Roger Smichen, Detectives Walsh and Malevich, and two other LAPD detectives who'd been assigned for the duration to the investigation.

After introductions were made, Morris asked his office manager Greta Lindstrom to make copies of Goodman's presentation from the flash drive the FBI profiler had brought. While they waited for these, Goodman poured himself a cup of coffee and helped himself to a bagel and cream cheese, and then engaged in small talk with Morris and other members of the team. Ten minutes later Greta brought in enough copies for everyone present, and MBI's computer and hacking specialist, Adam Felger, had everything set up for a video presentation. Goodman took one last bite of his bagel, used a napkin to wipe a smear of cream cheese from his lips, and was about to begin when Morris received a call from the mayor's deputy assistant, Doug Gilman.

"An unusual situation has arisen," Gilman said.

Morris excused himself from the gathering, and once he was out in the hallway with the conference-room door closed, asked Gilman if he was going to be happy with the situation.

"Doubtful," Gilman said. "I'm certainly not thrilled by it."

"What is it?"

Gilman hesitated, then said, "I believe you're personally acquainted with Philip Stonehedge?"

Because he wasn't expecting that name, it took Morris a moment before he remembered that Stonehedge was the actor starring as the serial killer in *The Carver* film, and that they'd spent time talking together in the actor's trailer. Even though it had been less than a day, it seemed like this had happened months ago.

"I met him yesterday," Morris said. "So?"

"So Stonehedge saw last night's press conference and decided he wants to tag along with you on this investigation. The studio that's making his latest film—the one you've been consulting on— has been calling the mayor all morning to make that happen, and they've succeeded. The mayor has given his blessing."

Jerry had called a half hour earlier to tell Morris that filming for *The Carver* was being shut down for a week. Now he knew why.

"How about Hadley?" Morris asked.

"The Commissioner signed off."

"Why in the world would they do that?"

"Because the studio will be paying the city two million dollars for this privilege," Gilman said. "I guess they see this as a unique promotional opportunity for when this movie comes out. Having Stonehedge stumping around, giving interviews about how he was on the team that tracked Corey Freeman's killer."

"I don't like this."

"Yeah, I didn't think you would. But it's only going to be for seven days. That's all we agreed to, and then you're free of him. Besides, according to Stonehedge you two have a good rapport."

That was a stretch. Morris had spent no more than twenty minutes talking to the actor, and his feelings had been pretty much neutral regarding Stonehedge.

"This isn't a game," Morris said, his voice growing tight from his growing exasperation. "Nor is it a Hollywood publicity stunt. We're trying to catch this maniac before he breaks open any more skulls."

"I know that, but Morris, we're talking about seven days. That's all. Besides, if you think about it it's not that big a deal. You cops have been having ride-alongs with actors for years."

A throbbing had started in Morris's temples, and he squeezed his eyes closed and slowly began massaging the area around his eyes with his thumb and index finger from his left hand as he held his cellphone with his right. "Not when we're dealing with a serial killer," he said. "We'll be putting Stonehedge's safety at risk—"

"He's been warned about that."

"Yeah, well, that's only one issue. Another is that we need to control the messages we give out to the media. What we put out there could be critical in capturing this killer. Not only does Stonehedge risk making this into an even bigger media circus than it's going to be, but if he says the wrong thing either on social media or in an interview, it could ruin our chances of catching this guy."

"He won't say anything," Gilman said. "At least he better not. Stonehedge signed a nondisclosure agreement that forbids him from saying anything about the investigation while it's ongoing. If he does we'll be prosecuting him, and he understands that." There was a deep breath and exhalation from Gilman, then, "Look, Morris, this is happening. There's nothing I can do about it, and nothing you can do about it. I called to give you a heads-up, but deal with it the best you can, okay?"

Morris applied more pressure as he massaged the area around his eyes. "Was he told this might be SCK?" he asked.

"No."

"When's he coming?"

"Any minute."

The office suite door opened and Morris looked up to see Stonehedge walking into MBI's lobby. He told Gilman he'd talk to him again later, and signaled for Stonehedge to join him.

The actor had on thick-rimmed eyeglasses, a fake prosthetic nose, scruffy blond wig, and had an equally scruffy fake mustache and beard attached to his face. He also wore badly faded jeans, a Los Angeles Dodgers T-shirt, and old running shoes. It was a decent disguise; the nose, wig, facial hair all looked real. If Morris hadn't been expecting the actor, he might've been fooled by it.

Stonehedge shot Morris a sheepish grin as he walked over to him and offered his hand, which Morris ignored. The actor seemed momentarily taken aback by the slight, but recovered quickly and acted as if Morris hadn't just dissed him. "You like my disguise? This is what I wear when I don't want to be recognized," he said. "I really appreciate you letting me do this." This last part was said as if Morris actually had any say in the matter.

"Why do you even want to do this?"

Stonehedge's grin turned a bit strained. "The scenes I shot yesterday were lousy. I was lousy. A ridiculous walking cartoon, nothing more than that. Jerry's going to have to reshoot those scenes. But if I can immerse myself in this for a week, I'll crack this nut, I'm sure of it, and I won't embarrass myself in this role."

"Really? Why do you think a murder investigation will help you do that?"

"Morris, man, don't kid a kidder. This isn't just a murder. The city of Los Angeles isn't going to hire you for a run-of-the-mill murder. This is the real deal. Am I right?"

Morris was going to try bluffing him and see if he could change Stonehedge's mind, but he accepted that the actor was too stubborn and he'd only be wasting his time.

"It could be," Morris admitted. "Here's how we'll do this. I'll allow you to observe as long as you don't interfere. I want you to be as good as invisible. Okay?"

"Not a problem, man. I'll blend into the walls. You won't even know I'm here."

"No tweets, no instagrams, no postings on Facebook. No social media, period. You do any of that, or leak anything to the press, and not only will I make sure you're prosecuted, but I'll break your jaw. I'm not kidding about that."

Stonehedge smiled wickedly. "Morris, man, first impression I never would've guessed what a badass you are. This is going to be great. Truly. And don't worry, I won't be mentioning a word about this to anyone. That's not why I'm doing this. My only reason is for my craft, that's it."

Morris didn't fully believe him since all actors were in effect professional liars, but nodded anyway. "Okay, then," he said, and he offered the actor his hand, which Stonehedge enthusiastically took.

"I might actually be able to help you with this, whatever this turns out to be," Stonehedge said. "I have access to people and organizations that you and the Los Angeles police department don't. Anything I can do to help, just say the word."

"I'll keep that in mind."

"So what are you dealing with here?"

Morris saw no reason to hide it any longer. It wasn't his call anyway. "Possibly SCK," he said.

The actor gave him a confused look.

"The Skull Cracker Killer."

For a fraction of a second, nothing, but Morris could the see the wheels turning in Stonehedge's eyes and then the precise moment that the actor connected the name to the news stories that came out of New York over five years ago. Immediately after that, the actor's jaw dropped.

"Exactly," Morris said.

Chapter Fifteen

More than a few eyebrows were raised when Morris brought Stonehedge into the conference room. Since the room was sound-proofed and the door had been closed, no one had heard their conversation in the hallway, nor did anyone recognize the actor in his disguise, so none of them had any idea who this scruffy-looking stranger was. It didn't go over particularly well when Morris told them. The Los Angeles police detectives all looked annoyed, Smichen amused, and Goodman concerned. The MBI team mostly hid their reactions behind poker faces, although Charlie Bogle couldn't help chuckling.

"Wow. Camera not only adds ten pounds like they say, but it must also give you a nose job, 'cause that's some beak you got in real life," deadpanned Dennis Polk, who was another member of the MBI team.

Stonehedge, who didn't know that Polk was a natural-born wiseass, tried answering him as if Polk had been serious. "This is a disguise so I'm not recognized when I go out in the field with you guys," the actor said. "The nose is a prosthetic."

"Never would've guessed that," Polk again deadpanned.

Stonehedge's face reddened as he realized Polk was being a wiseass. Bogle commented that Stonehedge was dressed like an actor trying to slum it with the police. "If he goes out wearing that outfit with any of us, the public's going to know something's not right."

"Very true," Morris agreed. He asked Polk where he bought his suits, then called Greta, made a guess on Stonehedge's shirt, pants, and jacket sizes, and asked her to pick the actor up a shirt, tie and a discounted suit off the rack at the same store Polk shopped at.

"Don't spend more than two hundred for it," he added. "We want him to look like one of us. Or at least like Polk."

"I'm impressed," Stonehedge said. "You nailed my sizes exactly. How about these sneakers? Okay if I wear them, or should I get some shoes?"

"The sneakers will be fine."

Sam Goodman had been mulling all this over, and finally he spoke up. "We at the FBI, and the same with the New York police department, have taken extraordinary precautions to keep this information from the public for obvious reasons, and I don't feel comfortable divulging it to a private citizen, especially an actor."

"I've got to agree," Walsh said. "That's all we need is Hollywood over there leaking stuff to TMZ."

"That's not going to happen," Morris stated. "Is it, Phil?"

"Not a chance," Stonehedge said.

Morris continued, "The reason it's not going to happen, other than the fact that Phil is giving us his word and he's an honorable man, is that he knows what the consequences will be if he leaks anything, which will include, but not be limited to, prosecution for obstruction of justice."

"This is still bull," Walsh grumbled. "If you don't mind, I'm calling my captain."

"Go ahead, but this wasn't my decision. Hadley already signed off on it."

Walsh stared openmouthed at Morris. "You're kidding," she said.

"Nope."

Goodman made up his mind. "I guess the federal government can bring charges also if Mr. Stonehedge interferes adversely with this investigation."

Stonehedge had taken all this in stride and even managed a disarming smile. "Everybody convinced I'll be behaving myself? We're good to go now?" he asked.

"Hold your horses," Polk piped in. He waved a thumb at Stonehedge, and said, "I'm giving three to one that Hollywood here either faints or pukes before this briefing lets up. Any takers?"

"Hmm," Bogle murmured as he considered the wager. Then he shook his head, "Nah, he's puking."

None of the Los Angeles detectives looked interested in wagering. Fred Lemmon, who was another of MBI's investigators, and who took it as one of his job responsibilities to act as a foil to Polk, stared intently at the actor as he sized him up. "You got a strong stomach?" he asked.

"Reasonably so."

Lemmon told Polk to put him down for twenty. "As long as you don't do anything to encourage him."

"Done. Anyone else?"

"Enough," Morris ordered. Then to Goodman, "Go ahead."

"Hold on!" Polk left his chair so that he could bring the trash can over to Stonehedge. Once this was done he took his seat again.

"Hollywood, when you puke, do it in the can. If you unload on our carpeting we're going to have words later, understand?" Then to Goodman, "I said my piece. Whenever you're ready."

"Thank you," Goodman said dryly. "First of all, SCK murdered twelve people in New York, not nine as was commonly reported. We hushed up three of his murders hoping we could flush him out. While we manufactured for the newspapers different circumstances for how these victims died, SCK did not rise to the bait and made no effort to take credit for these murders."

Goodman then proceeded to talk about the pattern to the killings—how they were all done in groups of three; always a forty-something year-old man, followed by a woman around the same age, and finally a twenty-something blonde girl. He showed pictures of the first three victims, and explained how they were killed within four days of each other.

"The first victim, an NYU psychology professor, murdered in his office on campus. The next victim was found in a back room at a boutique in Queens where she worked. The third, a student and part-time waitress, was found in her studio apartment in Brooklyn."

Goodman next showed crime-scene photos of each victim. While Stonehedge blanched at the sight of these photos, he held it together, leaving Polk still on the hook for possibly losing sixty dollars to Lemmon. After that, Goodman showed the next three victims, explaining how the first of these murders happened a hundred and thirty-four days after the last murders, and that these took place over three days. The next group were the murders that were hushed up, and there was a hundred and twenty-nine-day gap between these and the previous murders. As with the previous group, these victims were also murdered over three days. The final three murders happened a hundred and forty-one days later, and all these were done on the same day. While Goodman was showing the crime scene photos for these last murders, Polk commented that they'd picked the wrong name for the killer.

"Forget that Skull Cracker business," Polk said completely straight-faced. "He should be called the Pumpkin Smasher the way he left those skulls looking like smashed-up pumpkins. Am I right?"

"You're an idiot," Lemmon said.

"Nah, I'm a poet at heart," Polk argued.

"Idiot."

"Philistine," Polk countered.

"Enough," Morris warned.

Polk and Lemmon both swallowed back whatever it was they were about to say. Goodman waited several beats to make sure no one else had any additional comments before continuing with his presentation as if Polk hadn't interrupted him, and brought up photos of the four male victims on the same screen.

"All Caucasian, all close to the same age and size, all either with prominent bald spots or receding hairlines, all about twenty to thirty pounds overweight," Goodman said.

"They got different color hair," Bogle commented. "But they've all got these chunky, squarish faces, and there's something about their eyes also. Kind of smallish, squinty eyes."

"And they're mostly fair skinned," Morris noted. "And all white-collar guys."

Smichen pointed out that Corey Freeman was five feet eleven inches, which would be the right height, but that he was only a hundred and sixty-eight pounds. "He was trim and in good shape at the time of his death," Smichen noted. "Certainly not overweight. And he had a full head of hair."

Morris dug out a photo of Freeman that the realtor had used in an ad six years earlier. In the photo Freeman looked heavier and showed a receding hairline. "He must've gotten hair plugs and dropped twenty pounds since this photo was taken, but if I found it on the Internet, the killer might've also." He passed it over to Goodman who asked Morris if he had any recent photos of the victim. Morris passed one over, and Goodman looked preoccupied as he studied both photos.

"Anything wrong?" Morris asked.

Goodman looked unsure of himself as he shook his head. "You might be right, Morris," he said. "The killer could've latched onto the victim from this first photo, although I would've thought he'd abandon the killing once he realized his victim no longer matched his profile, but maybe not. Let me continue on with the presentation, and give this more thought later."

Goodman next brought up on screen pictures of the four women in their forties who were killed, all of them also Caucasians. One was blonde, two were redheads, and one had sandy brown hair. Two of them had their hair down to their shoulders, another had her hair cut in a short bob, and the fourth had tight, curly hair. The two ways they were alike were that they were all tall, and that they had thin, longish faces. Polk pointed out the obvious; no one else in the room bothered to do that.

When Goodman brought up the photos of the four girls in their twenties who were killed, the similarities among them were more pronounced. All had curly blonde hair that fell past their shoulders. All had slightly upturned noses and wide mouths. And all were what Morris's grandparents would've called *zaftig*. Not fat, but full-figured girls. As irrational as it was he couldn't help feeling a bit of relief seeing those photos together. Whether or not Rachel dyed her hair blonde, she'd never look like those girls. Natalie would be safe also. While she was slender like those other fortyish-year-old women, she was a good deal shorter than they were, and her face was shaped differently. More of a heart-shaped face than the longish ones these women had.

Goodman pointed out that the four young blonde victims were all between five feet six and five feet eight inches in height, and between a hundred and forty and a hundred and sixty-eight pounds in weight. No one felt the need to comment about their obvious physical similarities, not even Polk.

Goodman had one more screen to show them—a map of where the murders took place. Five of them had happened in Manhattan, three in Queens, and four in Brooklyn. The murders were numbered on the map, and they were scattered around with none of the three in any group occurring near each other.

"We weren't able to find any discernable patterns with the locations of the murders other than that they all took place within a mile of a subway station, although seven different subway lines," Goodman said. He took off his glasses so that he could rub his eyes. When he put them back on, he showed the room a grim smile.

"Now that I've gotten these preliminaries out of the way, let's dig into the meat," he said.

Chapter Sixteen

"Succinylcholine, or *sux*, is a muscle relaxer. Hospitals use it when they perform tracheal intubations. Veterinarians sometimes use it in the euthanasia of horses. This is not a sedative. It does not produce unconsciousness or anesthesia. Someone injected with a fairly small dose will suffer temporary paralysis. If his skull is then broken open, he's going to feel a tremendous amount of pain, and he's going to know exactly what is being done to him."

Goodman paused for effect. "Sux metabolizes quickly, and can be difficult to detect, but we got lucky with our first victim. He had a genetic abnormality that caused the sux injected into him not to fully metabolize, and because of that we found it in his blood. Since we were later looking for it, we were able to find traces of it in four other victims. We also found needle-sized puncture marks on all the victims; all of them were either injected in the arm, shoulder, throat, behind the ear, in the back of the neck, and in one case, under the left eye."

"Where would SCK get his supply of sux?" Morris asked.

"A hospital or surgical clinic, a racetrack, or a veterinarian office that handles large animals would be the easiest places, assuming that he doesn't purchase it directly from one of the manufacturers. We looked at all the possible sources in the city, but it didn't get us anywhere. It's not a class A substance, like an opiate, although it's far deadlier, and should be better controlled since it's a nearly perfect murder drug. The records we found were shoddy at best, and it's doubtful any of these places would've noticed if a package of sux had gone missing."

"Here's where we have a significant difference," Smichen volunteered. "The toxicology report came up clean on Freeman. I also didn't find any needle-sized puncture marks, and I checked carefully for that. As you said, if sux were injected into him, we might not have found it, but what I did find was that our victim was hit hard from behind with an iron pipe and that his wrists were taped together."

"Interesting." Goodman rubbed his chin as he considered this. "Obviously the killer used a different method to immobilize this latest victim, but that's not necessarily significant. It could be simply that he hasn't been able to locate a source of sux. Was the victim knocked unconscious?"

"If he was, he recovered consciousness before death. The killer didn't bother gagging him, and from the way he bit his tongue, gums, and lips, he was struggling."

"Then this still fits," Goodman said, relieved. "The serial killer I'd profiled whom you know as SCK needs his victims to suffer. After he had immobilized his victims by temporarily paralyzing them, he broke apart their skulls with a chisel and hammer, and then used the claw end of the hammer to dig out clumps of their brain. This is every bit as cruel a way to kill someone as it sounds. SCK could've used an animal tranquilizer if his goal was to leave a message with the way he murdered his victims, but it was important to him for his victims to suffer emotional trauma, fear, and great physical pain that would be made even more acute by the sux. If this latest victim had been unconscious during the killing, then there'd be no doubt that we would now be dealing with a different person."

"In some of the photos you showed I counted eight clumps of brain matter dug out. Was that consistent with each of the New York victims?" Morris asked.

"Yes. Why?"

"Ours had six clumps dug out."

"That's true," Smichen said.

"That might not be that significant," Goodman said. "This is over five years later and twenty-eight hundred miles away. SCK could've altered his signature for either a personal reason or to try to confuse us. As I'd hinted at earlier, he doesn't care about getting credit for his murders. He kills because the pressure builds to an unbearable level and then he needs to destroy victims who remind him of people he holds a tremendous amount of anger against."

Morris asked, "Who, parents and an ex-wife or girlfriend?"

"Possibly. Whoever they are I suspect they're dead now, and it wouldn't surprise me if SCK murdered them, or at the very least, severely injured them, although probably not in anywhere near as brutal a way as he did with these victims who've been serving as fill-ins."

"So he's looking for do overs," Lemmon said.

"Yes. Exactly."

Morris asked, "Why's he been quiet the last five years?"

"The million-dollar question."

"Could it be a copycat?"

Goodman shrugged. "It's possible," he said. "There are notable differences with this killing. I'll have the victim's remains shipped to the FBI lab, and we'll be able to tell if the same chisel and hammer were used, not that that would eliminate this killer being SCK if they weren't. It's been over five years, it would make sense if he had to ditch his other tools and buy new ones."

"Could this be a fluke killing unrelated to SCK?"

"Doubtful. We should be assuming it's either SCK or a copycat. There had never been a reported murder anywhere in the United States like these before SCK struck in New York, and none afterwards until this one. That two individuals could share this never-before-seen psychopathy seems highly unlikely."

The same dull throbbing Morris had felt earlier when Gilman had informed him that Stonehedge was going to be tagging along started up again as he appreciated what a mess this investigation was becoming.

"Let's see if I can clarify this," Morris said. "We could be dealing with SCK even though he killed Freeman differently than his other victims. Or we could be dealing with a copycat, which means someone in New York—either FBI, police, a witness, someone from the ME's office, or possibly dozens of other potential sources, leaked the particulars of the SCK killings to our new SCK. Or this could be totally random. Some very angry psycho holding a grudge against Freeman who just happened to stumble on the same bizarre method of murder that SCK used."

"Again, your last choice has a very low probability," Goodman insisted

"But not impossible."

"No, not impossible."

Philip Stonehedge spoke up then, "Pardon my interruption, but the original SCK could be the source of the leak, if it is a copycat. Let's say he got arrested five years ago and is now rotting in prison. He could've confided in a fellow prisoner who has since been released and is carrying out SCK's murders for him. Or it could be any number of similar scenarios."

"Not bad, Hollywood," Polk grudgingly admitted.

Morris took a deep breath as he made a decision. "We're going to have to investigate this on both ends," he said. He nodded at his MBI investigators—Bogle, Lemmon, and Polk. "You three take the first plane you can to New York and try to find out where SCK's been the last five years, and if it's a copycat, who leaked what to whom. Myself and our esteemed LAPD colleagues will investigate things from this end."

"What about Hollywood?" Lemmon asked. "You want us to take him with us?"

Morris shook his head. "No, Phil will stick with me." Then to Sam Goodman, "My guys are going to need full case folders so they know who to talk to in New York."

"Won't be a problem."

Morris gave his men who were still sitting at the conference table a quizzical look.

"I thought you three had a plane to catch?"

Bogle chuckled as he pushed himself away from the table. Lemmon reminded Polk that since Hollywood neither lost his lunch nor fainted he now owed him sixty dollars. Polk acted as if he didn't hear this, and as he reached the door, he belted out to the tune of *New York, New York*, "If you can kill them there, you can kill them anywhere." Lemmon commented that Polk was no Sinatra, no Bette Midler either, although in his opinion Polk looked more like Midler than Sinatra. Lemmon closed the door behind him, cutting off from those still in the soundproofed conference room what would surely have been a biting comeback from Polk.

For the next half hour, Morris strategized with the four LA police detectives. Roger Smichen was able to give them a four-hour window for when Freeman was killed, but it would help to narrow the window down, and it would especially help to know what time Freeman showed up at the house in Venice, and Malevich was going to keep digging for that information. The crime-scene specialists were able to lift over a dozen different fingerprints from inside the house. Given that the inside front doorknob had been wiped clean and that the only fingerprints lifted from the outside doorknob belonged to the realtor who had followed Freeman, there was little chance that any of these fingerprints belonged to the killer—but Walsh and the other two Los Angeles detectives were tasked to match the fingerprints with names, which meant fingerprinting every realtor and potential buyer who had entered the house. Once the Los Angeles detectives had left with their assignments, Morris asked Goodman, "When are you going to know whether we're dealing with the original SCK, a copycat, or something else?"

Goodman didn't need any time to think about his answer. "After the next two murders."

Chapter Seventeen

Henry was really beginning to love social media. *What a great way to stalk someone you want to kill*, he thought. Of course, that was only if they announce every little thing they do, like this Gail Hawes was doing.

Last night when he went to Susan's rented town house he snuck a look at her address book and got Hawes's address while Susan was off in the kitchen pouring them both snifters of cognac. She didn't invite him over just to *snift* cognac, but to see if he was feeling up to doing the *dirty deed*, as she liked to call it. It turned out to be a lot more difficult the second time to stay strong and resist the temptation she was offering, and he came within a heartbeat of giving in, but he meant the vows he made to Sheila. As much as his wife might like to claim otherwise, he did truly love her. Besides, what good is a man if he can't live up to his promises? So after their *snifts* of cognac (which to Henry tasted no better than lighter fluid) and a few smooches on the sofa while Susan maneuvered his hand so that he copped a feel of one of her plumlike breasts, Henry told her that he didn't think his heart was strong enough for them to continue down the path they were on, but given a few days to recuperate he was sure he'd be up to it. And so he left with Susan frustrated and unsatisfied, but alive, and himself with Gail Hawes's address.

After he cleaned, dressed, fed, and put his wife to bed for the night, he investigated Hawes because he decided he wanted her to be his next victim. Even though he'd only met her for a minute, she had rubbed him the wrong way, and it just seemed to make more sense to choose as his victims people who rubbed him the wrong way. As he thought about how that made a world of sense, he was hit by inspiration of how he'd be able to get her alone. His plan was still hatching in his mind and not yet fully formed, but one thing he knew for sure was that, for it to work, he'd have to be able to watch for when she left her apartment building. With that in mind, he performed some virtual spying by entering her West Hollywood address into Google Earth, and the satellite photo that popped up and all the subsequent "street view" photos showed that she lived in an attractive apartment building with extensive landscaping on a street filled with similarly attractive apartment buildings, all with extensive landscaping. Nice location, he had to give her that, but he couldn't see any good hiding spots to watch her building from, at least not without him sticking out like a sore thumb.

That was unfortunate. He hated the idea of scrapping his plan, because at this point it had become fully hatched, and it was a darn nice plan. But, as he often told himself, there's more than one way to crack an egg, so he next tried researching spy cameras with the idea of planting a camera so he could watch her building's entrance from several miles away. Twenty minutes of reading the instructions and trying to make sense of how to use one left his head spinning, and he accepted that figuring out these spy cameras was beyond him.

Henry wasn't about to quit that easily, and after some more pondering, came up with a new plan. He could dress up as a maintenance person, find a way to gain access to Hawes's building, and knock on her door late at night, but he quickly saw a number of ways that could blow up in his face. What if she recognized him before he was able to shut her up? She looked like a screamer to him. Someone with a healthy pair of lungs who'd be able to make sure everyone in the building heard her. But heck, even if he could shut her up fast enough, he didn't even know whether or not she lived alone. That would be all he needed—to shove a sock into her big mouth and knock her to the floor only to have a boyfriend or husband or roommate walk in on them.

First step had to be finding out whether Hawes was living with someone, and for that he searched for her on Facebook. Not only did he find her, but she made everything she posted public. And she posted about everything! At first, as Henry looked at her posts documenting every mundane aspect of her life, he felt a tinge of panic over whether she'd secretly taken a picture of him the other day and put that on Facebook also, but Hawes running into him and Susan seemed to be the only thing she'd done in the last few days that she'd kept to herself. As Henry read all the tidbits of her life that she made public, he learned her relationship status was "it's complicated," whatever that meant, and that she presently lived with her three best buddies—Persian cats named Hermione, Ginny, and Professor Snape. He also learned about the waitress with an attitude that she had encountered at lunch yesterday, saw copious pictures of her turkey lasagna that she had ordered, and a number of other annoying details of her life, all of which made him even more glad that she was going to be his next victim. Most important, he read about her plans for today, including what time she was going to be leaving her apartment. Thanks to that, Henry scrapped his idea about masquerading as a maintenance guy and went back to his original plan that he liked so much.

Henry used his iPhone to once more check her tweets and Facebook posts to see if she had changed her plans, but no, she was still on schedule. He was parked five miles away at a strip mall parking lot sipping on a mocha latte. Timing was still going to be tricky, but he decided to give it two more minutes, and then he pulled his car back onto the street and headed toward Gail Hawes's address.

He found a parking space two blocks from her apartment building. Earlier, he'd attached stolen license plates to his car, and later when he was done he planned to put back his Oregon plates. Henry had dressed in a suit and tie for the occasion, the first time he had done so in years. Before leaving his car, he checked once more whether Hawes had tweeted or posted anything new, saw that she hadn't, and hustled out of his car carrying with him a briefcase that had everything he required inside of it. He moved at a fast clip, almost jogging. Thanks to Hawes's need to tell the world where she was going to be eating lunch, he knew what direction she'd be walking, and sure enough he intercepted her less than a third of a block from her building.

"I know you, don't I?" Henry asked, his eyes squinting as if he were trying to place her.

She turned to him with a plastic smile etched on her face, but then she recognized him and her smile melted into more of an amused one.

"You're Susan's new friend," she said.

Henry smacked his forehead with his palm. "That's right," he said. "We ran into you just yesterday. You were pretty crafty the way you put two and two together."

She laughed at that. "A woman's intuition."

Henry held out his hand. "Howard Donner," he said.

"I remember," she said. "Gail Hawes."

"I remember," Henry said with a thin smile.

Mischief sparkled in her eyes as she asked, "How was your secret rendezvous with Susan?"

"If I told you I'd have to kill you."

She laughed at that. "A man of discretion. So what are you doing in my neck of the woods?"

"Your neck of the woods?"

"Yep. I live in that building right over there."

She pointed to her apartment building. Henry squinted in the direction where she pointed.

"Nice place," Henry said. "That's one of the buildings I've had my eye on."

"What do you mean?"

"I buy and manage apartment buildings. That's why I'm here."

Her interest in him perked up. As she appraised the suit he was wearing, which was an expensive one, and the briefcase he was carrying, also expensive, Henry could just about read her thoughts. *That's why Susan is interested in this ugly turd. He's loaded!* All at once, she started twirling her hair in a flirtatious manner. She even batted her eyes at him.

"Which building are you thinking of buying?" she asked.

"A twenty-unit one three blocks over on North Orange Grove. I got there a half hour early and thought I'd walk around the neighborhood and see what other buildings might strike my fancy." He gave her an embarrassed smile and added, "To be honest, I was also hoping to find a restaurant or bar with a restroom. My bladder's about to burst. Since you live right over there, any chance . . . ?"

"It could be arranged," Hawes said as she twirled her hair into a tight twist. Then she got sly. "But there's a price. You have to tell me all the juicy bits about your rendezvous with Susan."

"You've got me over a barrel," Henry conceded. "Deal."

So far no cars had passed them, and they didn't encounter any of the other apartment residents as Hawes led Henry to her apartment. Thanks to the large mocha latte he had drunk earlier, he really did need to relieve himself, and after he was done he lived up to his end of the bargain and told Hawes the full story of what had happened between him and Susan the other day. While he could see her disappointment over not hearing any particularly salacious details, he noted a calculating look in her eyes as she tried to figure out whether he was wealthy enough to bother seducing.

"How many buildings do you have in your portfolio?" she asked,

"Quite a few." He gave her the impression that he was adding them up. "Thirteen," he said. "With number fourteen to be added very shortly." He showed a surprised look and pointed behind Hawes. "What the heck is that?"

Startled, she turned around to see what it was that had alarmed him, and Henry used the opportunity to bop her on the back of her head with the iron pipe that he had taken from his briefcase when he used her bathroom, and had since kept hidden in his suit jacket. He didn't hit her hard enough to kill her or even to knock her out, but hard enough to leave her dizzy so she couldn't shout out for help while he shoved a sock into her mouth. The blow also left her unable to put up much of a fight as he bound her wrists together behind her back with duct tape. Once that was done he took his time moving her to the right spot on the floor, and then setting up his iPhone stand so that he could record what was going to be happening. Then he used the chisel and hammer he'd brought so he could keep the promise he'd made to her about what he'd have to do if he told her about himself and Susan.

Chapter Eighteen

Long Island, 1982

Henry wasn't much different at sixteen than he was at thirteen. He was still a quiet kid; still physically squat and awkward-looking, although he was wider and his hair was much longer making him look more than a little like a shorter and lumpier version of the singer Meatloaf. He had a tiny circle of friends—really only three, with Nancy Bower being his closest bud, as she liked to call him. He still struggled in math, barely passing each semester, still excelled in art, and still created his own comic books, although no longer superhero ones. Instead the comic books he drew were the stuff of nightmares. Horrific monsters doing horrific things to their victims. One major difference between thirteen- and sixteen-year-old Henry was that bullies steered clear of him, especially Brad Black, whose surgically repaired earlobe looked as if a blob of silly putty had been used to fill in the torn-off piece.

Henry, a sensitive boy, had a penchant for steering clear of trouble. As long as others left him alone, he was more than willing to do the same. This was why it was so surprising to Johnny Franco, quarterback and captain of the school's football team, and his two cohorts, also starters on the team, when Henry told them to quit picking on Gary Fleishman. At the time Franco had Fleishman, a scrawny fifteen-year-old freshman, in a headlock while Franco's two cohorts were in the process of removing Fleishman's corduroys.

"Mind your own business, fat boy," Franco ordered.

Instead of doing that, Henry told Franco again to let go of the kid they were picking on.

"If you don't I'm going to knock you down to the floor, and then I'm going to break both your arms," Henry stated calmly.

By this time a crowd of other students had gathered. Even though the incident with Henry and Brad Black had happened in middle school, Franco had heard the story about the odd ogre-looking kid who had gone all mental on Black and had left Black with half an earlobe missing. He let go of Fleishman, as did his two cohorts. Fleishman, for his part, gathered up his pants and fled to safety. It might've been over then if a crowd hadn't formed. Franco couldn't just walk away, not with how several of the kids in the crowd were jeering him on.

"What's to stop me right now from beating the stuffing out of you?" Franco asked, his voice a low, menacing growl, his eyes closing so that they were barely slits and his hands clenching into fists.

"Because if you try, I'll knock out your two front teeth."

That caused some more egging on from the other students. Franco turned to them making a *can-you-believe-this-moron* face, then sucker punched Henry in the jaw.

The last few years Henry's dad often told him that he was as strong as an ox, and that he should be playing football. "High school girls go nuts over football players, Henry, especially the cheerleaders. With how strong you are, you'd be a monster playing on the offensive line."

Henry didn't believe his dad about the girl part, and he had good reason not to. Whether or not he played on the school's football team, it was doubtful any of the cheerleaders or other girls would be interested in him as a boyfriend. His dad was also exaggerating about him being as strong as an ox, but he was still a deceptively powerful kid with heavy hands and a low center of gravity, and Franco's sucker punch didn't budge him. Instead, Henry immediately went for Franco's knees. In a flash he lifted Franco up and slammed the teenager to the floor, then sat on his chest. With one hard punch, he lived up to his word knocking out Franco's two front teeth, as well as two of his bottom teeth.

Franco's two football team cohorts jumped into the melee, and as they wrestled with Henry while Franco lay on the floor bawling, teachers rushed in to break up the fight.

Things got confusing then. Because of Franco's teeth being knocked out and his mouth being turned into a bloody mess, the school at first wanted to make this a police matter and have Henry arrested, but then as students came forward and the school's principal got a clearer picture about what had happened, he shut down that idea. These were three of the school's top football players, and if he went after Henry, he would have to go after those players even harder. The whole mess gave him indigestion.

"Why'd you get involved in the first place?" the principal demanded of Henry. "Did you have some sort of vendetta against Johnny? Is that it, you were looking for an excuse to hurt him?"

Henry's jaw dropped as he stared at the principal, not quite believing what he was asked. He stuttered in his confusion and anger as he told the principal that he had warned Franco and the other two to stop picking on Fleishman. "They were pantsing him right there in the hallway! What they were doing to him was humiliating! And Franco punched me first!"

There was no denying that Henry had a swollen jaw, as well as other lumps and bruises that he'd gotten while wrestling with the other two football players. There was also no way of getting around the fact that the students who came forward all claimed Franco threw the first punch. The principal, though, persisted, asking, "Are you friends with this Fleishman kid?"

Henry, still confused, shook his head. "I don't know him," he said.

"You should've found a teacher to handle the situation," the principal said coldly. "Because of your actions a fellow student has been seriously injured. That type of behavior won't be tolerated."

Henry was sometimes slow on the uptake, but he wasn't a stupid kid, and he understood then what was happening. At that point he refused to answer any more questions, which allowed the principal to get away with suspending him for two weeks while Franco and his two cohorts escaped punishment. After leaving the principal's office with his suspension starting immediately, he saw Aisley Martin hanging out in the hallway, obviously cutting class. Aisley was one of the goth girls in the school who wore all black, dyed her hair the same pitch black as her eye makeup, painted her fingernails blue, and her lips bloodred. Henry had had a crush on her for over a year, although he never would've been able to work up the nerve to talk to her. As he approached her, he tried to act as if she weren't there, or at least as if he hadn't been gawking at her a moment earlier. When she started walking alongside him, his face flushed and his heart thumped like mad in his chest.

"They suspend you?" she asked.

Even though she was walking less than a foot away from him, it surprised Henry that she actually talked to him. His voice noticeably cracked as he squeaked out that he'd been suspended for two weeks.

"That's bull. I bet they don't suspend those fascist jocks who started everything." There was a pause, then, "Mind if I walk with you? I'm heading outside for a smoke."

Even though Henry's heart now thumped so hard that he thought he might faint, he was able to croak out that he didn't mind, and so Aisley Martin continued to walk alongside him as they left the school building.

"I think that was so cool of you standing up for that kid like you did," she said.

"I don't like bullies," Henry said.

"Neither do I."

They continued on until they were half a block away from the school, then Aisley stopped so she could take a pack of cigarettes from her purse. "Do you smoke?" she asked.

Henry shook his head no because he didn't smoke, and then felt sick to his stomach as he realized that Aisley was really asking him to hang around and smoke a cigarette with her.

"Then we should get coffee sometime," she said. "Maybe after your suspension."

"Cool," Henry said, trying his hardest to sound cool.

"Cool," Aisley agreed.

That night Nancy Bower came over to visit. She'd blossomed from the thirteen-year-old girl Henry had first talked to. No longer pear-shaped, her braces gone, her skin having cleared up, and her blonde hair no longer oily but shoulder-length and curly, she was actually quite pretty, but she and Henry had long established themselves as platonic buddies.

"I missed all the fireworks earlier," she said. "You're all the school's talking about. What possessed you to take on three football players?"

Henry was at his desk hard at work on his latest comic book, the fourth in an apocalyptic series he called *Shriekers*, which had these horrific creatures that one day showed up and started following people around shrieking, and then ripping to shreds anyone whose heart rate goes up, or if their physiology in any other way indicates fear.

"I won the fight," he said. "And I've still got my teeth."

"You did, and you do," Nancy conceded. Her expression melted into one of concern. "You also got suspended, and you look like you've been hit by a truck. So why'd you do it?"

Henry shrugged. "I flashed back to when Brad Black and those others used to bully me like that. But I warned them. It wasn't like I started it. They should've listened to me."

"Are you okay? Your face looks pretty beat up."

Henry grinned at her. "You should see the other guys," he joked. "And it's not like they made me any uglier."

"You know I hate it when you talk like that. You're the sweetest boy I know, even if you do draw the most disgusting comic books." Nancy walked over to Henry's desk, her hand resting on his back as she looked over his shoulder. "Are you still working on volume three of your *Shrieker* books?"

"Nope, I had all this extra time this afternoon so I was able to finish it. This is number four."

Henry dug through his desk and handed Nancy a folder that held his most recently completed comic book, and she brought it over to his bed so she could stretch out on it and look at what he'd drawn.

"The artwork is so good," Nancy said as she studied the first page. "Clearly from a sick, depraved mind, but so, so good."

"Ha! Who's the one who got me reading H. P. Lovecraft?"

"I'm not saying I don't like it, just that you're clearly warped." Then more seriously, "You're going to be famous someday."

Henry blushed at that. "You think?"

"I think."

For the next fifteen minutes Henry worked feverishly on his comic book while Nancy read the one he had given her. Offhandedly, he commented that Aisley Martin was waiting for him when he left the principal's office.

That got Nancy's attention. "No kidding? The goth girl?"

"Yep."

"The one that you've been nuts about since forever?"

Henry blushed at that. "I wouldn't say I've been nuts about her," he argued.

"So what did goth girl want?"

"Not much. Only that she'd like to have coffee with me sometime."

"Congratulations," Nancy said, although she didn't sound congratulatory. "What do you know. My boy's in love."

That caused Henry to blush even deeper.

Chapter Nineteen

Los Angeles, the present

Henry didn't bring a change of clothing with him, so he stripped down to his birthday suit before using the chisel and hammer on Gail Hawes, and since he had positioned Hawes on her belly and she wasn't going to be able to see his nakedness, he didn't have to worry about feeling immodest. When he was done, he found a full-length mirror in her bedroom and checked himself over. Not a single drop of blood or piece of gore had splattered on him, leaving him impressed over how careful he'd been, especially given that it was such messy work.

He returned to the living room where Hawes's remains lay, and saw that two of her cats had surfaced. He recognized them from her Facebook photos as they stared at him with their accusatory pushed-in faces. Hermione and Ginny, with Professor Snape still in hiding. He noticed her laptop then on the dining room table (the room he was in was a combination living room and dining room) and an alarm went off in his head as he saw that it had been powered on.

He opened the laptop up and his heart turned into a cold, queasy mush on reading a Facebook post she had added about how she was going to be late for lunch because she had met up with a friend's secret lover.

Oh jeeze, he thought, realizing that she must've typed it up while he was using the bathroom.

For a long moment he stood stunned as he thought about the consequences of what she had done, then he broke out of his stupor and deleted the post. Even though it was now gone, Hawes's Facebook friends could've already seen it, including Susan. And even if they hadn't, and even if he had deleted the post, it still might exist somewhere on Facebook's servers. He didn't know how that stuff worked, but he knew that once something showed up on the Internet, it never fully disappeared. He had to assume that the police would eventually see it. Even though Hawes's post fortunately didn't include his name or (thank God!) a picture of him, it would provide the police a link back to him, as fuzzy as it might be.

What's done is done, Henry whispered to himself. Because of that annoying-as-heck Gail Hawes, he was going to have to do something now that he'd pretty much decided he didn't want to do. For a long moment he was seized with the idea of posting a photo of Hawes in her current state as a fitting final status update for her, but then shook himself out of that thought. It would be incredibly stupid to do something like that. As it was, it might be days before the police discovered her body, but if he were to do something that childish and petulant, they'd be here in minutes. He had to calm down and act smart. As long as he did, that post wasn't going to help the police, assuming that they ever found out about it.

Henry took a deep breath, and held it until he calmed down. Then he took the hammer and chisel to the bathroom and scrubbed them clean. After he had them wrapped up in cloth rags and stored away in his briefcase, and the duct tape cut from Hawes's wrists and the sock removed from her mouth, he put his suit back on and used one of the cloth rags to wipe fingerprints off anything he might've touched. He noticed that Professor Snape had finally made an appearance, and that all three cats were sniffing around the lumps of Hawes's brain that he had dug out. If he left them alone, they'd probably be eating it soon. He thought about grabbing them and locking them in Hawes's bedroom, but then he decided so what. Why should he care what they ate?

He looked out of the peephole on the front door until he was sure the coast was clear. Something made him turn around, and he saw that Professor Snape was staring at him in this most curious way.

"*Bon appétit,*" he told the cat before slipping out of the apartment.

"I've got to tell you, *sugar lips,* I've been going nuts all day thinking about your long beautiful legs and what it would feel like having them wrapped around me."

Henry held his breath as he waited for Susan's response, because she might've seen Gail Hawes's Facebook post, and if she did, she'd be asking questions about it. He had already figured out what he would say, but fortunately she didn't bring it up.

"So you've recuperated then," she said, her voice sultry.

"You better believe it. Right now I feel like I could go for hours. It's going to be torture waiting for you."

"Are you in the area?"

"Not too far away. I could be at your place at the drop of a hat."

"You might not have to wait then. Hold on a minute." It took less than a minute for Susan to get back on her cellphone and tell Henry that it was dead at the boutique and her boss gave her the okay to take off for an hour. "That should give us enough time for some serious afternoon loving," she said in that same sultry voice from earlier. "I'll meet you at my apartment in ten minutes?"

"You better believe it!" He hesitated, then added, "As long as you still haven't told anyone about us. My lawyer called today warning me that he was within a day of settling the divorce, but that I had to be careful."

"I haven't told anybody anything, I promise, Howard."

"Except for your friend yesterday."

"Well, I didn't tell Gail anything. She figured it out, the snoop! But she's not going to tell anyone anything."

That was truer than Susan could've realized. "I want you so bad right now," Henry said. "Seeing you naked is all I can think about. But I got to be careful with the divorce almost done. You didn't tell your boss why you're taking off for an hour?"

"I told her I needed to do some shopping, that's all."

"Then let's do it! I think I might explode if we don't."

"Oh, you'll be exploding all right." She giggled at her joke. "Several times in fact."

This was what Henry was counting on, and he was calling Susan from a lot closer than she could've guessed—almost right across the street from her boutique. At that hour it would be too risky to meet her at her rented town house, but he had already located where she had parked her car in the garage near where she worked, and at least five minutes ago there was nobody anywhere near it.

After he got off the call with Susan, he moved swiftly back to where her car was parked, and was relieved to see that there still wasn't anybody around. It didn't take Susan very long at all to hurry to her car, and she appeared breathless as she took her keys from her pocketbook. Henry waited until she clicked her door unlocked before emerging from where he was hiding and slamming her head against the door frame. The impact was violent enough to have killed her, but in case it didn't, he used his powerful hands to snap her neck. One look at her face left no doubt that she was dead.

He used her key to click open her trunk, and then he put her body inside of it. He had to bend her almost in half to get her to fit, but with a little elbow grease he was able to close the trunk lid shut. He felt some remorse killing her this way since he had already sat-isfied his latest Skull Cracker killing, and he had grown to like her over the last three weeks, more than he had even realized until just a few minutes ago. But he'd had no choice. He was convinced the police would uncover the deleted Facebook post, and then they'd find Susan. Even if she didn't know Henry's real name, they'd find him once she gave them a description. He grimaced hard enough that his cheek muscles began to ache. This was all Gail Hawes's fault, no one else's.

Even in death, Hawes was annoying as heck!

Chapter Twenty

Tracy Lacey, the owner of Lacey Properties was a short, round woman of sixty whose hair was dyed an orangey-red. She couldn't stop staring at Stonehedge in his disguise.

"You look so familiar," she said. "Where do I know you from?"

"Not sure, ma'am," Stonehedge said with a grin as he played up his role of detective. He was now wearing the cheap suit and tie that Morris's office manager had picked up for him.

"Do you go to open houses here in Venice?"

"I've been to a few."

"That must be it," she said, satisfied with that explanation. She then turned to give Morris a dubious look. "You're not police. I don't know if I should be talking to you about this."

He handed her the letter Gilman had arranged for him, which stated that he and the rest of the MBI investigators had been deputized by the Los Angeles Police, and that the mayor was entrusting MBI to investigate Corey Freeman's murder. Lacey read the letter carefully enough so that she could've been memorizing it.

"As the letter states, I've been authorized to look into this matter, but even without that authorization, I would've thought you'd want to see Corey Freeman's murderer caught."

"Of course I do," she groused half under her breath. "It just seems so peculiar, that's all, to be talking about things like this to people who aren't the police." She blinked several times as she looked at Morris. "Especially asking me to point fingers at someone."

"Are you telling me one of your other realtors had a problem with Freeman?"

Lacey looked as if she were suffering from a bout of gas before finally nodding. "Corey was a dear man. He'd been here seven years, and was genuinely well liked. I personally was very fond of him and cried like a baby when I heard the terrible news."

Her eyes became misty as she recounted this, and she seemed to struggle for a long moment before she was able to compose herself. "No matter how nice people are, there can be friction at times," she said. "A realtor's office can be extraordinarily competitive, especially when you have multimillion-dollar properties, like you do here in Venice. And sometimes there can be misunderstandings."

"One of the other brokers accused Freeman of poaching a listing?" Stonehedge asked.

Lacey looked a bit sick. "It happens sometimes, and quite by accident. A seller came in off the street and Corey signed him up and got the listing. One of our other brokers later claimed that he had given this seller his business card at a party, and so the listing should've been his. This was a four-point-two-million-dollar home, and by being the listing broker Corey earned a hundred and five thousand-dollar commission."

Stonehedge whistled softly. "I might be in the wrong profession," he said.

Morris shot him a look and then turned back to Lacey. "What's this other broker's name?"

"Glen Blakeman," she said as if it pained her greatly to divulge the name. "Glen's such a dear. I can't believe he'd hurt Corey over this."

"Blakeman have a temper?" Morris asked.

Lacey looked sick to her stomach as she nodded. "At times," she admitted. "Although he's really all bark and no bite."

"Did he make threats against Freeman?"

She looked even sicker. "He was just letting off steam. I'm sure he didn't mean any of it."

"Do you have Blakeman's schedule from yesterday?"

She shook her head. "The realtors here maintain their own schedules. Glen must've been out showing properties. He wasn't in the office yesterday."

"Anything else you can tell me about Blakeman?"

Lacey appeared absolutely crestfallen. "Glen's the listing broker."

"What?"

"The house where Corey was found, that was one of Glen's properties. He's the listing broker for the house."

* * *

Lacey wrote down Blakeman's cell phone number and home address, and handed these to Morris. There were two other brokers in the office, and Morris spoke to both of them and got the same story about the bad blood between Freeman and Blakeman.

"Who wouldn't be upset about losing that kind of money?" one of the brokers asked. "I have to admit, when I heard about Corey being found murdered and saw that the address was one of Glen's, the thought crossed my mind, but I guess I tried to talk myself out of it. So you think Glen killed Corey?"

"Too early to tell," Morris said.

When Morris tried calling Blakeman's cell phone, he got a message. He tried a second time, and again the phone rang through to voicemail, asking him to leave a message.

"Blakeman doesn't seem to be picking up," Morris said.

Stonehedge moved closer to Morris and in a soft enough voice so nobody in the office could hear him, asked, "Is it possible this isn't SCK? A hundred and five grand is a good reason to kill someone. Hell, I'd consider it for less."

Morris shrugged. "We'll find out." He next called Detective Walsh and told her about Blakeman. "Can you arrange for the LAPD to pick him up?" he asked.

"Will do."

Within seconds of getting off the phone with Walsh, Morris's cell phone rang. Gilman. Morris answered, and told Gilman that he was just about to call him.

"I've got a person of interest for Freeman's murder," Morris said, keeping his voice low. "This might not be SCK."

"Then your person of interest is wrong. We've got a second killing. This one in West Hollywood."

Gilman gave him Gail Hawes's address.

Chapter Twenty-one

Long Island, 1982

"I'm going to Super Comics after school. What do you say?"

Henry gave Nancy Bower an apologetic smile. "Can't," he said. "I've got plans."

"Don't tell me you're having coffee with goth girl again? You don't even like coffee."

"Who says?"

"You've told me that!"

"I like mocha lattes. That's where they put chocolate in the coffee."

Nancy rolled her eyes. "I know what mocha lattes are. So that's what you're doing after school, huh? Coffee club with goth girl?"

Henry's cheeks flushed pink. He said, "Afterwards we're going to her house. I'm going to show her my *Shrieker* comic books."

Henry and Nancy were sitting together in study hall. He dug out his latest completed comic book from his backpack and handed it to Nancy. As she flipped through the pages, she became demonstrably exasperated.

"You're kidding," she finally said. "You're making goth girl a shrieker hunter? Everyone else gets torn apart by them, but goth girl can kill them with a bow and arrow? You realize how stupid that is?"

Henry snatched the comic book away from her. "I liked the way I did it," he said. He pulled his social studies textbook from his backpack, and for the rest of study hall acted as if Nancy wasn't there.

For weeks Henry had been dreaming of this moment, and now that it was happening and he was actually alone with Aisley in her bedroom he could scarcely believe it. He pinched himself, and nope, he wasn't dreaming. He really was sitting on a beanbag chair and watching Aisley as she lay on her bed and read his full series of *Shrieker* comic books. He gave a quick look around to admire once more how cool her room was with the pewter skull, the pentagrams, the witch figurines, and the bats and other creatures painted on her walls, and then he was back to watching Aisley.

After that Henry couldn't take his eyes off of her. Aisley wasn't a skinny stick like a lot of the popular girls at school. Instead she had this breathtaking hourglass figure. Maybe a little plump, but to him she was perfect, especially her smooth, round, baby-doll face. She'd been reading his *Shrieker* books for an hour and was now on his last one, so of course he was anxious for her verdict, but simply watching her made him nearly breathless. His heart soared when a tiny smile crept over her lips. At that moment he experienced pure, unadulterated joy for the first time in his young life.

"You made me a shrieker hunter," she said. "So cool."

The next minutes were torture as Henry waited for Aisley to finish. When she did, she got off her bed, kneeled next to him, and kissed him on the cheek.

"These *Shrieker* books are so cool," she said. "I love them."

The thought of her lips having been pressed against his cheek and her close proximity made Henry dizzy. A hotness flushed his face as he fumbled awkwardly for her, trying to draw her in for a more passionate kiss.

"Whoa," Aisley said as she pushed him away and quickly got to her feet. "What do you think you're doing?"

Tongue-tied, Henry blinked at her several times before stammering out an apology. "I thought you liked me," he said in his confusion.

"As friends. Not romantically. I thought you were cool."

A redness glazed Henry's vision and a loud buzzing filled his head as he stumbled to his feet and gathered up his comic books and his backpack. He mumbled something to Aisley, but what it was he had no idea. He was only barely aware of leaving her room and clumping down the staircase to the front door, and it wasn't until he was nine blocks from her home that the buzzing in his head subsided. It was only then that he realized that he'd been walking to Nancy's house, and was in fact only three houses away.

When he rang the doorbell, Nancy's older sister answered. She didn't like Henry, always looked at him as if he were some sort of strange insect, and this time it was worse than any of those other times. But she still consented to yell for her sister that her oddball friend was at the door. "You better come down before he starts blubbering!"

When Nancy came to the door and saw Henry, she quickly stepped outside to join him and closed the door behind her.

"I'm so sorry, Henry."

He bit his bottom lip as he struggled to fight back tears.

"She didn't like you the way you wanted her to."

Nancy didn't say this as a question but as a statement of fact. Still, Henry nodded.

"Let's walk to Super Comics. It will cheer you up."

Henry still didn't trust himself to speak, and they set off on foot together to the comic-book store two miles away. After walking half a mile, Henry told Nancy that it was stupid that he was ever interested in Aisley.

"Those blue lips and black eye shadow make her look like a corpse," he said. "She's not anywhere near as pretty as you."

Nancy didn't say anything as Henry took her hand. They walked quietly for another block, then Henry said that they should date. "There's nobody I like better than you."

Nancy pulled her hand free. "Stop it."

"No, I mean it. You should be my girlfriend."

"I said stop it."

Her voice sounded different from what Henry had ever heard from her. As if she were talking to a stranger that she didn't particularly like.

"Do you have any idea how insulting this is?" she asked in that same cold, distant voice. "Goth girl rejects you so you come running to me as a consolation prize? We're friends for three years, and this is the first time you express interest in dating me!"

Henry couldn't think of what to say. A slow horror filled him as he realized he was on the verge of losing Nancy from his life.

"Why'd you even come to me that day in the cafeteria and ask if you could sit with me?"

He wanted to cut out his tongue as he half heard himself tell her that it was because Mr. Shapiro told him he should. At first Nancy stared at him dumbfounded. When she turned and walked away from him, he knew she would never speak to him again.

At first Henry felt too weak to move, as if his muscles had melted into goo. As if he'd been completely hollowed out and left barely as a husk. It wasn't until a half hour later that he was able to start trudging off toward his home, and it was then that he passed by the kid he had saved from humiliation weeks earlier, Gary Fleishman. Fleishman was on a bike, and he stopped to say hi to Henry.

"I never got a chance to thank you for saving me like you did. Standing up to those football jocks was amazing," Fleishman said.

Henry stared at him dumbly, not recognizing him or making sense of what this scrawny kid was saying. All at once hurt and pain and rage flared up inside of him, and he bellowed out a yell and started chasing after Fleishman, who had dropped his bike and was running as fast as he could to get away. As if he were running for his life. Which he was.

Henry never would've been able to articulate why at that moment he wanted so badly to beat Fleishman's face into a bloody pulp, but that's what he wanted to do, and he blindly chased after Fleishman for two blocks before Fleishman fell to the sidewalk skinning his knee bloody and crying out in fear. Henry, huffing and puffing, rolled Fleishman onto his back, then plopped down on his chest and brought his fist back ready to crush Fleishman's head as it were a grape. But a force stopped him from following through with his punch.

"What the hell are you doing, kid?"

Bewildered, Henry looked up to see that a man had grabbed his arm and was keeping him from hitting Fleishman. He broke free and ran off. The man who had kept him from killing Gary Fleishman made no effort to stop him, and Henry kept running, his chest aching as if it was going to break apart. It was only later that he realized that somewhere along the way he had lost his *Shrieker* comic books.

When Henry got home, he locked himself in his room and started a new comic book. This one had an anti-hero who killed his first victim (a scrawny kid who looked a lot like Gary Fleishman) using a sledgehammer to smash the skull into a gory pulp of blood, hair, brain matter and bone fragments. Henry decided to switch things up after that and have his anti-hero instead use a hammer and chisel to break open the skulls of those deserving his wrath, and once the skulls were broken apart, the anti-hero dug out the brains with the claw end of the hammer. His next two victims strongly resembled Aisley Martin and Nancy Bower.

Chapter Twenty-two

Los Angeles, the present

"Welcome, Howard."

"Hiya, Madame Asteria."

The young full-figured blonde fortune-teller offered Henry a warm smile and her right paw, which he took. Henry smiled right back just as warmly, hiding his disappointment over her not being as young as he had thought. From her website and the pictures he took of her outside this strip-mall storefront, she had looked like what he imagined a twenty-three year-old version of Nancy Bower to look like, but up close he could see the crow's feet creeping out from the corner of her eyes and the razor-thin lines pruning the skin above her upper lip. She was in her late thirties, easy, maybe even forty. He was just going to have to pretend she was twenty-three.

Of course, those photos making her look so much younger weren't the only fraudulent thing on her website. Her real name wasn't Asteria, Madame or otherwise. Three weeks ago he'd followed her from her psychic storefront to her apartment building in North Los Angeles, and found that her real name was Lois Grabenstein, which, to put it mildly, was not nearly as exotic a moniker as the way she advertised herself. Out of curiosity he searched on Google for the meaning of Asteria and found that it was the name of the Greek goddess of the stars, so at least she'd made a reasonable choice for her "psychic" name.

After letting Henry in, she had locked the front door and flipped the sign to *busy*, so he could've bopped her on the head when she turned around to lead him to the two satin-covered easy chairs sitting in the middle of the small room. Although the iron pipe was in the backpack that he carried (since killing Hawes and Susan, he'd changed into more casual clothes and moved everything he needed from the briefcase to his backpack), his fist would've worked fine. But he didn't do that. He was curious about what a psychic reading would entail. Maybe he was also a little frazzled after his im-promptu and rushed killing of Susan, and he wouldn't mind sitting in a comfortable chair for a few minutes to catch his breath, so to speak. Besides, he'd booked an hour with Madame Asteria, so why be in a hurry? He plopped himself onto the chair the psychic invited him to take with a sweep of her palm, and she lowered herself more daintily onto the matching chair facing him.

"Your name isn't Howard," she said.

He almost told her that her name wasn't Asteria, but he held his tongue and maintained his pleasant smile.

"It's similar to Howard, though," she said. Her forehead wrin-kled, and her eyes squinted to show that she was concentrating in her efforts to divine his real name. "Herman? No, not Herman. Her-bert. No, that's not it either. Henry, yes, that's it. Henry. That's your name."

She gave him a way-too-pleased-with-herself smile. *A parlor trick*, Henry thought. When she had called him Howard at the door he must've given her an unconscious signal that that wasn't his real name, and then when she rattled off those other names she was able to read his expression to know when she had it figured out. Not someone he'd ever want to play poker with, that was for sure!

"Very good," Henry said. "I guess you really are psychic, huh?"

"I have a gift, Henry. I sense your skepticism, but what I do is very real. Before we proceed any further, we should take care of my fee."

Earlier Henry hadn't yet decided whether to kill her right off or to play along for a while, so he had counted out the three hundred dollars that she charged for an hour-long psychic reading. He dug into his pocket for the money and handed her a wad of bills com-prised of tens and twenties. She gave it a cursory look before plac-ing it somewhere under the flowing pink robe she wore. He'd have to get the money back later so he wouldn't be leaving any finger-prints.

"Where's the crystal ball?" Henry asked.

She knew he was cracking wise, but she explained anyway that no psychic she knew of used crystal balls. "In my case I read auras," she said. "I'll also be aligning myself with your energy, and later during the reading I'll be asking to hold your hands. Now Henry, why don't you tell me why you wanted to see me?"

"As you said, I'm a skeptic. I'd rather you tell *me* my reason."

Her plump lips narrowed into a thin smile. "Very well." She took in a deep breath through her nose, and brought her hands parallel to her mouth so that her middle fingers touched. As she exhaled, also through her nose, she pushed her hands down.

"A cleansing breath," she explained, then for an uncomfortably long moment she stared at Henry in this weird way where her eyes seemingly became translucent. Henry wondered how she did that, and it made his skin crawl the way she looked at him. He strongly considered grabbing her and getting this latest Skull Cracker killing over with, but he stayed seated. In a perverse way, he was too curious about what she was going to say.

"You recently suffered a loss," she said at last. "A wife? No, not a wife. A girlfriend."

She was up to more of her parlor tricks, making wild guesses, and then reading his expression to see if she had guessed right. "Not a girlfriend," he said. "I'm married."

"A friend then."

He opened his mouth, but closed it without commenting whether she was right or wrong.

"A woman friend. She died after a long illness."

Before Henry could stop himself, he shook his head. If she wanted to think illness, he should've just let her think that.

"No? I had an impression of this woman being very skinny. In an unhealthy way. I thought illness, but now I see it more clearly. She died violently."

"In an accident," Henry said.

She looked like she was about to correct him, but she caught herself, just as Henry had done earlier. "You were with her when she died," she said. "I can sense her death heavily within your aura."

"I wasn't there," he insisted.

Again she looked like she wanted to argue with him, but instead swallowed back whatever she was going to say and offered him a sympathetic smile. "Nonetheless, her death is weighing heavily on you."

This had not only gone on too long, but was getting uncomfortable. Henry had no doubt that she was really just adept at reading his cues, kind of like a mind-reading act he'd seen on TV, but he didn't much care for it. With one quick lunge, he could grab her by the throat and throttle her until she passed out, and then once he had her trussed up, he could use the chisel and hammer to wake her up. But something wasn't right with the setup. He wasn't sure what it was, but something felt off to him.

"That may all be true, but that wasn't why I wanted to see you."

She did another of her cleansing breaths, and then did that cringe-worthy trick again making her eyes become translucent like a snake's. He wondered how the heck she did that. It didn't last long, though. Only a second or two, and then she was nodding to herself.

"You're here because of your wife," she said.

"What?"

"The impression I received of your wife was overpowering. She was hurt badly in an accident."

"That was five years ago," Henry murmured without fully real-izing he had done so. He wondered how she knew about his wife. Could she have researched him like he had done with her? But how? She didn't know his name, at least not his full name anyway. He had used a pay phone in Santa Monica when he scheduled the appointment. Then Henry remembered that he had mentioned his wife earlier. He must've subconsciously given her a visual clue then about what happened to Sheila. This Madame Asteria was one clever lady, he had to give her that.

"Your wife is in a great deal of distress. She sent you to me. Please hand me the items of hers that you brought and I'll sense the impressions I can from them."

She was referring to the backpack Henry had left by his chair. "There's nothing of hers in there. This is such a sketchy neighbor-hood, I didn't want to leave anything of value in my car."

He didn't know why he bothered giving her an explanation. He should just clobber her and get the killing over with, but something wasn't right about this. He wasn't sure what it was, but a whisper in his head was telling him that something funny was going on here.

She got up from her chair and kneeled beside him, smiling as she held out her hands so she could take told of his. It struck him like a thunderclap what his whisper had been trying to tell him. He understood it then as clear as day.

"You're filming this," he said.

It hadn't been anything overtly obvious. Subtle glances toward a mirror on the wall. A few other slight mannerisms that could've easily gone unnoticed. With the way her eyes momentarily shifted from his, he knew he was right. For a second she was going to try arguing that she didn't know what he was talking about, but as her eyes shifted back to meet his she must've realized it would be pointless. Without saying another word, she got back on her feet, walked over to the wall opposite to where she'd been sitting, and knocked on it. A moment later, the wall opened up exposing a hidden door that led to a hidden room, and a hipster type in his thirties walked out of it.

"I'm Devlin Pavlovich," the hipster said introducing himself to Henry and handing him a business card. "Executive producer of *Real Los Angeles Psychics*, which will be airing next fall."

At first Henry was too stunned to speak. A shudder ran through him as he realized how close he had come to attacking Madame Asteria in front of an audience. It was even possible with this being reality TV they might've stayed hidden and recorded the complete Skull Cracker killing. As the initial shock wore off, Henry wondered whether there was anyone else there other than this hipster and Madame Asteria. Because if that's all there was, he should be able to knock out the hipster and grab the psychic before she realized what was happening, and still go through with the killing.

Pavlovich mistook Henry's contemplative silence for outrage over having his privacy violated. Showing a guilty smirk, he said, "I apologize if you're feeling duped right now. I assure you that was not our intent."

Henry made up his mind after hearing scuffling noises coming from the hidden room, probably from a cameraman. The psychic and this skinny hipster with his wire-rimmed glasses and goatee he could handle. More than that, forget it.

"Really, huh? You had me fooled," Henry said.

Pavlovich showed more of his guilty smirk. "We're worried that if subjects know they're being recorded it will interfere with their psychic energy. When your session was over we would've introduced ourselves and asked you to sign a release form. Everything else was completely on the level."

Henry ignored him and asked Madame Asteria for his money back. She shrugged, and without any argument dug the wad of bills out from under her robe and handed it to him.

"My reading was sincere," she said. "Your wife is in danger."

Henry grabbed his backpack and got up to leave. His legs were rubbery as he trudged to the door. Another shudder chilled him as he fully appreciated the disaster that he had narrowly avoided.

Pavlovich followed him to the door. "Can I leave you the release form and have you consider letting us use your session? There's some good stuff there."

Henry pointed a thumb at Madame Asteria. "She's the psychic. Ask her what I'm going to say."

Henry had the door unlocked and was walking through it when Pavlovich asked him how he knew that there was a production crew recording him.

"I guess I must be psychic too," Henry told him.

Chapter Twenty-three

The detective who discovered Gail Hawes's body knew Morris from when he was on the force, and he met Morris and Stonehedge outside of Hawes's apartment.

"It's already a madhouse in there," he told Morris. "Forensics, crime scene, ME, and an FBI profiler are all present."

"How'd you find her?"

"A friend of hers called the station. The victim had written something on Facebook about running into someone's secret lover, and because of that she was going to be late for a lunch meeting, and then minutes later whatever she wrote was removed. According to her friend, it would be out of character for the victim, Gail Hawes, to remove anything she wrote on Facebook. When pigs sprout wings was how likely her friend put it. When she tried calling Ms. Hawes and got no answer, she called the station convinced something must've happened to her. Since we were on alert for possible female victims in their forties, I checked it out as soon as the call came in."

"What time was this status update written?"

The detective frowned at the question. "Status update? Is that what they call it? I wouldn't know. Facebook is Greek to me." The detective consulted a notepad. "The call came in at twelve fifty-five. I'm not sure when she first saw the victim's message."

Morris's mind buzzed as he thought about what this meant. This latest victim had seen SCK with someone she knew. Not only that, SCK was this mystery person's secret lover. They now had a concrete connection to SCK. If they found this person, they would have SCK.

"I need to talk to the friend who called this in."

"She was brought to the Hollywood station on Wilcox."

Morris called the station and soon had Hawes's friend on the phone. The woman sounded distraught as Morris questioned her about the exact time that she saw Hawes's status update. "This is so awful," she said. "Gail lived on Facebook. Everything she did, she posted. And it was such a strange message about running into a friend's secret lover, kind of a teaser, you know."

"She definitely said *a friend's secret lover?*"

There was what sounded like a stifled sob, as if the woman was struggling to keep from crying. "Yes, I'm sure of that."

"Any idea who this friend is?"

"No. Gail is—" A sob finally broke out as she remembered that Hawes was now in the past tense. It took several seconds before the woman was able to compose herself. Her voice sounded as if she were on the verge of tears as she said, "Gail *was* very sociable. She was always making friends."

"Did she say where she ran into this person? Outside her building? Someplace else?"

"She didn't say. Only that she was now running late because of it."

"How'd you know she was late for a lunch meeting?"

"Because Gail had posted a message ten or so minutes earlier that she was leaving her apartment to meet some people at a restaurant about a party she was going to be throwing. I think the place was local, only a few blocks from where she lived."

Morris thought about that, piecing together in his mind what must've happened. SCK had to have been waiting for her. Probably right outside her apartment building. Then when he "accidentally" bumped into her, he maneuvered her into inviting him to her apartment.

He told the friend, "Try to remember what time you saw Gail's status update about the secret lover. It's important."

"I think twelve thirty."

"When did you see that the message was gone?"

"I'm not sure. It's hard to think clearly right now. Wait." A half a minute later she was back on the phone. "I tried calling Gail right after I saw her status missing. According to my cellphone's call log, I tried calling her at twelve forty-seven."

Morris thanked the woman for her help, then got on the line with a sergeant at the Wilcox Avenue precinct, and told him that the woman was free to go, and that she should be escorted home. After he got off the phone, he told the detective they needed to be canvassing the area. "There's a good chance that sometime around twelve thirty the victim was outside this building with the perp."

The detective nodded. "I've got four patrolmen right now doing that."

"Door to door also in this apartment building. And we need to know if there are any surveillance cameras in the area."

The detective told Morris he'd get right on it.

"Do you realize what this means?" Stonehedge whispered to Morris as they entered the apartment. "A friend of this victim can point you to SCK."

"If the friend is still alive."

That thought appeared to stun the actor. "Oh, wow." He absently stroked his fake beard as he considered that. "You're right. SCK must know deleting the status update won't be enough."

Morris grunted in response to Stonehedge's comment. It was a small apartment, and because of the crowd milling about the room, Morris could see Gail Hawes's legs from the knees down and no other part of her. That was more than okay with him. He'd just as soon not see her broken apart skull if he could help it.

He spotted Smichen and Goodman standing among the crowd of forensic and crime-scene specialists. They noticed him also and made their way over to him. Smichen told him the murder looked mostly the same as Corey Freeman's. "I found a similar shaped hematoma on the back of her head. I haven't been able to find any traces of rust yet, but I'm fairly convinced the same object was used to incapacitate her. Residue found on her wrists, as with Freeman, indicating that after he knocked her dizzy, he taped her wrists together. Residue this time was found on her ankles, so he must've taped them together also. One difference, he gagged her. I found wool fibers in her mouth. Another difference, this time he clawed out eight lumps of brain matter. He must've remembered that was his preference. One final note, the victim had three cats who, among other things, nosed around the open skull, and contaminated the crime scene, but we should still be able to tell whether the same chisel and hammer were used."

"Okay, thanks." Then to Goodman, "Any doubts we're dealing with SCK?"

Goodman looked glum. "I'm thinking more that we could be dealing with a copycat. Her age is right, but let me show you a picture of the victim I found on her cellphone."

He handed Morris the iPhone, and it showed a selfie that the victim must've recently taken. She didn't have a thin, longish face like the other women in their forties that SCK had killed. Instead her face was more of a square shape. Whether it was SCK or a copycat at that moment seemed immaterial to Morris. Whoever he was, he was killing in a similar pattern, and Morris had more pressing concerns. He told Goodman about the deleted Facebook post.

"She invited him up here, and while he was off making a phone call or using the bathroom or whatever excuse he used to get her alone up here, she posted that status update, and he didn't know about it until after he had killed her. What are the odds that Hawes's friend who had SCK as her 'secret lover' is in cahoots with SCK?"

"Slim. Probably close to zero."

"That's what I thought."

Morris used the iPhone to bring up Gail Hawes's phone contacts and started calling in order all of the women who had phone numbers in the Los Angeles area. After each one answered, he identified himself, briefly explained why he was calling, and asked when was the last time that they'd seen Hawes. If any of them at first thought this was a prank, the severity of Morris's tone and the fact that he was calling them from Gail Hawes's phone quickly convinced them otherwise, and all of them ended up expressing a mix of concern and shock. Morris asked the ones who had seen her within the last week whether Hawes had recently caught them with a "secret lover," explaining that it was critically important for their safety and the public at large that they answer truthfully. He knew there was a chance that out of embarrassment or some other reason that one of them might lie to him, but he trusted his instincts to be able to tell if that happened. After twenty-six calls, he had worked his way to Susan Twilitter. When she didn't answer, he knew in his gut that she was the one. He brought up the Facebook app on Hawes's iPhone and found Twilitter's profile page. Unfortunately, there were no pictures of her, but he did discover the name of the boutique where she worked. He called the boutique and asked the owner about Twilitter.

"She's not here," the owner said, sounding worried. "Susie earlier asked if she could have an hour off, and I told her okay. That was two and a half hours ago. This isn't like her. She's always here when she says she's going to be. I've tried calling her, but she's not picking up."

Thanks to Twilitter having had a stolen recovery system installed in her car, it didn't take long for them to track her Honda Accord to the parking garage across the street from where Twilitter had worked. Before the patrolman on the scene pointed it out, Morris had spotted the blood on the pavement near the driver's side door. There wasn't a lot of it, only a few drops, but it was enough so it wasn't a surprise when they opened up the trunk and found Twilitter's body.

"SCK realized he had a loose end, and he cleaned it up," Stonehedge said.

Morris gritted his teeth but otherwise didn't respond to the actor's comment. Twilitter's body had been folded in half and crammed into the space so that her face was hidden inside of the trunk. Morris wanted to see what her face looked like, but he didn't want to disturb her body until the crime-scene team had a chance to go over it. Her pocketbook was still hanging on her shoulder, and Morris dug through it and found her driver's license.

"She's got the same type of face as those other women SCK killed," Stonehedge noted as he looked over Morris's shoulder. "Long and narrow. And she's skinny like those other women."

Morris had no doubt that Susan Twilitter was originally going to be SCK's victim, not Gail Hawes, but Hawes spotted them together so SCK decided to target Hawes. Then because of that Facebook message, he had to do an impromptu killing of Twilitter. Which meant he could've gotten sloppy. Someone else could've seen the two of them together, or possibly seen SCK while he was hiding in the parking garage waiting for Twilitter to return to her car.

"That realtor could still be SCK," Stonehedge said.

Morris gave him a puzzled look, his mind spinning too much about what he needed to do next to pay attention to what the actor had said.

"That realtor, Glen Blakeman. What if having over a hundred grand stolen from him triggered him into killing again?"

Morris was going to dismiss the idea out of hand, but as he thought about Stonehedge's theory it didn't seem impossible. He called Tracy Lacey and asked how long Blakeman had worked at her company, and she told him it had been four years.

"Where'd he work before then?"

"He was a stock broker on Wall Street. The poor man went bust in the 2008 crash, and was unemployed for a few years before moving out here to start over. Have you been able to talk to him yet and clear this up?"

Morris told her not yet, and then called the FBI profiler, Goodman, to tell him about the recent developments. "What are the chances Blakeman's SCK?" he asked.

"It's not impossible," Goodman said.

Chapter Twenty-four

The day's events had left Henry shaken, and he decided he could use a drink or two to settle his nerves. On the way back to Simi Valley, he got off the highway in North Hills and pulled into the parking lot for the first bar that he spotted. The place was mostly empty, and he took a booth.

"Hon, you look like you've been having a rough day."

This came from the waitress. A cute blonde who couldn't have been much older than twenty-five. Full-figured too. Henry flashed her his most charming smile. "You know the expression *man plans God laughs*?" he asked, chuckling softly over the futility of anyone ever believing that they could control anything. "It's been one of those days. Do you serve food?"

"Sure do, hon. Want me to get you a menu?"

"No need if you serve steak. Bring me your best sirloin, medium rare, with mashed potatoes, and a pint of something local. A pilsner would be perfect. Surprise me."

"I'll make sure the cook gets the steak on the grill right away, and I'll be back soon with a really nice pilsner that's brewed in Calabasas."

Henry watched her as she walked away, admiring her from the back. A very cute girl, and perfect for what he needed. Later he would leave a hefty tip. Not enough so she'd talk about it (or about him) to her coworkers, but enough so that she'd remember him. If it were at all possible, he would've liked to grab her tonight when she left work, except that would be far too dangerous. But that was okay. When he was leaving Santa Monica, he observed what had to be a very common occurrence these days, and that sparked an idea for how he'd be able to get his next victim. If that didn't work out, he could focus on this waitress. He was sure with a little planning he'd be able to grab her in the next day or two if it came to that.

She brought over the beer as promised, and he engaged her in small talk about what a long day it had been, getting her to talk about her day also, and coaxing a few laughs out of her over some of his corny jokes. The same when she brought over his steak. He continued chatting her up and joking around when he ordered his second beer, and then a third. By this point she had volunteered quite a bit about herself, including what time she had to show up at work, and how much she hated driving home in the dark when her shift ended at one each night. *Yeah, she wouldn't be hard at all,* Henry thought. If it came to that.

The three beers and the steak were helping him to relax, and he would've liked to have ordered a fourth beer. It was comfortable in the bar, very pleasant, actually, and he enjoyed chatting and joking around with Brenda, the blonde waitress, even if she might end up very soon being his next victim. She was certainly nice on the eyes, no denying that! But it was already past six, and once again he had left Sheila alone without arranging for anyone to look in on her since he didn't want people to know that he'd been gone all day. Yet the idea of having another beer was tempting. He was dreading going home and finding Sheila sitting in her filth, and much worse, seeing her loathing and those unspoken accusations in her eyes. Or if she actually deigned to speak to him, hearing her utter disgust for him in her voice.

Sighing, he signaled Brenda over, and asked for the check. When she returned with it, he gave her sixty dollars on a thirty-nine-dollar bill, telling her to keep the change for putting up with all of his bad jokes. From the way she touched his arm and smiled at him when she thanked him, he had no doubt that if he approached her late to-morrow night in the parking lot, she might be surprised to see him but she wouldn't be frightened by him. She also wouldn't know what hit her, at least not until it was too late. If it came to that.

No surprise that Sheila was where he had left her. Where else was she going to be? And of course she had soiled herself. Henry could smell it the moment he stepped into the house. He switched the TV to a local news channel, and carried Sheila to the bathroom so he could undress and clean her, and she refused to look at him while he did this. Once he had her washed and into a freshly laundered pair of pajamas he brought her to the kitchen and sat her in her wheelchair.

"What's it going to be for dinner, huh?" he asked. He waited for her to answer him, and when she didn't, he said, "Okay, how about I switch things up and make us some breakfast for dinner? Scrambled eggs and sausage? French toast?" Again no answer, so he set about making enough scrambled eggs and sausage for the two of them. Even though he'd had a steak dinner only a little while ago, he was already feeling like he could eat again, probably because it had been such a stressful and hectic day. Besides, he didn't want Sheila to have to dine alone.

The sausages were frying and he'd just cracked six eggs into a large bowl when he heard the words *Skull Cracker* from the TV. That drew him into the living room and he saw that the sort of funny-looking but tough guy from yesterday's press conference was giving another one. Henry had forgotten his name, but they soon showed it on the bottom of the screen. Morris Brick. They next brought up on the screen pictures of Hawes and the apartment building where she had lived, with Brick asking for anyone who had seen her outside her building with a man today, most likely around twelve thirty, to call the hotline number on the screen. It surprised Henry when after that they showed a picture of Susan and again asked for calls from anyone who might've seen Susan accompanied by a man over the last few weeks, and also if they'd seen a man acting suspiciously today around one forty-five inside the Santa Monica parking garage where Susan was found dead.

"That was damn fast," Henry muttered to himself. They'd switched back to Brick again, and Henry found himself staring intently at the man. *You're good, Brick,* he thought, *I'll give you that, and I'll be waiting with baited breath to see what you come up with next.*

That last thought was with a forced bravado, because he couldn't be sure whether he'd been seen at either the parking garage or with Susan, although he thought it unlikely. If he had been, so what? How could they track him from a police sketch to his home in Simi Valley? Certainly not if anyone'd spotted his license plates today since he had waited until he returned home and had pulled his car into the garage before replacing the stolen plates with the real ones. If the police did come up with a sketch that looked anything like him, he'd pack himself and Sheila up and they'd move somewhere else. Still, though, this Brick character was proving himself dangerous, and these new developments made Henry nervous enough that he only half paid attention as Brick warned that blonde women in their early twenties needed to be especially vigilant in the coming days, and to call the police if they notice anything out of the ordinary, especially if a stranger tries to get them alone. When his nerves calmed down enough so that he was able to make sense of what Brick had said, he snorted loudly.

"Fat chance. You're wasting your breath with that warning, Brick," he whispered to himself. "Plenty of young blonde girls out there for me to grab no matter what you have to say."

He started smelling smoke then, and it took him a few seconds to realize where it was coming from. "Ah jeeze," he swore as he rushed back into the kitchen and saw that the sausages had burnt to a crisp and were smoking up the room. He used a potholder to grab the frying pan and had to scrape the ruined sausage patties out of the pan with a spatula. "Why didn't you give me a shout that these were burning?"

Sheila didn't bother answering him as she sat bug-eyed, her savaged face twisted into a deathlike rictus.

Henry had had enough. "It's not my fault!" he shouted. "None of this is my fault, so quit acting like it is!"

He took several deep breaths as his anger subsided into guilt. "I'm sorry, okay?"

Still not a word from Sheila. Not even a blink from her, which Henry found amazing given all the smoke in the room. He opened up several windows, and then set about frying up a new batch of sausages, and once he had those underway, he prepared the scrambled eggs the way Sheila liked them. After he had the food spooned out onto two plates and her sausages cut up into tiny pieces, he rolled Sheila over to the kitchen table, placed a fork in her somewhat useable hand, and was relieved that she at least consented to eat. It took her over forty minutes to finish up what he had given her since she needed to chew her food into a fine paste before she could swallow, but once she was done he rolled her out into the living room and placed her in front of the TV. Then he hooked up his iPhone to the television's video feed and played the recording of what he had done to Gail Hawes. When it was over, he could see that Sheila's deathlike rictus had become more rigid.

"What is wrong with you?" she cried.

While Henry preferred Sheila talking to staying silent, it was always a weird effect when she did talk due to her paralysis on her right side, and after over five years Henry still hadn't gotten used to it. With only the left side of her mouth moving, it left her voice both hollow and heavy, and it left her speaking as slowly as she ate, like it was a great effort on her part to push out each word.

Henry felt his cheeks reddening as he looked at his wife. "I'm doing the best I can," he stated stubbornly.

"That is not who we agreed on!"

"I had to improvise," Henry explained. "That one saw me with Susan, so I had to switch things up. What's the big deal?"

"It's not the one I wanted! You are botching everything up!"

Sheila was furious with him. He could see that with the way the left part of her mouth twisted into a pinched, spiteful grimace. It always made him feel awful when she was furious with him.

"I had no choice so you'll just have to be satisfied with her," he said.

"What about that girl? Why didn't you record killing that girl?"

He wasn't about to tell her about the reality show. If he did, Sheila would find a way to blame that on him! "She was too old," he said. "At least forty, maybe older."

"You can't do anything right! You're useless!"

Henry could've argued that she had approved of Madame Asteria when he had showed her the psychic's website, and later the pictures he had taken of her, but he knew he couldn't argue with his wife when she got like this. He showed her on his iPhone a picture he had taken of the blonde waitress from earlier.

"I can grab her tomorrow night," he said.

"Before then."

"I can't do it before then. It's impossible."

"I said before then!"

"I'll find someone else tomorrow morning, okay? Someone who looks like her. They're a dime a dozen here in LA. Okay?"

Henry found himself holding his breath as he waited for Sheila to say something. She could be so damn unreasonable when she wanted to be.

"Kill that Susan first! Like you were supposed to!"

If he told her how he had snuck up on Susan and broke her neck in a quick attack, it would infuriate her. She would never forgive him for not breaking open Susan's skull with a chisel and hammer right there in the parking lot and digging out her brains.

"I'm not doing that. You'll just have to be satisfied with the one I killed for you."

"If you don't, I won't eat again! You will have to watch me die. Then you will be all alone!"

Henry crossed his arms over his chest. "Unless you accept the one I killed, I won't kill a girl for you tomorrow."

He was playing a game of chicken with his wife, but it was one that he knew he had the upper hand in, and he could see in her eyes the exact moment when she gave in.

"We have a deal?" he asked.

She gave him that angry pinched look again that made him feel so small, but she reluctantly agreed that they had a deal as long as he didn't screw this next one up also.

Chapter Twenty-five

Brooklyn, 2011

"I'm telling' ya, Henry, you gotta let me set you up with my wife's cousin. She's a doll. A real sweetheart, and I just know you two would hit it off."

Henry reached for one of the meaty chicken wing drumsticks and took a bite of it, savoring it. "These are the best chicken wings you can get anywhere in Brooklyn," he said. "Forget Brooklyn. Anywhere in the city. They don't cook these on a grill or in an oven. They've got an open pit barbecue out back, and they use mesquite wood to give it that smoky flavor."

"You're changing the subject."

"Just talking about the best darn wings I've ever had. You got to admit, it was worth the trip to Bushwick for them."

His buddy Joe took a long sip of his ale while he gave Henry a hard eye. "You've done too much work to throw in the towel after a few bad dates. How much did you drop? Fifty pounds?"

"Sixty-five," Henry corrected him. "I'm now a svelte two twenty. I might look like some sort of balding lumpy ogre out of a fairy tale, but at least I'm no longer a fatso."

Joe shook his head as if he were disappointed in his friend. "That's defeatist talk. You're a nice guy, Henry, and you're not that bad looking. At a certain age it's more important for women to meet a nice guy."

Henry had slipped up earlier. He'd learned long ago that people don't like negativity, or *defeatist talk*, as Joe called it. It was better to be a cheerful loser than someone who was always moaning *woe is me*. He knew his friend was wrong, though. As he had learned during his forty-four years on this planet, well, really thirty-one years starting that first time he was rejected (and so rudely) by a member of the fairer sex, women might find him a nice guy, and they might want him as a friend, but they certainly had no romantic interest in him, and that wasn't about to change. But he had nothing to gain by spelling that out to Joe, other than looking like a complainer, so he simply agreed with his friend.

"Okay, then," Joe continued, nodding, a dull glaze in his eyes from the three beers that he'd had. Joe was one of those tall, thin guys who showed the effects of his drinking after only a couple of beers. "I'll talk to my wife and get it set up." He gave a quick glance at his watch and pushed himself out of the booth. "And speaking of the wife, I gotta be heading home." He dug twenty dollars out of his wallet and dropped it on the table to cover his share, then pointed a bony index finger at Henry. "Don't ever forget, there's someone for everybody. See you at work tomorrow."

Henry watched as Joe tottered toward the exit. A good guy, but couldn't hold his liquor. Unsteady on his feet after only a few beers. Henry lifted up his glass and drained the pilsner he'd been drinking, and nearly snorted it out of his nose when a woman took Joe's place across from him, a big teasing grin stretching across her face. Not just any woman, but his dream woman. Sparkling blue eyes, wavy blonde hair, gorgeous face, and from what he imagined (since he could only see her from the waist up), a perfect hourglass figure.

"Trust me, you wouldn't be making a very good first impression if beer came out of your nose right now," she said, her grin turning impish.

Henry choked on the beer a bit, and coughed several times as it went down the wrong pipe, but he somehow kept it from blowing out his nose. He wiped his mouth with a napkin, and half expected this vision of beauty to be gone when he looked back up, but she was still sitting across from him. Still grinning.

"That would've been very gauche," he agreed. "Care for a wing?"

"Wouldn't mind one," she said. "I'm Sheila."

"Henry."

This had all happened so suddenly that Henry started thinking it had to be a setup on Joe's part. Women just don't approach him out of the blue like this. Maybe other guys, but not him.

"Did Joe set this up?" he asked.

"Joe?" she asked in between gnawing on the wing that she'd picked up. "Is that the tall skinny guy who was sitting in the booth with you?"

Henry nodded.

"I don't know him from Adam. But I've been waiting for him to get his ass in gear so I could meet you. You seem like a nice guy, Henry, and I really want to meet a nice guy."

Henry blushed at her compliment. "I don't want to appear ungentlemanly. Normally I'd offer to buy you a drink," he said, stretching the truth, since he'd never been in this situation before, "but it seems as if you already have one. Unless you'd like something else?"

Her eyes sparkled a tad brighter as she took a sip from the glass of wine that she had brought with her.

"You certainly are a gallant one," she said. "But this Chardonnay is fine for now. So Henry, what do you do for work?"

Henry couldn't help flinching at the question. With little enthusiasm, he said, "Word processing."

"Really? That's a thing?"

"Yep. I work for a law firm in Manhattan typing up briefs and other forms. It might not be glamorous work, but I do okay."

"Did you go to school for that?"

He could've told her that he'd gone to NYU for a bachelor's in political science thinking that he'd go to law school afterward, but that his grades weren't up to snuff, and that the word-processing job was just something that fell into his lap, but instead he shrugged and told her it was a job he got after college. "I never thought I'd be doing it for twenty years, but it got comfortable," he added.

"So I take it this wasn't something you've had a burning desire to do since childhood?"

Henry's cheeks burned redder as he saw the way she grinned, as if she were struggling to keep from laughing. He shook his head. "I'll show you what I wanted to do once upon a time when I was a teenager."

He turned to look for the waitress so he could signal for her. When he caught her eye and she came over, he asked for a paper napkin and to borrow a pen. With napkin and pen in hand he turned back to Sheila, except she was gone. Must've slipped out of the booth when his back was turned. Disappointing, but not a surprise. She had come over only to make sport of the ugly guy. His initial impulse was to crumple up the napkin and toss it to the floor, but instead he set about drawing Sheila from memory. This was the first drawing he'd worked on since his parents found his skull cracker comic books and made him see a psychiatrist, which was ridiculous since years later he discovered Japanese anime and found stuff more violent and gorier than what he had done. He could've blamed his losing interest in drawing on the way his parents had overreacted, but the truth was his interest had begun to wane before then. Maybe it was losing his *Shrieker* books, which he knew were the best things he'd ever do. Maybe it was because Nancy had promised him he'd be famous someday, and after that fateful day when she refused ever to talk to him again, he more than anything wanted to prove her wrong.

"Wowser, that's really good. Like what you'd see in a graphic novel, and not like one of those ten-dollar Central Park caricatures."

Startled, Henry looked up to see that Sheila was once again sitting across from him. "Where'd you go?" he asked.

Her grin turned mischievous. "You didn't think I ditched you?"

"The thought crossed my mind."

"Nope. Just something I had to do." She took the napkin that Henry had been drawing on and gave it a closer look. "Do you mind if I keep this?"

"It's yours."

She carefully placed the napkin in her pocketbook. It was one of those big bulky numbers. Something that could hold a kitchen sink. Henry wasn't sure, but he thought he caught a glimpse of a hypodermic needle.

"A big favor, Henry. With the Skull Cracker Killer prowling the streets a girl doesn't feel safe walking alone to the subway. Would you escort me?"

"Of course. Let me settle the bill."

She winked at him. "I'm going to use the little girl's room. How about I meet you outside?"

Henry felt like he'd suffered emotional whiplash, rapidly alternating between hopefulness to crushing despair to something close to euphoric bliss all in a matter of a few minutes, although after Sheila left the booth for the second time, he mostly felt confused. Dread began to creep in as he had a sinking feeling that Sheila really had ditched him this second time and he wouldn't be seeing her again. But he settled the bill, and trudged outside and stood waiting for her. When he saw her exit the front door (and now that he could see the whole package, he'd been right about her perfect hourglass figure!) and search for him, his heart somersaulted in his chest. He could've wept from joy, but controlled himself and instead gave her a small wave. She hurried over to him.

"My knight in shining armor," she said, teasingly. "I knew you wouldn't let me down."

They'd walked only half a block when Sheila stopped suddenly in front of an alley, her body tensing. "Did you see that?" she asked in a hushed tone.

"What?"

"There's someone down there who needs help."

Henry peered down the alley. It was too dark to see anything. "I don't think there's anyone there," he said, cautiously.

"I know what I saw."

"I'll call the police if you want."

"I'm not leaving some poor soul to possibly bleed to death down there."

She took off down the alley, which shocked Henry. This was crazy, but what was he going to do? Stay behind and let this woman who weighed at least eighty pounds less than him walk into possible danger? How gallant would that be?

He trudged into the alley after Sheila, pushing past her so that he led the way. It didn't take him long to reach the end of the alley, and aside from some garbage cans and a cat that scared the bejesus out of him when it darted past him, there was nothing else there. He turned to tell Sheila that, and caught a glimpse of what he thought was her holding a hypodermic needle, but before he could be sure of that she hid her hand behind her back.

"I could've sworn I saw someone." She said with this odd smile that Henry couldn't place. "I guess my eyes must've been playing tricks on me, huh?"

"It happens," Henry muttered, still confused about that hypodermic needle, because he was sure he had seen it. Did she want to come into this alley to shoot up? Was she a heroin addict? How could that be possible given how robust she looked?

Before he could spend more than a second or two pondering these thoughts, she asked him if he lived in the area.

He nodded. "A couple of blocks from here."

She took hold of his arm and leaned in close against him. "You really are a nice guy, Henry. How about we go to your place?"

Henry was still puzzled about a number of things, including what it was that she still held in her left hand. He decided he didn't care. Same with whether she was planning to shoot up at his apartment. He didn't care.

Arm in arm, Henry walked her out of the alley.

Chapter Twenty-six

Brooklyn, 2011

"Henry, my man, welcome back! How was the honeymoon cruise?"

Henry and Joe shook hands, and then embraced. Joe's lips momentarily quivered into a look of disapproval as he glanced at Henry's paunch, but whatever comment he wanted to make regarding Henry's obvious weight gain he kept to himself. Henry and Sheila had gone on a cruise to the Bahamas for their honeymoon, and the cruise had been one of those all-you-can-eat affairs. Henry had been planning on depriving himself and maintaining his diet, but Sheila, bless her, told him to go nuts; that she wouldn't mind it at all if he packed on thirty or so pounds, which he ended up doing.

"The cruise was a dream," Henry said. "One of the best weeks of my life."

That was certainly true. Henry might have even been willing to say it was the best week of his life, except he'd be hard pressed to pick any one particular week since he'd met Sheila as better than any of the others.

"It's definitely been a whirlwind," Joe said, shaking his head in amazement. "Amazing how life works. A month ago we're eating wings and drinking beer, and you're all down on yourself about how no woman is ever going to fall in love with you. Do you remember what I told you that day?"

Henry couldn't help grinning. "That's there someone for everyone," he said.

"And then what happened that night?"

Henry's grin stretched wider. "I met that someone."

Joe gave him a friendly punch in the shoulder. "I'm really happy for you, Henry. Sheila is definitely a looker, no question about that, and married life is definitely agreeing with you."

"Agreed on both fronts," Henry said, although it was a massive understatement.

His marriage certainly wasn't perfect. Sheila got moody at times (to put it mildly), and he would've liked more sex. They'd only made love three times so far—the night they met, one week later (and that night Sheila was completely wild, uninhibited, and insatiable, and had left Henry a quivering mess by the time they finished), and one evening during their cruise after Sheila had gotten sloshed on tequila shots. But even with those issues, which he considered minor, he was happier than he could ever have imagined. Before he met Sheila, his had been a lonely and unhappy existence, and he had resigned himself to it always being that way. So she gets moody, so they don't hump like rabbits, so they sleep in separate beds. So what? He had a beautiful woman to share his life with, and there were genuine moments of tenderness between them. Maybe not a lot, but there were definite moments. An unexpected caress, the times he'd catch her looking at him a certain way, her playful teasing of him, and just last night the way she surprised him by sitting on his lap when he was watching TV. No, it might not be perfect, but for Henry it was still close to paradise, and far better than the alternative hellish life he thought had been in the cards for him. And as far as the sex went, Sheila asked him to be patient, promising him that there'd be more nights where she'd be that crazed, insatiable sex goddess again (although she didn't put it in those words).

One of the law firm's partners came into the breakroom, eyeing Henry and Joe suspiciously, so they finished pouring their coffee, stirred in some cream and sugar, and headed back to their desks so that they could perform a full day of typing up briefs, contracts, and other legal documents.

The rest of the day Henry could barely concentrate on his work as he kept drifting into thoughts about how dramatically his life had changed. About how lucky he had gotten.

Like he had won the super lottery of life.

Chapter Twenty-seven

Brooklyn, 2011

Joe hustled through the crowd to bring two beers to the table; a pilsner for Henry and an IPA for himself. Henry, his face folded into a hangdog expression, barely looked up as he sat like a lump.

"Come on, man, buck up, it can't be that bad."

Henry could've easily disagreed with him, but instead he took a long drink of his pilsner.

"Look, there are always going to be bumps in any marriage," Joe offered philosophically. "These are things you got to work through. Everyone goes through it."

Henry knew not everybody went through what he was experiencing. He hadn't planned to talk to anyone about what had been happening between Sheila and himself—it seemed too much of a betrayal of his wife to do so, but Joe had insisted they go out for beers after work and he wouldn't take no for an answer. "Something's eating at you, Henry," Joe had said. "The way you've been moping around the office the last couple of days, you're not fooling anyone. So we're going to hoist a few, and you're going to spill your guts."

Henry had gone with his buddy to humor him. He couldn't imagine saying out loud the thoughts he'd been having, but as they sat drinking their beer, he mentioned how he didn't even know what Sheila did.

"What do you mean?"

"We've been married for three months, and I have no clue what she does for work. Or even if she works. When I try asking her, she tells me a little of this and a little of that, and then she gets mad if I push it."

Joe's expression turned serious. "That's odd," he said.

"She's got money," Henry said. "I have no idea how much, but her place on Central Park West costs a fortune. I'd need to be making ten times what I am now to afford it."

They were on their second beers, and Joe was already beginning to look a little bleary-eyed. He gave the matter some thought as he drank some more, then speculated, "Maybe she won the lottery?"

Henry shrugged, looking miserable. "Maybe that's it. All I know is I have no idea what she does when I'm at work."

What Henry said was true, but he had his suspicions. That first night they'd met, the thought had popped into his head that Sheila could be a call girl. That she had sat at his booth only to drum up business. After they had sex that first night, he was half expecting her to charge him for the night and was somewhat surprised when she didn't. He had felt guilty about having those thoughts, but when she later took him to her apartment on Central Park West (where they now lived) and she refused to tell him what she did for work, the thought that she might be a call girl, albeit a high-priced one, had once again popped into his head. She was certainly beautiful enough for that to be the case, and it would explain a lot of things; her lack of interest in sex and why someone as beautiful as Sheila would settle for Henry. After all, if she were being paid by guys all day for sex, why would she want any more from him, and why would she want anything other than a nice guy? If that was what it was—that Sheila was a high-priced call girl, and she simply wanted Henry for companionship when she wasn't working—he could live with that. But things had turned more ominous over the past week.

Joe pondered over what Henry had told him, and finally made up his mind. "A little mystery in a marriage isn't the worst thing," he proclaimed, before finishing off his IPA.

"I think I might be losing her," Henry said as he choked back a sob. Up until that moment he hadn't let himself admit that his wife might be about to leave him. He didn't think he could live if that happened.

"Sounds like you're jumping to conclusions," Joe said. He rubbed his bony jaw, giving the matter more thought. "I admit it's odd she won't tell you what she does, but you're making a pretty big leap there."

"Sheila has become so distant recently. The last three days she's gotten home past two in the morning, and she won't tell me where she's been."

"No kidding?"

Henry shook his head, afraid he might start bawling if he tried speaking.

"Call in sick tomorrow," Joe said. "Follow her. Find out what she's doing."

The next day Henry did as Joe suggested, paying the doorman fifty dollars to call him when he saw Sheila in the lobby. He got the doorman's call a few minutes after five, and he hurried from the bench in Central Park where he'd been camped out for the day, and spotted his wife as she left the apartment building, but then quickly lost her as she jumped into a cab.

He tried again the next day, this time renting a car. Sheila again left the apartment building a little after five, jumping into a cab, and this time Henry was able to follow her to a seedy bar in Queens. She was in there no more than forty minutes when a man exited the bar and stood outside of it as if he were waiting for someone. This man was about Henry's height and age, balding, and looking about thirty pounds overweight. Certainly not good-looking, but a sick feeling crept into Henry's stomach as he thought that this might be playing out the same as that night he had first met Sheila. He was proven right when a few minutes later Sheila left the bar and headed straight to this man the moment she spotted him. They walked together until they reached a car that they both then got in. Henry followed them to the Jamaica neighborhood of Queens and watched as the car pulled into the driveway of a small two-level house, and then as Sheila and this man entered the house together.

For the next half hour Henry felt like he was dying inside as he tried to figure out what to do. His first thought was to burst in there and catch Sheila in the act of cheating on him and play the martyr and tell her with shocked outrage that it was over, except the idea of losing her made him sick to his stomach. He accepted quickly that he'd rather she sleep around (whether she was being paid or not) than lose her. Even with the trauma Sheila had put him through the last few days, he couldn't go back to living alone, and he became terrified that if he broke into the house and confronted them Sheila would end things with him. He couldn't risk losing her, but he couldn't just drive away either. So he sat paralyzed in his fear and dread and despair as different plans of action raced through his mind. Finally, he decided he had to go in the house. He would physically pick Sheila up and carry her out of there on his shoulder if he had to, but he was taking her out of that house. Once he got her home, he would talk sense into her, and get to the bottom of what was going on. Somehow he would make Sheila see how much he loved her, and he would find a way to save their marriage. And maybe he'd also beat the heck out of her lover before he took his wife out of there.

The front door was locked and it appeared solid. Henry tried to break it open with his shoulder like he'd seen done on cop shows, but all he did was hurt himself. He rang the bell and got no answer. In his mind he imagined that his wife and this man were too busy making love in this man's bed to answer the door, and that thought left Henry seething. He raced around the house searching for a window or another door that he could enter through, and in the back of the house he found a flimsier-looking door that he was able to kick open on his third try. This door led straight into the kitchen, and that was where he found them, but not the way he expected them to be. Sheila lay crumpled on the floor not moving. The man was lying on his back near her, his eyes bulging open. He looked paralyzed, but his lips were trembling slightly as if he were struggling to say something.

Henry stumbled toward Sheila as he tried to make sense of what he was seeing. A hammer and chisel lay near the man, and a pool of blood seemed to be leaking out of the back of his head. Unless he was mistaken, a piece of the man's skull also lay on the floor.

Henry moved as if he were in a trance as he kneeled by Sheila, the room blurring around him and his blood ran ice-cold as he expected to find his wife dead. But she wasn't dead. She wasn't even unconscious. When he gently turned her onto her back, her left eye was blinking and the left part of her mouth was moving. As incredible as it was, she was trying to tell him something. He bent his ear to her lips and listened to what she had to say. Her voice was a faint whisper at best, and it took time for her to push out each word, but she told him what he needed to know. That if he called for the police or for an ambulance they would arrest her as the Skull Cracker Killer, and that he would never see her again.

He backed away from her, and that was when he spotted the hypodermic needle on the floor. Something made him lift up the man's head enough so he could see the back of his scalp, and sure enough a piece of his skull had been broken off exposing his brain. The room started spinning on Henry, and he sat heavily onto the floor.

He understood then that Sheila really was the Skull Cracker Killer, and knew why she had approached him that night in the bar. He also knew why she had slipped away from the booth when he had waved the waitress over. So that she wouldn't be seen with him. For whatever reason she'd changed her mind after they'd gone down that alley, but her plan had been to do to him what she started to do to this man. Whatever was in that hypodermic needle must've left him paralyzed, and she had tried using the hammer and chisel to break apart his skull just like the way Henry had drawn in his skull-cracker comic books when he was sixteen.

Joe's words came back to him. *There's someone for everybody.*

There was a reason why he drew those comic books and Sheila was now killing people the same way, just like there was a reason why she chose not to kill him in that alley. Because they were soulmates. Sheila must've sensed that, even if she didn't understand it at the time.

There's someone for everybody.

With a certain finality, Henry accepted the truth of this. His wife was a monster, but that wasn't going to change the way he felt about her, nor was he going to call the police. After all, he was more than somewhat monstrous on the outside, and even if he hadn't realized it until now, he had to be also on the inside for Sheila to have recognized that they were soulmates.

His dizziness had passed, and he moved over to Sheila and put his ear near her mouth. It took a while, but she instructed him on what he had to do.

Chapter Twenty-eight

Brooklyn, 2011

Henry did exactly what Sheila told him to do. He used a butcher's knife to cut off the man's head so that the police wouldn't be able to connect the man's death with the Skull Cracker Killer. After that he found a gym bag in a closet, put the head in it, also the skull fragment, and threw in a stack of plates to weigh the bag down. He then gathered Sheila's hammer, chisel, and hypodermic needle, and used one of the man's undershirts to wipe off any surface he or his wife might've touched. With that done, he wrapped Sheila in a blanket, and he raced her, the gym bag. and Sheila's ridiculously-sized pocketbook to the car he had rented.

On the way back to their apartment, he stopped and hurled the gym bag into Flushing Bay. He also stopped four blocks from their apartment to leave Sheila on the sidewalk. He hated doing this. He had no idea how long it would take for someone to find her, but he agreed with her that it had to be done this way. After leaving Sheila, he raced to their apartment because he had items of hers that he needed to get rid of along with the tools that she used as the Skull Cracker Killer.

She had always forbidden him from looking in her closet, but he found the scrapbook and diary where she told him they would be. A quick look in the scrapbook showed newspaper clippings about the killings she had done. The diary had, among other things, her personal thoughts about her killings. Henry read several entries, then found the one that she wrote after meeting him at the bar. The reason she had changed her mind about killing him was that there'd been several articles about the Skull Cracker Killer in which the FBI profiler insisted the killer had to be a loner and couldn't be married, and she decided Henry would be a harmless enough guy for her to attach herself to, and that by marrying him she'd help hide herself from the police. In the following entries, she wrote about how she found him repulsively ugly, but was also developing a certain affection for him, as well as a closeness. In a recent entry she wrote that she was happy in a way that surprised her to be married to Henry, and that she no longer minded the idea of making love to him, and that she was looking forward to doing so after her next round of killings. Sheila had directed him to burn the scrapbook and diary, but Henry ripped out several pages so he could keep them.

After he got rid of all the incriminating evidence (except the pages that he had ripped out), he returned the car and took the subway home. The cops were waiting for him, which was a relief since it meant someone had found Sheila. Still, he broke down when they told him his wife had been hurt and was at the hospital.

It turned out that Sheila was unconscious when she was found, so the police at first considered Henry a suspect and took him to the station for questioning. Things did not go well when they questioned him about where he'd been that evening, and he gave them a bogus answer about how he had rented a car that day so he could drive to Long Island and visit his parents' graves. The police didn't believe him, and Henry sweated up a storm as he realized that if they searched him they'd find the pages from Sheila's diary that he had taken. One of the detectives started asking him why he was sweating so much, and all Henry could think of to say was that he was worried about his wife, which only made the cops more suspicious. Henry could tell things were about to turn really ugly when a call came in that saved him. The detective who took the call must've been told that Sheila had regained consciousness and had claimed that her husband wasn't involved in what happened to her, because when he got off the phone he actually gave Henry a sympathetic look.

"That was the hospital," he said. "Your wife's awake. You should go over there."

"How is she?"

The detective looked away from him. "It would be better if you talk to her doctor."

Sheila had been taken to Mount Sinai. When Henry met with her doctor, he explained to Henry about Sheila's paralysis and the serious internal damage she suffered. The prognosis was that she'd live, but that she'd never recover full use of her body. That the paralysis was likely permanent.

Somehow Henry didn't mind that. It meant Sheila would never leave him. Also that she'd never kill anyone else.

It turned out Henry was wrong about the latter.

Chapter Twenty-nine

Los Angeles, the present

Morris had used Gail Hawes's Facebook entries, credit-card receipts, and cellphone call-log to create a timeline showing where she'd been over the last week, and was in the process of doing the same for Susan Twilitter when Natalie called.

"I've got a very unhappy dog here," she said. "He's been moping around all evening waiting for you to come home."

"I can imagine," Morris said. "I'll make it up to Parker tomorrow."

"I'm not entirely thrilled myself."

"I'll be making it up to you too. If not before then, on your birthday Saturday, definitely. I bet you thought I'd forgotten with all this craziness going on."

"The thought had crossed my mind."

"What's it going to be, your thirty-fifth?"

"You're a sweet talker, Morris."

"I can't imagine you being any older than thirty-five. Except we got a twenty-three-year-old daughter, so I'm not exactly sure how that works. But when I look at you, it doesn't seem possible for you to be any older than that."

"That's because you need glasses. Or maybe it's that old saying about memory making the heart grow fonder."

Morris checked his watch. "It's only been sixteen hours since I bid you adieu this morning."

"You sure? It feels like it's been days."

"I know." Morris rubbed his eyes as a tired sigh eased out of him. "We almost had him today, Nat. We know from her iPhone that when Gail Hawes left her apartment today, she turned left and walked about two hundred feet before running into SCK. If she had turned right instead, we would've had him on a surveillance camera. A damn flip of the coin. Right instead of left, and we'd have him."

"You think you're getting close," she said softly, not as a question but as a statement.

"We are. He's doing things he didn't want to have to do. The woman found in her car trunk, Susan Twilitter, was a rushed killing. We might get him from that. We're still pulling surveillance video from the area. And if Hawes saw Twilitter with SCK, someone else might've also."

"You're sounding like you might be getting obsessed again."

"Not obsessed. Highly motivated. I think we've got a chance to stop him before he kills his next victim."

"A young blonde girl."

"Yes."

"Okay. I understand," Natalie said, her voice soft, and as if she were trying hard to sound like she did understand. "Will you be making an appearance tonight?"

"I'll be trying to. Definitely by daybreak so I can pick Parker up."

"Did you remember to eat something for dinner?"

"I did forget," he admitted sheepishly. "The actor who's been tagging along with me started complaining about my stomach rumbling, and took off to pick up some fish tacos that he claims are *to die for*." Morris stared bleary-eyed at his watch for a moment as he tried to remember what time Stonehedge had left. "The restaurant is in Beverly Hills, and he should be back soon."

"*To die for*, huh? Sounds very Hollywood. But at least he's reminding you to eat."

"Yeah, at least he's good for something."

Charlie Bogle was calling. Morris begged off the call with his wife, promising her that he wouldn't be overworking himself into a stroke. When he answered Bogle's call, his investigator told him that he, Lemmon, and Polk, were checked in at their hotel in New York. "Your press conference tonight made the New York news," Bogle said. "The woman he killed, Gail Hawes, didn't look like she matched the other women SCK likes to kill. The one found in the car trunk did, though."

"That's because Twilitter was the SCK's original target. To make a long story short, Hawes saw the two of them together, so SCK moved on to her. Because of a Facebook post Hawes made, SCK had to eliminate Susan Twilitter also. He called Twilitter at work, most likely arranging to meet up with her, and then attacked her in the parking garage when she went to her car."

"I see." Bogle hummed softly as he mulled this over. "He's getting sloppy. Any surveillance cameras in the area?"

"None in the garage. The Santa Monica police are trying to pull whatever surveillance video they can."

"So you might have him already?"

"We might."

"It certainly sounds like things are breaking. Or at least they're about to."

"It does."

"Should we be getting on the first plane back to LA?"

"No. I still want you three to dig into this from the New York end. I got a name for you. Glen Blakeman. I'm not sure how serious he is, but find out what you can. Supposedly he was a stockbroker in 2008. Something happened five years ago to SCK. Maybe he got arrested, maybe he got into an accident, maybe he got sick. See if you can figure out which. Look for anything unusual happening before SCK's New York disappearance."

"Piece of cake," Bogle said. "New York has what, eight and a half million people? With two top investigators plus Polk looking into this, we should have this wrapped up by noon tomorrow. Or in five years."

"Try for noon."

"Will do."

Morris got off the call as Stonehedge returned carrying a large take-out bag. The actor brought back not only fish tacos, but sides of grilled squid in an olive and garlic sauce, roasted cauliflower, creamed brussels sprouts with pancetta, and a square pasta dish that Stonehedge said was a sunchoke and chestnut agnolotti in a brown butter and sage sauce. Morris skipped the squid but tried the other sides, and had to admit the fish tacos and the rest of the food was very tasty.

"Not a bad perk for having me tag along," Stonehedge said with a thin smile.

"Almost makes it worthwhile," Morris said, his expression inscrutable. He showed the actor the two timelines he'd been working on. "I'm trying to see where they intersect so I can figure out where Hawes ran into Susan Twilitter recently," he said in between bites of fish taco.

"You don't have much on Twilitter's timeline," Stonehedge observed.

"Unfortunately, she wasn't nearly as active on social media as her friend was. But she had a seven-hour gap yesterday where she didn't make any phone calls, and I'm guessing that's when she was with SCK. Hawes was in Santa Monica yesterday having lunch at Stephanie's Café."

"Twilitter lived and worked in Santa Monica."

"Yeah. I'm betting she met up with SCK somewhere near Stephanie's Café, and that's where Gail Hawes had the misfortune of seeing them."

The thought of this excited the actor. He asked, "What do we do now? Head down to this café and show a picture of Twilitter?"

"We'll wait until tomorrow afternoon when there's a better chance the same waitstaff is on duty. For now, we'll see if any surveillance video is found or whether the hotline brings in any plausible leads."

After the day's press conference, the hotline was busy for two hours generating forty-seven calls. Forty-three of them could be eliminated after a few minutes of talking, which left Morris with four calls he needed to follow-up on. These, however, seemed a low probability, at best, of leading anywhere, and Morris had decided to wait until tomorrow morning to handle them. The last hour a small trickle of calls came in, but these were from shut-ins looking for someone to talk to, or flat-out nuts.

A call came in from Walsh. Glen Blakeman was picked up in San Diego. "The detective I talked to told me he was acting squirrelly," Walsh said. "I know it's late, but if he's SCK I want to know it tonight."

It was late. Morris squinted at his watch, and saw it was already past ten. San Diego was more than a two-hour drive, which meant the earliest he'd be home would be three in the morning.

"I'm heading there now also," he told Walsh.

Stonehedge raised an eyebrow at Morris. "Where are we heading?"

"San Diego."

Stonehedge showed an amused smile. "Another perk of having me along," he said. "I'll chauffeur you in my BMW i8. At this time of night, I'll have us there in an hour and a half. Guaranteed."

Stonehedge kept his word. While the roadster never felt like it was going over sixty, Morris at times glanced over at the speedometer and saw that it was registering over two hundred kilometers per hour, which a quick conversion showed the car was speeding along at over a hundred and twenty miles per hour. He didn't complain, and they pulled into the San Diego precinct where Blakeman was being held an hour and twenty-eight minutes after they'd left.

Morris called Walsh and told her that he and Stonehedge had just arrived. Walsh seemed surprised to hear that. "Did that actor fly you down in a private jet or something?"

"Or something," Morris acknowledged.

"I'm still a half hour outside of San Diego. No reason for you to wait. You can fill me in when I get there."

"Okay."

The San Diego detective who had picked Blakeman up sat in with them as they joined Blakeman in the interrogation room where he was being held. Blakeman was a large, blubbery man whose eyes had a nervous twitch that left him blinking far too much as he sat staring at Morris and Stonehedge. He was also sweating badly enough that his shirt was drenched.

"I want a lawyer," he told Morris.

"You haven't been arrested yet," Morris said. "You're being held for twenty-four hours for questioning. If we can clear this up, you'll be released."

"I don't care. I want a lawyer."

"If you insist on that, you'll be booked and arraigned on charges for three first-degree murders, all strong candidates for the death penalty given the heinousness and exceptional depravity of the crimes. Bail will be denied, and the news will be reporting that you've been arrested as SCK."

Blakeman looked at Morris dumbly.

"The Skull Cracker Killer."

It took several seconds for Blakeman to react to that, and when he did it was as if he'd been punched in the face, and his blinking became so rapid that it looked like he was blinking out a Morse code message.

"That's who killed Freeman?" he asked.

"Him and two women today."

"What?" This news surprised him enough to momentarily slow his blinking. "The same guy also killed two women? That's not me. I swear it."

"Why'd you come to San Diego?"

Blakeman grimaced as if he were suffering from an awful toothache, and then his large round face melted into a look of utter hopelessness, and his blinking came to a stop.

"I panicked," he said, shrugging helplessly. "When I saw the news about Freeman being killed in one of my listed properties, I knew the police would be sure I'd done it, especially after I'd been shooting my mouth off to everyone in the office that I was going to bash Freeman's head in. I had no alibi yesterday, and so I came down here."

"When was that?"

"Last night."

"What were you doing yesterday?"

Another weak shrug. "I didn't have any showings scheduled. I spent the day smoking weed and watching videos."

"Porn," Stonehedge suggested.

Blakeman's expression was both embarrassed and sickly.

"Why'd you come to San Diego?" Morris asked.

"Maybe the weed got me paranoid, but when I saw the news about Freeman, all I could think about was escaping to Mexico."

"Why didn't you?"

Yet another half-hearted shrug. "Partly because I couldn't work up the nerve, and partly that I was hoping that the real killer would be arrested for Freeman's murder."

"What time did you get to San Diego yesterday?"

"I checked into my hotel around eleven."

"And you've been in San Diego the whole time?"

"Yep."

"Can you prove that you didn't drive back to LA today?"

Blakeman shook his head glumly.

"Where were you at twelve thirty today?"

That perked Blakeman up. "That was when one of those women was killed?" Tears of relief flooded his eyes as a smile broke over his face. "I had room service bring up lunch around one o'clock. Jesus. That should prove I'm innocent, right?"

At that moment, Walsh walked into the room. From the groan she let out, she must've sensed from everybody's expressions that she'd just spent two hours on the highway for nothing.

"If we can verify it, yeah," Morris said.

It took twenty minutes to verify it. On the drive back to Los Angeles, Stonehedge offered, "You win some, you lose some."

"All part of the job," Morris said. "You keep crossing off leads until you get one that sticks. My gut is telling me we'll be getting one soon that sticks."

Chapter Thirty

Portland, Oregon, 2012–2015

"What a first year we've had together, huh?"

Henry waited for his wife to respond, but as usual, since she got injured, she sat mutely in her wheelchair staring blankly at nothing in particular, her mouth twisted into a pinched, angry circle. Henry sighed. Eventually she'd accept what had happened to her and be grateful for this opportunity to start fresh. And they were starting fresh. A year ago they had met in a dive bar in Bushwick (even though the place had great wings) and now they were one month short of their first year anniversary and sitting together in the back-yard of their custom-built house in Portland, Oregon. Henry had even planted a garden. If things went well they'd be eating their own freshly grown tomatoes, cucumbers, peas, and strawberries later this summer.

It really had been a crazy, wild year, especially the last eight months. With the time that had passed, that bizarro night when Sheila got hurt seemed more like a bad dream than anything that really happened, especially now that they'd moved to the other side of the country. The months that followed that night, though, were difficult ones, as Henry was wracked with worry over his wife's health and whether the police would discover that Sheila had been the Skull Cracker Killer. Oddly, he never worried that he'd been seen entering that man's house or that the police would arrest him for killing that man and cutting off his head. He had somehow deleted that part of it from his own mind and had convinced himself that all he'd done that night was protect his wife from a man who had grievously injured her. The fact the man had hurt Sheila only during a desperate attempt to save his own life never occurred to Henry.

No question that Sheila had been grievously injured that night. The doctors told them the paralysis was permanent. The internal damage, especially to her heart, was worse than what the doctors had first feared. But they had also told them Sheila could still have a reasonably good quality of life. With dedicated physical therapy, she could strengthen her left side, and if she could control her stress and eat well there was no reason she couldn't live into her seventies.

So all of that was a relief for Henry. But there was still the fear that the police would somehow connect Sheila to the dead man in Queens. After all, Sheila had picked him up in that bar. But it turned out she'd been careful not to be seen with him, just as she had been with Henry at the bar in Bushwick. If the police were ever suspicious that there was a connection between the man's death and Sheila's injuries, they never talked to her about it. Instead, they seemed to fully believe that she had been assaulted on a sidewalk blocks from Central Park West where Henry had left her.

The media had a field day with Sheila's supposed assault, plastering her picture on TV and in the newspapers every day for a week, which scared the bejesus out of Henry. He was sure someone from the Queens bar would recognize her and come forward, but it didn't happen. Instead, there was an outpouring of public outrage over the city not having fixed the broken streetlight that Henry had left Sheila under since there had been another assault at the same location a month earlier. When a lawyer approached them about suing the city, Henry wanted no part of it. First, the idea of it seemed ridiculous, second, he just wanted Sheila to get healthy enough so they could pack up and leave New York before the police wised up, and third, he had discovered after that night that Sheila was far wealthier than he could've imagined. They didn't need the money, and they didn't need the risk of staying in New York a day longer than they had to, but Sheila wanted to sue and he was afraid it might look funny to the lawyer if he tried arguing against it. He could barely believe it when the lawyer was able to arrange a three-point-four-million-dollar settlement with the city (after his fees) less than two months later.

* * *

Henry let out a grunt and, with some effort, maneuvered his bulk off the lounge chair, stretched, and worked a kink from his back. He gave Sheila a quick look and noted her angry, sullen expression, and how twisted and thin her body looked. She must've dropped twenty-five pounds since the accident, and probably weighed at most a hundred and twenty. That was too light for her. Now that they were in Portland, things would change. They were only half a mile from downtown. He'd roll her to different healthy restaurants each day. They were going to become part of the community and make friends and enjoy their life here. New York would become nothing more than a faint memory. Only a whisper that they would ignore. Given enough time, they'd both believe those murders never happened— both the man Henry had killed and the ones Sheila did. This was going to be the start of a new day.

Henry squinted and shielded his eyes as he glanced up at the sun.

Yes, sir, the start of a new day.

Henry had been gone no more than an hour, and he blinked several times not quite believing his eyes when he saw that Sheila was smiling at him. Well, half smiling since the right part of her mouth stayed weighted down and only the left side was curled upward. This was only the second time since her injuries that he had seen her smile; the first time being after their lawyer told them what the city was offering for a settlement. Henry was about to comment about how he knew that the kitten he had bought his wife two weeks earlier would cheer her up when he saw the animal's small, fluffy body lying on the floor next to Sheila's wheelchair. Given how the animal's body was positioned and the way his little tongue lolled out of his mouth there was no question that the kitten was dead.

Henry grimly noted to himself how he'd been right about the kitten cheering up his wife, just that he'd been completely wrong about how the poor thing would do so.

"I see your left hand must be getting stronger," he said.

The left side of Sheila's lips twisted upward a tiny sliver more. She was obviously pleased with herself, but otherwise didn't bother to respond.

Henry picked up the dead kitten and brought it outside to their backyard. He left the kitten's body in the dead patch of weeds where he had tried planting tomatoes the first year they were there and retrieved a shovel from the shed. For two years he had tried growing vegetables with miserable results before finally accepting that instead of a green thumb, he was the kiss of death for plants. Worse than cyanide. He dug a hole for the kitten and buried the poor little thing.

Things hadn't worked out in Portland as he had hoped. He enjoyed the downtown area when he was able to go there, and he had little trouble shooting the breeze with strangers and making casual friendships, but his wife had been resistant from day one. After six months of seeing her mood only deteriorate, he tried to get her to see a psychiatrist, but she flatly refused. He tried talking sense into her, explaining that her depression was worsening but that it didn't have to be that way.

"If you send me to see someone, I'll tell him," she finally said in that painfully drawn-out manner that she had, as if it exhausted her to push out each individual word.

Henry felt the short hairs on the back of his neck stand up. "What would you say?" he half-heard himself ask her, knowing full well what she would say.

"About all of them I killed. About being the Skull Cracker Killer."

"He wouldn't believe you. Or she wouldn't believe you since the psychiatrist I made you an appointment with is a woman."

"She'll believe me. I'll tell her things to make her believe me."

"It wouldn't matter," Henry said. "Doctor-client privilege. She wouldn't be able to tell anyone since you're no longer a threat."

"I'll tell her about you. How you cut off Black's head after catching the two of us alone. That you injured me and left me on that sidewalk. She'll believe me, and there will be no doctor-client privilege to stop her from calling the police on you."

Tim Black was the man Sheila had picked up in Queens that night and tried to make one of her Skull Cracker victims, except that she didn't inject enough succinylcholine into him to fully paralyze him right away and he was able to fight back when she started to break apart his skull. Henry tried to decide whether she was bluffing or if she'd really tell a psychiatrist that lie. Or really half-lie. He wasn't sure, but he ended up cancelling the appointment, and he didn't bring up therapy or psychiatrists again, and over the next year and a half Sheila's mood darkened further. It was almost as if her mood had grown as twisted as her body had become.

It was three months after the kitten incident that Henry caught his wife looking at him in a way that caught him off guard. There was no dark anger or bitter resentment pinching her mouth. Instead she looked more the way she did before her injuries. There was almost a serenity to her features. Almost as if she were looking at him with the same kind of fondness he used to catch glimpses of during their early days together.

"Why?" she asked.

This confused Henry as he didn't know what she was asking. "Why what?"

"Why haven't you killed me yet?"

That shocked him. "Why in the world would I do that?" he asked incredulously. "You're my wife!"

"With my money you could get yourself another wife. Someone not crippled. Someone not insane."

"You're not insane," Henry insisted. "You had a rough patch, that's all. Besides, I married you for better or worse. We've had some of the worse, we'll have some of the better again. I'm sure of it."

Henry meant every word that he said. Actually, he understated it. Sheila wasn't just his wife, but the woman he was meant to share his life with. He knew that unconditionally. There was a reason why she'd spared his life in Bushwick, just as there was a reason he'd followed her to that home in Queens so that he could save her. Things might not be perfect right now, but having her in his life left him with a certain and undeniable contentment, and the thought of losing her left him paralyzed with fear.

"You really do love me," she said after a long while.

"Of course I do," he said. "And I know you love me also. I read your diary entries."

Her mouth pinched again into a tight, angry oval. "I told you not to read it," she complained.

"Too bad. I read it anyway. I know how you feel about me."

They stared at each other for several minutes, her mouth pinching into an angrier, smaller circle while Henry maintained a placid expression. He could've told his wife that he still had those pages from her diary, and that whenever he was feeling down he'd read those last entries she wrote about him, and it would give him hope for the future, but he kept that to himself.

Their staring contest ended as Sheila's pinched mouth softened and relaxed as whatever resentment she'd been feeling bled out of her. Once again she was looking at him with something approaching tenderness.

"I felt a connection with you from the start," she admitted. "I didn't realize it then, but that's why we walked out of that alley together. Not because I was trying to fool the FBI like I wrote in my diary."

"I know."

"And I do love you. Even if I don't show it."

"I know."

"I can't stand it, Henry. The pressure has gotten so bad. Like I'm being suffocated. It's so bad I can't even think. When I was killing them, it would make the pressure better, and I'd be able to breathe again. But now it's just awful."

Henry was tongue-tied, not knowing how to respond to that. A tear leaked from his eye and wormed its way down his cheek.

"I want to die, Henry. That's how bad it is."

"Don't say that. Please."

"If you love me like you say you do—like I believe you do, then you'll help me."

More tears leaked out of his eyes. Even Sheila's eyes had become liquid. "I'm not killing you," he said.

"Then kill them for me," she said.

He blinked at her stupidly, not quite understanding what she was saying at first. Then he involuntarily shook his head.

"If you really love me, you'll do that."

"You can't ask me to do something like that," Henry stammered out. "That's not fair. We're in Portland, Oregon, the center of the universe for alternative healing. Let me please try to help you that way."

For a long moment Henry was afraid she'd close up again, but Sheila surprised him by nodding.

"No psychiatrists," she insisted. "No therapists."

Over the next four months they tried crystal therapy, cranial massage, Reiki, and flower essences. Henry brought his wife to see acupuncturists, naturopathic doctors, and shamans. Nothing seemed to change her mood, and at the end of those four months Sheila refused to see anyone else, and then she stopped eating. Henry brought a nurse home to teach him how to force-feed her, but his wife was rapidly losing weight. Over the next two months, she became so skeleton-thin that Henry could see her skull shining through her scalp. He broke down sobbing in front of her, convinced that he was going to lose her.

"Please," he begged her. "Don't do this."

Her voice was weak and barely a whisper as she forced out, "Kill them for me."

Henry rubbed a thick hand under his nose trying to wipe away some of the wetness. He felt so icy cold then. Like death.

"You'll eat if I do this?" he asked.

"Yes."

"One person?"

"Three. I choose them."

"Then it's over? You won't ask me to do it again?"

"I promise."

There was no decision for Henry to make. He would lose his wife if he didn't agree to this, and he couldn't lose her.

"Not here in Portland," he said. "It's too small here. They'll suspect us if I kill them here."

He knew that was true. While he had made acquaintances and casual friendships, his wife hadn't, and he'd heard kids in the neighborhood calling her a witch. But there was more to it than that. He liked the area, and he liked the house, and he wanted to move back there when this was all done.

"Los Angeles," Sheila said.

Henry thought about it, and it made sense for that to be their killing ground. He made a phone call, and after arranging for a nurse to take care of Sheila during his absence, he bought a plane ticket for Los Angeles so he could find a house for them down there.

Chapter Thirty-one

Tallahassee, 1988

"Penny, dear, come on out. Your dinner's getting cold!"

Sheila felt a painful twinge in her stomach hearing her mother shout for her older sister. It was nicer at the dinner table without Penelope there, almost like they were a normal family, and she wished it could continue. She chewed another mouthful of macaroni and cheese, but just the thought of her sister made the food tasteless. She didn't know what trouble Penelope would cause, all she knew was that the peacefulness of the meal was going to end.

A clumping of heavy footsteps in the hallway made Sheila cringe, and she tensed as the footsteps continued on into the kitchen. She tried to stay focused on her food, but she couldn't stop herself from looking up when Penelope entered the room, and she cringed even more seeing her sister's face red with fury. This was going to be trouble!

"Look what the brat did to my George Michael record!" Penelope said, seething. She was holding one of her albums carefully by the edge. From the way she was showing them the album, Sheila could see the fingerprints all over it. "The little brat snuck into my room and got her greasy prints all over my record!"

"I did not!"

"Then how'd my record get all mucked up with your greasy little paw prints?"

"You did it!"

Penelope smirked angrily at that. "Peanut brain over there thinks we're all as dumb as she is."

"Peanut brain," their mother, Mrs. Proops, said, chuckling. "You're so clever with words, Penny."

"That is a good one," their father, Mr. Proops, agreed. "Such imagery. If we cracked open her skull what do you suppose we'd find? Only a peanut?"

"No," Penelope corrected him. "A brain the size of a peanut." She glared at Sheila. "A baby peanut at best. Something no bigger than a raisin."

"Then why not raisin brain?" Mrs. Proops offered.

"Because when you crack open a shell you need to find a nut of some kind," Mr. Proops said.

"A peanut isn't even a nut," Sheila said. "It's a legume. And those aren't my fingerprints! They're Penelope's! She's just trying to get me in trouble!"

"Look who's trying to act smart," Mr. Proops said. "Such a fancy word from a peanut brain. Like you know what a legume is."

"She doth protest too much," Mrs. Proops added.

"Peanut brain is too dumb to understand a Shakespeare reference," Penelope said, beaming over getting the reference herself. She brought the album close to her nose and sniffed it. "It smells like fried chicken grease. I'd bet anything peanut brain went to KFC today, greased up her paws on fried chicken, and then touched my album, being too stupid to realize she'd be leaving prints behind."

"It sounds like something she would do," Mr. Proops agreed.

"Peanut brain," Mrs. Proops said, chuckling more. "That really is a good one, Penny. You really are such a clever girl."

"So what about it?" Penelope asked Sheila, smirking again at her sister. "Are you going to keep denying it? Because I bet you were dumb enough to toss your KFC wrappers and chicken bones in the garbage, and if we look through the garbage cans we'll find it."

Sheila stared at amazement at her sister as she realized the lengths Penelope had gone to to frame her for this because she had no doubt that if they searched the garbage they'd find the greasy fried chicken remains right where Penelope had planted them. Penelope was five years older than her and had teased and tormented her for as long as Sheila could remember, and worse, all to their parents' delight as if they couldn't get enough of Penelope's *cleverness* and Sheila's humiliation.

"Nothing to say, huh?" Penelope said. "What's wrong, your

peanut-sized brain isn't smart enough to come up with any more excuses?"

"What about *walnut* brain?" Mr. Proops offered. "That would be more like the type of nut I would crack open. And the insides look sort of like a brain."

"A walnut would be too big for the little brat's head," Penelope said.

"Should we crack open her skull and see?" Mr. Proops joked.

"If we did we could replace her brain with a dog turd," Penelope said. "I bet she'd be smarter if we did that."

Mr. Proops laughed heartily at that. "Good one, Penny."

Mrs. Proops said, "Sheila, you're not going to make us look through the garbage cans, are you? Because if you make us do that and we find that you've been lying to us we'll have to punish you more severely than if you confess and apologize to your sister."

"Much more severely," Mr. Proops said.

Sheila felt sick to her stomach as she looked at the way her sister smirked at her. This could all be a bluff. There might not be anything in the garbage cans. What she wanted to do was make a run for it, but she knew she wouldn't get very far. At twelve, she was a skinny kid, while Penelope was a robust and athletic seventeen-year-old. If her parents weren't able to grab her, her sister would easily be able to outrun her and sit on her until her parents caught up to them.

"She's too much of a peanut brain to apologize," Penelope said. Sighing with an exaggerated sense of being put upon, she added, "I bet she's going to make us look through the garbage cans."

"You're really going to make us do that?" Mr. Proops asked Sheila, his expression showing his severe disappointment.

"I'm afraid she is," Mrs. Proops said.

They all went outside, and Penelope took on the task of dumping out each garbage can in turn and then using her foot to sift through the mess as she searched for the incriminating evidence. Of course, she made sure that the KFC bag and the bones from the fried chicken were in the last can that she dumped out.

"You could be a detective the way you figured this out," a beaming Mr. Proops told Penelope.

"Such a clever daughter," Mrs. Proops agreed. Then to Sheila, "Not very smart of you to make us go through all this trouble."

Penelope piped in, "What do you expect from someone with a peanut brain."

"True," Mr. Proops agreed.

"Part of your punishment will be to put the garbage back in the cans," Mrs. Proops said.

"Only part of it," Mr. Proops said.

"Get this mess cleaned up and then march your little behind right back into the house," Mrs. Proops said.

"You'll get your real punishment then," Mr. Proops promised.

Sheila didn't want to cry in front of them, but she couldn't help herself. This happened partly out of her frustration, but mostly because she knew how bad her real punishment was going to be once she returned back to the house.

"If you run away again, it will be so much worse," Mrs. Proops said.

"The same if you bother any neighbors or strangers complaining and spreading lies like you tried before. If you do that, I promise you it will be much, much worse," Mr. Proops threatened, his lips pressing down into a harsh scowl.

"Maybe this will teach you not to be a sneak and a liar," Mrs. Proops said.

"And to leave your sister's things alone," Mr. Proops added.

"It won't teach her anything," Penelope said. "When you've got the brain the size of a peanut, it's impossible to learn anything."

They headed back into the house then, leaving Sheila alone to scoop up the rotten food, dirty tissues and other trash with her hands so she could put it all back into the garbage cans. Before they disappeared back into the house, she heard her mother again chuckle over "peanut brain" and compliment Penelope on her clever expression. Once they were gone, the floodgates opened and Sheila started sobbing uncontrollably because she knew the awful things they were going to do to her once she finished scooping up the garbage and they had her alone inside the house. What they called her punishment. She thought again about killing herself. This was something she thought about a lot these days. She emptied out a plastic bag and tried to work up the courage to use it. A resoluteness took over and she put the bag over her head, twisted it around her neck and held it tight, but the inside of the bag smelled heavily of fish, and soon her lungs were hurting and she started coughing, and like a coward she pulled the bag off her head.

After the coughing fit passed, she finished picking up the garbage and headed inside for her punishment.

Chapter Thirty-two

Tallahassee, 1990

Sheila was asleep when they grabbed her, and during the first few seconds was too groggy to fully realize what was happening or to put up much of a fight while they wrestled her onto her stomach. She was fully awake, though, when they pulled her pajamas off of her. The fear pounding through her made her hyper alert to their heavy breathing and their stench of beer, sweat, and body odor. When she opened her mouth to scream, one of them shoved a rag into her mouth and then taped her mouth shut, gagging her. She tried squirming and fighting them as she lay helpless on her stomach, but they easily overpowered her and taped her naked ankles together, then pulled her arms back and did the same to her wrists. After that they flipped her onto her back, and Sheila could see that her attackers were Penelope and two of her delinquent friends, Tommy Morales and Jimmy Connelly.

"I see your sister's a natural blonde," Jimmy Connelly whispered. "How about leaving me alone with her for five minutes?"

"She's filthy. You don't want to stick your dick in her."

"Maybe I do," Jimmy Connelly insisted.

"Maybe I do too," Tommy Morales said.

Sheila always knew her sister hated her. She never knew why, although after years of trying to figure out the reason she accepted that it was simply Penelope's resentment of Sheila being born, and her no longer being the only child in the family. Her mother used to laugh about how as a baby Penelope loved her little sister so much that she would try to squeeze the stuffing out of her and would have to pull Sheila away otherwise Penelope would've succeeded. What Sheila now saw in her sister's drunken face went beyond hate. They were going to do things to her that were even worse than her *punishments*, and then they were going to kill her. Sheila could see that as clear as day in her sister's eyes.

"Not here," Penelope said.

They picked her up and hustled her out of the house and into the trunk of Jimmy Connelly's waiting Camaro. The trunk was closed on her, leaving her in the dark in that dirty, smelly, greasy space. As the car drove off, Sheila accepted that they were going to drive her to the woods and spend hours doing terrible things to her before killing her, and she found herself oddly at peace with that. At least it would be over. All the fear and anguish would be ending soon. Also all of her hatred toward Penelope for not ever loving her and treating her the way a big sister was supposed to treat her little sister. And so too the choking hatred that she felt toward her parents for their willingness to always take Penelope's side and look for any excuse to inflict their *punishments* on her.

Sheila lost track of time as her thoughts wandered to odd little questions, like whether her parents would be sad at all when they found out that she had been murdered, and whom Penelope would focus her meanness on after she was gone, and what it would be like to be dead and not have to worry about being tormented any longer. They could've been traveling for ten minutes or for hours; Sheila had no idea which it was when the car came to a stop. All she knew for sure was it was still dark out when they opened the trunk and took her out of it. She didn't squirm or fight them any longer. She just wanted them to be done as quickly as possible so it would be over. That was all she wanted. For it to be over.

They dumped her on concrete, which surprised her. She was sure they were going to take her to the woods. In the moonlight she could see the way Jimmy Connelly leered at her.

"I still want time alone with her," Jimmy Connelly said.

"And I told you no. She's too filthy for that."

Sheila was surprised to hear fear in her sister's voice. What happened next surprised her even more as she watched her sister pull Connelly away and Tommy Morales reluctantly follow them. Shortly after that she heard their car start up, and then the sounds of it driving away. They were actually leaving her alive! Whatever homicidal impulses that drove Penelope when she and her friends snatched

Sheila from her bed must've faded after they had put her in the car trunk, causing her to change their plans.

It was too dark out for Sheila to see where they had left her. All she knew was that the concrete was rough on her skin and a light rain had started, which made her shiver. Soon she was shivering uncontrollably; partly from the chilliness in the air and the rain, partly over what she'd been through, but mostly because she realized that she'd be able to send Penelope to prison over this. Maybe she'd be able to send her parents to prison also. Their *punishments* were always done in private without any witnesses, and it would've always been her word against theirs and Penelope's. Three against one. Nobody would've ever believed her, especially with the lies all three of them would've told about her. But this was different. Strangers were going to find her. The police were going to be called. Penelope wasn't going to be able to lie her way out of this, and the authorities might now believe her about her parents and their *punishments*.

As Sheila thought about this, she started shivering so badly that she had moments where she thought her heart might give out and she might die. But she didn't die. Eventually a calmness took over, and she realized she didn't want Penelope behind bars. Or her parents either.

It was hours before it started getting lighter out. From her vantage point, she couldn't see that they had left her right outside of the middle school that she attended. She even drifted off at some point, and was woken up when Principal Brownell covered her with his suit jacket.

"My God," he said, his face ashen. "Sheila Proops, is that you? What in the world happened?"

As gently as he could, he peeled the tape from her mouth and removed the rag that had been gagging her, but Sheila refused to tell him. She also refused to tell the police and instead kept asking that they bring her home. Mr. Proops had already left for work, so Mrs. Proops was asked to come to the school with a change of clothing for Sheila (by this time they had given Sheila gym clothes to put on and had wrapped her in several blankets). Mrs. Proops was at a loss to explain how Sheila had ended up gagged, bound, and naked outside of the middle school, and seemed legitimately flabbergasted over the news. But she didn't insist that Sheila tell them what had happened. Instead she asked if the police officers and school officials would leave her alone with her daughter. After they left, she demanded Sheila, "What kind of nonsense are you up to now?"

"Penelope did this to me," Sheila said.

Mrs. Proops blinked several times. Her color paled as white as milk. In a harsh whisper, she said, "You're lying!"

"I'm not lying. Penelope and her lowlife friends Jimmy Connelly and Tommy Morales grabbed me out of my bed, stripped me naked, tied me up, and threw me into the trunk of Jimmy Connelly's car. They were going to kill me, but Penelope must've changed her mind."

Mrs. Proops had recovered somewhat. In the same harsh whisper as earlier she said, "You have grown to become quite a liar. If you tell anyone this outrageous story the consequences for you will be quite severe. Do you understand me, young lady?"

Sheila shook her head. "If I tell them what Penelope did, they'll believe me, and they'll send her to prison. They might even believe me now about the *punishments* you three give me. You and dad might be joining Penelope in prison."

Mrs. Proops again blinked several times as what Sheila had told her sank in. "What do you want?" she forced out in a strangled voice.

"I want you to take me home."

Mrs. Proops conferred with the police and the school officials, and they agreed that it would be best if she took Sheila home with the understanding that she would try to get her daughter to confide in her about what had happened. During the ride home, Mrs. Proops gripped the wheel so tightly that veins bulged from her hands and her knuckles turned bone white.

"How dare you threaten us the way you did!" she yelled at Sheila, a hysterical edge in her voice. "You stupid, peanut-brained ingrate! Whatever discipline we've had to give you was for your own good! And if Penny did that to you, it was a harmless prank! You're going to threaten to ruin your sister's life over a harmless prank?"

Sheila spoke calmly and carefully the words she had rehearsed in her head as she had lay bound and gagged outside of her school, because she had fully expected her mom to say what she did.

"If you ever call me peanut brain again, I will tell the police what Penelope did. If you say anything that I don't like, I will tell the police. You better tell Dad that. And Penelope also. Because the same goes for them. And none of you are getting any second chances."

Mrs. Proops didn't say another word to Sheila. When they arrived home, Sheila found a quart of ice cream in the freezer that was Penelope's favorite and was being saved for her, and she brought it to the den and ate it while watching TV. When Penelope came home from her job as a cashier at a fast-food restaurant, Mrs. Proops was waiting for her, and she dragged Penelope to the back of the house so that she could have a word with her. Penelope avoided Sheila the rest of that day.

Mr. Proops came home at his usual time, but from the way he looked at Sheila when he stuck his face into the den, it was obvious that he had already had conversations with Mrs. Proops over what had happened.

"Sheila, honey, could you join us in the kitchen?" he said with a sickly smile. "We would like to have a family meeting."

Mrs. Proops and Penelope were already sitting at the kitchen table. Mr. Proops and Sheila joined them.

Mr. Proops said to Penelope, "Do you have something that you'd like to say to your sister?"

Penelope looking somewhat ghastly said, "I'm sorry if what we did last night upset you. It was only a joke."

"There you have it, honey," Mr. Proops said. "All done in innocent fun. How about you forgive your sister and let's drop this nonsense. After all, no harm no foul."

"You've got to be kidding."

"Now, Sheila, let's be reasonable here." To show that he was also willing to be reasonable, Mr. Proops spread out his hands with his palms up. "You can't expect us all to live with something like this hanging over our heads, can you?"

"Father, you can be a funny man when you want to be," Sheila said, icily. "I meant what I told mother before. None of you are getting any second chances, and if you say another word about me forgiving Penelope or you or mother, for that matter, that's it, I'll be speaking to the police."

Mr. Proops exchanged a quick look with Mrs. Proops, and it chilled Sheila because she knew what was behind it. *Should we just kill the brat, and be done with her?* But just as quickly those looks faded, leaving both their faces aged and defeated. The police were going to be following up on today's incident, and because of that they knew they couldn't get away with killing her, even if they had the nerve to try it.

"What do you want?" Mr. Proops asked.

"For all of you to leave me alone," Sheila said.

She got up from the table then and went back to the den and continued watching TV. As with earlier that day, the thoughts buzzing through her head kept her from paying attention to the program she was blindly watching.

Chapter Thirty-three

At 7 A.M., Bogle, Lemmon, and Polk met NYPD detectives Frank Thompson and Pete Childs, and FBI special investigator Julie Crasmore at the FBI's lower Manhattan office. All three of the MBI agents looked badly in need of coffee, which made sense since it was only 4 A.M. Los Angeles time. Polk in particular had a ragged appearance—skin an unhealthy gray, eyes bloodshot, and thick bags giving him a basset hound look. Still, after introductions were made, hands shaken, coffees poured, seats taken around the conference table, and blueberry muffins grabbed, that didn't stop Polk from ogling Crasmore.

"Jesus, I must be seeing things," he said between bites of his muffin, crumbs tumbling out of his mouth. "When did the FBI start hiring knockouts?"

Crasmore, other than wrinkling her nose, ignored him and spoke directly to Bogle. "I talked with Sam Goodman last night. He's not convinced what you have in Los Angeles is SCK. He thinks it might be a copycat."

Bogle shrugged. "It might be a copycat, but from what I've been told you guys kept a tight lid on the specifics of how SCK operated."

"That's right," Thompson said, gruffly.

"So if it's a copycat, someone told him SCK's secret, and that someone might be SCK himself."

"What do you propose?" Crasmore asked.

"We attack this from two angles. Angle one, make a list of everyone in New York who knew SCK's methods, and since Polk is such a charmer—"

"That I am," Polk agreed, more blueberry muffin crumbs tumbling out of his mouth.

"He'll interview everyone on the list, and see if any of them spread any tales they shouldn't have," Bogle continued. "If they did, Polk will figure it out. He's got a certain way about him for worming out information."

"You better believe it," Polk said.

"No kidding. After a while, the guilty party would rather confess than spend another minute with him," Lemmon offered.

"We all got our ways," Polk said.

"Angle two," Bogle continued, "is we try to figure out what happened to SCK. That means going back to his last killing and looking at all arrests and accidents from that day to three months after when you expected SCK to kill again. Not just arrests leading to five years in custody, but longer stays since SCK might've revealed his trade secrets to a cellmate who decided to carry on the tradition."

"Why accidents?" Childs asked with a smirk. "You think SCK's been in a coma for five years?"

"Who knows? Anything's a possibility with this mess. If he was hurt badly enough, maybe he was in rehab all this time. Or he could've ended up in a nursing home, and confided in an orderly who was as much of a psycho as SCK. All I know is we got to do this systematically. SCK didn't just disappear. Something happened to him five years ago."

Crasmore thought this over. "SCK ending up in prison is probably our best bet, but you're right, we also need to look at accidents, illnesses, and assaults that led to extended hospital stays. This is going to be a tall order, but it makes sense." She gave Detective Thompson an apologetic smile. "Frank, you mind working with Polk on getting that list together and helping out with the interviews?"

Thompson gave Polk a sideways glance. "As long as he doesn't get any crumbs in my car," he grumbled.

"I can't make any promises," Polk said.

Crasmore pushed herself away from the table and stood up. "Let's see if we can finally crack this damn SCK case."

Chapter Thirty-four

Los Angeles, the present

Morris woke up with Parker sitting on his chest licking his face.

"Gah," Morris spat out as he held the dog back with both hands. "Sardine breath!"

This made Parker more enthusiastically try to bull his way forward, his rear end wiggling like crazy. Morris squinted at the clock next to the bed and saw that it was just after seven. He spotted Natalie by the open door.

"You're enjoying this," he said.

"Somewhat. But it was an accident. Parker was waiting quietly outside the door, and he squeezed his way through before I realized he was there."

Morris successfully wrestled Parker away and maneuvered himself off the bed. He rubbed the bull terrier's muzzle. "Are you ready for a day of crime fighting?" he asked.

Parker responded with one of his excited piglike grunts.

After he showered, shaved, and dressed in the same wrinkled suit he wore the day before, although with a fresh shirt and a different tie, Morris kissed Natalie good-bye and took Parker with him. On the way to the MBI offices, he stopped off for a coffee and bagel and cream cheese, and picked up a bagel, bacon, and egg sandwich for Parker, which the dog greedily devoured.

Stonehedge was waiting at MBI. The actor had on the same disguise as he did the previous day, and he gave Parker a careful look. "Is this bring your dog to work day?" he asked.

"Whatever you want to call it. I often bring Parker to the office with me," Morris said. "At least the days that my wife doesn't take him with her. Best dog in the world, no question about it, but not the kind you can leave at home all day by himself. He's also a su-perlative judge of character, and offers certain other advantages in my kind of work. With some witnesses, Parker proves to be very disarming, and they relax with him around. Others get more ner-vous when they try lying in front of him. I can't explain why the latter happens, but it does."

The dog watched attentively as Morris handed Stonehedge a strip of bacon that he had removed earlier from the sandwich.

"Give him that, and he'll be your friend for life."

Stonehedge did as Morris suggested, and somehow avoided having one of his fingers snatched off in the process. As promised, the dog gave the actor one of his piglike grunts and wagged his tail.

"How'd you come up with the name Parker?" Stonehedge asked. "Are you a wine enthusiast?"

Morris gave him a confused look.

"Robert Parker, the wine critic? Or did you name him after the other Robert Parker, the author of the Spenser detective books?"

"I named him after the other Parker books," Morris said. "The ones written by Richard Stark." He showed a guilty smile. "That's right, he's named after a stone-cold criminal, but one with a strong code of conduct."

The actor looked deep in thought, as if he were trying to dredge out a stubborn fact from his memory. "A movie was made with Lee Marvin from one of those books, right? *Point Blank*?"

"That's right."

Morris's cellphone rang. Doug Gilman.

"I heard from Hadley that the Santa Monica police weren't able to pull any useful surveillance video," Gilman complained sourly.

"I wouldn't know. I only just got to the office."

"Yeah, well, that's the story. And what do you mean you're just getting to the office? It's eight o'clock already."

"True. But I needed to go to San Diego late last night to cross off a potential suspect, and didn't get home until three."

"We want this psycho caught before he completes his cycle. You know, killing a blonde twenty-something girl. There's a lot of fear out there, Morris."

"I understand that. And I want to catch this psycho as much as anyone, but the odds are he's already finished his cycle and we just haven't found the body yet."

"Let's hope that's not true. Whatever extra resources you need, you give me a call, okay? The mayor is hot on this."

"I understand."

"Did the hotline generate anything of interest?" Gilman asked, his voice sounding more weary than his earlier petulant tone.

"It brought a lot of shut-ins and crackpots out of the woodwork, but it also gave us a few leads to follow up on. I'm sure more calls came in overnight, and more will be coming. Doug, we'll catch him. Either because of a mistake he made here, or from the New York end."

"Sooner will be better than later."

"No kidding."

That seemed as good as any place to end the call. Morris checked in with his office manager, Greta, who, after welcoming Parker with a hug, gave Morris a stack of messages, which included the same news that Gilman had given him regarding the police coming up empty on finding any useful surveillance video. As he had expected, more calls had come in to the hotline overnight, and Morris spent an hour calling these people back. One of them was a psychic who claimed she had a suspicious client the other day.

"He gave me a fake name. He told me his name is Howard, but his real name is Henry."

"What's his last name?" Morris asked.

"He never gave it."

"Are you a blonde?"

"Yes. A natural."

"Your age?"

"Forty-one, but I'm told I look younger."

Morris started to draw a line through her name, but stopped halfway and asked whether the man had threatened her.

"No, not exactly."

"What do you mean not exactly?"

"He didn't do anything that a typical bystander would think was threatening, but I found his psychic energy extremely threatening. There was a lot of disturbing violence in it."

Morris heard Parker let out a soft moan, and looked down to see the dog stretching as he lay on his side by Morris's feet. "Did he say anything that could be construed in any way as a threat?" he asked.

"No, nothing he said. Only his energy."

Morris finished drawing the line through her name. None of the other callbacks went any better.

At eleven o'clock he met Adam Belkins at the parking garage in Santa Monica where Susan Twilitter was murdered. Of the four hotline calls from the other night that had shown a modicum of promise, Morris had crossed out three of them that morning after more detailed questioning, but Belkins might actually have seen SCK while he was lying in wait for Susan Twilitter.

Belkins, a thin man in his late twenties who was dressed sharply in a light gray suit, stood by the pedestrian entrance of the parking garage waiting for Morris, tapping his foot impatiently.

"I was in a rush yesterday when I saw someone kneeling by a car," he said after he exchanged greetings with Morris, gave Stonehedge a nod as if he recognized him but couldn't quite place where he knew him from, and noted that Parker looked like one cool dog. "I thought he was checking one of his tires and didn't think anything more of it until I saw you on the news last night. I wish I had gotten a better look at him."

Morris had him take them to the location where he had spotted this mystery man, and it was where Susan Twilitter's car had been parked. Stonehedge volunteered to kneel by the car that was currently parked in that spot, and Belkins positioned the actor so that he was in the same spot and bent down as much as the man Belkins had seen. Once that was done, Belkins moved to where he was standing when he had spotted this mystery man, which was sixty feet away.

"I had just come up that staircase," Belkins said, nodding to a staircase to his left. "My car was parked in that empty spot next to where those two vans are now. For some reason I looked over my shoulder, and that was when I saw him. It was just a quick glance, and it barely registered. Again, I thought it was just someone checking a tire."

From where Belkins was standing, he wouldn't have been able to see much of SCK while he hid behind Susan Twilitter's car, especially if it had been just a quick look. All Morris could see of Stonehedge was the top of his head and the outline of his shoulders. Still, he asked Belkins to describe the man he had seen.

Belkins shook his head. "I don't think I can."

"Any impressions?"

Belkins considered this for a moment. "He was big. Wide. And a round head. Like a pumpkin."

"Color hair?"

Belkins shook his head. He squeezed his eyes tight as he tried to remember more about the fleeting glance he had seen. "Hard to say. Maybe light brown? I think he had a bald spot."

"His race?"

"White. I'm pretty sure of that."

"What was he wearing?"

"That would be a wild guess at best. His shirt might've been dark blue. Or maybe gray. Possibly a polo shirt. Or a golf shirt. Again, I'm just guessing here." Belkins made a disgusted face. "It never occurred to me that he was hiding there. I really thought he was just checking his car."

That seemed to be all that Morris was going to get out of Belkins, and he thanked him for coming forward.

"I just wish I could've told you more."

"It's a lot more than we had."

"Yeah, maybe, but it's awful thinking what he did to that woman here. And to those other people also. I wish I'd been more on the ball and realized what was going on. Maybe if I had been, I could've stopped him from killing that woman."

Morris didn't say what was obvious to him. That if Belkins had tried approaching SCK he'd probably be dead now also.

After leaving Belkins, Morris, Parker, and Stonehedge walked the four blocks to Stephanie's Café. As Morris expected, Parker was a big hit among the waitresses working there. When he showed them photos of Gail Hawes and Susan Twilitter, two of the waitresses remembered seeing Hawes two days earlier, but none of them could recall seeing Twilitter.

"We should split up," Stonehedge suggested to Morris. "If you give me one of Susan Twilitter's photos, I'll take the blocks south of here and show it around to the bars and restaurants and see if she ate at any of them with SCK two days ago."

Morris agreed that made sense, and he gave the actor one of the photos he had brought of Twilitter. Twenty minutes later he got a call from Stonehedge.

"I found the place where they ate," Stonehedge said. He gave Morris the address, telling him it was on the same block as the parking garage.

"Don't question anyone any further," Morris said.

"Don't worry. I'll be waiting outside the place for you, and I'll keep my mouth shut."

Parker gave a little yelp as he sensed Morris's excitement, and happily sped up his gait to keep pace with Morris's half jog. Stonehedge was waiting where he said he would, a hard grin etched on his face as he leaned against the outside of the restaurant.

"A waitress recognized Twilitter's picture right away. She started to volunteer more information, but I asked her to wait until you got here."

"What kind of information?"

"That she was here with someone."

Morris nodded. "You did good," he said. "I might make an investigator out of you yet."

"I almost wouldn't mind that. It's more honest work than I've been doing," Stonehedge said, his grin tightening. He led the way into the restaurant, which was really more of a dark, dingy bar with some tables up front and booths in the back for more privacy. It was a place for people having an affair who didn't want to be seen, and even though it was at the height of the lunch hour the restaurant was mostly empty.

Only one waitress was working then; a young, slight girl, very pretty even with all the piercings and her hair dyed an unnatural bright red. She'd been biting her bottom lip in a nervous way when she first saw Morris and Stonehedge approaching, but when she caught sight of Parker her mouth relaxed into an easy smile, and she scratched Parker behind the ear.

"I love these types of dogs," she said to Morris. Her expression became more worried again. "That picture I was shown, was that the same woman who was killed in the parking garage yesterday?"

"Yeah."

"Wow. I saw something about it on TV, but I wasn't paying close enough attention. I didn't recognize her until your partner showed me that picture."

She gave Stonehedge a more thoughtful look. "You remind me

of someone, and I couldn't think of who it was until just now. That actor. Philip Stonehedge."

"A good-looking guy," Stonehedge volunteered.

"Dreamy," the waitress agreed.

"A damn good actor also."

The waitress made a face at that. "Nah, he's a ham, but I still wouldn't kick him out of my bed."

"Hmm," Stonehedge murmured.

"You told my associate that Ms. Twilitter was eating here with someone?" Morris said, steering the conversation back to the reason they were there.

The waitress gave Morris a blank look.

"The woman in the photo," he said.

"Yeah. I remembered her right away when I saw her picture. She came in by herself and took one of the booths in the back. She looked worried, like she was afraid she was going to be stood up, but she ordered for both herself and the person she was waiting for. A salad for herself and a cheeseburger for her friend."

"And the guy showed up?"

"I'm pretty sure he did, although I never saw him. If it was a *he*. She was alone when I took the order and brought the food. Same when I brought over the check. She also left by herself. But both the cheeseburger and salad were eaten, and both drinks were empty, and on her way out I asked if her date ever showed. She didn't say anything, but the way she smiled at me, I think he or she must've shown up."

"You didn't go by the table to see if they wanted anything?"

"She told me not to. That they wanted their privacy. So I only came over to give her the check when she waved for it."

"Strange," Stonehedge said.

"Yeah, I know," the waitress agreed. "That's what I thought. But it happens sometimes."

"Where do you think he went when you brought over the check?" Morris asked.

The waitress shrugged. "If it was a he, the men's room. If it was a she, ladies' room."

"How was the bill paid?"

"Cash. She handed me thirty dollars when I came over with the check, and told me to keep the change, which ended up being a nice tip. Almost ten dollars."

"Did you see a large man walk in after you brought the food over? Wide body? Round head like a pumpkin?"

She thought about that and shook her head. "If he did come in, I missed him. He could've come in through the back door. If he did, I wouldn't have seen him."

"Any other waitresses working then?"

"No, just me. I was handling both front and back, and that woman was the only one sitting in the back. Rudy was working the bar. He might've seen this guy. He's got the day off, but I can get you his cell number."

A woman at one of the front tables had stood up and was giving the waitress an annoyed, impatient look. The waitress smiled apologetically at Morris and told him that she needed to get back to work.

"There's really nothing else I can tell you. I'll get you Rudy's number right after I take care of Queen Bee over there."

She gave Parker one more scratch behind his ear and walked away.

Chapter Thirty-five

The driver made a face as she looked from Henry to her iPhone, and then back at Henry again. "This photo doesn't look like you," she said.

She was right. The photo didn't look much like him because it wasn't him. The picture Henry used when he registered last night for the ride-sharing service Pooled was of a man at least ten years younger than him, sixty pounds lighter, and with much thicker and longer hair. Of course, Henry used a fake name also. Still, if someone squinted hard enough at the photo, he might be able to imagine this man becoming Henry if he were to go completely to pot.

"A confession. That picture was taken before I got sick," Henry said in a pleasant enough tone. "A thyroid disorder. I've gained some weight since then."

"You really should update your photo. It's a safety issue."

Henry's pleasant smile dampened with a touch of melancholy, showing that he'd been properly chastised. "You're a hundred percent right," he admitted. "My vanity on display."

The driver stared at Henry for several more seconds before making up her mind. "Where are you heading?" she asked.

"East Hollywood."

Henry brought his gym bag into the car with him. He started to give her the address, but she stopped him and demanded that he enter it into the app, which he did. Once the car pulled away from the curb, he commented that he didn't blame her for being overly cautious. "The stories in the news about that maniac on the loose are frightening," he said.

"They are," she agreed, a noticeable shiver running through her.

"But I don't think you've got anything to worry about. They say he's going to be killing a blonde girl next. Unless you're dying your hair?"

"Nope. I'm a natural brunette." She laughed nervously. "Finally an advantage to not being a blonde in Los Angeles."

"I can't speak about that," Henry said. "My wife's a blonde, but we're not from here."

"I figured as much. New York, right?"

"Myself, Long Island originally. My wife's from Florida. But we've been living in Portland, Oregon, for a number of years. If I knew you were going to be having this trouble down here, we'd have stayed there, especially since according to the news last night this maniac also likes to kill men my age who are somewhat over-weight, which I am. Okay, maybe I'm more than somewhat over-weight, but who knows whether this killer has a cut-off limit for what his male victims have to weigh? Or that the killer is even a he? Maybe the killer's a she." He smiled playfully and added, "Maybe I should be the one worried sitting back here."

She laughed at that. "Oh sure, you've got a lot to worry about with me. And I guarantee you the killer's a guy. No woman would be doing what he's doing."

"You might be right," Henry said, smiling to himself at seeing how much more at ease she had become. She only saw him as a doddering, fat, middle-aged man, and certainly no threat to her. Yes, he was quite pleased with how this was going, especially given how the news last night made it so much harder for him to get his next victim.

Of course, finding a twenty-something year old full-figured blonde to kill wasn't the problem. Los Angeles had a ridiculous number of those types of girls for Henry to grab, and picking one off a street corner would be as easy as picking an orange from an or-ange grove, at least if he didn't have to worry about getting caught. With all the surveillance cameras out there, hidden and otherwise, and now every twenty-something blonde girl looking at guys like him as potential deranged killers, getting caught was a very real worry. Henry knew he had to be more cautious than earlier, and equally important, he had to be smarter about how he went about it. If it wasn't for Sheila (well, if it wasn't for Sheila, he wouldn't be doing this in the first place, would he?), he wouldn't much care if he went to prison or simply just died. But Sheila needed him, and because of that when he grabbed a girl he had to be a hundred percent sure it was safe doing so.

The idea he was now working on had come to him yesterday when he was stopped at a red light in Santa Monica. He had watched a car pull up to a twenty-something girl loaded with packages, and even though it wasn't a taxi, and the driver and the girl didn't seem to know each other, she had gotten into the car anyway. Henry had rolled down his window and heard enough of their conversation to realize that it was some sort of ride-sharing service; something that she had ordered with her iPhone. He had heard about these companies but never paid much attention to them. In Portland he walked everywhere, and in Los Angeles he drove everywhere. Besides, he was an old-fashioned guy, and if he needed to pay for a ride, he'd rather use a taxi. But when he saw that girl get into the car, it gave him an idea of how he could grab his next victim. Last night, he read up on one of these services called Pooled to understand how it worked, downloaded the app to his iPhone, and registered with a fake name and bogus photo. Earlier today he bought a blonde wig to make it even easier to find his next victim. After all, how would Sheila know that he'd put a blonde wig on the girl before cracking open her skull?

As Henry sat back, he was amazed at how easy this was working out. When he had pressed a button on the app signaling that he wanted a ride, he had no intention of making his driver his next victim since he expected it to be a guy. His only purpose for trying out the service was to observe in person how it worked since he expected to find his victim by pretending to be a driver. But when the app sent him a picture of his driver and he saw it was a girl the right age, he thought, why not? He had the blonde wig in his gym bag, and as long as her body was close enough to what Sheila needed, why not? As it turned out, her body was exactly what Sheila wanted. He might feel a little guilty draping the blonde wig over her head and pulling that type of deception on his wife, but he'd be able to live with that.

The address he had given her was to a shuttered nightclub on a dusty stretch of road that had nothing nearby. Henry had passed it when he had driven to see Madame Asteria, and after he left her psychic storefront he drove back to the empty building to give it a closer look. The back lot behind the building would be deserted enough for him to do what he needed to do, but it was also obvious that power had been cut to the building and that it had no active security system. He'd easily be able get inside of it and have more privacy if he desired.

As the car approached the shuttered nightclub, the driver asked him if he was sure of the address.

"The place looks out of business," she said.

"It is. I'm thinking of buying the building and want to give the place a looksee. Pull up in back, okay?"

"Sure. Oh, do you want me to send you the picture I took of you?"

Henry wasn't sure he heard that right. "Excuse me?"

"I always take photos of my fares and send them to my dispatcher. It's a safety precaution. The picture I took of you is pretty good, and would make a good replacement for what you registered on Pooled."

She reached back and handed him her iPhone, which showed the photo she'd taken. Henry hadn't even realized she had done this. He felt a numbness spreading along his forehead as he handed the device back to her. He tried to decide whether she showed it to him because she was suspicious of him or was just being friendly. Whichever it was, it didn't matter. He wasn't going to be able to kill her. Just as well. He might as well look for a blonde victim so he wouldn't have to lie to his wife later.

"No thanks," he said. "I look like I've got three chins in that photo."

"You really need to replace what you've got up there. I guarantee you that you're going to find drivers who won't pick you up because of it."

"I'll keep that in mind," Henry said curtly.

She parked behind the building. A perfect, isolated location, all for nothing. He wouldn't even be able to use it with another victim since this woman would now make the connection.

"Do you want me to wait for you?" she asked.

"Sure," he said.

Since it was expected, he got out of the car and made a show of inspecting the building as he walked around it. When he returned to her car, he asked her to take him back to the same spot where she had picked him up. He almost recommended that she buy herself some lottery tickets since it was clearly her lucky day, but he wisely bit his tongue instead.

Chapter Thirty-six

New York, the present

"Caucasian, big, wide body, round head like a pumpkin, bald spot, dark brown hair," FBI agent Julie Crasmore said to Morris over Bogle's cellphone, repeating the description of SCK that Morris had given her. "How much credence do you give this witness?"

"I don't know. He's not a flake. He did see SCK hiding behind a car, but from sixty feet away, and as he said, only a fleeting glimpse. But the lighting's good, so there's that. I'd say it's a sincere description from the witness. But maybe not fully reliable."

"Except it's better than anything we've had," Crasmore said with a sigh. "You found where SCK dined with one of his victims?"

"We did. A restaurant in Santa Monica. Only one waitress was working then, and she didn't see him, probably because he slipped in and out through the back door. We're still trying to track down the bartender who was working that day."

"Any surveillance cameras in the area?"

"None. He parked in a garage less than half a block from the restaurant. He was careful in picking the place. We'll get something on the news tonight about him being there with Susan Twilitter, but I'm not hopeful on us getting any leads from it."

"Well, then, we'll have to see what we can find from our end."

Crasmore handed Bogle back his cellphone, and once Bogle was off the phone, Crasmore suggested they change tack.

"Let's assume this description of SCK is good, or at least mostly good. Let's also assume that you're dealing with the same SCK in Los Angeles, and not a copycat. Pete, how about you and Lemmon look at anyone who was arrested and later incarcerated who could fit SCK's description?"

Childs nodded. "Sure, how about yourself?"

"I'm going to pull every damn major crimes file, and with Bogle's help, we're going to see if anyone matching SCK's description could've been involved."

Crasmore and Bogle decided to start with crimes that happened near the date they had forecasted SCK to start killing again based on his previous pattern, and then work their way forward and backward from that date. Twenty minutes after they pulled the first batch of files, Crasmore tossed one of them to Bogle. Several photos were in the file. The first one showed the victim before she had been attacked. Blonde, hourglass figure, very pretty. The other photos showed her crippled, her body unnaturally twisted.

"I had a thought when this case went down that SCK could've done it," Crasmore said.

Bogle scanned the report. "She was thirty-five. That puts her older than the girls SCK likes to kill," he said. "Also, she'd be out of sequence. SCK was supposed to have killed a forty-something, balding, overweight guy next."

"There's that," Crasmore agreed. "But about her being older, it was dark where she was attacked, and if you look at her photo she could've passed for twenty-five."

"Yeah, maybe, but he didn't crack her skull open and dig out her brains."

"True. But whoever attacked her hurt her pretty badly."

Bogle nodded without much enthusiasm and tossed the file aside. The victim, Sheila Jones, might've fit the twenty-something blonde-girl profile, but that wouldn't have been the type of victim SCK would've been searching for then. Forty minutes later the case file Bogle had grabbed made him sit straight up. Crasmore noticed his reaction.

"What?" she asked.

Bogle maintained a perfect poker face as he finished reading through the file and handed it to Crasmore. It was an open case about a man in Queens who was found in his home decapitated and his head missing. His driver's license photo was included in the file. He was forty-four, and he resembled someone SCK might've targeted.

"Look at the date of when he was last seen," Bogle said.

The victim, Tim Black, was discovered in his home four days after Sheila Jones had been attacked, but the last time anyone had seen him alive was at a bar in Queens earlier that same night Jones was found on a Central Park West street.

"SCK could've been responsible for both of them," Bogle said. "There could be a thin, forty-something-year-old woman also killed that night whose body was never found."

Crasmore had finished reading the file, her face tense as her lips tightened into a hard grin. "That sonofabitch left Sheila Jones alive," she said.

"At least she was alive five years ago."

Bogle searched through his pile of discarded files for Sheila Jones's.

Chapter Thirty-seven

Los Angeles, the present

Earlier Henry had picked up a pair of binoculars at a sporting goods store, and he used them to get a better look at a woman who had wheeled a grocery cart loaded with bags out of the discount super-market and had stopped in front of the building so that she could fiddle with her purse. She was blonde and looked like she was the right age. She wasn't as full-figured as Sheila wanted. Actually on the skinny side, but if he was careful with how he positioned her body before he recorded cracking open her skull he'd be able to fool his wife. When he saw that she had taken a cellphone from her purse and was fiddling with that, he drove out of the parking lot across the street from the discount supermarket. Before leaving the house that morning, he had replaced his Oregon plates with stolen ones, so he didn't much care if the market had an outdoor surveil-lance camera that might capture his license-plate number.

It took him all of thirty seconds to pull his car up in front of the supermarket. Up close he could see she was as young as she had looked through the binoculars. She also turned out to be skinnier; her jacket had made her look rounder. It was going to take some sleight of hand on his part to fool his wife, but he'd figure out a way. He rolled down his window and waved her over.

"Miss, you haven't seen this lady around here?"

Henry held out his iPhone showing a picture of a random middle-aged woman that he'd gotten from a dating website. The blonde girl, trying to be helpful, came over to his car and gave the picture a look before shaking her head.

"There was nobody else standing here when I came out of the

market," she said with an apologetic smile. She was actually very pretty, especially when she smiled. Even with her skinnier body.

"Drat. I was sent to this location to pick her up, but I got stuck in traffic. She must've gotten a ride from someone else." Henry let out a heavy sigh and shook his head. "I'd hate to make this a wasted trip. You're not looking for a ride, are you?"

She hesitated before telling him that she was, but that she'd already requested a pickup from Uber. Henry smiled at her, partly for show, and partly because he found it endearing that she was just too nice to walk away from him and appear rude.

"If your driver gets stuck in the same traffic I did, it's going to be a while before he gets here. You don't want your groceries to spoil in this heat. How far do you need to go?"

"I don't know . . ."

Henry brought up on his iPhone his fake Pooled profile, and flashed it to her, making sure to do it fast enough so she wouldn't notice that he wasn't a driver. "I drive for Pooled," he said. "We're cheaper than Uber, and in my opinion, nicer and better. Since I don't want to leave empty-handed, I'll give you a discount like you wouldn't believe."

Somewhat reluctantly, she said, "About ten miles."

"Five dollars then. How's that sound?"

Again reluctantly, she admitted that it sounded good.

Henry flashed her his most disarming smile, "Deal?"

That coaxed a smile out of her. "Deal," she agreed.

"Good. Why don't you take a load off and get in back, and I'll move your groceries to the trunk."

She did as Henry suggested, and he left the car to take care of her groceries. There was some risk in him doing that, but with her in the car it was doubtful a bystander would remember seeing the two of them together. He moved quickly anyway to load up the trunk, and was huffing a bit by the time he got back into the car. She gave him her address, and he was quite proud of his ingenuity as he drove out of the supermarket parking lot.

At first it had been harder to find women to pull this scheme on than he would've thought. This was when he was driving around shopping areas in Hollywood and Beverly Hills. It took him three hours to find two women loaded with packages who matched Sheila's requirements and who he caught using their cellphones to request rides (or at least that's what he assumed they were using them for), and neither of them wanted anything to do with him. In fact, he could tell one of them was a heartbeat away from calling the police. He almost gave up after that, especially after seeing the flaw in his idea. For his plan to work, he needed the woman he picked up to want him to take her home, but there was no telling where any of these pickups would want to go. It was very possible that they would want to do more shopping. Then inspiration hit and he had the idea of staking out supermarkets. Anyone leaving a supermarket would want to just head home so they could put away their groceries. Once Henry adjusted his scheme, he more easily found potential victims. The first three women he approached turned him down, but he could tell that two of them almost accepted his offer. The fourth did accept, but the building she lived in had a doorman who got a good look at Henry when he helped carry her groceries to her apartment. That was when he realized he needed to adjust his scheme once more and stake out discount supermarkets instead of the higher end, ritzier ones. It didn't take him long after that to get this lady he now had in his backseat.

"How long have you been doing this?"

Henry had been so lost in his thoughts that he almost didn't hear her. "Not long," he said. "I'm retired, but this seemed like a good way to meet people. So here I am."

"That must be nice," she said. "Being retired and doing what you want."

"Eh, too much time on my hands sometimes. Let me guess, you're an actress."

He gave a quick peek in the rearview mirror and caught her blushing.

"Hopeful actress," she said. "Part-time waitress."

"You'll make it. You got the looks. Not that I'm trying to hit on you or anything. Jeeze Louise, you're young enough to be my daughter, and besides I'm married and there's no more faithful guy in the world than me. But the moment I saw you, I thought *what a looker*, she's got to be an actress."

"Thanks, but I haven't had much luck yet. Not sure I ever will."

"It's a tough business," Henry acknowledged. "But trust me, someday soon your name will be in the papers."

"I hope you're right."

The address she had given him was for a small three-story brick apartment building that looked like it had been built in the sixties. The front showed six units, each with a small balcony and a cheap air conditioner sticking out of the wall. There were probably six more apartments in the back of the building. Certainly not the type of place that would have a doorman. Or where anyone would notice Henry walking in and out.

He was able to park on the street in front, and he left the car quickly so he could grab the bags from the trunk. The blonde followed him out of the car, and she told him he could just leave them on the sidewalk and she'd take care of them.

"Uh uh," Henry said. "No way I'm leaving these for you to carry by yourself. That's not the way I was brought up. Besides, this neighborhood looks sketchy to me. You leave any of these down here so you can carry these up one at a time, and the odds are the others will be gone by the time you get back down."

She relented. Henry could tell she didn't feel comfortable doing so, but still she relented. She was probably too nice a person to do anything else.

"At least let me take one of them," she said.

Henry let her take one while he carried the other three. Of course, she had to have a third-floor apartment, and there was no elevator. He was breathing heavily by the time they reached her door. Later, after he had her subdued, he'd return back to his car for his gym bag.

She opened the door for them, and he was disappointed to see that there was a young girl sitting on the sofa watching TV. This girl couldn't have been much older than eighteen. She had dark, black hair, looked Hispanic, and was much skinnier than the blonde. When she saw Henry carrying the three bags loaded with groceries, she jumped off the sofa and took one of them from him. As he followed her to the kitchen, he played out in his mind how he'd subdue both of them, and decided he could do it without either of them being able to scream out for help. But then as he put the bags down on the kitchen countertop, he saw the little boy. Not having any kids himself, or ever spending any time with children, he wasn't great at judging their ages, but he had to think this pint-sized runt couldn't be any older than three. Now he had to decide how much of a monster he truly was, because he'd have to be a darn insidious one to also kill a three-year-old boy, and if he was going to kill these two dames, he'd have to kill the boy also, given the way the kid was staring at him and memorizing his features. With a heavy sigh easing out of him, he decided he wasn't enough of a monster to do that.

"Shrek," the boy said.

"What was that?" Henry asked.

"You're Shrek!" The boy pointed at Henry and started laughing as if he'd just told the funniest joke ever. "Shrek! Shrek!" he screamed, repeating the punchline.

"Connor, you apologize to this man right now!" the blonde woman ordered.

Connor started giggling. He yelled *Shrek* one more time before running out of the room.

"I'm so sorry for that," the blonde told Henry.

"Boys will be boys," Henry said.

She kissed him on the cheek and handed him twenty dollars. "You're a nice man," she said.

"You don't know the half of it," Henry said.

He put the twenty-dollar bill on the kitchen counter and left the apartment.

Chapter Thirty-eight

Morris and Stonehedge had tracked Rudy the bartender to a private pool party in Brentwood where he was working, but he insisted that he didn't see Susan Twilitter's lunch date.

"Things don't pick up at the bar until after five, and that day was slower than most. If he came in through the front door instead of the back, he probably slipped in while I was catching Laker highlights on ESPN. I wish I could help you, but I didn't see the guy."

Morris had tried some additional questioning, but it became clear that Rudy had nothing to give them. Since it was almost three o'clock then, they picked up several sandwiches from a nearby shop (a meatloaf on sourdough for Parker), and they ate these as they headed back to the MBI offices.

"What next?" Stonehedge asked in between bites of his prosciutto and mozzarella panini.

Morris shook his head. "I don't know. I'm not putting out the description we got. It's not reliable enough yet. Maybe a new lead will come in through the hotline." He paused for a moment, then asked, "I need to run an errand. It's my wife's birthday Saturday, and I'd like to stop off at a jewelry store and pick her up something. Mind coming in with me and giving me your opinion?"

As if he were insulted, Stonehedge said, "You're figuring I must know jewelry since I'm an actor?"

"Exactly."

Stonehedge dropped his insulted act and smiled broadly. He winked at Morris. "You're right, I do. My favorite gift to give a lady after hooking up. Let's go to a place I know on North Canon Drive in Beverly Hills."

"I don't want to spend more than three hundred."

"You won't have to. I'll get you something nice there well below cost." Another wink. "It's part of the deal I have with them for all the mentions I give them in interviews."

"Will they recognize you in that getup?"

"They've seen me in it before."

"Okay, then."

Stonehedge smiled thinly. "Another perk of having me tag along."

"They're beginning to add up," Morris admitted.

Traffic was light to Beverly Hills. The jewelry store turned out to be one of those where you either need an appointment or you need to be a favorite customer to get buzzed in. When Stonehedge pressed the buzzer, he announced himself to a woman named Carol and told her that he would be bringing a friend in with him. "He's got a well-behaved bull terrier. A beautiful dog. Would it be okay if he brings his pet in also?"

"Of course, Mr. Stonehedge."

The door buzzed open.

Morris whispered to Stonehedge, "Are you sure they're going to have something in my price range?"

The actor gave Morris another wink and pushed through the door. Carol was waiting for them inside the shop. A sleek and absolutely gorgeous brunette. She made no mention of Stonehedge's disguise and instead took his hand warmly as she greeted him. Her greeting to Morris was friendly, but more professional, and she gave Parker a quick pat on the head.

"Can I get any of you Prosecco, coffee, tea?" She gave Parker a slight smile. "Sparkling water?"

"I'll have a cappuccino with whole milk," Stonehedge said.

"Black coffee, sugar," Morris said.

"And for the dog?"

"A biscuit if you have one," Morris said as a joke.

"Certainly, I'll be right back."

Outside of Carol, there were two other customers in the store, both being waited on by salesclerks. One of the clerks was a fit man in his sixties with well-groomed salt and pepper hair, the other a similar looking man, but with a goatee and about thirty years younger. Both were dressed in expensive-looking dark gray suits that had to be custom tailored. The older man smiled at Stonehedge before returning his attention back to his customer.

"That's Antoine, the owner," Stonehedge said in a reserved whisper to Morris. "Great guy. The other guy working is his son Jules."

Morris was studying one of the display cases. "I've never been in a shop like this before," he said.

Carol returned with refreshments, which included three butter cookies for Parker. "The closest I could find to a dog biscuit," she said with a dazzling smile to let Morris know she was in on the joke. Then to Stonehedge, "What can I show you?"

"My friend is looking for a gift for his wife."

"Earrings," Morris said.

"Something deeply discounted as a favor to me," Stonehedge said. "No more than three hundred dollars."

"I'm sure we can find something," Carol said with another dazzling smile.

She took them to one of the display cases and pulled out a tray loaded with what looked like very expensive earrings.

"What color are your wife's eyes and hair?" she asked Morris.

"Green. Natalie's a dark brunette. Very slender woman."

The door buzzed as she picked up a pair with emeralds and diamonds that looked like they cost a fortune.

"Normally these would be eighteen hundred dollars, but I think we can arrange a price of three hundred dollars for one of Mr. Stonehedge's friends. What do you think?"

The door was buzzed open. Quickly, Parker was on his feet, growling and tugging at his leash. Morris looked over at the door as a middle-aged woman came tumbling through it and fell onto the floor, and was followed by two men brandishing large handguns with silencers attached, their faces hidden by ski masks. One of them came rushing toward Morris, his gun trained on Parker. The other dragged the woman who had fallen to the floor with him as he made his way to the other end of the showroom.

"You hold that leash tight, pal, or your dog takes one in the head, then you take one right afterwards."

Morris pushed hard on Parker's back, ordering the dog to lay down. Parker reluctantly complied, but continued to growl.

"You won't have any trouble from us," Morris promised.

The other robber had made the owner and son put their hands flat on the glass case. "I'll make this simple," he announced. "You got one minute to hand over three of those million-dollar Roger Dubuis watches. It takes you longer than that, I shoot this lady in the face."

He pointed his gun at the face of the woman Antoine had been helping.

"Please, Antoine," the woman pleaded, her color dropping to a sickly gray.

"I don't have those watches," Antoine said in a voice that was little more than a squeak. "Whoever told you I did misled you."

"You've got forty seconds," the robber said. "After I shoot her, your son gets a bullet in his eye."

The woman started crying. Antoine's skin color had turned as gray as hers.

"The watches are in the safe," he said. "I need to go to the office to get them."

"Smart man," the robber said. "You two get out from behind the counter," he ordered, referring to Jules and Carol. "All you nice folks lie flat on your face while me and Antoine conclude our business. Let's see if we can end this with none of you getting killed."

The robber closer to Stonehedge was focused intently on Morris and his dog, and the actor stepped forward and started to throw a right jab at him. The man must've seen this punch out of his peripheral vision, because he whipped his gun around slashing Stonehedge's cheek open with the barrel. The actor stumbled back several steps, both hands going to his injured cheek.

Morris could see through the openings in the ski mask the robber's eyes glazing into a look of violence. This was a stone-cold killer, and before Morris could do anything to stop him, the man shot Stonehedge in the leg, and the actor collapsed onto the floor moaning. Parker stayed on the floor, but his growling grew louder. The man pointed his gun at Parker's skull, his eyes still glazed.

"Shut that dog up or I'll blow his head off," he snarled.

"I've got him under control. You don't have to shoot him." Morris glanced over at Stonehedge and saw that the actor was bleeding profusely from his bullet wound. "Let me tie a tourniquet around his leg. He could bleed out if I don't."

"Do you think I care? Because of this dumbass playing hero, this has turned into a twenty-five to life if I get caught. Let him die."

"A felony murder would still be worse."

"Not for me." His attention turned to Carol. "Sweet cheeks, thanks to hero boy over there everything has changed. Me and you are going to the back room together for some privacy." He yelled out to his partner. "You got a problem with that?"

The other robber's voice was a tight growl as he said, "None. I'll get my crack with her after you're done."

Carol shrank back. She looked like she wanted to scream, but was too terrified to do so.

"Missy, you get your ass out here now before I pull you out of there by your hair!"

Morris stepped forward, his hands pressed together into a pleading gesture. "You don't want to make this worse than it is," he implored.

The man swung his gun toward Morris, but before he could get a shot off, Morris took one more quick step forward while simultaneously flashing out with both his hands; his left grabbing the man's gun hand by the wrist and twisting it around, while with his right he struck the man in the jaw with an open palm. As he did this, Parker lunged forward and locked his jaw on to the man's knee and started shaking it as if he were trying to rip his leg off. All of this took less than two seconds, and before the other robber could react, Morris had the gun ripped out of the man's hand and fired off a shot, hitting the other robber in the shoulder, which sent his gun flying out of his hand and him falling backward to the floor.

Morris punched the robber he was tangled with twice in the jaw. The first blow dazed him, the second knocked him out. Morris grimaced as he looked over at Stonehedge and saw how badly the actor was bleeding, but he needed to defuse what was happening across the room before he could attend to Stonehedge. The customer who had been threatened earlier had picked up the gun the other robber had dropped, and now stood over him with both hands holding the gun shaking as she pointed it at him, her body trembling as she tried to work up the nerve to shoot him.

"You don't want to do that," Morris said, as he took the gun away from her. He checked that there was a bullet in the chamber, then handed it to Antoine. "Cover him until the police come. If he tries to get up, shoot him in the chest." As he ran back to Stone-hedge, he ordered Jules to call the police and have an ambulance sent over. That they had a shooting victim in critical condition.

He used his tie as a tourniquet to staunch the actor's bleeding. Stonehedge looked awful, but was still conscious.

"Am I going to die?" he asked Morris.

"Sometime in the future, but not today unless your ambulance gets hit by a bus."

"That's good to know."

"The studio is not going to be too happy with me letting you get shot like this."

Stonehedge laughed weakly. "They're going to be thrilled with the publicity they get from this."

"I suppose you're right."

"How bad's my face look?"

"It's a mess. You're going to have quite a scar, but it will give you character."

Carol had come out from behind the counter so she could sit by Stonehedge and rest his head in her lap. Morris made sure the rob-ber he had knocked out was still knocked out, and he rubbed the bruised knuckles on his right hand as he retrieved his dog, who had moved over to the other robber so he could stand guard over him and growl.

Chapter Thirty-nine

On his way back to Simi Valley, Henry stopped at the same restaurant in North Hills that he had eaten at the night before. The same cute blonde waitress, Brenda, once again waited on him, and she showed him an adorable smile when she recognized him.

"I guess you just can't get enough of us, huh?" she asked. "You must be a glutton for punishment."

"I'm a glutton for your beautiful smile. It warms my heart just to see it."

He ordered the same steak dinner he had the other night, and the same locally brewed pilsner, and added a shot of bourbon. When Brenda brought over the drinks, he told her a few more of his corny jokes, and did the same when she brought over the steak. His heart, though, just wasn't in it. He was only killing time, avoiding going home any sooner than he had to. He was only half done with his steak when he waved Brenda over for the check.

"Time for me to go home and face the music," he said.

She scrunched up her eyes, not understanding what he meant.

"The little woman is not going to be happy with me," he explained.

"I find that hard to believe."

"It's true," he said. "I disappointed her. And I'm going to hear about it when I get home."

"She must be a hard woman to please."

"One could make that case," he agreed.

As with the other night, he left a hefty tip, this time a few cents over twenty dollars.

When he arrived home, he didn't say a word to Sheila, nor her to him. He simply carried her to the bathroom, undressed her, scrubbed her clean in the bathtub, and put her in pajamas that were freshly laundered from the other night. It wasn't until he had her in her wheelchair and in the kitchen that he spoke, asking her what she wanted for dinner.

"Are you going to make me beg?" she said in the painful way she had of speaking since the accident, where each word had to be pushed out as if it took every ounce of strength she had. "Show me the recording!"

"I didn't kill anyone," he said.

Her body became even more rigid, and her mouth twisted into the pinched, angry circle that he knew so well. She looked at him as if he had betrayed her in the worst possible way, and that made him lose his temper as well. He was trembling as he told her that he had tried to find someone, but it just wasn't possible.

"Those police press conferences have put every blonde girl in the city on edge. Every single one that I approached looked at me as a potential serial killer. There was just no way of getting any of them alone."

Of course, he was lying. There was that skinny blonde girl with the three-year-old boy and the eighteen-year-old babysitter. He could've killed all three of them if he was monstrous enough.

"You're lying," Sheila accused.

"I killed three people for you already! Three and a half if you count that man in Queens, since you left him half dead! Isn't that enough?"

"You know it isn't."

"How am I supposed to know it isn't? You make these insane requests of me. That's it, I'm done! You just have to get over this craziness!"

Sheila clamped her mouth shut and looked away from him.

"Fine," he said. "Be mad at me. I don't care. We're going to live like normal people for a change. I know you're hungry. What do you want for dinner?"

After she didn't answer him, he told her he was going to make things easy for himself and make her a fruit smoothie. He proceeded to add yogurt, almond milk, a banana, strawberries, a spoonful of honey, a pear, and vitamin powder to the blender. Once he had the concoction blended together, he took a sip, approved of the way it tasted, and placed the glass in front of his wife with a straw in it so she could drink it on her own. She didn't waste any time using her somewhat good hand to knock the glass to the floor.

"Fine. You want to be that way, tomorrow I'll pick up tubing and syringes for force-feeding, and we'll do it that way."

Henry took two beers from the fridge and brought them out to the living room, leaving his wife in the kitchen. He was brooding too much to pay attention to what was on TV. This changed for several minutes during the ten o'clock local news when they ran a story about Morris Brick's heroics during a failed armed robbery of a jewelry store in Beverly Hills.

"You're a busy man, Brick," he muttered to himself.

After the story finished, he was soon back to his brooding. Later, after the local news ended, he went back to the kitchen and stared silently at his wife. She knew he was there, but she continued to act as if he didn't exist.

"Do you want me to put you to bed, or would you like to watch some TV?" he asked.

No answer and no indication that she heard him.

He was past his brooding, and his nerves felt jangled. He couldn't stand the silence from her. He couldn't stand the thought that she'd rather die than acknowledge him.

"This is crazy," he implored, his voice cracking. "You know I love you and would do anything for you as long as it wasn't something completely nuts. Please, stop this!"

"If you really loved me, you would've done this for me," she said in her painfully slow manner of speech.

"It's not fair for you to want me to do this!"

"If there was something that was making you feel like you were suffocating, I'd do whatever you needed me to do so you could breathe again."

Henry stared silently at his wife for several minutes, his mouth moving as if he were slowly chewing gum. Then he went back to the living room and stared blindly at the TV. At twelve thirty he got up from the sofa, and without saying another word to Sheila, he left the house.

Chapter Forty

Sheila was carrying a hammer when she entered her sister's bedroom. She couldn't help smiling seeing Penelope's alarmed expression. Her sister had every right to be worried about her walking into her room holding a hammer. She wasn't the same skinny little girl that Penelope and her parents had once terrorized so thoroughly, but was now a more robust eighteen-year-old, and probably as strong as her sister. Stronger, actually, thanks to all the hate filling up her heart. She doubted it would be much of a contest if they ever got into a physical fight.

"What are you doing in here?" Penelope asked. She'd been sitting on her bed, smoking a joint, and reading one of her trashy gossip magazines when Sheila had interrupted her, and her expression was dopcy enough that Sheila started laughing so hard that tears ran down her face.

"You're really not very smart," Sheila said between gasps of laughter. All at once her laughter dried up, and she wiped the tears away from her eyes. "It's so ironic that you used to call me *peanut brain* since you're the one with almost nothing inside your skull. The question you should be asking me is why did I bring a hammer with me."

"I know why. You think you're going to hit me with it."

"No, that's not it, dummy. Guess again."

Penelope's mouth tightened as anger flared in her dull eyes. "I'm getting off this bed and taking that hammer away from you," she said in a soft, menacing voice. "Then I'm going to shove it so far up your ass that the doctors will never be able to get it out."

"I wouldn't try doing that. Not with you being so deathly allergic to bees."

Penelope had started to get off the bed, but she sat back down. She took another hit from her joint and stubbed it out, all the while keeping her gaze focused on Sheila. Slowly she let the smoke leak out through the side of her mouth. "What does that have to do with it?" she asked.

"I'll explain in a minute. But first let's talk about what you just threatened to do to me with this hammer. You and mom and dad used to like to stick things into me, didn't you?"

Penelope blinked several times. "You're nuts," she said, her voice now as dull as her eyes.

"My *punishments*? You've forgotten about them already?"

"Whatever mom and dad did to you was because you kept misbehaving."

Sheila laughed again, but it was a sour, painful laugh that left a dull throbbing in her temples. "What mom and dad used to do? Are you that delusional that you've forgotten you used to join them? That you used to come up with ideas of what they should do to me? And this would be after you'd break things and blame it on me so you three could inflict your *punishments* on me!"

Penelope's eyes narrowed, and her body tensed as if she were again considering jumping off the bed and attacking Sheila. In a way Sheila would've liked that to happen since it would've given her an excuse to drive the hammer through one of Penelope's eyes. But she had a better use for it.

"Don't forget about the bees," she said.

Penelope blinked two more times as she remembered there was something about bees that she needed to worry about. She again settled back onto the bed.

"Whatever was done was for your own good," she said. "And it was years ago. How long are you going to keep crying about it?"

Sheila almost threw the hammer at her sister's head. It took an almost Herculean effort on her part not to do so. But, as she kept telling herself, she had a much better use for it.

"You three did those things to me from when I was a very little girl until I was fourteen. It was only after you kidnapped me that I was able to make all of you stop!"

"That was only a prank," Penelope insisted.

"A prank? You and your two trash friends grabbed me from my bed, stripped me naked, tied me up, and threw me in the trunk of a car, and it's a prank?"

"That's all it was. A harmless prank," Penelope stubbornly said.

"No, that's not what it was. You three were going to take me into the woods and do worse things to me than stick this hammer up my ass. And then you were going to kill me. But you chickened out."

Enough of a glimmer showed in her sister's eyes to prove to Sheila that she had been right about what she had thought, but Penelope still persisted in claiming that Sheila had blown a prank into something much bigger than it was.

"A mountain out of a mole hill. That's what you always do. Make a mountain out of a mole hill."

"Enough," Sheila said, holding up her left hand, palm facing her sister. "This is getting tiresome."

"You bet it is!"

"Yeah, it is," Sheila agreed. "Let me tell you about the bees, although if you weren't such a dull-witted cretin I wouldn't have to tell you about them."

"You better watch your mouth. I've had it with your insults."

Since entering the room, Sheila had slowly positioned herself by the wall where right outside her mother's prized rose bushes grew.

"My insults are the least of your problems. Getting stung by dozens of bees is what you should be worrying about. Haven't you been wondering why there's been a buzzing noise coming from this wall for over three months?"

"You're full of it," Penelope said.

Sheila put a finger to her lips and shushed her sister. As the sounds of their talking faded, a silence grew in the room. Sheila kicked the wall and an angry buzzing could then be heard.

"There are bees in the wall?" Penelope asked, a slow panic forming in her eyes.

"Duh."

"How?"

"I put them there. It wasn't even that hard once I read a book on beekeeping. Not even that expensive either. I was able to buy a three-pound package of bees in Crawfordville for only forty-nine dollars. Getting them in the wall wasn't that hard either. All I had to do was drill a hole from outside near the rose bushes, and then spray sugar water inside of it. Bees really like sugar water. After that I made a hole in the package that lined up with the one in the outside wall, shook it a little, and left it alone overnight. By morning, the bees settled nicely into their new hive."

Penelope's mouth dropped open into a dumbfounded expression as she processed what Sheila had told her. "If any of those bees had gotten into my room, I could've died," she said.

"That's right."

"Why would you do something like this?"

Sheila had to bite her tongue to keep from laughing. How dumb could Penelope possibly be?

"To make you tell me the truth about why you kidnapped me that night. Because if you don't tell me the truth right now, I'm going to punch a hole through the wall and hundreds of angry bees are going to swarm in here. And they are going to be pissed off angry. Bees don't like having their hive disturbed."

"I already told you the truth!"

Sheila raised the hammer high enough so she'd be able to swing down with enough force to break through the sheetrock

"Stop! Stop!" Penelope's eyes shifted from her sister's. "We were going to take you someplace private and have some fun, that's all."

"There was a shovel in Connelly's trunk. The blade kept digging into my side. Your plans were to bury me after your fun."

Penelope shook her head, but otherwise didn't say anything.

"Why'd you chicken out and change your plans?"

Penelope said something in a low murmur that Sheila couldn't hear.

"You better speak up. I'm not fooling with this hammer!"

"Tommy's got a big mouth. I didn't trust him not to talk."

For a long minute neither sister spoke. Then Sheila demanded, "Why?"

Penelope shifted her eyes back to Sheila, her expression showing her confusion over her sister's question.

"Why what?"

"Why'd you and mom and dad hurt me so much? I couldn't have been older than five when all that started!"

Penelope thought about it for several seconds before shrugging. "Because you were helpless."

It took Sheila a few seconds to make sense of that. It really wouldn't have mattered what Penelope had said, but that answer made what Sheila was about to do so much more rewarding, especially given the matter-of-fact way in which she said it. Sheila let out a primal scream as she swung the hammer into the wall, trying to let out all of her hate and disgust and loathing. The hammer's head tore deep into the wall, and when Sheila pulled the hammer loose, dozens of unhappy bees flew out of this new opening. Sheila was stung several times, but she didn't care. She stood and watched as Penelope sat paralyzed in fear. Bees buzzed quickly around her face, some landing on her arms, neck, and head.

"Maybe none of them will sting you," Sheila said. "But you better sit awfully still, because if you scream, or even move as much as a twitch, I bet you get stung. And you better not swat at any of them."

Sheila kicked the wall and more bees came out. Several bees were now crawling over Penelope's face. If somehow none of the bees stung her, there was a good chance she would die of fright.

"Remember, don't scream," Sheila said. "And no matter how much you're dying to, don't swat at them."

She left the room, slamming the door behind her as hard as she was capable of. It didn't take long after that—maybe a second, maybe two—for Penelope to scream out, but it quickly became a strangled noise, and seconds after that there was a loud thud. Sheila waited ten minutes and then went back into the room. Penelope was lying on the floor. From all the large swollen red lumps on her face, neck, arms, and legs she'd been stung at least several dozen times. All Sheila could think as she stared at her dead sister was that she hoped it had been sheer agony for Penelope.

Dozens of bees were still swarming the room, but they had calmed down somewhat, and none of these stung Sheila as she moved her sister to the wall where the beehive was located. She used her T-shirt to wipe off the hammer and then while holding the head of the hammer with her T-shirt so she wouldn't leave any prints, she placed the handle in her sister's right hand and closed the fingers around it.

It would be a mystery as to why Penelope would do something as stupid as to use a hammer to investigate a buzzing noise in the wall, especially given her allergies, but let the police prove it was something other than that.

Satisfied with how things looked, Sheila left the room again so she could call 9-1-1. Some bees had escaped with her into the house. Good. Maybe her parents will get stung by them when they return home. At least she could hope so.

By pressing down on her bee stings, Sheila was able to generate genuine tears, and her voice shook with pain as she told the emergency operator about the tragic turn of events that had just occurred.

Chapter Forty-one

For the first five weeks following Penelope's death, neither Mr. Proops nor Mrs. Proops said much of anything to Sheila. She'd catch them at times staring at her, but whatever suspicions they had they kept bottled up, at least during those five weeks.

It was only after they had collected Penelope's life-insurance settlement, because surprisingly, at least to Sheila, they had taken out a two-million-dollar accidental-death policy on her, that they voiced their suspicions.

"I'd like you to explain something to us," Mr. Proops said to Sheila as Mrs. Proops stood next to him, neither of them looking very happy.

"I'm eating. Can't this wait?" Sheila said between bites of corn flakes.

"No, it can't."

Sheila rolled her eyes. "Fine. What do you want me to explain?"

"Not here. Outside."

"Fine. Whatever."

Her parents led the way to the rose bushes outside of what had been Penelope's room. Mr. Proops got on his hands and knees and crawled behind the bushes.

"There's a hole in the wall here," he yelled out.

"If you say so," Sheila said.

"There certainly is one! I've got my finger sticking inside of it."

"Okay."

Mr. Proops crawled back out, making sure to avoid the branches covered with thorns. Once he was on his feet again, he dusted himself off.

"That hole looks like it was made by a drill," he said, his eyebrows bunched in an accusatory look. "How do you suppose it got there?"

Sheila shrugged. "I have no idea."

"You made it," Mrs. Proops said, her breathing shallow as she stared at Sheila.

"Why would I have done that?"

"You made that hole and you got those bees into it!"

Sheila stared with wide-eyed innocence before giving any indication that she understood Mrs. Proops accusation.

"You're saying I murdered Penelope? By using bees?"

"That's exactly what I'm saying!"

"And you think this also?" Sheila asked Mr. Proops.

"Somebody drilled that hole," Mr. Proops said, his eyebrows bunching even more.

"Well, if somebody really did drill a hole there and figured out a way to get bees into it, I think the police would figure it was the parents who were collecting on a two-million-dollar life-insurance policy they had taken out on their dead daughter. I have to admit that I've been wondering about that policy ever since I saw that letter you received from the insurance company. Why would you have taken out that policy if it wasn't so that you could murder Penelope and collect all that money? And just between us, how did you get a whole hive of bees into the wall?"

Mr. Proops eyelids lowered, but he otherwise didn't respond. Mrs. Proops slapped Sheila hard enough across the face to leave a mark.

"You're nothing but an ingrate," Mrs. Proops forced out. Her lips pressed hard enough together into a spiteful line that wrinkled the skin around her mouth, making her look thirty years older. Then she smirked nastily and said, "A peanut-brained piece of trash. Penelope was so much better than you."

Sheila smiled at that. A hard smile that felt like it had been permanently plastered onto her face. Like it would take a chisel and hammer to remove it.

"Mother, you know what I find interesting about you accusing me of such a bizarre thing? You're the one who spends hours fretting over your rose bushes. If there was a beehive in that wall, wouldn't there have been a lot more bees flying around here? Why didn't you notice them? Unless you did this?"

Mrs. Proops right hand flashed out as she slapped Sheila again, this time the crack from the blow sounding almost as loud as a gunshot.

She took a step forward, her breath sour in Sheila's face. "I want you out of my house now," she said.

"You heard your mother," Mr. Proops said. "We won't tolerate you here any longer."

Sheila's lips were still locked into that same icy, harsh grin. Nothing in the world could've gotten that grin off her face then. For the next thirty seconds she stared with pure, unadulterated hatred at her parents. Mr. Proops was unnerved enough by it that he stumbled back a step, but otherwise stood his ground. At the end of those thirty seconds, Sheila turned from her parents, went back into the house to collect her pocketbook and a few other belongings, and then left for the bus stop without saying another word to either of them.

Chapter Forty-two

Tallahassee, 1998

Sheila's parents had a habit of sleeping in the buff, so it was easy enough for Sheila to inject Mr. Proops in his right shoulder without having to fool with pajamas. She would rather have injected him in the eyeball, but she was afraid he'd scream if she did that and wake up Mrs. Proops. When she saw the reaction from injecting a dose of succinylcholine into her father she realized he wouldn't have been able to scream if she had done what she wanted. The needle had woken him up, but other than opening his eyes all he did was flop for a brief moment like a fish that had been reeled out of the water, and then the paralysis took over.

Damn, she thought, on seeing how fast the drug had worked. She moved over to the other side of the bed, and jabbed Mrs. Proops in the cheek with the other hypodermic needle she had brought. As with her father, Mrs. Proops also woke up and flopped for a second before the paralysis froze her.

The room was dark, mostly just in shadows. Mrs. Proops' eyes were also open, and Sheila wanted her parents to see her, so she turned on her mother's night table lamp.

"Hi, there," Sheila said. She kept her voice low even though nobody passing by outside would've been able to hear her—assuming anyone would be passing by her parents' house at two in the morning. "Long time, no see, huh? What's it been, four years? You're probably wondering why you can't move. Simple reason for that. I injected both of you with a drug I stole from the hospital where I work. If I had injected you with a fatal dose, your respiratory system would've shut down completely and you'd be dead now, so don't fret. This paralysis is temporary. From what I've read, in a half hour or so you'll be able to wiggle some of your fingers, and a half hour after that you'll be able to move around, although sluggishly, like one of those zombies from *Night of the Living Dead*."

She walked back to Mr. Proops' side of the bed, and she lowered her face so that she was staring eyeball to eyeball with him. Her fingers searched out one of his nostrils, and after she had gripped several of his nose hairs, she yanked them out. He lacked the muscle control to wince from the pain, but from the way his eyes jerked in their sockets, there was no doubt that it hurt him. Sheila straightened up.

"I did that for my benefit," she said. "From what I've read about this drug, it's not an anesthetic, so it won't numb any pain; in fact, it actually makes you feel more uncomfortable, more distressed. I wanted to see that for myself, and dear father, the reaction I saw in your eyes told me everything I wanted to know. Anyway, it's a relief to know that you're going to be feeling everything that will be happening."

She had brought a large paper bag with her, and she dumped the contents onto the bed. Four scented candles, a bottle of massage oil, and several copies of the type of newspapers that you get from adult bookstores, the ones that advertise services and products. Sheila placed two candles on each night table and lit them. With that done, she rolled Mr. Proops toward Mrs. Proops. It wasn't easy rolling all that dead weight, and she had to flip him over three times before she had him lying partway on top of Mrs. Proops, and then she had to yank and pull on him before she had him positioned the way she wanted him. The exertion left her breathing hard, and she needed to stand for a moment to catch her breath.

"That will do," she said, nodding to herself as she approved of her handiwork. She took the massage oil and squeezed out a large puddle of it next to her parents, and then squeezed a lot more of it all over them.

"This stuff is highly flammable," she said. "Not very smart to be using it when you have lit candles around, especially when you spread these obscene adult newspapers all over the bed. Oh well, if people weren't doing stupid things, like Penelope punching a hammer through a wall to find out why she was hearing a buzzing noise, these types of dumb, tragic accidents would never happen."

Sheila reached past Mr. Proops' exposed buttocks so she could grab the adult newspapers and spread them over the bed and on the floor. With that done, she reached for one of the candles on Mrs. Proops's night table so that she could knock it onto her massage oil-drenched parents, but she stopped herself and instead kneeled so she could look into both her parents' faces.

"You were right about Penelope. I drilled that hole and encouraged a box of bees that I had bought to go into the wall and build a hive. I was also the one to break open the wall with the hammer. You should've seen how petrified with terror Penelope was as those bees crawled over her face. What a dummy she was. Here she was, deathly allergic to bees, and after hearing a buzzing in her wall for three months, it never occurs to her that there might be an active hive in there. Makes you wonder what we might've found if we cracked open her skull. A peanut? A raisin? A dog turd?" Sheila leaned in closer, her voice soft as she whispered, "I'll tell you a secret. Whenever I need to cheer myself up, I think about the way Penelope looked with those bees swarming over her. Sometimes when I need to treat myself to a special memory, I visualize the way she looked after being stung by all those bees; her face and body covered with all those swollen red lumps."

Even though Mr. and Mrs. Proops were paralyzed, their eyes still darted around in their sockets and Sheila could see the fear in them. She breathed in deeply and smelled the fear that their bodies exuded. It was definitely palpable; a sweet, sickly smell, and she breathed in deeply again, letting that odor fill up her lungs. In a way it was a shame that the drug left them unable to speak. Not because she had any questions she wanted to ask them, because she couldn't care what either of them would have to say. She wanted them to be able to talk only so that she could hear them beg for their lives. Even more so, she wanted to hear them scream when she set them on fire. The thought of them being unable to scream while being burned alive seemed particularly off-putting to her, as if she were going to be cheated in a way.

"It wasn't very bright of you to keep that spare key under the fake rock outside," she said. "Especially if you thought I was devious enough to kill Penelope the way I did. You should've been smart enough to realize that I'd also be coming back to kill both of you, although to be fair, it wouldn't have mattered if you had found a different hiding place. The latch for one of the kitchen windows has been broken for years, so I could've gotten in that way, but I do thank you for making it easier for me."

A thumping noise from outside stopped Sheila. She lifted her head and listened intently and heard the noise again and realized it was either a snake or some other critter hitting the glass patio door. She smiled to herself over letting something like that spook her. She lowered her head again and this time stared directly into Mr. Proops' eyes. She had no interest in saying another word to her mother. The faster that woman went to hell, the better. But Sheila did have something more that she wanted to tell her father. Because she knew what he had been planning.

"Let me tell you another secret," she said. "I snuck into the house a month after you kicked me out, and I found the insurance policy, and what do you know, you bought the same accidental death coverage for each of us. I wondered about that for all of five minutes before understanding why. You were planning to kill me for the money, but it would've looked funny if I was the only one you bought the coverage for, so you bought it for all of us. I guess I was lucky that I killed Penelope while you were still working up the nerve to kill me in some sort of accident. And guess what? Before joining you tonight in your boudoir, I searched through your desk, and sure enough, you've still been maintaining that policy. Still planning to kill me for the money, dear old father? I guess you waited too long."

The fear exploding in his eyes right then was really something remarkable. Sheila watched it for a moment, and then stood up. Instead of knocking over one of the candles, she adjusted several of the newspaper pages so that when one of the candles burned down a quarter of an inch, it would set a page on fire, which would set more of them on fire, which would shortly after that ignite the bed. Sheila moved to the door, but she found she couldn't walk away. Instead she had to watch the candle burn down. Once the newspaper caught on fire, she left the room and fled from the house.

She had parked her car (a beat-up Honda Civic that she'd

bought with a hundred and fifty thousand miles on it) four blocks away because she didn't want any of her parents' neighbors to see or hear it, and she was almost a full block away before she heard the crackling noise that the fire made. She looked over her shoulder and saw the blaze. The house had been a tinderbox and it had gone up fast. She wished again that her parents had been capable of screaming. It would've been so nice if she could've heard them scream.

Chapter Forty-three

Los Angeles, the present

Henry waited until the blonde waitress was only a few feet from her car before stepping out from the darkness.

"Brenda, thank God I caught you," Henry said.

The waitress spun around to face him, startled, and was about to scream when she recognized Henry from the last two nights. "What are you doing here?" she asked.

"I left something really valuable inside the restaurant. I was so worried I wouldn't get back here before the place was locked up for the night."

All at once Henry's knees buckled and he clutched at his chest. Then he pitched forward face first onto the dirt surface of the small parking lot behind the restaurant.

"Oh my God, oh my God," Brenda gasped out as she rushed forward to Henry. She got down on her knees next to him and put her hand against his neck to search for a pulse, and was surprised to feel it beating as fast and strong as it was. With a surprising quickness, he grabbed her by the wrist and yanked her down and rolled on top of her. He pushed his left forearm into her throat to keep her from screaming, and then punched her hard in the nose, breaking it. Her eyes fluttered for a moment before rolling up into their sockets. She was out cold.

Henry moved quickly as he picked her up and carried her to his car where it was parked in the shadows. Aside from Brenda's car, there was still another in the parking lot, and Henry wanted to get out of there before that person finished locking up the place. He didn't bother tying up or gagging the waitress. Given how hard he had hit her, she was going to be out for a while. He dumped her in the trunk and moved fast to get behind the wheel, and he burned rubber as he tore out of the parking lot. After a mile or so, he forced himself to slow down. He had to remind himself that there could be extra patrols on the road because of SCK.

He had the radio tuned in to a news station, and the big story that night had been about Morris Brick single-handedly foiling a Beverly Hills jewelry-store robbery. Heck, they were even giving the story more coverage that night than the Skull Cracker killings, and they were going into a lot more detail than the earlier report he'd seen on TV. If what they were reporting was true, Henry could understand why. Supposedly Brick took the gun from one of the robbers as he beat the man unconscious and then in a split second shot the other robber, disabling him. What made it an even bigger story than Brick's heroics was that a famous actor had gotten shot during the ruckus. Henry had never heard of this actor before, but the news reports made a big deal over him, and of course, Brick was also credited with saving this actor's life.

Henry tugged at his lower lip as he thought about Brick being like Superman. Or maybe more like Batman. And this was who he had to have chasing after him? The news report had played a few comments Brick made at an impromptu press conference, and one of them was about the Skull Cracker Killer. According to Brick they were following up on a lead from New York that was looking promising. He refused to say anything more about it other than he expected this to lead to SCK's arrest. Henry had thought about that and decided Brick was trying to play some sort of mind game on him. There were no leads in New York or elsewhere they were following up on. Brick was only trying to get under his skin and scare him into making a mistake, and no matter how good Brick was he wasn't going to be able to do squat. After tonight, Henry was done, and SCK would no longer exist. He and Sheila would wait an appropriate amount of time to move back to Portland so as not to attract any attention, and that would be the end of it.

Something Henry had recently read popped into his head. An article about how the police could trace the location of someone's cellphone. He couldn't remember whether the cellphone had to be turned on for the police to do this, but then again, he had no idea if the waitress had a cellphone with her, and if she did, whether it was turned on or not. He pulled over and opened up the trunk. She was still out cold. He dumped the contents of her pocketbook into the trunk, and sure enough, she did have a cellphone and it was turned on. He turned it off, then dropped it to the asphalt and smashed it several times with his heel. After wiping off any prints he might've left on it, he flung it as far as he could while making sure not to get any fingerprints on it.

He couldn't help chuckling to himself over how sloppy he'd been and the potential disaster he'd narrowly avoided. Even if the police couldn't trace the waitress's phone, if she had woken up, she could've used it to call for help.

Wow, he thought. He looked up toward the night sky. *Someone's got to be looking out for me!*

Once he was back in the car, he changed the radio to an easy-listening music station and whistled along with the songs that they played. During the twenty-minute ride back to Simi Valley, he passed at most a dozen cars, none of them police cars. By the time he pulled into his garage, he was feeling relaxed and at times had even forgotten about the waitress he had stored away in the trunk. Not completely of course, but enough so that he had moments where none of this seemed quite real.

When he opened the trunk, she was not only awake, but had gotten her hands on the tire iron that was back there for changing a flat. She surprised him with how quickly she leapt from the trunk like some sort of crazed banshee, almost as if her legs were spring coils. Her face was a bloody mess, but that didn't stop her from clobbering him pretty good with the tire iron, hitting him right above his left ear. The blow dazed him enough that he almost fell to the floor. She should've used the opportunity to keep hitting him. If she had done that, she would've lived. Instead, in her panic she ran to the garage door and tried to lift it open. If she had pulled the manual release handle, she would've escaped, but as Henry got his bearings and watched her struggle to open the door, he realized she'd probably never seen a garage door rigged up with an automatic opener, which would make perfect sense for an apartment dweller. At the last second, she noticed the red handle attached to the trolley mechanism. As she reached up for it, Henry ran at her. He sort of stumbled into her, hitting her with his shoulder, and the force of the blow knocked her face first into the door and sent her sliding to the garage floor.

As she lay unconscious, Henry went back to the car and got the tape and rag out of his gym bag. His ears were still ringing from the tire iron she'd bounced off his skull, and he had to steady himself for a moment before he moved back to her. After he taped her wrists and ankles together and stuffed a rag into her mouth, he left her alone in the garage. He was still feeling too woozy to carry her inside the house.

Sheila's eyes held a feverish, expectant look in them as Henry walked past her. She didn't say anything to him, but Henry knew she was dying to ask him about the commotion she'd heard coming from the garage.

Henry was still staggering a bit as he made his way to the bathroom. For several minutes he splashed cold water onto his face, and when his eyes could focus, he studied himself in the mirror. Maybe he was imagining it but his left pupil looked larger than his right. He grimaced as he gingerly touched the area above his ear where she had hit him and could feel how swollen the lump had already gotten. That waitress had clocked him pretty good, he had to give her credit for that.

Henry found a bottle of extra-strength Tylenol in the medicine cabinet, spilled several tablets into his palm, and made a face as he stared at them. He was nauseous and wasn't sure he'd be able to keep the Tylenol down, but he swallowed the tablets anyway. He stood for a moment wishing the room would stop spinning on him, but he knew that wasn't going to be happening anytime soon. Gritting his teeth, he staggered out of the bathroom and went to the utility room where he found a plastic tarp that he'd used when he painted some of the rooms after they bought the house. He brought the tarp out to where Sheila was sitting and spread it out on the floor. Then he went back to the attached garage.

He still wasn't feeling strong enough yet to be able to pick up the waitress, so he dragged her by her feet into the house and onto the tarp. His thinking was still cloudy, and he only then remembered that his gym bag was still in the car, so he had to go back to retrieve it. When he returned, Sheila was staring keenly at the waitress.

"She has to still be alive," she said in her slow, painful way. "It's no good if she's already dead."

"She's alive," Henry said.

"What did you do to her? Her face is a mess."

"What I had to."

"Clean her up. I need to see what she looks like."

Henry swallowed back the cutting remark he almost let loose. After what he'd been through that night, Sheila was going to be picky about this? But there was no point in arguing with her. He left the room so he could bring back a bucket of warm water, soap, and a washcloth. The waitress stirred slightly as he washed her face, but otherwise was still out of it. Once he had her cleaned off, Sheila nodded her approval.

"Wake her up," she ordered.

Henry slapped the waitress lightly on her cheek until her eyes fluttered open. Then he rolled her onto her stomach and used the hammer and chisel on her.

Chapter Forty-four

"Honey, someone's ringing the doorbell."

Morris groaned as he stirred awake. For several seconds he tried to pretend Natalie hadn't told him about the doorbell, but when it rang again he forced his eyes open and stared groggily at the alarm clock kept on the shelf by Natalie's side of the bed.

"I can't make out the time," he croaked out hoarsely.

"It's ten minutes after two."

Morris groaned again, and then with a concerted effort swung his legs off the bed. "If it's a reporter, I might kill the guy. Or gal," he said.

"Under the circumstances, no court would blame you."

Morris moved in a shuffling gait as he headed out of the room, his leg muscles stiff. He almost tripped over Parker who was lying outside the door, but at the last moment he awkwardly hopped over the bull terrier.

"Some watchdog you are," Morris groused.

Parker opened an eye and his tail thumped once half-heartedly, but otherwise he didn't move. Morris appreciated how exhausted Parker had to be, and he continued on to the door. A peek through a side window showed Walsh standing outside ringing the bell.

"You weren't answering your phone," Walsh explained to Morris after Morris had let the detective inside his house.

"I was getting too many calls from reporters."

"I can imagine. Quite a night you've had, and sorry to say it's just getting started. SCK might've grabbed a waitress from a restaurant in North Hills."

"When?"

Walsh checked her watch. "Around an hour and ten minutes ago."

"How likely is it SCK?"

"Someone grabbed her unless the owner of the place did something to her and is trying to put the blame on SCK. I'll tell you more on the ride over." Straight-faced, she added, "Nice boxers. The little hearts are cute. How about you put some clothes on?"

Morris had answered the door wearing boxer shorts and an undershirt. He told Walsh he'd be right back, and he left her to get dressed. This time when he stepped over Parker, the dog didn't bother to open his eye and his tail barely moved.

Natalie was sitting up in bed waiting for him. Even in the semi-darkness of the room, Morris could see her worried expression.

"You're heading out?" she asked.

"Yeah, I have to. SCK might've just grabbed another victim. This time in North Hills."

"I see." She tried smiling, but it was a weak effort, and her concern only deepened. "I wish you didn't have to go. You were so exhausted earlier."

"I still am," Morris admitted as he slipped on a pair of trousers. "But I have no choice in the matter. I'll be careful. I won't work myself into a stroke. I promise. Maybe I'll be able to take a nap on the way to North Hills. Annie Walsh will be driving."

"Awfully nice of her. Will Parker be joining you?"

"Doubtful. The dog's a slug right now pretending to be dead to the world."

"When you get back, wake me, okay?"

"Sure, of course," Morris said, knowing full well he wasn't going to be disturbing Natalie if she was sleeping. He finished buttoning his shirt, and moved over to his wife's side so he could give her a kiss. She made it linger longer than she normally would've, in her own not-so-subtle way to motivate him to come home as soon as possible.

A test of true love, Morris thought smiling to himself as he grabbed a tie and his suit jacket on his way out of the room. If Nat had tasted his bad late-night breath, she didn't show it, and if hers tasted anywhere near as bad as his, he didn't notice it. He remembered again at the last second to step over Parker, and he hurried to join Walsh by the door. The detective had two coffees that she'd picked up from a twenty-four-hour convenience store waiting for them in the car, and she pointed out that there was sugar and half and half in the paper bag. Once they were underway, Walsh explained what had happened.

"The waitress who might've been taken is named Brenda Maguire. The owner of the restaurant, Jack Conway, and Ms. Maguire were alone together closing up the place, and he told her around one that she could take off. Fifteen minutes later he finishes up what he had to, but when he goes outside, her car's still there."

"So she got in someone else's car. It could've been someone she knew. She could've gone with this person willingly."

"She's not answering her cellphone, and they found blood near her car."

"How much blood?"

"Drops."

"So she was forcibly abducted," Morris said.

"Unless the owner of the place is lying to us about what happened."

"What about Ms. Maguire? Does she fit SCK's profile for his next victim?"

Walsh was grim-faced. "Pretty much perfectly."

"If this is SCK, he took her someplace private to kill her. Where does she live?"

"An apartment in North Hills."

"You need to send a patrol car there. The psycho might've taken her to her own apartment to kill her. Also you need to put a trace on her phone."

"Both have already been done. Her apartment's empty and two patrolmen have been stationed inside of it, and her phone's not showing up in a trace."

"He must've destroyed it," Morris said after he thought it over. He took several sips of his coffee and added, "I'd also flood as many extra patrol cars in North Hills as the department can manage."

"That request has already been made."

"Anything else you can tell me?"

Walsh shook her head. "That's all I have."

Morris drank more of his cheap convenience-store coffee, savoring it as if it were the finest French roast ever brewed. Whatever grogginess he'd been feeling earlier was gone, and his mind raced with different thoughts of how this might lead them to SCK. He only half heard Walsh as the detective asked him something.

"I'm sorry, I missed that."

"I was just asking if things went down in that Beverly Hills jewelry store the way they've been reporting it."

"Pretty much."

"Damn good shooting then."

"Not really. I was aiming dead center for his chest."

"Damn lucky shooting then."

"I can't argue that."

"Something I found awfully conspicuous in the reporting was why they shot Hollywood."

Morris grimaced at the thought of that. "He tried playing the hero and coldcocking one of the robbers. It didn't work out the way he had hoped."

Walsh sighed. "It seldom does," she said.

"Very true."

It was an eighteen-mile drive from Morris's home in West Hollywood to North Hills, which normally would've taken thirty-six minutes if you drove the posted speed limits. Walsh kept her lights flashing and her foot heavy on the gas, and she got them to the restaurant in a little less than fifteen minutes. There was a small mob of police and forensics already there by the time Walsh pulled into the restaurant's front lot. Morris wasn't surprised to see Detective Greg Malevich at the scene, but he was surprised to see Gilman gabbing with the detective. The mayor's deputy assistant was no longer dressed in an expensively tailored suit, but in worn jeans, a Loyola Marymount sweatshirt, and tennis sneakers. He was also looking worn out, and as exhausted as Morris had felt earlier. Morris stopped off to have a word with Malevich, who told him that he'd hit a dead end trying to track down whoever Corey Freeman thought he was meeting at the house in Venice where he was butchered.

"All I've been doing the last twenty-four hours is beating my head against a wall," Malevich said.

Morris nodded. "Pretty much the same as myself," he said. "We'll touch base tomorrow morning and see where we're at. In the meantime, let's see what we got here."

Gilman joined in, saying, "I'll tag along also. Morris, when you're done here, we'll talk."

They continued on to the back of the restaurant where floodlights had been set up, illuminating the back parking lot as bright as day. One of the members of the forensics team came over to show them the trail of blood drops they found, half of which had already been scraped off the ground.

"The drops started over here," she said, pointing to a marker that was roughly six feet from Maguire's car. "And end over there by the last marker. There was a good deal more blood at this first location."

"He must've attacked her over here and carried her to a car parked near that last marker."

"Most likely."

Morris squinted at one of the floodlights illuminating the area. "Can we turn those lights off?" he asked. "I'd like to see how dark it would be back here without them."

The lights were turned off. Gilman commented that someone could've been standing ten feet from the first marker and Brenda Maguire wouldn't have seen him. "And if a car was parked over by the end marker, she wouldn't have seen that either," he added.

The lights were turned back on. Morris asked the forensics specialist whether they'd found anything other than blood.

"Only blood so far," she said. "If it had rained recently, we might've gotten lucky with foot or tire prints, but the dirt's packed too hard to leave any. We'll be scraping up all the blood and seeing whether it's from one or more sources."

Morris thanked her for her help, and she went back to work while Morris, Walsh, Malevich, and Gilman went inside the restaurant to talk to the owner. Conway was sitting in the bar area with another detective, both drinking coffee. From what Morris could tell, Conway was looking either devastated or very guilty, and he couldn't decide which it was.

Conway looked up at the group approaching him and offered a bleak smile. "I've got a fresh pot brewing. Can I get any of you coffee?"

Morris told him he'd take some with sugar. Walsh and Malevich also accepted the offer, while Gilman told him he didn't need anything. While Conway went to get the coffee, the detective who'd been talking with him filled them in on what Conway had said.

"Pretty straight story," the detective said. "Conway owns the place, and also works the bar. The place closes at midnight. He had one person working tonight in the kitchen. Chad Brady. According to Conway, this Brady finished cleaning up the kitchen around quarter to one and then left. My partner visited Brady at his home in Simi Valley, and I got a call from him fifteen minutes ago. Brady was alone with his wife, and no sign of Ms. Maguire. He was cooperative and allowed my partner to check his car, both inside and trunk. No blood. My partner's convinced he's clean, and according to when his wife claims Brady arrived home he left here no later than a quarter to one."

"Did he see anything unusual when he left?"

The detective shook his head. "My partner tried asking him about any cars parked here that shouldn't have been, but Brady claims he wasn't paying attention. That he was beat after a long night in the kitchen and just wanted to get home."

"So that leaves us with Conway. He seems pretty shook up. Or pretty guilty."

"I'd say pretty shook up. His story is as straight as it gets. Ms. Maguire finished up around one, and he told her she could leave. He stayed another fifteen minutes handling the day's receipts, and when he saw Ms. Maguire's car still in the back lot, he knew something was wrong and he called 9-1-1."

"Anywhere inside here he could've stashed a body?"

"No. We searched the place thoroughly."

"How about his car?"

The detective stopped to think about that. "We didn't check his car," he admitted.

Conway came out of the kitchen carrying a tray with three mugs of coffee, cream, milk, and sugar. After he brought those over to the table where Morris and the others had gathered, Morris asked him if it was just him, Brenda Maguire, and Brady working there that night.

"That was it," he said. "Friday nights and weekends I have two waitresses working, and I bring in another bartender, but weeknights are slow."

"Did Ms. Maguire have any beefs or problems with any of your other employees? Or customers?"

"No. Never. Brenda's a sweetheart. Feisty as hell, but as nice and friendly a person as you'll ever meet." His face crumbled a bit, and he wiped a thumb over a tear that had leaked out of his right eye. "I should've walked her out to her car tonight. With those stories about that psychopath on the loose, I should've made sure she got to her car safely."

Morris didn't ask him why he didn't do that. It would be rubbing salt in the wound to do so, and besides, the answer was obvious. It's impossible to believe you or someone you know could be affected by a psycho like SCK until it happens, especially when you live in a quiet community like North Hills.

"Anything unusual happen here the last few days?" Morris asked. Conway shook his head.

"Did you see anyone here fitting the following description—Caucasian, big, wide body, round head like a pumpkin, brownish hair, bald spot?"

"That's half my clientele," Conway said.

"Anyone new like that the last few days."

Conway shook his head. "I don't know."

"Give it some thought."

Conway gave it some thought and shook his head.

"Did Ms. Maguire have any customers recently that she found odd?"

Conway started to shake his head, but stopped himself. "Brenda told me about a guy who stopped in by himself the last two nights. Ordered sirloin steak both times. She liked him. Thought he was funny. There was something else."

Conway bit his thumbnail as he thought about what that something else might've been. Then his eyes widened. "Jesus," he swore. "I can't believe I'd blacked this out. The guy was a New Yorker. Or at least Brenda told me he had a New York accent."

Morris felt his pulse quicken. "Did you get a look at him?"

"No, or if I did I didn't pay any attention to him. The last two nights were particularly slow and I spent time working on the books and taking care of other business away from the bar."

"Could he have paid by credit card?"

"I don't know. I can check the last two nights' receipts."

"Why don't you do that now, and make us a list of everyone who used a credit card the last two nights. Leave off anyone who didn't spend enough money to have ordered the sirloin steak."

"Sure. Of course."

"While you're doing that, how about giving us your car keys and allowing us to search your car."

Conway looked at Morris dumbly for a moment before he realized why Morris wanted his car keys. His expression deadened then, but he took a key off his key chain and tossed it to the table.

"Do what you need to. I'll get the list for you," he said without looking at Morris or any of the others at the table.

They checked Conway's car. The trunk was empty, and there was no blood in either the trunk or inside the car. One of the patrolmen used a slim jim to unlock Brenda Maguire's car, and her trunk was empty also.

Gilman pulled Morris aside. "If SCK ate here, he didn't pay by credit card," he said.

"You never know. This psycho's already made mistakes. He might've made one here. Anyway, that's what we do. We follow all leads until we exhaust them."

"What about that lead from New York I heard about? That SCK might've left one of his victims alive?"

"My investigators in New York are trying to track her down."

"How likely was she attacked by SCK?"

"I don't know. The same night five years ago when they were expecting SCK to strike again, a man in Queens gets his head chopped off, and this woman is attacked so brutally that it left her crippled. And both of them fit SCK's victim profiles."

"Except there should've been a middle-aged woman attacked also that night."

"Polk, with NYPD's help, is looking into that, seeing if a victim might've slipped by the police's notice."

Gilman rubbed his jaw as he considered what Morris had told him. "Then goddamn it, let's find that potential surviving victim," he said. He hesitated, then added, "The mayor wants to publicly acknowledge you saving people's lives today in Beverly Hills. The optics aren't right to do that now, but when they are, we'll be making a big deal out of it."

"After SCK's been apprehended."

"Yeah, after that." Gilman hesitated again before saying, "Is there anything we can do to help this Brenda Maguire, like offer a reward for her safe return?"

Morris grimly shook his head. "If SCK took her, she's already dead."

"But maybe he's not the one who abducted her?"

Morris didn't bother saying what they both already knew.

Chapter Forty-five

Evan Goldberg thought he was making good time as he raced his road bike along a remote stretch of Mulholland Drive and passed one of his landmarks. A quick glance at his watch showed that he was right. Five twenty-eight. He was two minutes ahead of his best time so far. As he turned a corner, he caught a glimpse of a coyote only fifty feet or so from the road. He'd seen coyotes in the area in the past when he'd ridden at dusk, but never during any of his early morning rides. Seeing a coyote out at dawn would've been unsettling enough, but Evan could've sworn the animal was trying to drag something into the woods.

He almost rode past this, but he had an unnerving feeling that what the coyote was trying to drag away wasn't a large dog or some other animal, but a human body. That he had actually caught a fleeting glimpse of a human leg. He turned his bike around and rode back to where he'd seen the coyote. The animal was almost fully behind a tree, but it was definitely dragging something. Evan got off his bike and headed toward it, moving cautiously through the brush. He picked up a large rock, saw another one, and picked that up also as he continued on toward the coyote. When he got within twenty feet of the animal, it turned toward Evan and bared its fangs. Whatever the coyote was dragging was hidden in the brush and tall grass. Evan started yelling at the animal to get away. At first it stood its ground, and continued baring its fangs, but when Evan threw a rock at it and hit it squarely in the side, the coyote let out a yelp and backed up about ten feet. When Evan threw another rock at it, the coyote took off running.

A coolness flooded Evan's head as he moved closer to whatever it was lying in the grass. "Oh Jesus," he whispered when he got within five feet of it and saw that it was a naked woman. At first only her legs and waist were visible, but that was enough for him to see the bite marks and torn flesh that the coyote was responsible for. He moved a step closer and was able to see that her skull had been cracked open like an egg, and he almost passed out.

Chapter Forty-six

Henry left Sheila by the computer while he headed off to the kitchen to make them scrambled eggs and bacon for an early breakfast. Normally he would've insisted that she stay in bed longer, or at the very least, given her a bath and dressed her before putting her anywhere, but for the last hour she'd been bugging him nearly nonstop to leave her by the computer. He guessed that she wanted to see whether they'd found the waitress's body yet. Fine. He wasn't going to argue the matter if it was that important to her. Besides, he was too beat to argue with her. It was 4 A.M. by the time he returned home after dumping the waitress's body, but even though he was tired and still woozy from the blow he'd taken to the skull, he was also too restless to sleep. Maybe he dozed for a minute or two, but that would've been it, and by 6 A.M. he gave up the fight completely.

He fried up the bacon first, then broke a half dozen eggs into a bowl. This way he'd be able to add in the bacon grease when he cooked the scrambled eggs. Once he poured in some milk and shook out a healthy amount of pepper, he went about whipping all this up with a fork. He wanted to feel relief that this was finally over, but there were certain things that were troubling him. First, there was Sheila insisting that he remove that poor girl's clothing after he'd killed her. Wasn't it bad enough what he did to her? He had to leave her to be discovered like that? He didn't like it one bit, but he decided it wasn't worth fighting Sheila over. If it was that important to her for that girl to be found naked, fine, as long as this was finally over. What had Henry most troubled, though, was the look he caught on Sheila's face when he left her by the computer. It was a look that told him this wasn't over. Well, like it or not, it was! He'd kept up his end of the bargain, and she was damn well going to keep up hers! He was going to fight her tooth and nail over it if he had to.

He had zoned out for a minute, and realized he had overcooked the eggs. Eh, it didn't matter. They'd still be edible, especially with all of the bacon grease he'd added. He spooned all of it out onto two plates, then went to retrieve Sheila.

"You find what you were so anxious to see?" he asked, not bothering to hide his annoyance.

She surprised him with what she had up on the computer. It wasn't a news report about SCK's latest (and last) victim being found in brush along a remote stretch of Mulholland Drive. Instead it was an article profiling Morris Brick, and Henry felt a chill as he saw how fixedly Sheila was staring at a photo of Brick, his wife, and his college-aged daughter.

"You need to kill them," Sheila said in her excruciatingly deliberate way as she pushed out the words through the half of her mouth that worked.

"What in the world are you talking about? We had a deal!"

"You messed things up!" she accused, her mouth forming that familiar pinched, angry circle. "It took too long to kill the last one, and the first two weren't right."

"Uh uh. I did the best I could. I'm not killing anyone else. Especially not those three."

Her look softened, and her eyes reminded him once again of how they used to look during their early days together.

"I know you tried," she said. Her eyes searched deeper into his. "But I'm still suffocating, and I'm not going to be able to breathe freely until you do this for me. I need you to do this for me. Then it will be over. I promise."

Henry rubbed a thick hand over his face. At that moment he felt more lost than he'd ever felt in his life.

"Brick's wife and daughter don't look anything like what you asked for before," he claimed. "And Brick isn't some soft, white-collar guy. None of them match."

"But they're what I need now. If you kill them, I can live, otherwise it will be like I'm being strangled to death."

Henry blinked back several tears. "I can't," he said, his voice choking on him. "It's not possible."

"You can do it," she promised him. Although it took her a while to get all the words out, she explained to Henry how he was going to kill them.

Chapter Forty-seven

New York, 2009

The apartment manager stared aghast at Sheila's application. "Your last annual salary was only eleven thousand dollars?" he asked, his voice trembling in his growing incredulity.

"That's right. That was when I was in Tallahassee working as a hospital orderly. I only moved to New York last week and haven't had a chance to look for a job yet."

"I see." He dropped the application onto his desk as if it were something diseased. "Miss Jones, this is Central Park West. As I explained when I showed you the apartment, the rent is six thousand dollars a month. That would be for each and *every* month. I suggest that you confine your search to the Bronx. Or perhaps Jersey City."

Sheila broke out laughing. After all, one minute he was acting like he'd cut off his left arm to bed her, and now like she was nothing but dirt. "I'm sorry, but you look so much like you just bit into a lemon." She wiped a tear from her eye. "I was only having a little fun. That job was back in 1998. That was when my parents died tragically leaving me a good deal of money."

She took out her cellphone, made a call, and after a short conversation, handed the phone to the apartment manager, Montgomery Hellinger.

"My bank," Sheila explained. "When you have as much money as I do, you're given concierge service. She'll confirm the amount I have in my account."

Mr. Hellinger spoke briefly over the phone before handing it back to Sheila, his cheeks reddening.

"I apologize for my rudeness earlier," he said with the proper amount of contrition.

"Don't fret another second about it. As I said, I was only having some fun. If you'd like, I could have you speak to someone at my brokerage firm. I have almost the same amount of money there also."

"That won't be necessary." He compressed his lips as he manufactured a grave look. "I would like to offer my condolences. I know it's not easy to lose your parents no matter how many years have passed."

"Thank you. We'd been estranged for a while before the fire that took their lives," Sheila said. "Four years had passed since I'd last seen them, and it was a surprise that they had me listed as their sole beneficiary."

"You poor girl."

"The money has helped," Sheila said. "With what they already had and their life insurance and the insurance from their house burning down, it added up to quite a lot, and since then I've made some smart investments. Or I guess I should say lucky investments, because I had no idea what I was doing."

"I sincerely doubt that," Hellinger remarked with his earlier jaunty smile back in place. "You impress me as someone who always knows exactly what she's doing."

"Why, Mr. Hellinger, you're making me blush!"

"Monty, please."

So he was back to flirting with her. Good. She guessed his age at close to forty. Trim, tall, good-looking in a Ken doll kind of way. Not that she had any interest in him romantically. So why was she so glad he was flirting with her again? She wasn't going to string him along so she could cut his throat or garrote him like all those other men over the past eleven years. That was the promise she had made to herself when she decided to move to New York. No more killings. Well, whatever her reason for enjoying his attention, it didn't matter.

"Monty," she said, smiling demurely.

"So you're from Tallahassee," he said, flashing her a more wolfish grin now. "I was wondering where you got such an exquisite tan."

"Well, I was originally from Tallahassee, but since receiving my windfall I've been traveling the world. This tan is from four months in southern Thailand where I spent many hours at a nude beach, so no tan line, in case you're wondering. To tell you the truth, this is the first time I've been back to the United States in almost eleven years."

"Quite the adventure," Hellinger said. His grin turned almost obscene in its lasciviousness. "I could only imagine the places you've seen and the things you've done."

"Oh, I doubt your imagination could possibly be wild enough for that. Monty, you'd be shocked. Beyond shocked. Your hair would turn white! But now that I'm in New York, I plan to be a good girl."

"One of these days, you'll have to test me," Hellinger said, a growing hunger in his eyes as he stared unrepentantly at Sheila.

"Maybe one of these days I will."

There were several more minutes of intense flirting before Hellinger had her sign a one-year lease, and she wrote a check for the full year so she wouldn't have to be bothered with remembering to send monthly payments.

"Ms. Jones," he said with a twinkle in his eye as he handed her a key. "I say this to all our new tenants, but I've never meant it as much as right now. I am very glad to have you join us here."

The reason he'd been calling her Ms. Jones instead of Ms. Proops, and the reason she'd signed her lease with the name Sheila Jones was because she had bought herself a new identity after collecting the money from her parents' estate. Only months after it had been transferred to her, she was in Miami and after some inquiries was introduced to an individual who could handle such matters. She didn't necessarily want this new identity because she was afraid the police would one day come after her for murdering her sister and parents (although she thought it would be a prudent thing to do for that reason too), but more because she wanted to leave her old identify as horrifically abused Sheila Proops far behind. This man with the gold front tooth and greased hair and teardrop tattoo offered her the diamond package for twenty grand.

"Passport, driver's license, birth certificate, Social Security card, high school diploma. All as good as the real thing," he had promised her.

"Deal," she agreed.

When it came time to picking a new name, he suggested she keep Sheila since it would be familiar to her, and for a last name to use something popular, like Jones. That way she'd blend right in. She agreed that made sense, and two weeks later she had her new papers, and Sheila Proops ceased to exist while Sheila Jones soon afterward boarded a flight to São Paulo, Brazil.

After that it was a whirlwind of foreign cities and dead bodies. Rio, Buenos Aires, Bogota, Lima, Sidney, Tokyo, Seoul, Cape Town, Frankfurt, Nice, Rome, and too many others to remember before spending the last three years traveling through southeast Asia. Sheila couldn't even remember all the men that she'd killed. None of the murders were planned. All of them had been spur of the moment. Pure impulse. Most of these men had been interested in her sexually, but not all of them. A few had only wanted to hang out with her to drink, share drugs, or swap war stories. Early on, Sheila had either bludgeoned these men, choked them to death, or sliced their throats with a handy kitchen knife. Later she started carrying a switchblade, so their deaths might not have been as spur of the moment as she might've liked to have believed.

None of these men deserved to die. None of them did anything to hurt her or seemed particularly awful. It surprised her at first the utter lack of remorse she felt after killing them. In fact, if she felt anything at all it was only a sense of relief from the anger that had been choking her, but this relief would be fleeting at best. Invariably the next day when she'd fly off to a new country or region, she'd promise herself she wouldn't be killing anyone else, although she'd still hold on to her switchblade.

Even though it was only two weeks ago, she could barely picture the last man she had killed. A wealthy French industrialist— she remembered that much. Also that he was married and that he had a chest covered with coarse, black hair. He had coaxed her to his hideaway for a night of passion and hedonistic adulterous sex. Like a fool, he had allowed Sheila to tie his hands to the bedposts, and she used a butcher's knife to split him open from his sternum to pelvis. That much she remembered.

As with all her other murders, she got away with it, or at least seemingly got away with it since she never hung around after any of them. Maybe the police were after her for butchering this French industrialist, or perhaps police in one of the other countries were looking for her, but if they were, she had no idea about it. Unless police or Interpol one day came knocking on her door, it appeared as if she'd somehow gotten away with all of it. In a way that would make sense since all the murders were so random and senseless, and while others might've seen her chatting with her victims in nightclubs or at parties, it would always be days or sometimes even weeks later when she'd find herself alone with one of these men. And their rendezvous were always handled so discreetly.

After the last one, she had an epiphany of sorts. She couldn't keep doing this. It was time for her to start afresh and have a different life. She had to find a more productive and longer-lasting way to get rid of the anger that was eating away at her insides as if it were cancer. That was when she decided to move back to the United States and not kill anyone ever again.

As she walked out of Monty Hellinger's office, the apartment manager asked her what she was going to do now that she was in New York.

She smiled at him, because at that moment her anger wasn't suffocating her, and she believed that she could close the door on her old life and that the possibilities for a new life were endless.

"This is a fresh start for me," she confided. "After I get my apartment furnished, I'm going to find a job. Maybe as a hospital orderly. It's certainly not glamorous work, and I don't need the money, but I need the stability. And maybe later I'll go to college. In any case, I plan to drop all my bad habits once and for all."

"Hopefully not all of them," he said with a wink.

"Well, maybe for old times' sake I'll hold on to one or two of them."

"That's the spirit. And perhaps you'll let me buy you a drink sometime, and you can tell me some of your stories and we'll see if my hair turns white?"

"Perhaps. We'll see."

Chapter Forty-eight

New York, 2010

Sheila briskly knocked on the office door and walked in without waiting to be invited. She had been surreptitiously watching Professor Levine's office and knew he was alone, and she also knew that his office hours were ending in the next five minutes and that it was doubtful anyone else would be coming by.

Professor Levine stared up from a stack of papers looking like a startled owl, his eyes first darting toward Sheila's chest (she had gone braless that day and was wearing a tight T-shirt under her suede jacket, which she had left open), and then reluctantly moving up to meet Sheila's eyes. The look he gave her was a mix of inquisitiveness and annoyance, with a hint of lust.

Sheila smiled innocently at him as if she hadn't caught him ogling her breasts, and said, "Professor, I know your office hours are ending soon, but I was hoping you'd have a few minutes for me."

"Certainly," he said, clearing his throat. He gestured for Sheila to take the chair to the side of his desk, and she did so. That day she had also worn a miniskirt, and she crossed her legs so that the professor would have to be left wondering whether she had worn underwear. His eyes moved quickly to her legs, hoping to catch a peek of what her crossed legs were hiding before once again settling back to Sheila's eyes. She continued to smile as if she hadn't caught him doing this.

"You're not in one of my classes, are you?" he asked, his face scrunched up into a forced perplexed look. "I'd have to hope I'd remember you if you were."

She laughed good-naturedly, again acting as if she didn't catch the way his eyes had lingered on her naked legs.

"No, not yet, anyway," she said. "That's what I would like to talk to you about. I had a difficult time of it growing up, and didn't have the opportunity to continue on with my education after high school, and I've been thinking for years about enrolling in college and majoring in psychology. One of my concerns is how much older I'll be than most of the students here."

Completely straight-faced he said, "My dear, while twenty-five would certainly be older than most of our undergraduate students, I don't see that being a problem."

"Aren't you kind, but I'm thirty-three."

A hint of a smile showed through his poker face. "Impossible!"

"Sadly it's true."

His smile stretched a fraction of an inch. "Well, you had me fooled. But if that were true, which I'm not saying I absolutely believe, it would simply mean you'd be bringing more life experiences into your studies." He pursed his lips. "Why are you interested in psychology? For career opportunities?"

"More to better understand myself."

Sheila uncrossed and re-crossed her legs, and smiled inwardly as she caught the professor's eyes once again darting downward and discovering that she was going commando that day.

"What I'm particularly interested in is better understanding the irresistible impulses I have," she said. "Once certain desires take over, I find myself helpless against them."

Professor Levine swallowed hard as his eyes fell once again to Sheila's naked legs, his cheeks mottling pink and white.

"Are you by any chance having one of these desires now?" he asked.

"I'm afraid I am. Professor, if I was a student, or even if I was enrolled in the university, I'm sure it would be highly inappropriate for me to sit on your lap and continue this discussion. But since I'm neither, I assume there would be nothing improper about me doing so at this time?"

He cleared his throat, and said, "Quite right, my dear."

Sheila smiled impishly as she got up, walked over to him, and lowered herself daintily onto his lap.

"Now isn't this much cozier," she whispered into his ear while jabbing the hypodermic needle into his neck that she had earlier kept hidden in her jacket pocket. His body stiffened, but before he could otherwise react, she injected him with succinylcholine. Although fear and surprise registered in his round, owlish eyes, his body instantly went slack, and she guided him onto the floor. She rejoined him after retrieving the hammer and chisel that she'd brought in her backpack, and sat down onto the floor next to him.

"I did come by here two weeks ago to talk to you about enrolling in the university and majoring in psychology," she told him. "I was sincere about that part of it. But the moment I saw you, I was struck with one of my irresistible impulses. I hoped it would go away, I truly did. But it didn't. In fact, it only grew worse, and soon all I could think about was what I wanted to do to you."

Since he had no muscle control, his head had rolled to the side. Sheila took hold of his chin and moved his head so he had to look at her.

"I won't bore you with the details, but what I had told you about having a difficult time of it growing up isn't the half of it," she said. "I understand fully what's behind this compulsion driving me. While you only superficially look like my dad, I guess that's enough, and I so much need a do over. I can't help thinking that if I do the things to you that I wanted so badly to do to him, then I'll stop feeling all this pressure pushing down on my chest, and I'll be able to breathe easily for the first time in years. I've read enough psychology books and am self-aware enough to understand that I'm simply projecting my feelings about my dad on to you, and that none of this is fair. That you might be a genuinely nice man who'd never do things to a daughter that my dad did to me. While I logically understand all that, it doesn't help. But what I'm sure will help is if for the next half hour or so I trick myself into pretending you're my dad."

Sheila took one last look at the terror flooding Professor Levine's eyes, and then rolled him onto his stomach. She undressed completely so she wouldn't get any blood or gore on her clothing, and then used the hammer and chisel in the way that she'd been dreaming about, all the while saying things to the professor that she'd always wanted to say to Mr. Proops.

Her estimate about the time she would need with him had been almost exactly on the mark. Thirty-five minutes later she snuck out of the professor's office without being seen, and soon after that out of the building. If anyone looked at her as she strode through the campus, it was only to catch a look at her legs, or maybe her ass.

She was amazed at how complex the subconscious mind could be, and how she could be doing things for over a year without fully understanding why. The reason she had moved to New York and gotten a job again as a hospital orderly wasn't so that she could start fresh as she had believed. It was because she was getting so little relief from killing all those men the way she was killing them, and she instead needed to discover this way to have a do over with her dad. Which meant she needed a job that gave her access to succinylcholine. She might not have understood any of this until very recently, but she understood it now.

She was grinning from ear to ear by the time she left the campus, and when she arrived at Washington Square Park, she broke out giggling and did a somersault on the grass, landing flat on her back. As she stared up at the hazy sky, she realized that for the first time since she was five she could breathe easily. All the pressure that had been squeezing her chest was gone. She started crying then. Tears of joy.

Chapter Forty-nine

New York, 2010

The woman was tall and skinny like Sheila's mom had been, and she also had a similar longish, thin face, but otherwise she really didn't look much like the late Mrs. Proops. Her long, brown hair fell well past her shoulders, while Mrs. Proops had worn her blonde hair in a short bob cut. Her nose and chin were completely wrong also, and her lips in contrast were far plumper than Mrs. Proops' razor thin ones. She was also younger than Mrs. Proops had been at the time of the fire—as with Professor Levine, this woman was more around the age of Mrs. Proops when Sheila was banished from the Proops' family home. Still, as Sheila spotted this woman unlocking the door to a small boutique, she knew this was the woman she'd been looking for even if she hadn't been consciously aware that she'd been looking for anyone.

Subconsciously, though, she had to have been out searching for a replacement for her mom, even if she hadn't realized it until right then. That had to be what sent her to this quiet street in Queens, and it also had to be why she had brought a dose of succinylcholine in her ridiculously large pocketbook, as well as the hammer and chisel that she had wrapped up in a hand towel.

The fact that this woman had just unlocked the door to this boutique and flipped the sign from *closed* to *open* at 6:45 P.M. must've meant three things: (1) she was coming back from dinner, (2) nobody else was working there, and (3) nobody else was in the store. This woman who was meant to be a substitute for Mrs. Proops so that Sheila could have a do over was all alone in there.

Sheila gave a quick look around before crossing the street and entering the store. The woman had started folding blouses, and she looked up to smile at Sheila. Sheila smiled back at her and picked up a blue-and-green patterned shirtdress. She held it out in front of her, and the woman commented that it would look nice on her.

"If you'd like to try it on, there are dressing rooms in the back." The smile the woman offered Sheila was much nicer than any she'd ever seen from her own mom. "That would be very pretty on you. It would bring out your blue eyes, which are lovely."

That almost ruined it for Sheila. Almost. For a brief moment she saw this woman very differently than as a substitute for her mom. Even her voice had been nice, with none of the shrill hysteria that her mom's voice had always held. But then she turned from Sheila so she could continue folding the blouses, and the light hit her in such a way that everything went back to being perfect.

"I think I will try it on," Sheila said.

The woman smiled again at Sheila and told her to give a yell if she needed any help. Sheila promised her she would do so.

Sheila found herself trembling in anticipation as she stood in the back dressing room and removed her clothes. She hadn't realized just how much she needed to do this until right then. Bringing a hypodermic needle and wearing only her bra and panties, she left the dressing room and stuck her head out of the back area so the woman could see that she was mostly naked and also to make sure that nobody else had entered the store.

"The dress was a little too snug on me, could I try a medium?"

"Of course."

The woman dutifully searched through a stack of the shirtdresses before pulling one out and bringing it to Sheila, again a warm smile stretching over her lips. When she held out the dress, Sheila grabbed her by the wrist and yanked her forward, jabbing her in the arm with the hypodermic needle before the woman could otherwise react. As with Mr. and Mrs. Proops and Professor Levine, the woman's body went slack within a second of being injected with succinylcholine. Sheila lowered her to the carpeted floor, then pulled her fully into the back area so that nobody passing by the store's front window would be able to see her. She then took a deep breath to calm herself, put her clothes back on, and went back to the front of the store so she could lock the door and flip the sign back to closed again. If anyone had entered the store before she'd been able to do this, she would've killed this person too. Nobody was going to stop her from having her do over!

With the store locked up and the substitute for Mrs. Proops paralyzed and helpless, Sheila again removed her clothes. She had been careful with Professor Levine and didn't get so much as a drop of blood on herself, but it wasn't worth taking any chances. Besides, it was exhilarating doing this naked. At the end with Professor Levine, she had actually obtained an orgasm for the first time in her life. If she bothered to examine the psychological reason for this, she knew it would be mixed up with how her parents and Penelope would always strip her naked before her *punishments*, but she didn't care to delve any deeper into it.

She used the hammer and chisel and said all the things to this woman that she had always wanted to say to Mrs. Proops, and at the end she obtained an orgasm that was so powerful that she almost blacked out. As it was, it left her whole body throbbing with pleasure, and it was minutes before she was able to put her clothes back on. Also, as with Professor Levine, at the end of it she felt freer than she could ever remember feeling.

The store had a locked door in the back dressing room area, and Sheila found a key on the woman that unlocked it. The door was to a stockroom, which also had a bathroom and a door that led to a back alley. Sheila was glad about the bathroom, both because it gave her a chance to wash off the hammer and chisel before wrapping them back in the hand towel, and that unbeknownst to her she had gotten several blood smears on her face. After she washed her face clean, she slipped out the back door.

Chapter Fifty

New York, 2010

"Excuse me, but you didn't use soy milk for my vanilla latte like you were supposed to. I know skim milk when I taste it."

The young blonde woman's words to the barista might've seemed relatively polite, but her tone was petulant and nasty enough to draw Sheila's attention. Up until that moment Sheila hadn't noticed her, but the woman could've been a dead ringer for Penelope. Even the same dull-eyed stare!

This time it was no accident. Sheila was in Brooklyn only because she was looking for a Penelope substitute. She knew that she needed a do over with her sister to complete the cycle, and that once that was done she'd be able to close the door forever on her past and start fresh with a clean slate. As she eavesdropped on their conversation, she heard the barista patiently explain that he used soy milk, and the Penelope look-alike insist that he was a liar, and that she could tell the difference between soy and skim milk.

"Unless you want this dumped all over your counter, you better give me what I asked for," the blonde threatened, her voice so eerily like Penelope's that it gave Sheila goose bumps.

The chastened barista made her a new vanilla latte, and after she took a sip of it she told him she'd be taking her business elsewhere in the future. "Someplace where the employees aren't so braindead that they have to argue with customers," she added, her eyes an angry dull-eyed squint.

Sheila shivered as she heard this, realizing how perfect this was going to be. She'd been careful over the last several minutes to watch this Penelope look-alike out of her peripheral vision so she wouldn't be caught staring at her, and after the woman left the coffee shop, Sheila forced herself to remain seated for another minute before leaving the shop to follow her.

She caught sight of the Penelope look-alike before she had made it to the next block. The blonde was walking at a fast clip, and Sheila had to do likewise so that she could stay within a half a block of her, but she was able to follow her for several blocks to Thirty-third Street without the woman realizing it. When the Penelope look-alike turned to go into one of the four-story brick apartment buildings lining the street, Sheila started sprinting. She made up the distance between them quickly, and was able to reach the glass security door before it had completely closed. She was breathing hard as she slipped into the building, but she could still hear the blonde's high heels clacking on the wooden steps above her. Sheila was wearing sneakers, and she raced up the staircase and caught sight of Penelope's doppelganger as the woman unlocked the door to one of the apartments and went inside of it.

Sheila had no idea whether this woman lived alone, had a roommate, a significant other, or even kids, but none of that mattered. She needed this *do over* as badly as she needed her heart to pump blood through her body, and she didn't care how many other people she'd have to slaughter if it came to that. The young blonde woman in that apartment was hers.

She waited until she had her breathing under control, and then took the hypodermic needle from her bag and held it as if it were a switchblade. Then with a great sense of calm washing over her, she walked over to the blonde's door and knocked on it. When the woman answered and saw it was Sheila, recognition glimmered in her eyes.

"I know you," she said, her mouth moving about as much as if she were working a ventriloquist's dummy. "You were in that coffee shop. What the hell are you doing following me?"

Sheila jabbed upward with the needle, sticking it into the blonde's throat. Before she could inject the succinylcholine, the blonde had grabbed Sheila's arm and had swung her hip out so that Sheila went flying over her. A loud *oomph* escaped from her as she landed heavily on her back, her wind knocked out. As she struggled to get up she heard the clicking sound of the door being closed shut, and then she was grabbed by her hair and forced back to the floor. The next thing she knew the blonde was sitting on her chest, her knees pinning her arms down. The woman's eyes seethed with fury as she pulled the needle from her throat.

"You dumb psycho bitch," she said, her breath sour in Sheila's face as she leaned forward. "Who sent you here?"

Sheila started crying. She couldn't help herself. She had been so close to reclaiming her life, and now it was like she was twelve years old again with Penelope sitting on her chest so that she could torment her.

"You're crazy, is that your story? Guess what? I don't care what your problem is. Let's see about this drug you wanted to inject me with so badly."

At that moment the blonde was no longer simply a Penelope look-alike to Sheila, but the real thing, and Sheila couldn't let it end this way, not after all the years of torment and abuse she had suffered. Summoning up every ounce of strength she was capable of, she wildly bucked her body and was able to free her left arm. The blonde missed as she tried to grab at Sheila's freed arm, and Sheila poked her in the eye.

"You crazy bitch," the blonde cried out as she grasped at her eye with both hands. Sheila used this opportunity to push the woman off of her, and to scramble for the hypodermic needle that she had dropped. She was still clutching at her injured eye when Sheila stabbed her in the shoulder with the needle and injected a full dose of succinylcholine into her. Almost instantly the woman's body went slack.

Sheila lowered herself to the floor and lay motionless next to this paralyzed woman until the thumping in her chest subsided. Once she felt as if she had recovered enough, she stripped herself naked and had her long awaited *do over* with Penelope, because as far as she was concerned this woman was Penelope.

Chapter Fifty-one

Brooklyn, 2011

She had gone insane. That was the only explanation Sheila could come up with. Less than a half hour ago she had him alone in that alley all ready for the slaughter. It would've been easy and safe. Nobody had seen them together in that Bushwick bar, and nobody would've stumbled on them in that alley. But instead of injecting him with a dose of succinylcholine when his back was turned, and then having another do over with good old dad that she so desperately wanted, she had put the needle away and invited herself to his apartment for sex. Since then they'd been seen together by enough people to where it would no longer be safe to kill him, and now she was standing naked in front of him, which had to mean she was actually planning to have intercourse with him, and she couldn't understand why.

If he hadn't drawn that picture of her, she would've made him her next victim, but that picture changed things somehow. It was very beautiful in its own way, but it also touched her that he saw her like that instead of as simply a pretty face, nice set of tits, and a tight ass. Or as just an enormous bag of money. But that wasn't the only reason she didn't kill this lumpy, toadlike man. It couldn't have been.

He still hadn't taken off any of his own clothes. Instead he sat on his bed fumbling awkwardly with his top shirt button while looking absolutely stricken. Almost like he might drop dead of a heart attack at any moment.

"Would it be okay if I turn off the lights?" he asked.

"Oh for God's sake."

She stepped forward and ripped his shirt open, popping off the buttons. He looked like he was on the verge of tears as she pulled the shirt off of him, and then yanked off the undershirt he wore underneath. Half naked he was even doughier and more repulsive than she had imagined.

"Can we talk first?" he pleaded.

"You have me naked and willing, and you want to talk? I'm betting you don't do this very often."

He looked away from her ashamed. "No, I don't," he said. His voice lowered to a whisper as he admitted, "This will be my first time."

"How old are you?"

He tried smiling, but it didn't stick. "Forty-four."

She sat next to him on the bed. "You never used a prostitute?" she asked.

He shook his head, his cheeks reddening. "I didn't think it would be right to do something like that."

Sheila understood then why she didn't kill this man in that alley. Even though he was the right age and, as long as she squinted, had enough superficial physical similarities, she still wouldn't have been able to imagine this man as her dad, especially after seeing the picture he had drawn of her. She was going to have to find someone else for her next Mr. Proops do over, because, as she was learning, the release she got from these killings didn't last very long. After only a few months she'd start feeling the compulsive urge to have her do overs again with suitable replacements for dad, mom, and sister. Maybe even later that night she'd search for another substitute for her dad, but it wasn't going to be this man.

Her voice softened as she asked, "What do you want to talk about?"

"Why did you choose me?"

She looked at him confused, at first wondering if he could've been asking why she had picked him for killing, at least initially. Did he see her brandishing the hypodermic needle in that alley? Or when she was in his bathroom minutes ago, could he have looked through her pocketbook and found the hammer and chisel that she had wrapped up in a hand towel? Did he somehow figure out that she was the Skull Cracker Killer?

"What do you mean?" she asked cautiously, her muscles tensing as she wondered whether she might have to kill this man after all, even if it wasn't safe.

"You're beautiful," he stammered out. "Beyond beautiful, really. Anyone would think that. I know I'm ugly. I've been told that my whole life. The little hog ogre. That's what they called me throughout school. I don't kid myself about it otherwise. I've accepted it." He hesitated as he stared down at his hands before adding, "You could've gone home with any guy in Bushwick. Forget Bushwick, any guy in the city. So why me?"

Sheila relaxed as she put out of her mind the violence she'd been briefly considering. She also realized then why she'd gone home with him, and why she was willing to have sex with him. He may have been repulsively ugly, but she felt a certain affinity with him. A closeness that she'd never felt before. He might not have been repeatedly violated and tortured as a child (under the guise of *punishments*), but she was sure in his own way that he had suffered. She had a wicked thought then. The FBI profiler had been so damn smug the other day when he was talking on TV about how the Skull Cracker Killer had to be a loner who was incapable of intimacy or having a relationship. This dummy who thought he was so damn smart even got her sex wrong, claiming that SCK could only achieve sexual release through *his* killings. Well, maybe she'd prove him wrong on all fronts! Maybe she'd even hook up with this poor schnook for good. Even though this Henry character looked like a squashed toad, the idea of that appealed to her.

"Why not you?" Sheila asked. "Sometimes you just find yourself attracted to a nice guy who shows by a picture he drew of you that he sees you in a way nobody else ever has. How about we get those pants off?"

Chapter Fifty-two

Los Angeles, the present

Morris answered the phone on the first ring. Since he was expecting the call and didn't want to wake Natalie, he flopped in Rachel's vacant room when he got home at 4 A.M. Even though he'd been dead tired, he hadn't been able to fall into a deep sleep since he knew the call was coming. Instead he had one of those restless sleeps where he was not sure when he woke that he'd really slept.

Morris talked briefly on the phone, got the location of Brenda Maguire's body, and told the detective that he'd be there as soon as he could. Since he'd been expecting to have to leave at a moment's notice, he'd slept in his suit to save time, only taking off his suit jacket and loosening his tie. He swung his feet off the bed, and heard a rustling next to him and realized he'd had company for the night. Parker lay on the bed stretching all four legs, his thick tail thumping the mattress. Morris could vaguely remember letting Parker into Rachel's room so that the dog wouldn't wake Nat. He also remembered ordering Parker to stay on the floor as if he actually expected the dog to listen to him.

With a snort, Parker flipped himself to his feet, jumped off the bed, and proceeded to yawn and stretch more vigorously. Morris watched him for a moment, then held out his palm so that the dog could push his muzzle into it. As Parker did this, he let out a couple of his piglike grunts.

Morris checked his watch, which he'd also worn to bed, and saw it was only a quarter past six. "You're expecting to accompany me today, aren't you?" he said in a low voice so that Nat wouldn't be able to hear him in the neighboring bedroom. He rubbed Parker's muzzle and got another grunt from the dog. "What you really want is bacon. I know your tricks. But you earned it yesterday, even though you were a godawful watchdog last night."

Morris grabbed his suit jacket and left the room with Parker tagging close behind. His mouth tasted awful, and he decided he could spend two minutes brushing his teeth and washing his face. He grabbed his toothbrush and toothpaste from the master bathroom and took it downstairs so he wouldn't wake Nat. After a quick scrubbing of both his teeth and face, he opened the downstairs bathroom door to find Nat standing on the other side of it, her hands on her hips. Even though she was paler than she usually was and her long dark brown hair was tangled and in disarray, she was as beautiful as Morris had ever seen her, and as always, her beauty brought a small lump to his throat.

"I was trying to be quiet so I wouldn't wake you," Morris apologized.

"I must've heard Parker plodding down the staircase," she said. "Let me guess, you camped out in Rachel's room when you got home?"

"Guilty as charged. I felt bad enough that you were woken up at two, I didn't want to wake you again at four, especially knowing that I'd be getting a call a couple of hours later. It's your day off, I wanted you to be able to sleep late. Sorry you weren't able to."

"It's not your fault, it's just hard to sleep when you're not lying next to me."

Morris understood that. Whenever he had to sleep apart from Nat, he always had a restless time of it.

"Tomorrow," he promised. "We'll both sleep late on your birthday."

"Deal." The fragile smile she'd been showing him weakened. "They found that girl's body?"

"Yeah. Off of Mulholland Drive. I'm heading there now."

"You're taking Parker?"

Morris nodded, and Parker on hearing his name let out one of his excited grunts.

"Good," Natalie said. "You look beat, I'm glad you'll have the company. And I'm holding you to your promise. We're not leaving the bed tomorrow until noon."

She gave Morris a tender pat on his cheek, and then reached in for a kiss. After the kiss ended, she asked Morris if he was going to get something to eat that morning.

"I'll stop somewhere for a breakfast sandwich." He gave the bull terrier a solid thump on the side. "This little guy definitely earned himself some bacon for yesterday."

Another happy grunt from Parker.

"You're not going to get into any more shoot-outs in jewelry stores?"

Morris forced a grin. "Hey, it wasn't a shoot-out. Only one of us fired."

"You know what I mean."

"I know what you mean. I'll be safe. No more Beverly Hill jewelry stores for me. How about you? Any exciting plans for your day off?"

She thought about it and shrugged. "Nothing too eventful. At least nothing more exciting than maybe getting a massage."

Chapter Fifty-three

There was already a small mob of police and forensics at the scene when Morris pulled up to the remote stretch of Mulholland Drive where Brenda Maguire's body had been found. No media or spectators yet. Too early in the morning for that. At least that was one small break.

Morris left his car with Parker on a leash, and spotted Walsh, FBI profiler Sam Goodman, and Gilman gathered together, all of them standing in brush about twenty feet from the road. The forensics team was camped out forty feet past them near a tree, which must've been where the body was left. He didn't see Malevich, but he saw other detectives and officers that he either knew or recognized.

Walsh nodded to him as did Goodman. The mayor's assistant separated from them so that he could intercept Morris. Gilman was back to wearing a custom-tailored suit, although it now looked loose on him, as if he'd lost weight over the past three days. He didn't look too happy that Morris had brought his dog, but he probably wouldn't have looked too happy about anything at that moment. When he got close enough, Parker leaped on him, resting his two paws on him as he grinned in a way that only a bull terrier could, his tail wagging. Morris yanked the dog off of him.

"He likes you," Morris said.

"Strange." Gilman frowned at Parker, but he still conceded to give the dog a scratch behind his ear. "I'm a cat person."

"You have him fooled. I'm guessing you didn't get any sleep last night."

"That obvious?" Gilman asked. "You're right, I didn't. I spent the night trying to figure out how we were going to handle this if the worst happened, which it has. Yourself?"

"Maybe a couple of hours. I'm not sure."

Gilman nodded, more to himself than to Morris. "This is bad. Worse than the others, if you can believe it. A coyote got to the body. I don't even want to think about it." He blanched then as he must've thought about it. "I was really hoping we'd be able to rescue her," he said dejectedly.

Morris clapped him on the shoulder. "We're going to get him," he promised. "Sooner than later."

"I hope you're right. I don't want this psycho bastard killing anyone else in my city." Gilman clenched his jaw, fighting back either a sob or anger, Morris wasn't sure which. The mayor's assistant got whatever emotion he was fighting under control, and asked Morris whether they should keep this from the media. "We could probably hide this from them for another four to eight hours. Any advantage in doing so?"

"None. Let's get this out there after the body's moved. Maybe someone saw something."

Gilman morosely told Morris that he was heading back to his office, and he'd handle the media. Surprisingly for a cat person, he gave Parker another pat on the head before walking off. Morris moved on to Walsh and Goodman. Walsh informed him that they were still waiting on the medical examiner, Roger Smichen, and filled him in on the rest of it.

"She wasn't killed here. Forensics already determined that. The sonofabitch dumped her out here naked."

"Something sexual?" Morris asked Goodman.

"Doubtful," the FBI profiler said. "Most likely he got his DNA on her clothing."

"When Roger examines her, he'll be able to tell us whether she was sexually violated," Walsh said.

Morris heard a couple of horn beeps, and looked up to see Roger Smichen pulling up in his new Prius. A minute later the ME gave them a wave as he jogged past them to get to the body.

"SCK broke her nose," Walsh continued. "There are other bruises, and abrasions that look like she was dragged over cement. Roger should be able to tell us more, such as any defensive wounds. Unfortunately, if she did struggle with SCK, forensics wasn't able to find any of his skin under her fingernails." She showed an angry, strained smile, and added, "A coyote got to the body and whatever SCK had clawed out from her skull wasn't found at the scene. The animal did other damage to her. A cyclist spotted the coyote dragging her over to that tree, and chased it away."

Morris couldn't help grimacing thinking about that. "Where's the cyclist now?" he asked.

"You know Charlie Dunlop out of West Hollywood, right? He interviewed the guy and told him he could go."

"That's too bad," Morris said. "I would've liked to have talked to him before he had a chance to regroup." Morris then asked Goodman, "Any chance SCK could've been this cyclist? Maybe trying to get more of a thrill from this kill by being the one to call us in on it?"

"No, that's not why SCK's doing this. He doesn't care about credit for his murders, or playing mind games with the police. These killings are very personal to him, and performing the act is all that matters to him."

"Unless he's changing his tactics," Morris said. "Like taking off this woman's clothing."

"I'm sure he did that out of necessity," Goodman said.

"This cyclist isn't SCK," Walsh argued stubbornly. "I got his particulars from Dunlop. Evan Goldberg. Twenty-four. Average height, skinny, full head of hair, and in not a single way matches the description you got from your Santa Monica parking lot witness. Dunlop did the right thing. Goldberg had nothing else to tell us."

"Okay, I'm not going to argue otherwise," Morris said, although he still planned to talk to Goldberg in person. "Any traffic cameras on Mulholland?"

Walsh shook her head. "I already called up the precinct about that. None."

"That's a damn shame."

"If he was speeding, yeah."

Goodman cleared his throat to get Morris's attention. "I had an interesting conversation with an FBI colleague, Julie Crasmore, out of New York. She told me about the lead your people are trying to track down, and unless I completely missed with my profile, I can't think of any situation which would've had SCK cutting off that man's head in Queens. Not unless something very unexpected happened."

"That's what I'm betting on," Morris said. "Something very unexpected happening that night that made SCK need to hide that he was involved in Black's murder by getting rid of the head. The timing of it is suspicious. Two brutal crimes happening the night SCK was expected to strike next, and you have both victims matching his victim profiles, followed by SCK disappearing."

Goodman stroked his chin as he considered what Morris had said. "I guess it's possible," he agreed. "At least it's not impossible."

"My gut's telling me finding Sheila Jones gives us our best chance of finding SCK. I need to talk to Roger. Either of you willing to watch Parker?"

Walsh volunteered, and Morris handed her Parker's leash. Fifteen feet from where Smichen and a group of the forensics team were gathered, Morris saw a marker in the tall grass showing where the skull fragments were left. A thin trail of blood could also be seen from that spot leading up to where the body was eventually dragged. From the pictures he'd seen of Brenda Maguire and the description he'd been given, she weighed around a hundred and thirty-five pounds, and he was surprised that a coyote would've been able to move her.

"Anything you can tell me that I don't already know?" Morris asked as he approached the ME.

Smichen shrugged. "Other than that the coyote made a mess of the crime scene? How about that she's been dead for at least four hours? Does that help?"

Morris glanced at his watch. "She was abducted around one last night, so SCK killed her within two hours of taking her, which is about what I would've expected. Any defensive wounds?"

"Some of her nails are splintered. Abrasions on her hands and fingers look like she was dragged over a cement surface. If you find the location, we might find forensic evidence there if he didn't scrub the area carefully enough."

"Was she sexually assaulted?"

Smichen shrugged again. "No obvious signs, but I won't be able to tell you for sure until I complete my examination, which will be done in my lab. I'll call you as soon as I have anything."

Morris saw that Greg Malevich had arrived at the scene and was talking with Walsh. He left Smichen so that he could divvy up among Walsh, Malevich, and himself the restaurant customers they needed to check out from the list that the owner, Conway, had made from his credit-card receipts over the last two nights.

Chapter Fifty-four

"What are you doing here?" Claudia Franzetti asked Natalie after the two of them ran into each other in the office building's lobby. "Friday's supposed to be your day off."

Natalie smiled guiltily. "I thought I'd catch up on some paperwork."

Claudia wagged a finger at her. "That's not it. I've been watching TV. You're worried about Morris. This is what you do every time you're worried about him. You hide out here."

Natalie laughed. "You should be a detective yourself."

The elevator arrived, and both women got in it. Their offices were both on the seventh floor. As the elevator got underway, Claudia asked, "This creep your husband is looking for, is he going to find him?"

"Morris always finds them."

"Jesus, I hope so. What this creep is doing to these poor people gives me the shivers." Claudia smacked her forehead. "I almost forgot, tomorrow's your birthday." She smiled impishly. "What's it going to be, number thirty?"

"Ha! You're sounding like Morris."

"Lucky man, your husband."

"Although he claims I look thirty-five."

"He needs his eyes examined."

The elevator arrived on their floor and the door opened. As the women separated to their respective offices, Claudia called out, inviting Natalie to lunch later. "My treat," Claudia said with a big grin, "the least I could do given that tomorrow is your big 3-0."

"Deal," Natalie agreed, smiling, but by the time she unlocked her office door and walked inside, her smile had faded. Claudia was right. She was worried about Morris. It was bad enough hunting the last serial killer, that twisted monster Vincent Rubosto, almost killed Morris, but last night she had to find out he was almost shot to death in a Beverly Hills jewelry store. Of course, she knew logically that that had nothing to do with his investigation, but still, she had every right to be upset about it. And of course, when Morris told her about it, he downplayed the event, making it sound as if he were never in any danger. It wasn't until she saw an in-depth report about it on the news that she realized how deadly the situation had become, with the store owner and others telling the reporter that the robbers were about to murder everyone in the store before Morris took charge. And then after that he had to run out of the house at two in the morning after not sleeping the night before. Even though he was perhaps the toughest and most capable man she'd ever met, she had every right to be worried!

Her phone rang almost the second she sat behind her desk. When she answered it, a man's voice asked if she were Natalie Brick.

"Yes, speaking," she said, her guard up, thinking this might be a reporter.

"Thank heavens I got you," the man said. "Erica Pines has been telling me you're the absolute best therapist in LA, and that's what I need. If you could squeeze me in, I'd be eternally grateful. Insurance isn't an issue, I've got money."

Natalie hesitated. She wasn't taking on new clients, but seeing someone that day would help take her mind off worrying about her husband, and Erica was one of her dearest clients.

"How long have you known Erica?" she asked.

"Years. Great gal. The absolute best."

"What would you like to see me about?"

"Oh, jeeze, my marriage. Things have gone completely nuts with my wife. I am so desperate to talk to someone about it. If you can squeeze me in, I'll be there at the drop of a hat."

The desperation in the man's voice helped Natalie make up her mind. "Sure. How about two o'clock today?"

"Oh, wow, thank you. That'd be swell. I'll be there."

"What's your name?"

"Howard Donner."

Chapter Fifty-five

"This Sheila Jones has been like a ghost since she left New York," Bogle told Morris over the phone. "Not a trace of her."

"What about tax returns?"

"She never filed any. IRS has nothing about her in their system."

"That's odd," Morris said after chewing and swallowing a mouthful of his chicken salad sandwich. At that moment, he was sitting in a booth at a downtown diner that allowed him to bring Parker along, and the bull terrier was trying to guilt him into giving up some of his sandwich, acting as if he hadn't just gobbled down an order of meatloaf.

"Tell me about it. Whatever credit cards she had expired with her New York address as her last known address. FBI's helping us with the banks, but so far no luck, and they haven't been able to get as much as a whiff of her. No forwarding address when she left New York, and she didn't tell any of her neighbors where she was moving. From what I can tell, nobody in the building knew her. I tried getting a look at her apartment application, but they tossed it years ago. I did get a Key West address for the apartment manager who took her application, but haven't been able to get a phone number for him. We might have to have a face to face with him. Okay if Polk flies down there?"

"Sure. If nothing else, it gets Polk out of your hair."

"That it does. One of the nurses at the hospital where she was sent after her attack thinks she was married, but she wasn't able to tell me more than that. New York hasn't computerized their marriage licenses, and it's a shot in the dark, but Lemmon's been at City Hall since they opened this morning going through them one by one. If she's married and we can get the husband's name, maybe he'll be easier to track down. But other than that, I'm out of ideas."

"What about her hospital records? Were they sent anywhere?"

"No such luck. She carried them out with her when she was discharged."

"It sounds like she went out of her way to make sure no one could find her after she left New York," Morris said. "Maybe she knew her attacker and didn't want him coming after her again."

"Maybe it's something like that," Bogle said, sounding unconvinced.

"Keep digging," Morris encouraged.

"Yeah, that's what I love doing. Digging a hole that goes nowhere. How about on your end? What have you been up to?"

Morris broke down and tossed Parker the rest of his sandwich. The dog was a champion moocher. He had to just accept that. With about the same enthusiasm that he'd heard from Bogle, he said, "First thing this morning I saw SCK's latest handiwork up close. Since then I've been chasing after leads that are going to the same place as that hole you've been digging."

Chapter Fifty-six

"This is a nice office," Henry said, nodding approvingly. "Really pleasant. And this easy chair, so comfy. I'd like to thank you again for squeezing me in. Very nice of you."

"Happy to be able to do so, Howard." Natalie sat in an identical easy chair arranged at a forty-five-degree angle to her client's. Earlier, she'd worn jeans, polo shirt, and sneakers to her office, but after lunch with Claudia she swung by her house so that she could put on a blouse, skirt, and shoes, and be in a professional attire for seeing a client. "Let's discuss your issues with your marriage."

"I need to fill you in about my history so this makes sense." Henry took a sip of the chamomile tea Natalie had made for him when he first arrived, and then held the cup so that it warmed both his hands. "I like this," he said. "I never had chamomile tea before. Heck, I don't think I ever had any tea other than what they serve at Chinese restaurants. But I'm procrastinating, which doesn't make much sense since my history is staring you right in the face. It's no secret that I'm an ugly guy, and I was just as ugly a kid."

Henry smiled inwardly as he waited for her to argue with him about that, but she didn't, and he appreciated it. He guessed most therapists would've tried convincing him that beauty and ugliness were subjective and that inner beauty was what really mattered, and he would've just found that condescending as well as a lie. This one, though, just looked at him in a caring and empathetic way that seemed sincere, and waited for him to continue, and he liked that.

"It might surprise you to know that my parents weren't ugly," he said. "My pop was sort of doughy and lumpy like me, but he was also this strapping tall man. Big, wide shoulders, someone who looked like a brawler. He might've been one in his younger days, I don't know, I only knew him as a gentle and decent man, a guy who worked as an assistant dispatcher for the New York subway system. If you made a life-sized clay model of him, and squashed it down about ten inches, you get me, but with him, he looked like he could've been a movie star. My ma was a dainty thing. Petite and slender, like you. Different than you in that she was fair skinned and a redhead, and not as beautiful as you, but still very pretty. With them as my parents, somehow I ended up like this."

"You used *weren't* to describe them. Are they still around?"

"No. My ma died of cancer when I was twenty-two, and my pop, well, even though he wasn't even fifty and I always thought of him as being as strong as an ox, he dropped dead of an aneurysm only a month after she was buried. I guess he didn't want to live without her, and I can't blame him for that."

"I'm sorry."

"Thanks, I appreciate it. They were good people, both of them. But I brought them up more so you could understand my background. As a little kid, you don't think of yourself as ugly, even when all the other kids are always teasing you about it. You still think that someday you're going to grow up and be at least okay looking, at least enough so that a nice woman falls in love with you, especially when you got parents as good-looking as mine. The old ugly duckling growing into a swan story. But with me that never happened. As I grew older, I only got uglier, and it didn't take me long to learn that women found me physically repugnant."

Henry took another sip of his tea, more to see if she'd try arguing with him about the last thing he had said. Maybe he would've preferred an argument this time, but she wasn't about to demean herself by lying to him about something so obvious. He could understand that, but still, he breathed in deeply and let out a hurt sigh before continuing.

"After a while I became okay with that, and accepted that I would live my life alone. About six years ago I let my best friend convince me to lose weight, get a better haircut, yada yada. This was back when I lived in New York, and I ended up dropping about seventy pounds, all of which I've since put back on. I also bought new clothes, saw a hair stylist, and used a tanning salon. After all that, I went on a few blind dates, and each of these women when they met me looked as if I was pulling some sort of cruel joke on them. So on the very night that I was about to give up for good and accept what fate had dealt me, I met my future wife. The most gorgeous woman I ever could've imagined. My best friend Joe who pushed me into doing all this used to tell me there's someone for everyone, and I used to think he was full of it until I met Sheila."

Henry put his tea cup down on the table next to his chair and held his hands out in a *what-are-you-going-to-do* kind of gesture. "If I had never met Sheila, I'd be okay living out the rest of my life alone, but I can't go back to that now. It's not just the loneliness part of it, but that she's the one and only person in this world who was meant to be with me, and somehow I found her. I can't lose her now. I can't."

"You're afraid she's going to leave you?"

Henry's expression turned dour. "Yeah, but not the way you think. She can't walk out on me. After we were together only four months she had an accident that left her a cripple, not that I'm holding her hostage or anything. But I'm afraid she might die if I don't do the things she demands of me. It's more than I'm afraid. She threatens to die if I don't do these things, and I believe her. And her demands are so unreasonable, but what choice do I have? Whew! I've been keeping all that bottled up. It feels better than I would've thought to let it out."

Natalie tensed, her voice stilted as she asked how he knew Erica Pines.

"I don't know her," he said. "That was a white lie on my part. She left you a Yelp review. A lot of your clients have. They seem to really love you, and I can understand why. You're good at what you do."

"Leave my office immediately!"

Henry made a face at that. "Or what? You'll scream? I don't think so, especially not after you see a photo I took a couple of hours ago."

He struggled for a moment to pull an iPhone out of his pocket, then after fiddling with it he held it up to Natalie so she could see a photo of her daughter Rachel lying in a car trunk with her wrists bound by duct tape and a gag in her mouth.

"I'm a pretty strong guy," Henry said. "Quick, too. I'd have no problem overpowering you, but the problem would be getting you to my car afterwards. There's just no way I could do that without someone trying to stop me. So I need you to cooperate."

Natalie's voice trembled as she said, "You expect me to leave here willingly with you?"

"Yeah, that's what I'm expecting. If you don't, I'll beat you unconscious, maybe kill you, and then I'll drive away and do terrible things to your daughter. If you survive what I do to you here, you'll have to live knowing that you did nothing to try to save her. And if you try screaming now, it won't last very long. I promise you. So are you going to be a good girl?"

Natalie's face crumbled.

"Good. Here's what we're going to do. We're going to leave your office together, walk to the end of the hall, go down the fire stairs, all seven floors, and when we get to my car, you're going to climb into the trunk without a fuss. If you say a word to anyone, your daughter's dead. If you try fighting me or drawing any attention to us, ditto. Understand?"

Natalie bit hard on her lip to keep from crying. Even though she knew the answer, she couldn't help herself from asking in a sick whisper, "Why are you doing this?"

Henry shrugged. "It's one of those things you do for love. As I explained earlier, I got no choice. Now stand up."

Natalie did as she was directed, although she had to reach back for the chair for support to keep from falling. Henry joined her and clamped his hand tightly around her narrow wrist.

"Remember what I told you," he said. "I'm not joking about any of it."

He tugged her along after him as he headed for the door.

Chapter Fifty-seven

Morris's cellphone rang. Bogle calling from New York.

"Good news?" he asked.

"Good news indeed," Bogle said. "Lemmon, bless him, found the marriage certificate. Husband's name is Henry Pollard, and he's been filing tax returns like a good citizen. We've got an address for him in Portland, Oregon. But take a look at his New York driver's license photo."

Morris brought up the photo that arrived right before Bogle called.

"His license has him as only five foot six, so he's not tall, but he's certainly got a wide body," Bogle said.

"And a round head like a pumpkin," Morris observed.

"I bet he's got a prominent bald spot too."

"I bet you're right," Morris agreed.

"What if his wife tracked him to that house in Queens, and walked in on him while he was breaking open that guy's head? It might explain why things went south with him chopping off the guy's head to hide that it was SCK. It might also explain why that same night he ended up crippling his wife."

"That's a pretty big assumption," Morris said.

"It is, but it feels right."

"Let's find out first if he's in Los Angeles."

Chapter Fifty-eight

Morris agreed with what Madame Asteria had told him over the phone several days earlier. At first glance she did look much younger than she was, and could easily be mistaken for someone in her twenties. He was confused, though, about the presence of the thirty something year-old hipster dude who was with her inside of her psychic studio and had introduced himself as Devlin Pavlovich, a TV producer.

"I have no interest in doing any interviews or being on a reality TV show," he told Pavlovich.

Pavlovich smiled in a nervous, twitchy sort of way, possibly because of how Parker was staring at him. "That's not why I'm here," he said. "You called Madame Asteria about looking at a photo to see if it's the same guy that she had called you about. I saw him also. In fact, I can show you a video recording of him."

"Why's that?"

His smile grew more nervous and twitchier as Parker continued to stare at him without blinking once. "I'm producing a reality TV show about Los Angeles psychics."

"You recorded him via a hidden camera?"

"That's right."

"Did he ever find out about it?"

"He figured it out. It upset him when he did."

"Am I being recorded now?" Morris asked.

"No, certainly not."

Morris wasn't sure whether Pavlovich was lying to him, but if he was there wasn't anything he could do about it at this point. "Why don't you show me that recording," he said.

Pavlovich glanced quickly at Parker, and said, "The equipment is in a room behind this wall. It's a small space. You should leave the dog out here."

"I'll keep this handsome guy company," Madame Asteria volunteered, and she got down on her knees so she could wrap her arms around the dog's neck and give him a hug. Parker looked embarrassed by this, but also as if he was enjoying the attention.

Pavlovich pushed next to a large mirror on the wall and a door opened, revealing a hidden room. Inside was a camera, a video monitor, and other equipment. Pavlovich played the video recording that showed Henry Pollard. He was older, of course, than his driver's license photo, but it was the same man.

"I'm going to need a copy of this," Morris said.

"Of course."

When Morris walked back into Madame Asteria's studio, the psychic looked up at him as she hugged Parker and could tell from Morris's expression that it was the same man. She studied him knowingly. "I felt it so strongly at the time," she said. "All that violence swirling around him. It was so thick, I could almost taste it. If he didn't realize that he was being recorded, he would've killed me."

Even though she didn't ask it as a question, Morris nodded anyway. It didn't take a psychic to know that was true.

Chapter Fifty-nine

"My favorite fish tacos. Morris, you're a good man."

As Morris had guessed, the private hospital room was already overflowing with roses, daisies, carnations, and at least three dozen elaborate floral arrangements.

"I figured you wouldn't need any more flowers," Morris said.

"You guessed right. The flowers that have been coming in the last few hours are being donated to other rooms." The thick bandage covering Stonehedge's cheek and the swelling and redness of the skin around it gave the actor's grin a sardonic quality. "The studio's replacing me on *The Carver*. I'm hearing they're already talking to Ronald Degragio."

"I never heard of him."

Stonehedge's grin stretched wider and grew a touch more sardonic. "The guy's a stiff."

"You seem awfully chipper given that news."

"It's the drugs they got me on. Some really potent stuff. Anyway, I can't blame them. The bullet not only nicked my femoral artery, but shattered my femur. With enough physical therapy, I might be walking in a couple of months, but I can't expect them to shut down production for that long. It's not all bad news, though. They're going to rewrite the part of the Carver's last victim, make it a heftier role, and let me play it in a wheelchair. The studio's still going to squeeze every drop of publicity they can out of this."

Parker had been staring at the bag containing the fish tacos. He let out an impatient grunt.

Morris said, "The dog's a champion moocher. Ignore him."

Stonehedge shook his head. "I owe him also for yesterday." He fished out one of the tacos from the bag, and tossed the bull terrier a piece of Ahi tuna.

"Sorry you're going to be missing out on playing the *Carver*," Morris said.

Stonehedge gingerly touched the bandage covering his cheek. "Thanks. I consulted this morning with a plastic surgeon. No matter what they do, this is going to leave a prominent scar. I should be looking sinister enough to play another serial killer sometime down the road. So Morris, now that we finished with these niceties, let me guess your real reason for coming here. You want to tear me a new one for the dumb stunt I pulled yesterday."

"That was pretty dumb," Morris agreed. "But no. I came here to tell you we know who SCK is."

"No kidding?"

"No kidding. We're keeping it quiet until we arrest him, but that should happen soon."

"Wow. Thanks for letting me know. Are you going to be there for the arrest?"

Morris shook his head. "I'm done. The rest is for the police. As soon as I leave here, I'm heading home, taking a nice, long hot shower, and getting some sleep." He paused, then added, "I wanted to let you know that even with that incredibly stupid stunt you pulled inside that jewelry store, you did okay on this investigation. It wasn't so bad having you tag along. You had some good ideas."

"I'm telling you Morris, we make a good team."

"I'm not going to disagree. Get better soon, okay?"

The two of them shook hands, and Morris led Parker out of the hospital room.

Chapter Sixty

Henry pulled into Morris Brick's driveway, and hustled out of the driver's seat so he could open the garage door that he had earlier left unlocked. While Brick's quaint English cottage home sat on a quiet West Hollywood street, and the property was surrounded by tall hedges and a small banyan tree, giving it a good deal of privacy, Henry would still be exposed to anyone passing by. Perspiration coated his forehead and dampened his shirt as he drove into the garage and hurried out of his car so he could close the garage door after him. He had to hope no nosy onlooker had seen him do this, and he felt breathless for a moment. A bleak smile twisted his lips as the thought struck him about what an inopportune time this would be for him to have a heart attack. He had to admit it unnerved him being in the lion's den, so to speak. But he also had to admit Shcila's plan made a lot of sense. Morris Brick might be tough as nails, but a chisel and hammer would shatter his skull just like anyone else's.

Henry took several slow deep breaths. Once he felt steadier he opened the trunk and looked down at Natalie Brick, who stared back at him with a mix of fear and defiance. She didn't try screaming for help, which showed she still had her wits about her. She had earlier complied with his orders, climbing into the car trunk and allowing him to bind her wrists and ankles together and to gag her. There was a moment when he had fumbled with the duct tape and she could've tried escaping, but she had believed his threat about what he would do to Rachel if she disobeyed him. At the time he couldn't help marveling over the love this woman must have for her daughter. Anyway, that one moment had long since passed. If she screamed now with the gag in her mouth, nobody outside of the garage would hear the muffled noise she would make.

Henry dumped her onto his shoulder as if she were a bag of sand. The woman was barely a wisp and couldn't have weighed more than ninety pounds. Earlier when he had brought Rachel to the house, he had left the door connecting the garage to the den unlocked. He had also forced her to give him the security code for the alarm system, letting her know in precise detail how he would kill her if she gave him the wrong code, which would be in an even more horrifying manner than how he would actually be killing her later.

He carried Natalie into the house and placed her on the carpeted floor next to Rachel, who was also gagged and bound. Both mother and daughter's eyes filled with tears as they craned their necks so they could look at each other.

Touching, Henry thought as he watched their reunion, and then shook himself out of his stupor. He wasn't out of the woods by any stretch. He had to move his car, which meant he'd be exposed when he left the house and also later when he came back, but it had to be done. He couldn't have Brick coming home and finding a strange car in the garage. He moved to the front of the house so he could unlock the front door and lift a slat on the closed window blind so he could peek out and see that the coast was clear. After that he hurried back to the den and into the garage.

His gym bag had everything he'd be needing later, and he left it on the garage floor, then changed into the paint-stained dungarees and T-shirt that he wore whenever he did projects around the house. This way if anyone saw him later when he came back to the house, they'd think he was a painter or handyman doing work there. After putting on these work clothes, he reversed his earlier maneuvers: opening the garage door, pulling his car out, closing the door, and then driving three blocks away where he had earlier spotted plenty of on-street parking.

Blood roared in his ears as he walked back to Brick's house. This was the part of the plan that he dreaded most since there was a chance Brick could've returned home during the ten minutes it took Henry to dump his car. It would be one thing to clobber Brick on the back of the head while the man walked unaware into his house, it would be something else entirely to walk inside there and come face to face with him. Henry was so preoccupied by this possibility that he at first didn't hear Brick's neighbor chasing after him as she tried to get his attention. It was only after he had walked halfway to Brick's front door that he heard her.

"Excuse me, excuse me," she repeated as she hurried to keep pace with him. "What do you think you're doing here?"

Henry turned and found himself blinking stupidly at a skinny woman in her sixties wearing tight Lululemon yoga clothes, her short hair dyed an unnatural yellow. Clearly a sun worshipper who didn't believe in sunscreen given how leathery her skin had become, almost like a saddlebag.

"I live next door to the Bricks," she said, her expression more combative than suspicious. "I saw you driving away from here a few minutes ago."

"What? I'm doing some work here," Henry stumbled out. "I had to drop off supplies."

"Natalie didn't mention anything to me about you," she said, a hint of doubt weakening her combativeness. "Isn't it late in the day to be starting a job?"

Henry shrugged and was able to manage a pleasant smile. "No choice. I had to finish another job first, and this is the earliest I could make it. Better late than never, right?"

More doubt showed in her eyes as she began to believe there was a chance Henry was telling her the truth. "Do you have a business card?"

"What? Of course." He winked at her. "Maybe you might be able to make use of my services at a future date. Especially if the Bricks are happy with what I do for them."

He made a show of working his wallet out of his back pocket, all the while taking a step closer to her. Her guard had weakened enough that it actually seemed to surprise her when he grabbed her and swung her down to the ground. Or maybe her surprise was over how quick he had been. Whichever it was, he didn't bother to ask her, and instead he covered her mouth with his hand to keep her from screaming. He had to give her credit the way she fought like a devil possessed. She had sunk her teeth into him and tried to tear out a chunk of his flesh, but he outweighed her by at least a hundred and fifty pounds, so she had no real chance. It didn't take long for him to roll on top of her. Soon after that he had his hands around her throat, strangling her, and he watched as her eyes bugged out as if they were going to pop right out of her head. A minute or so after that he saw the exact moment when they became as lifeless as glass.

Their tussle had mostly been hidden by the hedges. The only way anyone was going to see them was if they walked up Brick's driveway, but still, Henry knew time was of the essence. That at any moment someone could appear. If not a delivery man, Brick himself. Henry's legs felt rubbery and unsteady as he carried the dead woman to the front door. A muffled cry sounded behind him as he brought her into the house. From their vantage point in the den, they must've both seen him. Brick's wife and daughter. It didn't matter. He had more pressing concerns.

Henry left the dead woman in the kitchen. A growing sense of panic filled his chest, his heart palpitating wildly. This was the first time he had looked into the eyes of any of his victims, and he didn't much like it. It didn't help either that he was still feeling woozy from the tire iron shot he took the other day. No doubt he was suffering concussion symptoms. Absently, he looked at the hand she had bit and slowly made sense of the fact that he was bleeding. He realized then that his DNA must've been in her mouth, and drops of his blood were probably left both outside and in the house. He decided it didn't matter. The police didn't have his DNA on record, and after today he wouldn't be doing any more killing. The fact that they'd have his DNA wouldn't help them catch him. Still, though, the way things had gone had left him feeling unnerved. He just wanted to be done with this.

A thought stopped him. Why should he wait for Brick? Sheila had demanded that he kill them in the same order as those other victims. Brick, his wife, then the daughter. But how would she know? He could take care of those other two now; that way he'd be able to kill Brick right away and get out of this darn house all that much faster. It would also give him something to do besides waiting around and getting more and more nervous. He thought it over some more and made a decision. He didn't look at either Natalie or Rachel as he walked past them so he could retrieve his gym bag from the garage.

He dragged Natalie into the middle of the room and flipped her onto her stomach, then fiddled around with the iPhone stand so the recording would also capture Rachel in the background. This way, it would also help convince Sheila that he killed them in the order that she had insisted on. Once that was done, he took the chisel and hammer from the bag, held the spiky end of the chisel against the back of Natalie's head, and swung the hammer back so he could generate enough force to break apart her skull with a single blow.

The daughter let out a strangled scream, but that wasn't why Henry stopped the hammer suddenly when it was an inch away from the chisel. He did this because he knew Sheila would somehow see through him and know that he cheated, that he didn't kill them in the order she had demanded. And that she would then force him to kill three more people before this could be over.

Sighing in his defeat, Henry dropped the hammer and chisel to the floor. He flipped Natalie over, and moved her so that she was against the wall and next to her daughter. A tinge of guilt fluttered inside him as he saw the way both their faces were crumpled in terror, but what was there to say?

He took the iron pipe from the gym bag and moved to the door that led to the garage. He tried not to look at either of them as he waited for Brick. Sooner or later, this would all be over.

Chapter Sixty-one

Morris tried Natalie again after he left the hospital, and once again he reached her voicemail. He left a message, saying, "I was hoping third time would be the charm, but I guess no such luck. I should be home in twenty minutes and am heading straight to bed, but wake me when you get home. I hope you're having a relaxing time at whatever spa you ended up at."

On the drive back to his home in West Hollywood, he called Walsh to see if there were any updates.

"Nothing yet," Walsh said. "I've got a couple of officers with me at his house in Simi Valley, and as soon as he makes an entrance we'll have him in cuffs. His garage floor has a cement surface, but I'm holding off for now bringing in forensics. I don't want a circus here. I want him surprised when he finds us waiting for him."

"Anything from the wife."

"She's not talking. I'm not sure she's able to. I don't know if she was able to understand me when I tried questioning her. He'll be back sometime today to take care of her. It won't be long. I'll call you when we have SCK in custody."

"Okay, thanks."

Morris's exhaustion hit him then. Like his namesake, he thought, smiling thinly. He just wanted to lie down and close his eyes. His mind drifted toward Natalie as he thought about how surprised she was going to be when he gave her the earrings and matching necklace. Antoine had insisted that he take them as his appreciation for what Morris had done, and he only put up a token fight before accepting them. He imagined Nat smiling brightly wearing her new jewelry, and the thought of her like that brought a lump to his throat. No question about it, he was a lucky man.

Parker was lying on the passenger seat next to him, but as Morris pulled into his driveway the dog sat up, his ears straight up, and a harsh growl rumbled out of him. Morris stared at the dog for a moment and felt an iciness pushing deep into his skull. He called Walsh.

"Someone's inside my home," he told Walsh. "Someone who's not supposed to be there."

"Are you sure?"

"Yeah."

"You think it could be SCK?"

"I don't know."

"Is your wife home?"

"I don't know. She wasn't answering her phone, but I thought it was because she was at a spa."

"Okay, stay put. Don't go in there. I'm sending over some cars."

"Have them keep their sirens off. I'm going in through the back. If SCK's in there, he'll be waiting for me by the garage entrance."

"Morris, stay out of there—"

Morris disconnected the call, and turned off his phone. He took hold of Parker's snout and quieted the dog's growling, then opened the automatic garage door and drove in. Parker again started growling, this time more fiercely, but Morris again quieted him. He left the garage door open and took from his trunk a slim jim that he kept in case he ever needed to open a locked car. If he could've kept Parker locked in the car, he would've but he knew the dog would start barking if he tried that, so he took Parker with him as he snuck out of the garage and ran for the back of the house.

He used the slim jim to break the latch on the laundry room window. He needed to replace that window anyway. Again he shushed Parker and warned the dog to be quiet, and then he noiselessly opened the window and started to crawl through it. Out of the corner of his eye, he saw the pipe swinging at his head, and he twisted enough so that it instead glanced off his left shoulder. It still hurt like hell and sent him crashing to the floor. Henry Pollard was on him in a second, his weight heavy on Morris as he fought to break free. He caught a glimpse of Pollard raising the pipe to smash it down on his skull when Parker leapt through the window and in a flash grabbed Pollard's thick meaty wrist in his jaw. Pollard shrieked and fell backward. Morris scrambled to his knees, and climbed on top of Pollard while the man fought a losing battle to free his wrist from the bull terrier. Morris noticed the swelling on the side of Pollard's head, and he punched him there as hard as he could, almost breaking his hand. Pollard shrieked again, then his eyes fluttered, and his body went limp. Morris punched him again, this time in the jaw, and got no reaction from Pollard.

Morris hobbled to his feet and forced Parker to let go of Pollard's wrist. His right hand throbbed, and he realized he must've broken a bone when he punched Pollard the second time. His knees hurt from when he landed after falling through the window, and his shoulder ached and he knew something wasn't right there either, but he forgot about all this when he heard a muffled sound over Parker's growling. He staggered as fast as he could out of the laundry room and his blood chilled ice cold when he found Natalie and Rachel both gagged and bound in the den. They were alive, though, and from what he could see, unhurt. Still he had to fight to keep from sobbing. It wouldn't do either of them any good for him to break down then.

Parker used the opportunity of Natalie and Rachel being helpless to lick both their faces as he went back and forth between them, whimpering.

Morris removed their gags. He kissed Natalie's forehead, then Rachel's, and told them that he was getting a knife to cut them loose. "I have to cuff that sonofabitch first, but he's not hurting anyone ever again."

Morris stumbled away from them, and found a pair of cuffs in his office. Pollard was still out cold as Morris cuffed his wrists together. He fought back the urge to bash Pollard's skull in with the pipe that the psycho had brought, and instead went back to his wife and daughter and cut them free. They then huddled together, all three of them breaking down sobbing as they hugged. Parker bulled his way into the middle of the group, licking whatever faces he could.

Chapter Sixty-two

"I should be in the hospital," Henry complained as he sat cuffed in the interrogation room, his voice not much more than a mumble due to his injured jaw.

Walsh shrugged and said, "When we're done here. Unless you don't want to talk to us now."

"As good a time as any." Henry's lips folded into a severe frown as he looked around the room. "I'm surprised Brick isn't here."

"He's with his family. You met his wife and daughter when you abducted them."

"Yeah, but still, I would've thought he'd want to be here." He raised an eyebrow. "Unless he's observing this from behind that two-way mirror."

"He's not back there."

"That's too bad," Henry said as if he were truly disappointed.

Walsh had been standing with her arms crossed, but she took a seat across from Henry and dropped a folder onto the table. "We've already got enough to convict you for two of the murders," she said.

"The neighbor I left in the kitchen," Henry said.

"That woman's name was Leanna Crowley. You admit to killing her?"

"Yeah, sure. It would be pretty silly of me saying otherwise."

"Forensics also found evidence at your home linking you to Brenda Maguire."

"That was the blonde waitress?"

"Yes. How much do you want to bet that the hammer and chisel you brought to Morris Brick's home also ties you to Freeman's and Hawes's murders?"

"A bet? Sure. A million bucks that it does."

"You admit you murdered them too?"

"Yeah, why not? You got me dead to rights. I killed them all. The ones here and the ones in New York."

"Susan Twilitter also?"

"Yeah, her also."

"Your wife had no involvement?"

Henry squirmed in his seat. His voice held a cautious note as he said, "That's absolutely true. Sheila knew nothing about what I was doing."

"Except that you told Natalie Brick that you were killing them for your wife."

"I made that up. Sheila had nothing to do with any of this."

Walsh pulled from the folder several creased and weathered pages that had been torn out of a diary over five years earlier. "We found these when we searched your home. What your wife wrote implicates her for the New York murders."

Henry winced noticeably as he stared at the pages he had kept as a souvenir.

"Nothing to say about that?"

Henry's eyes shifted back to meet Walsh's. A dull, inscrutable look had formed over his face. An impenetrable mask. "I wrote that," he said. "I'd like to see you prove otherwise. And fat chance you'll ever get a sample of Sheila's handwriting to prove otherwise since she's paralyzed now on her right side. I'm done talking."

Chapter Sixty-three

As Morris had thought, an X-ray showed that he'd broken a bone in his hand. His doctor was fitting him for a cast when he got a call from Polk.

"Sheila Proops," Polk said.

"What?"

"That's her real name. Sheila Proops. Monty remembered that she was from Tallahassee."

"Monty?"

"Montgomery Hellinger. The apartment manager who took her application so she could get into that swanky Central Park West apartment. Once I found out she was from Tallahassee it wasn't hard to get her real name. And guess what, she worked as a hospital orderly there. I bet she worked as an orderly also in New York. If she had, that would've given her access to that drug that paralyzes people. What did Goodman call it? Sux? I'll bet also we find out she was the original SCK."

"We won't be finding out anything. We're bowing out now. Give all this to your FBI contact in New York. Julie Crasmore."

"Ah, you're no fun."

"Right now I'm not. I'm in the middle of getting a cast for my hand."

"How'd that happen?"

"Punching SCK's lights out."

"I didn't hear about that. All I heard was we had SCK in custody. How'd you end up being the lucky one to punch his lights out?"

"He took Nat and Rachel and was going to butcher them. Me also. And the psycho succeeded in killing my neighbor."

"You're kidding?"

"Unfortunately, no."

"Wow. I'm sorry about your neighbor. Everyone else okay? Other than your hand?"

"Nat and Rachel survived physically unscathed. I've got a few other bumps and bruises, but I'll be fine."

"Jesus. Well, if you want to know why SCK was targeting her victims, I'll send you photos of her parents and sister, all long dead."

"I'm guessing the victims resembled them."

"Bingo. Give the man a prize."

"I don't need to see them. I've had enough of SCK."

"Haven't we all."

Chapter Sixty-four

Saturday, Morris and Natalie stayed in bed as planned. Rachel had slept over in her room, partly because Natalie had insisted that she do so, and partly so that she could take care of Parker for them.

Neither of them spoke as Natalie lay nestled against Morris, her head resting against his uninjured shoulder. They both seemed to crave the silence, and Morris was more than content with feeling Natalie's body against his, even through the pajamas they were both wearing. He certainly didn't want to bring up anything that would remind her of what had happened the other day, and he knew any conversation would circle around to Henry Pollard and his equally twisted wife, Sheila Proops. Sometime in the future they'd have to talk about what they'd gone through, but not that day.

At noon Rachel knocked on the door, and carried a tray into the room with blueberry pancakes and freshly brewed coffee.

"I figured you two could use some nourishment," she said.

"Thank you, dear," Natalie said. "This is so sweet of you."

"Well, it is your birthday," Rachel said.

"How'd you keep Parker from barreling in here?" Morris asked.

"We just got back from a two-hour walk. Right now I've got him tied up outside gnawing contentedly on a rawhide bone. Later I'll be barbecuing him a steak. He earned it."

Morris hadn't told anyone about how Parker had jumped through the window and grabbed Pollard's wrist so that he could keep the maniac from smashing in Morris's head. He didn't want either Natalie or Rachel to know how close he had come to dying, especially not Nat. He knew they'd find out eventually, but he wanted some space before that happened. From what Rachel had said, and the gleam in her eyes as she looked at him, there was no

question that she had found out about it. The police probably figured it out from the bite marks on Pollard's wrist, or maybe Pollard
told them about it. However it came out, Rachel must've either read
about it in the newspaper or seen it on the news. She was tough,
though, like him. If it fazed her at all to learn about it, she didn't
show it. Not that Nat in her own way wasn't tough. It took an amazing amount of strength to willingly get into Pollard's car.

"He likes his steak medium rare," Morris said.

Rachel smiled at that. If Nat was confused about what Parker
had done to earn a barbecued steak, she didn't ask about it.

"I checked the home messages," Rachel said. "Most are from
reporters, which I've deleted. You had a few from someone from
the mayor's office. Doug Gilman. He sounded annoyed that you
weren't responding to his text messages, so I called him back for
you. The mayor wants you at a press conference tonight so he can
give you an award."

Morris shook his head. "Not tonight. I've got plans. Could you
call Gilman back for me?"

"Sure."

Natalie said, "Sweetie, thanks again for breakfast."

"Don't mention it."

Rachel left them to their pancakes, coffee, and silence.

Postscript

Jason Dorsage shook with outrage as he watched yet another news story about Morris Brick, the hero. He lifted his Beretta nine-millimeter semi-automatic pistol and aimed it at the TV, but instead of pulling the trigger and laying waste to the TV, he used the remote to shut it off.

He knew the hatred he'd been feeling toward Brick the last two days was completely irrational. Brick couldn't possibly have known how he had ruined Dorsage's detailed plans for his next Rube Goldberg machine. It was possible Brick had seen a video of one of Dorsage's other Rube Goldberg contraptions—after all, several of these videos were on YouTube and had garnered millions of views, and had made Dorsage famous enough so that corporations paid him tens of thousands to build these contraptions featuring dominos, playing cards, ping pong balls, remote control toy cars, and other common household items for their events. These past contraptions he'd put together, though, had become nothing more than insignificant frivolities to Dorsage. The sequence of events that Dorsage had been carefully working on for over a year would've been something very different. Something real. Something horrible and beautiful that would've left thousands dead in Los Angeles and the city in flames. It would've been something Dorsage could've been truly proud of, but now his plans were ruined because of Morris Brick.

Of course, Brick couldn't possibly have known how important Alex Malfi was to Dorsage's plans when he foiled that jewelry store robbery at Antoine's of Beverly Hills. Now Malfi was in police custody being held without bail, and probably wasn't going to be getting out of prison for at least twenty-five years. Dorsage's plans wouldn't be able to wait that long. They were so beautiful, so intricate, and now thanks to Brick's meddling, they were garbage.

Oh well, Dorsage thought, back to the drawing board. This time he was going to make sure Brick was in the middle of whatever he came up with.

ACKNOWLEDGMENTS

I would first of all like to thank my editor, Michaela Hamilton, as this book wouldn't exist without her. I first met Michaela in 2012 at the Cleveland Bouchercon, and that meeting led to a series of emails and phone calls during the fall of 2015, and it's because of Michaela's generosity of spirit and guidance that this new Morris Brick series was born.

Thanks also to John Lutz, Reed Farrel Coleman, Paul Levine, and Vincent Zandri for taking time out of their busy schedules to read *Deranged* and providing their generous blurbs.

In advance I'd like to thank the Kensington team who'll be supporting this book and doing their magic to make it shine: Lauren Jernigan, Michelle Forde, Alexandra Nicolajsen, and Vida Engstrand.

A big thanks also to my college buddy Alan Luedeking who, as with all my books, muddled through my initial draft and helped smooth out the language.

As always, I'd like to thank Judy, my wife and best friend, for her encouragement and support, and for also helping to make my manuscript more readable.

Don't miss the next exciting Morris Brick thriller

CRAZED

Coming soon from Lyrical Underground, an imprint of
Kensington Publishing Corp.

Keep reading to enjoy a tantalizing sample excerpt . . .

Chapter One

Seattle, the present

Griffin Bolling broke out laughing, partly from outrage, but mostly from the lunacy of what he was reading.

"What's so funny?"

Griffin looked up to see that the soft, feminine voice asking this question came from the slight redhead who had taken his latte order fifteen minutes earlier. At the time she had blushed a nice pink as she flirted with him, making sure he knew she was interested. In her petite, tiny way, she was cute, and with the way her hair was pulled back into a ponytail, she looked like a fresh-faced teenager even though she had to be in her early twenties. She must've left the cash register to bus tables so she could continue flirting with him. Now she stood off to his right with this funny, lopsided smile, hopeful that he would show the same interest in her that she obviously had in him.

"The latest insanity concerning Sheila Proops," Griffin said.

She stared at him blankly, not making a connection with that name. He smiled inwardly at her reaction. That was the thing with these Seattle slackers and hipsters. They were so insular. If it didn't have anything to do with their local scene, they had little interest.

"I'm reading about how they're not going to prosecute her for any of the Skull Cracker killings."

Her eyes scrunched up as she gave him more of a confused look. "That happened in Los Angeles?" she asked.

"And in New York five years before."

"But I thought they caught the psycho who did those murders?"

Griffin could've explained that the guy they arrested was Sheila Proops's husband, and while they had him dead to rights for the

Los Angeles killings, anyone who'd been following the story carefully knew that Sheila had to be the one who killed the twelve people in New York. The problem the authorities had was the dumb slob husband took the blame for all the killings, and that they couldn't find enough evidence to charge Sheila. So she was going to skate on twelve murders that anyone with half a brain knew she had done. But Griffin didn't bother saying any of that to the girl. Instead, he smiled wickedly at her and told her that he thought she was cute as hell. "What time do you get off work?" he asked.

That caused her to blush even deeper than before, leaving her cheeks almost the same red as her hair. "Three o'clock." It was only nine-thirty and a hint of impatience and disappointment showed in her eyes. She moved closer so she could tell him slyly, "But if I put on a good enough act that I'm coming down with something, maybe I'll be able to cut out earlier."

She winked at him as she faked a faint cough.

Griffin held out his hand to her. "Trent," he said. He'd been using the name Trent Regan since coming to Seattle nine months earlier.

"Zoe," the redhead said. Her small, slender right hand disappeared quickly into Griffin's. He couldn't help noticing how warm her flesh felt. A thought struck him. A thought so deep and profound that it startled him and had him almost laughing out loud.

"Is something wrong?" Zoe asked, concerned.

Griffin recovered quickly and flashed her a wolfish grin. "The feel of your skin took my breath away," he said.

That caused her to blush even deeper, her cheeks now blood red.

The manager of the coffee house, a heavyset thirty-something dude with a buzz cut, neck tattoos, and a dozen face piercings, must've had the hots for this redhead given the way his voice sounded as he called out from behind the counter that he needed her to take over at the cash register. Zoe's cheeks blew up like a chipmunk's showing her annoyance at the way her boss had intruded on their moment. Griffin shrugged in a what-are-you-gonna-do kind of gesture, and he watched as she reluctantly left him. Then he settled back in his chair and took a sip of his latte and thought more about the delicious idea he'd had. That he was going to kill Sheila Proops.

Ever since arriving in Seattle, he'd been drifting aimlessly, wallowing in a low-grade depression, his mood more often than not matching the weather of this dreary city. He worked day jobs here and there, and supplemented his income by ripping off the women he slept with, almost always tourists. There was no shortage of women coming to Seattle on vacation or for business who'd spot him in a coffee house, bar, or nightclub, and let him know that they wanted to hook up with him for the night. But he'd never really gotten much satisfaction from the sex part of it, and had badly fallen into a rut since coming here, not killing a single person. There just no longer seemed any point to it. But as he thought about snuffing out Sheila Proops's life, he felt inspired, truly, the desire that had been absent for so many months once again burning deep inside him. He could feel his true self that had been missing for almost a year coming to the fore. The phoenix reborn.

As Griffin imagined all the things he was going to do to Sheila Proops, he found himself growing rock-hard between his legs. He was going to take his time with her, that he knew for certain. And she was going to deserve every single torment that he inflicted on her. While he was able to kill thirty-nine people in the shadows without anyone suspecting it (well, really thirty-eight, since he wasn't even a teenager when he killed his first victim, and there were certainly some who suspected him for that one—but he was so young at the time, and he more than learned his lesson since then!), this twisted broad only murdered twelve people, but she had to do so in a way that screamed out for attention! Why? For the notoriety? Griffin's jaw clenched and his lips hardened to thin, bloodless lines as he thought about it. It was infuriating, it really was. Yeah, she deserved everything that he was going to do to her.

He was so caught up in his thoughts that he only half noticed the blonde woman who placed a business card on his table before sashaying past him on her way out of the shop. He looked up to see the door closing behind her. A few seconds later he caught a glimpse of her through the front window. She turned briefly to look his way and give him an impish smile, and then she was gone. He remembered her from when he had first come into the place. Professionally attired in a gray skirt that fell past her knees, a white blouse, and high heels. She'd been sitting alone at a table diagonally across from him. While he hadn't taken the time to study her, he had the impression that she was roughly his age (thirty-two), very attractive, and had long, slender legs. She had been so tunnel-focused on her laptop computer that he didn't think she had noticed him.

He picked up her business card and read what she had scribbled on the back of it:

My meeting lets up at 1. You don't have to wait until three—
Claire

He smiled as he sniffed the card and picked up the lilac scent of her perfume. After so many months lost in the wilderness, he deserved a treat. A going away present. But which was it going to be? The willowy blonde with the long, slender legs or the petite fresh-faced redhead? Decisions, decisions. He would have to flip a coin.

Chapter Two

Los Angeles, the present

Parker, an all-white bull terrier with the exception of a small black smudge on his left ear and a slightly larger smudge on his tail, lay on his side on the kitchen floor by Morris Brick's feet, one eye open, his ears perked up. Morris noted between bites of oatmeal that the dog did not look happy. He couldn't blame him. Three weeks ago Morris had switched to eating a healthier breakfast, which meant no bacon, sausage, or scrambled eggs to mooch. Morris used the big toe on his right foot to rub the dog's chest. Parker consented to half-heartedly thumping his tail once.

"You're going to hold a grudge, huh?" Morris said.

Parker's open eye shifted to peek at Morris, but otherwise no reaction. All at once he lifted his bullet-shaped head, and his tail began thumping more enthusiastically.

"*Buon giorno*," Natalie announced cheerfully as she entered the kitchen. Parker's tail thumped against the floor more rapidly and he let out one of his piglike grunts. Natalie gave Morris a quick kiss, then dropped to a knee so she could hug the dog around his thick neck.

"You'd never guess by the way he's acting now, but he's been sulking ever since we got back from his walk. B-a-c-o-n with-drawals."

"You gave him a can of his f-o-o-d?"

"Of course."

"That should be enough for him."

"You can be a cruel woman, Nat."

She smiled at that. "But just."

"No question. I've got more oatmeal warming on the stove. Would you like some? With a sliced banana and cinnamon?"

"That would be lovely."

Natalie kissed Parker on the snout and took a seat at the table while Morris got her breakfast.

"*Grazie.*" Natalie flashed him a dazzling smile. After twenty-four years of marriage, she could still bring a lump to his throat and make him weak in the knees. He was a lucky man, no question about it. His wife was still the same slender, dark-haired beauty he'd fallen in love with all those years ago, while he has always been a funny-looking guy with big ears, thick, long nose, spindly legs and a short, compact body. The type of guy who should own a bull terrier. People had to wonder how they ever ended up together, but the answer was simple. He got lucky when she somehow fell in love with him also.

Morris finished his breakfast, his spoon scraping the bowl. He wondered briefly how the oatmeal would taste with crumbled up bacon mixed in, but he forced the thought out of his mind. He smiled thinly, thinking how Parker must be sending him psychic messages.

"I'll get coffee started," he offered as he took his bowl and spoon to the sink.

"It's nice getting a later start today," Natalie said.

It was almost ten and usually they were both out of the house by seven; Natalie, so she could see clients at her private office where she worked as a therapist, and Morris so he could run Morris Brick Investigations, more commonly known as MBI. But since Natalie had her eight o'clock and nine-thirty appointments cancel on her, and since operations at MBI were running smoothly and Morris didn't have anything scheduled until one, they'd decided to take it easy this morning, which was a luxury for both of them.

Natalie waited until Morris brought the coffee to the table before commenting on how in nine days they would be jetting off to Rome. While it was ostensibly a statement, it was really a probing question. Was he as excited about their upcoming vacation as she was? Morris hesitated just enough before nodding to give away that he had concerns.

"This will be our first real vacation in years," Natalie said. "Two weeks in Italy. Rome, Sorrento, Florence, Venice, and Milan. This will be a dream for us, Morris. You'll love it as much as I will. I promise."

Morris forced a smile. Nat was right, of course. Outside of a four-day trip upstate to wine country they hadn't been on a vacation in years. Nat was also being kind in not mentioning that this would make up for the honeymoon they'd never had. Back when they had married, he was a rookie on the force, busting his ass to make something of himself. A year later they had Rachel, and money became too scarce to go on any sort of extended vacation. After Morris was promoted to detective they started saving some money, but whenever they'd plan a big vacation Morris would get caught up in a case and they'd have to cancel their trip. In fact, they had this very same trip planned three years ago when the Hillside Cannibal case broke, and by the time Morris caught up to the twisted monster, Vincent Robusto, who murdered and ate the internal organs of his eleven victims, they were in no shape to go anywhere. Then a year and a half ago Morris retired from the force and started MBI, and with all the hours he was putting in to get his fledgling firm off the ground, any sort of vacation seemed impossible. But now things were humming along nicely at MBI, and Natalie convinced him the place wouldn't collapse if he was gone for two weeks. That they could finally go on the trip that they'd been waiting twenty-four years to take.

"MBI will still be standing when we get back," Natalie said. "You'll be leaving it in good hands with Charlie Bogle. Now maybe if you'd picked Polk to run the place while you were gone, you'd have something to worry about!"

"I'm not really worried about MBI," Morris conceded. "More about leaving this little guy for two weeks. He's mad enough at me as it is for the current b-a-c-o-n situation."

"Parker will be fine. More than fine. Rachel will be spoiling him rotten. Like daughter, like dad."

"What are you talking about? I've been tough as nails with the little guy. I barely let him mooch anything from me these days."

"Ha! I bet you've been thinking of frying up b-a-c-o-n and crumbling it into your oatmeal just so you'd have an excuse to give him some each morning."

Morris made a harrumphing noise. "The thought never crossed my mind," he insisted. His expression softened. "And Nat, I really am looking forward to Italy."

"Good." She hesitated before adding, "And you'll be careful with the cases you take?"

"I promise. Nothing that will make me cancel this trip."

ABOUT THE AUTHOR

JACOB STONE is the byline chosen by Dave Zeltserman, an award-winning author of crime, mystery, and horror fiction, for his new thriller series featuring serial-killer expert Morris Brick. His crime novels *Small Crimes* and *Pariah* were both named by the *Washington Post* as best books of the year, with *Small Crimes* also topping National Public Radio's list of best crime and mystery novels of 2008.

His horror novel *The Caretaker of the Lorne Field* was short-listed by the American Library Association for best horror novel of 2010, a Black Quill nominee for best dark genre book, and a *Library Journal* horror gem.

His Frankenstein retelling, *Monster*, was named by *Booklist* as one of the ten best horror novels of the year and by WBUR as one of the best novels of the year.

His mystery fiction is regularly published by *Ellery Queen Mystery Magazine*, has won Shamus and Derringer awards, and has twice won the Ellery Queen Readers Choice Award.

Dave's novels have been translated into German, French, Italian, Dutch, Lithuanian, and Thai. His novels *Outsourced*, *Small Crimes*, and *The Caretaker of Lorne Field* have been optioned for film and are currently in development.

www.ingramcontent.com/pod-product-compliance
Lightning Source LLC
Chambersburg PA
CBHW020440270626
47155CB00022B/688